THE FADING FLOWER

THE
FADING
FLOWER

A HISTORICAL NOVEL

NEMEN M. KPAHN

THE FADING FLOWER

Copyright © 2014 Nemen M. Kpahn.

Certain characters in this work are historical figures, and certain events portrayed did take place. However, this is a work of fiction. All of the other characters, names, and events as well as all places, incidents, organizations, and dialogue in this novel are either the products of the author's imagination or are used fictitiously.

iUniverse books may be ordered through booksellers or by contacting:

iUniverse
1663 Liberty Drive
Bloomington, IN 47403
www.iuniverse.com
1-800-Authors (1-800-288-4677)

Because of the dynamic nature of the Internet, any web addresses or links contained in this book may have changed since publication and may no longer be valid. The views expressed in this work are solely those of the author and do not necessarily reflect the views of the publisher, and the publisher hereby disclaims any responsibility for them.

Any people depicted in stock imagery provided by Thinkstock are models, and such images are being used for illustrative purposes only. Certain stock imagery © Thinkstock.

ISBN: 978-1-4917-4046-0 (sc)
ISBN: 978-1-4917-4047-7 (e)

Library of Congress Control Number: 2014917022

Printed in the United States of America.
iUniverse rev. date: 10/16/2014

CHAPTER 1

———◆◆◆———

"Samuel-I hate this country."

"That sounds funny to me. Maxwell how can you hate a country whom you have sworn to defend? We are soldiers and soldiers we are."

"I know Samuel it is not my country that I hate, but the way people in authority treat those of us who guard and protect them that sets me on edge at times-"

"Maxwell such talk is dangerous, you better be careful who you utter such comments to otherwise you will remain a Master Sergeant forever or you might end up in Belle Yalla prison. For me, I do not want to remain a Staff Sergeant for the rest of my life. One day I like to become a Warrant Officer, Lieutenant or even a Captain."

"How long have you been in the army?

"You should know the answer since we enlisted on the same day, were assigned to the same platoon and squad during our basic training."

"Ha ha I remembered well the soggy bed and Sergeant Zazay our training commandant who singled us out for punishment."

"And when we were forced to miss our GI boogie for stealing cassava tubers from a poor farmer patch."

"Now it has taken you 4 years for you to become a Master Sergeant, at this pace it will take us 15-20 years to become a commissioned officer---whats your last name?

"Forkpa..........

"What sort of name is that?

By the way who gave you that Maxwell name?

Your name should have been Korlubah Zazay Forkpa"

Hypocrite! And what should your name be.........? Gonkarnue Gweh Dahn instead of the civilized bible name Samuel."

"Maybe it was my recruiter who could not pronounce my Gonkarnue name."

"Hi man instead of waiting for 15 years to get a promotion I guess there is a better way to get one sooner."

"And what brilliant idea is that that you have not brought up for the past four years we've been sleeping outside suffering Mosquito bites."

"NCO speak up now or forever hold your peace."

Samuel's voice sounded sonorous as a clergyman.

"By the authority vested in me our names are now changed to......

"Who vested you with the authority ? Samuel managed to whisper in between fits of laughter?

"And what are you changing my name to?"

"Samuel your question puzzles me." Maxwell laughed.

"From today your name is Samuel Benedict Richards; no more bush sounding name like Dahn. Pronouncing such a country name makes me hungry."

"And you- the name Forkpa is unbecoming of a superior officer. How would you like to be called Capt. Eugene McCritty?

That sounds much better."

"Changing the name is the easy part but convincing the personnel director whose uncle is the Defense Minister James McCritty is the serious part. How do you expect to change that bush accent of yours?"

"Maybe the Palm Butter my wife is cooking will help us practice our new accents to match our names to sound like someone from Crozerville."

"Mine said she wanted to cook Palaver sauce."

"Ok, we go first to your house…..No, yours first then mine cause my sister in law brought something special.

You know the unique 90% proof gin distilled in Nimba County. If you get too drunk to go home my wife can call your wife to come and take you home. Good our wives are friends also. But on a serious note my friend something need to change in this country. I know right? but we can discuss that later."

"Samuel things cannot continue like this."

"And what you want to do about it? I warned you such talk is dangerous. If you continue to talk like that and I am your bosom friend you know what does that mean for me my friend?"

"Ok my lips are sealed my friend."

"Make a wish. What is your dream job?"

"To become the Commanding General of the Armed Forces of Liberia."

"Samuel that also is my dream job. We have the same

aspiration. There can be only one Commanding General and there are two of us."

"Man lets go I am beginning to hunger. Neither of us can rise above the rank of a Captain so let go for our food and drink."

Samuel slapped his friend on the shoulders. Maxwell Forkpa and Samuel Dahn were both well built men who appeared to be in their mid twenties. None of them were born in a hospital so they did not know their exact ages.

CHAPTER 2

The day was a hectic one for students at the university. An important visitor from one of the countries known as the Iron Curtain was visiting the country as part of the new policy of President Roberts to open his country up to the rest of the world. Liberia, the President reckoned was a sovereign country that could choose her friends in any part of the world who shared her attributes of respect for human dignity. The hawk nosed Bulgarian President Vladimir Patolva smiled pleasantly as he strolled along with President Roberts around the university campus. He was being given a guided tour by the head of the school. The tall Bulgarian announcement that his country would donate tractors to the Agriculture College brought thunderous applause from the students. Across the road, Liberia's cultural Ambassador and her troupes danced vigorously under the hot midday to entertain students and onlookers. This visit was a normal routine in many parts of the world. Unprecedented for Liberia firmly entrenched in Washington's camp in the twilight struggle of the cold war to be giving a state visit to a communist head of state. Taking him even to where the best minds of the country were being educated was a crime. Under the administration of his predecessor a benevolent pro western despot, such an event was unthinkable. Here was President Roberts in his characteristic white suit holding a cane smiling with a communist President!

To the old elite and to the American Embassy on the other side of town this visit was to say the least sacrilegious. Among the many faceless students milling around the main campus of the University of Liberia communication specialists from both east and west buttonholed each other. Men in suits and dark sunglasses spoke into Walkie talkies. Washington needed a dossier on each aspect of the visitor's stop- overs since this visit did not amuse the US government in any way. Even though Liberian Government officials were keen to downplay the significance of this visit Washington to the say the least was not amused. President Roberts was treading on dangerous grounds. In a fight one did not differentiate much between an enemy and neutral bystander. Allies were the important thing and President Robert instead of being a steady friend now drifted into the role of an innocent by stander much to the chagrin of his traditional ally. Something never to be done soon. The agency was ordered to act.

CHAPTER 3

Soon after the visit of the VIPs, somewhere on the campus a diverse group of student leaders were locked in a clandestine meeting. Most of the student leaders belonged to tribal stock hailing from interior counties. Adonis Vonleh hailing from the northeastern county of Nimba, Flomo Kekurah, the rotund fellow with a perpetual happy grin on his face hailed from Bong County. His boyish features and sheer exuberance did not always mean success for the many endeavors he engaged in. His outrageous optimism was based simply on a robust outlook on life, a character trait which was both a blessing and a curse. His boundless enthusiasm inspired his friends into action. Yet this very optimism made him overlook any crack in his plans; since he believed everything would turn out for the best. Prof. Gabriel Martins was a young professor recently returned from the United States where he studied Political Science on a government scholarship. Now Associate Professor of Political Science at Liberia College, Prof Martins was the most intellectual among the group. Thomas Weah, the muscular firebrand student leader from D. Twe High School in the borough of New Kru Town was a man of action born in the raw, gritty world of poverty; he cared little for long intellectual discourse.. All he wanted was action and he craved confrontation with the powers that be hoping for the chance to take to the streets to vent his spleen. Weah's stout muscular physique had developed fighting at an early age in the borough where people relished the chance to watch a fist fight along the coastal sand. Elizabeth Iris Reeves, the lone female member of the group was a petite firebrand. This small bone frail looking girl possessed an iron will. A determined activist Liz wanted a radical change in society" so that the majority of the people" in her words "could have a share in the country's wealth." Her forbears were settlers from Savannah, Georgia, and she a granddaughter of the powerful Speaker of the honorable House of Representatives. Liz was born with a silver spoon in her mouth, cocooned into money and influence yet for some strange reasons she rebelled against that world. Liz as her friends called had a very light complexion and in most of their meetings always found herself seated beside Adonis. Emory Lomax, the tall lanky dark-skinned chap hailing from the upriver settlement of Arthington was the most youthful of the group. He fell somewhere between the intellectuals and the action oriented camp. The boyish Chemistry major possessed a ceaseless penchant for expensive clothes, and starched cuff link monogram shirts. The group was meeting to discuss their strategy to confront the government under a leftwing progressive label.

Since his return from the states, Prof. Martins had been trying to form a pressure group to advocate for change. This pressure group has long searched for an issue which possessed the propensity to capture the imagination of the Liberian people and galvanize them into agitation. So far their main tool was pamphlets produced in dingy underground cells whose distribution remained confined to a few scattered student populations. Most students used the leaflets as toilet paper anyway to effect change. After more than a century of being in power, the Whigs Party has become an entrenched institution whose tentacles shaped every sphere of national life. It was a cozy arrangement which benefited the elite and brought peace and tranquility to a nation whose majority population was content to allow the people to do their own thing as long as the price of a bag of rice remained affordable. It's a perfect system. But the young people in heated discussion now hated this hegemony and longed to break it through agitation. Many of those in the echelons of power were aware of the activities of the young people but they were not too perturbed. Boys will be boys, girls will be girls. It has always been like that. Young people agitate to change the order. Soon they were co-opted with jobs, money and foreign travels to be a part of the system. Enamored by these privileges they would fight to maintain the system in later years. Many of them fondly reminisced in their air-conditioned offices about their own youthful days. Soon these university students who were making noise in the eyes of the elite would become a part of the classiest elite in Africa.

Watching the student leaders with eagle eyes from afar was Police Director Paul Noring. A giant of a man; light skinned, huge and impatient he grew up along the banks of the St Paul River near Crozierville, raised by an austere disciplinarian father. Growing up in a home where he was expected to rise up at 4 am to feed and water the hogs, fetch water for his parents and hew wood to stoke the fire before going to school this reflected in his outlook on life. In the modern world of child rights this treatment could be described as torture. But for Emmanuel Noring there was no other way to make his son grow into a man except through hard work and discipline. The only way to success the old man affirmed was through hard work. Though not a rich man Emmanuel instilled in his children Spartan discipline. It seemed for his lack of material wealth God blessed him with sturdy, hardworking sons and a daughter. Noring the head of Police still maintained that habit from childhood of being an early riser. He was first cousin to the President: though he had no consuming interest in politics he leaned to the right and was not in favor of many of the changes in government being introduced by his cousin. "Give a man an inch and he would soon demand a yard" Director Noring would often say. A dedicated man Director Noring would be in his office on the hill at least thirty minutes or an hour before his younger assistants and deputies arrived. He did not hesitate to call them lazy young men without control. His assistants often laugh and promise to do better knowing no matter what they did it would not be enough to satisfy their middle -aged boss.

7 am Director Noring was already busy at his desk going through a dossier he compiled on what he called trouble- makers and saboteurs being given sanctuary by the very government which they sought to undermine. Amelia come and see." The Assistant Director of Public Affairs at headquarters, a young woman rushed to the boss office since her office was just next door.

"I do not know what has gotten into the children now a day. Someone once said yesterday they ate rice, today they chew on rights. Look at this; can you imagine the Speaker granddaughter being one of the saboteurs? Look at this." He pushed the intelligence report highlighting the date and place where the student leaders were meeting. Amelia peered over the report. "Daddy little girl has all she needs so she can have time to play mischief. She should have been on some farm hewing wood and fetching water"

"I wonder whether she sits and think about what will happen to her along with the rest of her family if the change she is fighting for comes?

What has she got in common with a Yarkpawolo?

"Director I do not know what has come over the young people nowadays. But the Bible says in the last days perilous times shall come when children shall be disobedient and disrespectful."

"I wish Rob was not such a gentleman and allow me to keep her with the rest of her crew in the hotel at South Beach prison. The stench of the urine there away from her velvety bed will make her have a rethink."

The two officers burst out laughing. "I know a better way. I will have to meet both her father and grandfather to inform them what daddy's sweet little girl is doing. But we have to keep a close eye on those student radicals. Things are not what they always use to be."

The Police Director beeped his deputy in charge of operations.

"You see all of these papers on my desk here. How would you describe them? Seditious, libelous to say the least" the bespectacled career officer graying at the temple replied after glancing at the papers.

"What concerns me most is not the contents of these pamphlets; after all how many persons read them let alone grasp and act upon their message of rebellion. But my concern is how these students can be able to operate a miniature printing press underground without us knowing where their printing press is."

The two men along with the Director became silent.

Long pause followed, later the Operations Director spoke up. "What we need to do is to send a covert agent to gather intelligence from the group. I already have a secret agent among them which you know; otherwise we will not have the chance to get hold of these. But even he at present does not know where their machines are kept. Be patient boss, I can assure you we will soon lay hands on those machines.

CHAPTER 4

For the next couple of days, one bad news after the other assailed the youthful pro democracy activists. An early morning scoop on a safe house in Sinkor led to the discovery, seizure and subsequent destruction of their typewriters, mimeographing machines, ribbons, sheet, photocopiers, correction fluids and other subsequent propaganda producing materials. State radio was virtually close to them. The other alternative electronic media was the ELWA Station which broadcast straightly religious programs and shied away from controversy or anything remotely political. Forced to resort to underground leaflets; the Police have managed to find their materials, confiscated and destroyed them. Demoralized, their meetings became erratic and people drifted into other things. Has democracy been dealt a death blow in Liberia while still in its infancy?

The students still met to plan and agitate. Now and then a student was expelled from a school for being overtly political but the opposition still searched for the galvanizing issue to take their campaign from the ivory towers of academia into the laps of the common man on the streets. Searched they did but it was like scratching the surface of a huge boulder with a piece of rock. Bewildered and confused inward while their agitation gained momentum abroad especially among Liberian exiles in the United States, it appeared the status quo in Liberia would remain as it has been the case since time in memorial in the nation's history.

And then the President inadvertently placed the issue in their laps when he increased the price of a bag of rice. The rationale according to President Roberts was to support local farmers and increase food production especially rice. It did not help matters that the President's brother was one of the major rice dealers in the country. Nepotism! Insensitivity to the plight of the common man! The Congo people were selling the country to foreigners! Activist screamed and their claims rang a bell, for the first time the issues at stake affected the common man especially urban dwellers who relied on imported food as the mainstay of their daily diet.

Somehow through the connivance of a loquacious producer at the state broadcasting institution Professor Martins managed to get on the airways lambasting the government for neglecting the common man. "They do not care for we natives!

Boom everyone in the country began talking about the unjust Rice price. The progressives who rank now swelled with civil society activists wanted to demonstrate to show their opposition to the "arbitrary" hike in the price of rice. A jittery government promptly banned any attempt to demonstrate against the new Rice price. Religious leaders appealed for calm from both the government and her opponents. But sensing the momentum on their side the student leaders and their supporters could not back down. Leaflets announcing the date and venue of the planned march circulated in the streets courtesy of an unnamed embassy near the capital. Government spokesperson appeared regularly on ELBC urging citizens to go about their normal business and forget about the plan illegal march.

Maxwell Forkpa and Samuel Dahn were busier than ever doing sentry duties at the Executive Mansion with little time for themselves to think let alone care what the impact of the upheavals would have on their lives. Their frequent duties at the Mansion sometimes together and in between shifts provided them with valuable knowledge that would prove valuable in a few months unknown to even themselves.

———•◆•———

Noring was pleased that for the first time Cousin Rob showed spine by banning the proposed march on April 14, through his Justice Minister. Early on the morning of the proposed march Director Noring cruise the streets in his Police car urging people through loudspeakers to go about their normal business. Shop owners who close their shops as a precautionary measure were ordered to open their stores. By mid morning all seemed calm but yet a palpable sense of tension reigned in the air. The month of April was a good one for demonstrations. It marked the end of the hot, dusty Dry Season and commenced the beginning of the unpleasant Rainy Season. April, the twilight zone between the two extremes possessed a mild weather.

The opposition determined to make their voices heard through the streets along with their supporters congregated in small groups trying to march. These small groups were quickly dispersed by Police. The government banned on the march remained in force, riot Police were highly visible on the streets. Opposition leaders on bicycles playing cat and mouse game with the security forces urged their supporters to come out onto the streets. Each side stuck to her guns not willing to consider a compromise.

By the time the Director drove around the city from Broad Street to Paynesville through Somalia Drive and back to the city center through the Congo Town route, he was quite satisfied that the government had prevailed in maintaining law and order.

He returned to Police headquarters still restless in his office. He just could not concentrate sitting at his desk. Director Noring set out originally to cover the short distance to the university; instead he drove his Landrover to the city center for the second time. Loud speakers mounted on his speeding vehicle equipped with siren and lights flashing warned people to keep off the streets. Traversing Broad Street, he detoured to the university through Carey Street.

A small group of would be student agitators were bottled up inside the university trying to break out to the street. This did not cause the Police Director much concern because of the small number of persons involved. What worried him though was the small group of onlookers standing on the main sidewalks of the boulevard jeering at his men. Wasting no time Director Noring snatched a megaphone and began yelling into it.

"This is an illegal gathering. All of you standing are order to disperse! I think we all need to get some rest. There are children to take care of."

If the crowd heard him it did not acknowledge his warning with a response. An incensed Noring drew aside from his men and the crowd. He dialed the President's private number. There was no response.

"Make sure you get the President back on the line," he snapped at one of his bodyguards handing him his mobile gear.

"Korlubah get back to headquarters and bring more riot control gear."

"Sir the President is on the line.

"Good, yes Mr. President, no problem. No visible sign of trouble on the university campus. If you stand on your balcony you can see them. I want to use force to quell this small group of trouble -makers along the sidewalk before the situation gets out of hand. I want to nab their leaders now!

"Take time with those young people bottle them inside the university, seal the place but use no force'. The Police Director cursed under his breath. "What Mr. President?"

Yes I will make sure your instructions are carried out."

A standoff ensued between the group of onlookers and the Police. In the standoff the number of Police kept increasing and soon the motley crowd began to slowly drift away.

By now it appeared tension subsided. The dire radio warnings may have taken effect. Law and order have prevailed over the evil forces of anarchy.

For Adonis and other leaders of the opposition, Director Noring was proving to be their nemesis. In spite of appeals from religious leaders urging restrain, the opposition could not let this golden opportunity pass by. While they had no access to the state monopolized airwaves forced to spread the activist relied on the popular appeal of their cause to bring the people to the streets. But now they were checkmated effectively bottled up inside the university campus. The number of Policemen outside the main entrance at the Capitol Building and those at the lower entrance leading to the Foreign Ministry were perhaps equal to the number of protestors inside. The diehard student protestors were just too few to break through the Police cordon to spill out onto the streets where they hope their ranks would swell.

Desperate, the student leaders were huddled in an impromptu meeting. Worrying them was the fact some of their numbers have started to slip away. "You know what? We can make a frontal assault, that is, we can rush on the Police and before they realize it we would have broken onto the streets".

"But"?

"But what"? We all know this is an illegal march. Yet

we have to somehow find a means of taking our case to the people."

Weah's suggestion was typical of him, confrontational and militant".

"Maybe we can call off the whole thing" Flomo suggested

"You want our supporters to think we are spineless? There has to be a way," Liz mused.

The discussion edged on fruitlessly. Disappointment loomed on the faces of the student leaders. The leaders themselves were starting to dawdle from the meeting in front of the Law building. Suddenly Liz's eyes brightened. Adonis! Prof. Martins! We can send someone to check the Jallah Town's back route. If there is no Police presence we can leave from here in small groups, then assemble on the streets below to get to the Bye Pass at Maternity Center Junction".

"Too farfetched" Prof Martins replied.

Adonis remained silent turning the idea over in his mind. Jallah Town's high slopes were covered with grass and overhanging rocks. One had to struggle to find a foothold among the rocks, and the houses precariously situated on them which dotted the steep slope posed an added problem. Too difficult to crisscross the rocks without being noticed by the Police. "Let us start going now. What are we waiting for?

Weah asked rising to his feet. Liz and Weah were in favor, Prof. Martins was against.

"Let's give it a try" Adonis suggested in a voice that did not inspire much confidence.

One of the protestors flipped on his transistor radio. The confident voice of the Information Minister bellowed urging citizens to go on with their normal businesses.

"The few hooligans who wanted to create trouble" in his words have been arrested.

For Adonis, Flomo, Prof. Martins, Liz, Jackson Weah, and others their moment set for personal triumph had turned to personal failure. The sense of personal failure tied Adonis stomach to a knot. Weah heading a group of hotheads was freely exchanging insults with riot Police stationed outside the gates. Adonis under one of two university palaver huts watching the main gate felt a hand on his shoulders. Fear and defiance was mixed in the pretty face staring at him. Her eyes asked the question "so what do we do now? Unspoken, her question stabbed Adonis wavering heart.

"Prof. Martins we are heading down! Adonis ran to the gate drawing Weah aside. He whispered to him. "Keep the Police busy with your boys". He winked, Weah winked back.

Adonis was speeding ahead with Liz close at his heels. "Adonis please wait for me". Even a casual observer could tell these two young people had an attraction for each other far beyond the normal camaraderie of activism. Thrown together by their shared commitment to change albeit from different social backgrounds. The two were inseparable. Adonis held Liz by her hand attempting to lift her up. The look on her face made him freeze. Liz wanted to walk by herself and not be carried even though the rough path laden with stones hurt her delicate feet. Through narrow doorways, bathrooms, kitchens, through slippery meandering paths they trudged on. The residents of the area knew their zone well. There was actually a maze of pathways leading below through the ram shackled structures built without plan or sanitation. Receiving insults and or cheers the activist plowed on. A boy of thirteen years led the small group down. Adonis held close to Liz hands' to protect her from falls. One slip and there was nothing but instant death on the tarmac below. With time, the charcoal black road below drew closer. And lo they reached the glorious ground below. Traffic was almost nonexistent. Their discovery was an eye opener. Since their pathway to the main boulevard has been blockaded by Police, this dangerous back route offered a chance to circumvent the blockade. An alternative route fraught with danger, but oh they have gained access to the road. Adonis in excitement grabbed Liz waist "Let us get back."

Liz's petite body stumbled across a boulder as they ascended a steep slope. Adonis grabbed her in time.

I am sorry."

In Adonis hurry to get back to the top he had forgotten the frailty of the lady beside him who had never experienced hardship in her life before.

"Do not worry Adonis".

Adonis waited as she picked dirt from her denim jeans. If coming down the slope was hectic, climbing up was nerve racking through the depressed neighborhood.

Back up on the main campus, it was an angry Weah who confronted them.

"Adonis I thought you and Liz wanted to run away leaving us to confront the Police."

"No, Weah Liz lowered her voice to a conspiratorial tone.

We have found a way to escape the Police."

Liz whispered struggling to regain her breathe.

"Impossible to escape the Police Liz! More and more Policemen are surrounding the campus.'

We will use a route behind the girls' dormitory. All we need to do is jump over the fence to incur their wrath. Flomo, Emory you and your boys will keep the Police busy with chants and abuses while the rest of us make our way down un -noticed by the blue boys".

"No way. You expect me to sing while the rest of you get away? No way, I am no baby sitter. I want to be at the very front of the demonstration. Please Michael you have to keep them busy before they notice we are getting away".

"No".

"Please you are so good at it. The police did not notice our departure please".

Emory scowled, grimaced but finally relented. The students at the entrance of the fence small in numbers were a vocal bunch confronting the squad of baton welding tear gas toting police keeping them busy while the main body descended slowly in small groups down the Jallah Town Hill. Within minutes a small group of students gained access to the main road and were marching to the Bye Pass, their ranks swelling with each minute. Prof. Martins looking scholarly and dignified wore a stiff business suit under the hot, tropical sun. His hair was combed neatly as if he was headed to a dinner gala. Most of the student protestors though wore jeans and T-shirts. Some wore bandanas on their heads. Adonis looked resplendent in a plaid white shirt worn over a pair of soft gray trousers. Liz in jeans was at the front of the demonstration risking their very lives. Many people came out of their houses out of curiosity. Soon the hustlers, Passer bys, the pimps, the Grona boys, the market women began to join the students who were determined to march to their de facto party headquarters located in the central business district of the city. At this initial stage, the crowd was still manageable, but there was no Police presence to counter their illegal march. The police were so intent on keeping the demonstrators inside the confines of the university campus that they did not notice it was actually a small group of students performing diversionary tactics to keep them away from the comrades gathering below.

Soon the demonstrators reached the main boulevard now growing bigger by the minute.

Chanting anti- government slogans the crowd was by now blocking parts of Crown Hill and adjoining Streets continuing down to a two storied building situated between Gurley and Buchanan Streets intersection.

Adonis Vonleh, the poor boy from a no name background stood on the balcony turned impromptu stage to address the huge, youthful crowd. The large crowd overflowing into the streets pleased and worried the organizers of the protest. Rice oh Rice the king of crops had rallied the people more than any single issue.

Adonis voice railed against nepotism, greed, corruption, favoritism and the high price of rice implemented by the government to benefit the President's brother. He raised his clenched fist. The crowd showed their appreciation with thunderous applause. Adonis perspired as his voice steadily rose higher.

And then Liz mounted the stage to speak. Petite and intense, her fiery rhetoric further stirred the crowd now hurling insults at the President William Roberts. Then Prof Martins's booming voice announced power to the people! Yet his words were too erudite for the common people. Speaker after speaker denounced the government's new increment in the price of a bag of rice which was a diabolical strain on the common people calling on President Roberts to reduce the price of a bag of rice. It seemed angels themselves joined in the applause when Prof. Martins declared that if their Progressive Alliance Union Party was to govern the country, a bag of rice will be sold for $10.

Using megaphones the Police repeated their ubiquitous warning.

"This demonstration is illegal. You are hereby ordered to disperse!

The sound of the Police megaphones annoyed the crowd. A new mood of defiance slowly began to sweep through the crowd.

"Let us march to the Mansion itself!

Someone in the crowd shouted. The crowd surged onto adjoining streets. As the mob of people began to spontaneously drift towards the UN Drive some pattern started to emerge. Instead of an orderly group marching to their party headquarters demanding political rights led by student leaders, the mass of people began to produce leaders some with dubious motives. The better organized protestors remained at their party headquarters listening to the speech making while those on the fringes did their own thing. The thin line dividing riot Police and demonstrators blurred in the confusion. Teargas canisters landed immediately following the Police warning in the de facto party headquarters from whose balcony the progressives addressed the crowd. Soon the intoxicating blinding fumes spread unto the balcony and into the building. All hell broke loose. Volleys of teargas reeked the air. Police using water cannons and electric batons charged the crowd. The crowd responded with fury pelting the Police with stones and broken bottles. Mayhem and pandemonium broke out as an unruly crowd and Police officers fought in the streets.

Blinded by teargas Adonis crawled on his knees. His eyelids appeared to be burning as if sprayed with pepper water.

The Police ill trained for such a massive outpouring of dissent by the citizenry continued to shoot volleys of teargas straight into the confused incensed crowd. Soon the generous use of teargas began to affect the Police themselves. Pandemonium, teargas, stones, broken bottles, stones, clubs, batons interacted as the Police retreated only to recharge the crowd which fought back with everything it had. People were running in all directions falling over one another in their mad rush to escape the blinding fumes. Adonis ran downstairs. Even in his semi blind state Adonis recognized a body lying on the ground. Recognition brought horror. He struggled to lift the small body from the ground while bleeding from a cut on his face. Weak and filled with nausea Adonis did not know where he got the strength to pick up the body and rush ahead away from the melee around him seeking refuge in a strange house where he lay his burden down.

Inside a cramp apartment on Front Street in one of the old Pioneer styled zinc structures

Adonis and another fellow with bushy beard were keeping what amounted to a vigil on the girl breathing in spasmic gasps in the hot low ceiling room. All sorts of thoughts were passing through Adonis mind as he watched the helpless looking girl.

After what seemed like eternity Liz re -opened her eyes for the first time.

"Adonis where am I?

Adonis heart leapt for joy. Liz was still alive!

"Oh she is alive,' the giant remarked beside.

He disappeared from the room appearing shortly later with bottles of warm soft drinks which had to be put to her lips before she could drink because she was so weak.

Adonis mind whirled around in a circle, the exciting exit from the university, the swelling crowd some of whom were mere rabble rousers and hooligans filling the ranks of the activists demonstrating for change. The euphoria and speeches at the party headquarters; and then the ugly confrontation and teargas! The crash on his skull and the mad rush and search for Liz and then the intense fear for her safety thinking the fragile rich urban girl had been mortally wounded. Now with Liz opening her eyes inside this seedy place it seemed the heavens had opened to shower their blessings on him. If even all went wrong with the demonstration today and Liz was alive everything was well with him.

"She needs to rest and relax a little" Adonis heard the giant say.

"You have to stay beside her while she gathers her strength. I need to go back to hustle. Today the Robert government will fall. I will make sure of that," with that their rescuer darted outdoor.

"You heard him Adonis. Today the rotten Robert Government will fall. I want to be there to see it fall, to be one of those to make this happen. I will be proud tomorrow to tell my grandchildren if even I have some to tell that that the power they enjoy today was a result of people power of whom I was one. Get up and let us go now!

Adonis remained motionless like a man in a trance.

"Adonis you do not take me serious. I know. I know I am a rich spoilt girl but I am not your play toy. If you do not rise this minute I am leaving".

Still Adonis did not move. He looked into the eyes of the tired beautiful young woman and he sensed for the first time something more than the camaraderie of activism. He felt a strong desire to love and protect her.

"Liz it is still too dangerous to go out there. All hell has broken loose. Looters and men with guns are out there. I know I love you and want you safe."

"Adonis stop talking and kiss me."

"What?

"You heard me right."

Adonis brought his lips down on her, their lips touch and the warm feelings and sensations enveloping him was too sweet to describe. His hand moved swiftly to her soft breast. She let his hand lingered. When he attempted to probe more she stopped him with a smile.

"Adonis there will be time for that. I have love you from the first time I saw you. We shall have children who will grow tall in freedom. But now that freedom has to be won. Get up and let us go."

Adonis remained rooted to the spot. Liz rose swiftly from the room banging the door so hard rocking both the door and frames. She rose swiftly. Before Adonis could stop her she was already out door with Adonis chasing behind her. The streets were still in motion as they left it. Looters were breaking into stores and making away with their loots. She was like a Gazelle running down Randall Street unto UN Drive not heeding Adonis call to stop.

Inspector Noring by now has been able to pinpoint the location of one of the leaders of the protestors. One of his plainclothes officers has spotted Adonis Vonleh and the rebellious granddaughter of the Speaker entered a house. With his men, thinly spread the Police Director still sent men to apprehend the rebellious pair. For once Speaker Reeves rebellious grand daughter was going to pay for her recklessness. His agents armed with pistols burst into Wesseh's room arresting all of the occupants of the house. But the couple they wanted was no where around.

In the heat of the event Inspector Noring found it

impossible to get the Defense Minister Murphy Jenkins on the line. Rushing to his residence in Sinkor, he found the sixtyish man with grizzled salt and pepper hair adding more ice cubes to his scotch soda watching T.V.

"Minister Jenkins hell is breaking loose. People are getting ready to march to the Mansion. We need your permissions to bring soldiers to the streets to quell the anarchy reigning on the streets"

"Noring you know the rules. Civil defense is a matter for the police. Armed invasion is a matter for the army. Soldiers must not interfere in civilian matters. Riot is for the police. You should be in touch with the Justice Minister. The framers of our constitution were wise in separating our powers."

"Minister forget about the finer intricacies of the law, we are in serious trouble. We need soldiers; we are teetering on the brink of disaster."

Out of frustration while Noring rattled on about the deployment of troops Minister Jenkins roared.

"Noring get the hell out of my room! Go and do anything you want to do. Just let me watch my documentary and catch some sleep. I was with the President up to 1 am this morning."

Inspector Noring wanted to blow the face of the eccentric old man serving as Defense Minister, who happened to be one of the best Defense lawyers in the world. His father and grandfathers before him were prominent in government

The cozy relationship existing between business, the government and the legal fraternity along with a low literacy had kept the chains of rebellion from breaking out before.

In his quiet surrounding the Defense Minister, did not know that the regime that guaranteed his comfortable lifestyle was hanging on a thread. Director Noring rushed to the BTC Barrack so see Chief of Staff Albert Gayflor putting together a small group of men numbering less than thirty armed with M-1s, M-16s and Uzi submachine pistols together. The Police Director used Gayflor's men to add to the officers who still kept their discipline to mount a barrier between the demonstrators heading to the Mansion and the few men blocking their path. The soldiers soon began taking positions behind makeshift barricades around the Ministry of Information.

The number of demonstrators heading down Camp Johnson Road at the moment was small since many have turned to the most lucrative aspect of the demonstration which was looting. The group coming towards him was determined and the number of men with him was even smaller. Each second brought them closer to the thin line of men blocking their path.

Finally, a few feet separated the Police men behind their makeshift barriers and the small, but growing number of protestors confronting them. Both sides it seemed were waiting for their numbers to swell. The crowd began to increase and the Director knew it was time to act before the numbers became uncontrollable.

President Robert cocooned in the Mansion with his government teetering on its last leg faced a dilemma: an ill equipped police and military force reluctant to fire on demonstrators yet without non- lethal means of crowd control. With law and order breaking down and rioters and looters running amok in the capital, the seriousness of the situation at last dawned on the President. He picked up the phone to talk to his long time friend, the arch dictator Ahmed Sekou Toure to request for assistance which the latter swiftly responded to. Within hours, airborne Guinean troops were heading to Liberia.

Adonis was running like a crazy man behind Liz while looting continued relentlessly. "Monkey come down we tire with your nonsense!

The invigorated demonstrators chanted showing clearly that some now wanted regime change. The tone of the protest has changed from protestation about rice to demanding change of government.

Adonis could not keep up let alone catch up with the nimble girl. Perhaps it was the crash of the baton on his skull caked in congealed blood which slowed his speed. Adonis could stop her and she was soon lost in the crowd. He persevered in his chase. Protestors recognizing him made way for him to pass. He fought his way through the crowd knowing the girl whom he now realized he loved as a woman not merely as a fellow activist was somewhere at the front of the crowd confronting the security forces somehow. People were singing and dancing, while others were ransacking government offices nearby in a melee of confusion.

Director Paul Noring drenched buckets of perspiration. His ever trusted megaphone was in his hand warning the crowd to disperse. The crowd ignored the warning surging ahead. The Director and his men held their ground. It was a dangerous situation. If the crowd rushed ahead it could eventually empower the grim faced soldiers holding semi automatic rifles and Policemen holding pistols. But it was certain those at the front of the demonstrators would be mowed down by gunshots before this happen. Who was prepared to be the first to die? A tense stand up developed as both parties held their ground in a stalemate. The crowd was neither dispersing nor was it moving forward towards the pointed guns. But the singing and dancing and looting continued. Elderly people across the country clenched their teeth. They could not understand what the youth of the country wanted. The younger generation wanted change and change very fast. The President wanted change, but his pace of change was too slow for the liking of those who yearn for change and too fast for the custodian of the nation's heritage who wanted things to remain just as they were.

Disperse! This is an illegal demonstration! We all could go home and rest, we had had enough activities for a single day

The small area of governmental control was near the Presidential palace where Noring was issuing his ubiquitous disperse order.

Down with corruption, down with nepotism! Do not stand in the way of the People! The voice of the People is the voice of God! Leave our path as we go to the President!

And let us go!

The crowd surged forward and soon the jittery men manning the barrier opened fire with automatic rifles not shooting straight into the crowd but above their heads mostly. A blood thirsty soldier while his friends shot into the air fired directly into the crowd sending two demonstrators to the ground bleeding. All semblance of order broke down. Not willing to be mowed down by gunfire leaders ran. Volleys of teargas being shot into the crowd aggravated the situation in an almost repeat scenario of what occurred earlier at the proposed party headquarters.

In the stampede which ensued something sharp like a metal stung Liz above the shoulders. She fell down. Tired but knowing she had to get up, she wanted to rise, she attempted to rise. A large step pressed her down and another and another. Liz lost the strength to rise as more and more weight pressed her down until she could not feel anything anymore. She fell into a sleep from which she could never rise from, her blood soiling her clothes.

Liberia a bastion of peace lost her innocence that very day on April 14.

The next morning broken glass, shattered windows, broken bones, shattered limbs and breach of peace stared the nation in the face. Bolstered by Guinean troops, shaken by the action of his protégés whom he had personally invested in, the struggle for power between the reformers and the conservatives swung decisively in the direction of the conservatives. The leaders of the protests were rounded up and charged with treason. A commission of inquiry was set up to look into the causes of the riot.

CHAPTER 5

Prof Martins, Emory Lomax, Thomas Weah, Adonis Vonleh and others stood in the dock arraigned before the Criminal Court A at the Temple of Justice in Monrovia to answer to the charge of Treason. Clean shaven and clothed in orange jumpers with leg chains attached to them they resembled school boys apart from the manacled chains on their legs.

The accused listened impassively as the prosecution read the long charges against them coaxed in difficult to understand legal jargon. But the words treason, sedition, rebellion,etc. were generously sprinkled in the terminology of the Assistant Justice Minister for litigation. He also served as lead Prosecutor Clarence Jones. Clarence graduated from Yale University with a cum laude degree in Law. Tall and clean shaven one could not see his prematurely graying hair beneath the white powder Whig he wore in the hot courtroom, a situation not helped by the long black robe placed over his three piece suit. His Uncle was the Minister of Justice and he was anxious to prove that he was a lawyer of repute not only resting on the laurels of his illustrious ancestors. It surprised many that the government could choose one so comparatively young to lead her charges against the accused instead of the Justice Minister himself who was one of the best Lawyers in the world.

The old man laughed during a meeting in Careysburg with the President when the Speaker of the House of Representatives made the point to him.

"Think for long my friend. Do you expect me a graying old man to lead the charges against those young boys when TV cameras from the world are focused on the courtroom?

Imagine an old man prosecuting those young boys? It would be the old people ganging up against the beauty of youth creating unnecessary sympathy for them as I levy my charges? No, we need one of their own, somebody who looks like them to prosecute them. Beauty always lies in youth."

The seasoned lawyer with the receding gums laughed. The President concurred with his Justice Minister's thought and that was how Clarence Jones landed the job of lead government Lawyer assisted by Lawyers of tribal stock from the counties of the accused to assist him.

The defense lead Lawyer was Richard Daniels, a middle age Lawyer gifted with a booming baritone voice . From his youth the appeal of the legal fraternity held a special enchantment for him. Even at such an age when most of his friends concerned themselves with music and girls he spent his time reading old law books and words such as "let me clarify "or" I say this to say" occupied a lot of his vocabulary. He wasted no time in studying apprenticeship law and finally matriculating to the Louise Arthur Grimes School of Law which was one of the region's finest. However, he always possessed an anti establishment bias which ruled him out of holding a top lawyer position from the government or large business corporations despite lucrative offers from them. Preferring instead to defend people whom the government considered her enemies. Something which made his personal fortune small and earned the perpetual scorn of his wife who could not understand why her husband courted poverty instead of riches. Now this case defending the enemies of the state was his toughest challenge yet. Even though most of his clients were opposition leaders and state operatives who had lost favor with the powers that be and in the rare cases they were taken to court, the man carried a general disdain for partisan politics and politicians in general.

Court room procedures and processes are hard for the ordinary person to understand as the trial opened. The statement which the members of the jam packed courtroom understood universally was the plead "not guilty "entered by the defense to the applause of those watching the trial from outside the windows of the courtroom soon interrupted by the sound of gavel and a loud voice calling for order. The opening day of the trial was not dramatic. As soon as the pleas of the defendants were taken the judge announced a date for the trial. Women cried as the prisoners were matched into sealed up vans for their trip to the Post Stockade Prison.

Most of the prisoners were dejected. Alone in their

cells cut off from one another without access to radio, newspaper or television each man was lost in his own thought wishing desperately that the world would not forget them knowing full well that the penalty for treason in Liberia was death by hanging. President Roberts had shown the nerve to take tough decisions when he allowed the mandate of the court to be carried out in the case of ritualistic killers with high connections to be hanged in 1979. The question which Adonis wanted so much to know was the where about of Liz. Why was she not among those being tried for treason? Had her connections seen her off the hook? Where was the girl of his dreams? Emory informed him while being driven back to prison that he had seen Liz last at the demonstration leading to the Presidency. Adonis anxiety for Liz dented his own concern about his fate. Nobody could give him any answer. The more he asked about the girl;,, the more of nuisance he became to his friends because everyone was fed up with his persistent questioning about someone whom they could not account for. The security agents he asked merely laughed at him.

CHAPTER 6

On the other side of town nestled in the lap of luxury, grief raw and inconsolable invaded this bastion of opulence in the prosperous eastern suburbs. Businessman Fred Reeves eyes were swollen from sharing so much tears over a beloved but wayward daughter.

"If children only knew the grief their actions sometimes caused their parents they would think twice before doing certain things" remarked granny Mae to her son. The house was full of guests who had come from far and wide to sympathize. All of the members of the Reeves clan from Louisiana, Clay Ashland around Monrovia and from further afield as Fortsville had all come to console the powerful Speaker and his son for the loss of their daughter and granddaughter.

"She had all in the world to live for why did she have to throw her life away chasing the dream of those country a----s for? Everything I own belongs to her. With her brilliance she could have gone to Harvard. Why? Why? Why?

Fred continued to ask pressing his head in the palm of

his hands. His older brother John was standing over him tapping him on the shoulders.

At the back of the house Liz mother was covered in ashes. Her long beautiful hair hang loosed. Dark icicles formed beneath her eyes. Groups of mourners arrived by the hour. With the entrance of each group the wailing started afresh. Claudia looked haggard. Her younger sister Willete was urging and pleading for her to take a bite of the bread she dipped in tea for her to eat a little something. The grief being felt by the family was profound knowing they could not see their Liz again at least not in this present life. The fact that she died for a cause which was inimical to the interest of the family rubbed salt into the wounds of grief. The why question floated on everybody lips. Outside the tastefully furnished mansion food was being cooked on a huge open fire for the mourners who descended in droves to the Reeves Family Residence. Everyone who came arrived to grieve, and grieved they did. Here there was no such thing as private grief, grief touched the lives of everyone. The burden of grief had to be shared equally.

It was amazing the ability of Africans to share and combine emotions particularly among the women folks. One moment they were rolling on the ground wailing loudly for Liz, the next moment they were talking and laughing sharing anecdotes of her short eventful life and gossiping about their husbands. Even in her grief Liz mother was able to direct the servants to make sure everyone who came had to something to eat. Friends of the Speaker came in their droves, but many did not stay long because the dead girl had died trying to overthrow everything they represented. But of course everyone wanted to be on the good side of the powerful Speaker at the same time enjoy the confidence of the President. However, there was genuine admiration among some of the mourners for the courage of Elizabeth Iris Reeves for standing up for what she believed even though what she believed in did not appeal to these conservative people who made up the ruling class.

Elizabeth Iris Reeves battered body sewed together with the best skills of a private exclusive funeral home placed in an expensive bronze casket was laid to rest at the family's private cemetery in Clay Ashland, the home of Seven of Liberia's President with so much tears that even the angels who watched from above wanted to cry.

It was only after the burial the family had time to mourn alone for the voice of the daughter they would no longer hear. The pain of the Reeves Family painful as it was, was not limited to them because families were privately burying their dead in other parts of the city for fear of reprisals from the authorities. A sea of pain and lost enveloped the nation.

CHAPTER 7

All this was taking place unknown to Adonis his life continued confined to the dull monotony of prison. The door of his prison cell opened with a clang. He found himself in the presence of a beautiful well dressed aristocratic looking woman.

"Trouble maker you have a visitor. I do not know why madam would waste her time to come and see a bad boy like you." The prison guard did not hide his contempt for the prisoner.

"Remove the handcuffs from him."

"Madame Speaker I please cannot do that. This man is a dangerous man who could attack you when we remove the handcuffs."

"Remove the handcuffs officer. I cannot talk to this young man while he is bound and in chain. I must talk to him like a free man."

"I have to seek permission before I do that. In fact I have to sit down right here to make sure nothing will happen to you in his presence."

The visitor flashed a brilliant smile.

"Officer that will not be necessary. I am perfectly safe talking to this young man."

Recognition dawned on Adonis. This lady smiled just like Liz. In addition their eyes and chiseled noses were the same. This was Liz mother by Jove!

The lady opened her bag and brought out a couple of us dollars bills. "Officer if I need you I will call you-:-"

"Madame if anything happens…_"

"Nothing will happen officer_".

The obstinate bravado had gone out of the officer's voice. He palmed the bills and soon the handcuff clanged opened.

The woman looked at Adonis deeply without saying a word wondering what to say to this young man before her. For a moment her resolve crumbled. Why has she come to see this boy for? Perhaps her husband was right in being dead set against her ever seeing this soon to be convicted man.

It was Adonis who broke the oppressive silence.

"Mama where is Liz? Where is she? Is she alright?

He asked in rapid succession.

"She is in her grave thanks to you and your friends."

"What? Adonis asked in shock. He burst into uncontrollable wailing. Prison guards with drawn guns rushed into his cell. Liz mother remained sitting watching him impassively.

"Madame leave now this boy's head is not straight."

Claudia waved the officers out of the room. Adonis crying face was pathetic to see. The spasm of his cries came from deep with his stomach. Why did she have to die? He asked between fresh outbreaks of tears. It seemed wherever Liz death came up the question why immediately came to mind.

Could this young man be faking grief to earn her sympathy? Claudia watched him as if detached from his grief .A spasm of emotion tore through his body.

"What did I do to you young man for you to take my daughter to her early grave?

Elizabeth before you and your friends poisoned her was such an obedient lovable child. What did my family and I do to you for you to help take away what we love so much?

Adonis remained mute. Tears flowed freely down his face without him attempting to wipe them away. The both of them were united in their grief but the gulf that divided them was still too deep.

"You country people will not be satisfied with anything. We brought you Christianity, civilization and education and look at what you have repaid us with? Look at the country now and you will weep."

"How can we be satisfied madam when we have drunk deep from the prurient spring of education? You think having tasted education we will be satisfied to be your houseboys, cleaning women and continue to receive token gestures?

No madam. You grief is my grief. Most of us in this life our actions are driven by some element of self interest no matter how altruistic we make it appear to be. But that was not the case with Liz. Her beliefs were central to her."

"Tell me young man. How did my daughter die?

"I wish I knew exactly how she died."

Adonis related to Claudia how he took Liz to the apartment, how she ran out and finally how she ran out of their hiding place and his valiant but unsuccessful attempt to stop her."

Tears were rolling down their faces.

"Madame what I want is contrary to what you want. But I can tell you one thing. We both loved Liz dearly. Now I wish I could have died instead of her. As I hear about her death right now the pain of it in this prison is almost too great for me to bear. And madam take it from me I am not saying this because this is what I think you want to hear, but these words of mine are from the bottom of my heart."

Adonis began to sob.

"Young man I do not understand your fight but may God help you as you bear the penalty for your sins."

"I know Liz is in heaven now looking down at me and for her sake I shall continue the struggle in her memory."

Liz mother touched him slightly on his arm and dabbed handkerchief on her face to wipe away the tears from her eyes. Soon the prison guards came to put the chains back on.

Miles Spider was a cold warrior to the bone. A man uneasy with peace viewing every peace overture from the Soviet Union as a ruse to gain tactical advantage in their twilight struggle with the capitalist west carried his beliefs with missionary zeal. No other evil had befallen mankind than the accursed thinking of Marx and Engels in the form of Godless communism seeking to overwhelm the forces of freedom represented by the capitalist free enterprise system practiced in the United States. An absolutist, Miles believed communism must be nibbled in the bud by whatever means possible in any part of the world. Miles would not rest his war and he was willing to do battle in any part of the world where communism reared its ugly head especially in the dark continue of Africa among newly independent states. Liberia had had close historical links to his country; it puzzled him that the government of President Roberts had the audacity to become a leading member of a communist front organization like the Non Aligned Movement giving aid to communists masquerading as freedom fighters in Angola, Mozambique and other places on the continent. Soon if present trend continued Liberia would fall into the communist sphere of influence thus enslaving the freedom loving people of the country.

America the beacon of freedom would lose some strategic assets in this country. Though Liberia was geographically a small nation, it possessed an influence far beyond her size. Newly independent states came to her shores to seek advice as Africa's oldest republic. Losing this country to the communist as it was headed under the administration of President Roberts would be a major loss of face for Washington. Reared in the austere tradition of the conservative Christian right Mile's politics and religion were fused together as one. To prevent Liberia from becoming a socialist nation this reason brought the American evangelist Danny Craven to Monrovia. Every detail of visitors from the eastern bloc and rogue states heads of government that visited the black republic was crammed in the briefcase of Miles safely stored at his home in north Virginia since his decision to visit Liberia.

True to form, the cold warrior arrived in the country on a direct Pan Am flight from New York's JFK Airport to Liberia's Robertsfield Airport as Evangelist Danny Craven. A team of senior local clergymen were on hand to welcome the distinguished American clergyman. This nation was reeling from the unprecedented civil disturbances of the rice Riot of April 14. The youthful opposition leaders spearheading the call for change have been arrested and were being tried for treason. The nation had extended itself, after the violence which shock the country and terrified the elite; a somber reflective mood prevailed. Would Prof. Martins, Adonis Vonley, Emory Lomax and student other student leaders imprisoned in the aftermath others be found guilty of treason and hanged as was specified in the law? Could the forces of law and order adhere to the longing for change and introduce radical reforms to ameliorate the dichotomy in society between the haves and have nots? Or would they react with even more repression as the result of the threat against their authority by a people longing for change? These and many other questions plagued the nation in 1980 when Evangelist Danny Craven plane touched down at the airport. The Evangelistic smiled. He greeted the men assembled to welcome him just outside the glass at the arrival terminal. Danny looked each clergy man in the eye and flashed a brilliant smile. He took time shaking the hands of the dignified men with thick lips and curly hair one by one by their names which he memorized. The raw heat and humidity hit with a bang.

"Welcome to the sweet land of Liberty Evangelist Craven."

Bishop Ted Roland the tall, dark skinned bespectacled head of the Episcopal Church of Liberia announced in his well modulated baritone voice.

"We hope the Lord will use you mightily to save souls in our land."

"Hallelujah brother, the Lord do move in mysterious ways and I know this crusade will bless this wonderful land."

"This way sir," the frocked tall dark Methodist Bishop pointed leading the way to a large stationary van. The ignition started and the engine zoomed to life. Soon the team was headed to Monrovia. The American Evangelist took time introducing the members of his team which included singer Al Kane along with his backup singers, Evangelist Philip Murphy and Prayer Warrior Shiela Kims. The drive from the airport to Monrovia was a lovely drive through coastal mangroves, through low bush dotted with Palm and Rubber trees and tall grass. A narrow single lane highway snaked its way through lush vegetation dotted with isolated homesteads. Danny Craven watched the fleeting shadows and relaxed to admire the scenery. His attention glued to the enthralling scenery was being constantly distracted by the enthusiastic babble of the ministers rattling on and on about their burning desire to save the souls of their countrymen and how the arrival of the distinguish clergy man will aid in that process. "Every generation has a Moses and I believe reverend God has sent you to be the Moses of our generation to raise up disciples for the Lord in our troubled nation."

"Yelp, yelp," the Evangelist mumbled without much conviction. Rev. Adolphus Sayewah, the affable leader of the Baptist Convention eyes rested on their guest watching him keenly. Quickly Danny Craven realized he must say something. More was expected of him than just yelp.

"This is true. Our Lord said the harvest is plentiful but lo the laborers are few." Shiela Kims chipped in for him. Rev. Saywah observed the clergyman.

"Our master said we should go ye into the world and make disciples of all men baptizing them in the name of the Father, Son and the Holy Ghost Mathew 28:19. I hope the Lord will use me to make disciples of all manner of men in this great country."

He muttered with all the sincerity his voice could muted. The Liberian clergy man smiled. The ice has been broken. Now the conversation became more Lord centered. The Evangelist laid a portable bible on his lap allowing his staff to interact with the clergy men while he continued to admired the scenery and concentrate his considerable mental abilities on the elements he needed to contact for the purpose of his mission. Two boyhood friends-military men from the east hailing from the east had been under Washington's radar for years. The country needed an inexperienced person to take over the reign of power.

The prosecution and defense teams rested their case and allowed the jury of two women, and seven men all belonging to the establishment to decide the verdict. The jurors spent the first days of their deliberation debating the upcoming party caucus. All of the conservative jurors were horrified by the events of April 14. The verdict was a foregone conclusion: Guilty as charged. The only point of debate was whether the culprits would face life imprisonment or the death penalty. The pulse of the nation beat faster and faster on the side of the young idealist though; yet people were appalled at the violence of that unforgettable date.

The verdict of the reason trial was tomorrow. Somber religious music dominated the output of ELBC the day before the announcement of the verdict of the treason trial which had tore the nation apart like no other trial in the history of this peaceful nation. Everybody knew something had to be done, but nobody knew exactly what to do. In churches, mosques and shrines around the nation; clergymen and women, imams and zoes prayed for peace. Even in beer bar revelers prayed to the force of the universe. It was a time of national upheaval, uncertainty never seen before in the sublime, almost perpetually peaceful nation. The stakes were high. To further raise the stakes, the civil erudite President had proclaimed a state of emergency. Security forces were given sweeping powers to do anything necessary for the security of the nation.

Inspector Paul Noring pleased that the trouble- makers were locked behind bars where they rightfully belonged was in a tight corner. His intelligence unit informed him that there existed the strong possibility of widespread social disorder if the anarchists were hanged. Perhaps the court could sentence the defendants to death, and then the President could commute the death sentence to a long prison sentence diffusing the situation. A man with his eyes on the lookout for anything out of the ordinary scrutinized one of the posters of an American evangelist who entered the country yesterday posted at the entrance of the police headquarters. Evangelist! Evangelist! Evangelist! He kept turning the word in his mind sipping black coffee later at his office. The evangelist smiling face, his healing crusade sounded altruistic; saving mankind from hell fire. Coming into the country at this time of trouble, something was out of place. The Director kept picking his teeth. Danny Craven coming to polarized nation to bring healing. He kept pacing the room his right fist in his left palm. Inspector Noring flipped on the TV. Why now? Why now? He kept muttering to himself.

Back home he kept thinking about the American evangelist and his healing crusade. Realization slow and powerful dawned on him. He ran outside to the garage alarming his wife who ran after him.

"Noring are you going mad? Must it be you alone who must tote this government business on your head?"

Too focused on his thoughts Mr. Noring did not respond to his wife's verbal jabs. He must make haste because if he responded he would get into a verbal exchange with his wife whom he knew would always have the better of the exchange. He started his trusty red Ford pickup and as he reverse out of the drive way he responded.

"Monica I need to see the President immediately. When I come back I will explain".

"But you are not properly dress, lookat your clothes….

The last words were lost on the Director as his van zoomed out of his leafy Barnersville yard at high speed headed to the Presidency. Family links were even stronger than governmental links and it was his responsibility to help take care of his auntie's son.

CHAPTER 8

Evangelist Daddy Craven could not contain his joy. The long awaited invitation from the President for which they rejoiced at earlier was official. CIA agent Miles Spider aka Evangelist Danny Craven hastily prepared his kits including a particularly powerful miniature camera, an ultra light microphone, and a laser gun. Satisfied with his packing, Miles examined his false teeth. Again satisfied, he selected a pristine white monogram shirt and conservative blue suit for the occasion. The excited agent fumbled through a large time-honored King James Bible checking his watch for the umpteenth's time. Across the street, an unmarked Police vehicle parked unobtrusively observing the scene. Miles Spider drew the curtains of his room apart. A black Mustang that had not been in the vicinity before was parked across the street of his Ducor Hotel. He laughed: the goons tilling frequently changed cars. This invitation from the Liberian President was uplifting. The word has been going around that the President was loathed at the particular time to meet with Americans since there were rumors were flying around that the Americans were dissatisfied with the new independent nationalistic trend of President Robert wanting a change of government. At last intense lobbying by local clergymen along with the President's own pastoral tendencies won out allowing the President to meet the US Evangelist in his official residence. Of course, the President could have agreed to meet him in his home town at Careysburg where he entertained his friends and spent the weekends. But that would not serve the purpose of the cold warrior. He wanted a meeting with the President at the Presidential Palace. Now that the invitation had come; he struggled to contain his emotion. The ability to detach oneself from emotion and do the job necessary for God, Country and Family was one of the most prized character traits of an agent.

Minutes later, the veteran agent accompanied by Rev. Korlubah, other senior clergymen and Rev. Sayewah had transformed into Evangelist Danny Craven, distinguished, affable, clean shaven, and a conservative friendly man with a burning passion for bringing healing to a nation being torn apart by itself. Camera flashed and zoomed. Danny Craven smiled as the long sleek limousine conveying him sped through the narrow winding streets of the capital down Broad Street onto Gurley Street and UN Drive. As they journeyed to the Mansion the narrow road gave way to a a more spacious boulevard leading to the seat of power.

Danny Craven was absolutely involved in the meticulous study of God's word evidenced by his deep meditative mood. He mapped out his route from the back of his car chauffeur driven van reading his bible

The main entrance to the fenced seat of the Presidency was surprisingly very lightly guarded. Vendors selling cigarettes and mints were even trading right at the entrance. Furthermore, commercial cars were depositing passengers right in front of the building. The low iron fence encircling the mansion could be jumped over by a teenager. Pedestrians strolled passed the large building from all directions. The limousine carrying the American evangelist approached the Mansion from the lower direction of the impoverished densely populated Buzzi Quarter and branched right heading straight to the box sized architecture of the Executive mansion which looked dark yet made outwardly transparent by an outer screened through which one could see part of the Mansion wall. Below the arched pathway through which they drove to the main entrance the visitor noticed the beautiful flower garden of neat manicured lawns which added a touch of class to the somewhat austere surrounding of the rigid formality of power. Miles Spider's casual nature possessed an instant aversion to formal rigidity.

Chaperone by a phalange of bodyguards, the evangelist and his Liberian gospel minister companions. Evangelist Danny Craven was received with respect and cordiality. The elevator discharged the guests into an ornate styled room furnished in an elegant taste. The view and luxury of the room astounded Miles Spider who imagined the country to be a mosquito infected backwater. Gold embroidered chairs filled with soft, rich red plumes pillows occupied the center of the room. There were also leather chairs equipped with hand rests. Large embroidered drape curtains covered the sliding windows enhancing the colors of the white mannequin ceilings and silver chandeliers hanging above. The sweet scent of Hibiscus and aloe flowers permeated the Presidential suite with their enchanting aloes. Thick wall to wall carpets met one shoe as soon as one exited the polish tiles of the hallway. One could almost see an image of oneself in the veneer wood lining both sides of the Presidential desk courtesy of the premium quality varnish used on it. Soft electric lights hidden behind chandeliers filled the room made even more comfortable by split air-conditioned system. In a corner to the right of the President's chair, a large volume of books filled the shelves of a large cupboard like shelf. Above the shelf hanged portrays of past Liberian Presidents. Few men possessed the aura, the aura of a dignified African statesman as the dark man sitting behind the desk. His face was somber and round; bespectacled he wore a creamy white suit with dovetailed collars. His shoes matched his clothes. President Roberts have done away with the long tail three piece western suits which have been trademarks of the powers that be in Liberia for so long.

"Welcome Evangelist Craven, this office has heard much about your good works. The Lord is using you to accomplish much, it my fervent hope that the Lord will use you to bring healing and reconciliation to our troubled land."

The President smiled and extended his hand for a handshake. "Thank you President Roberts for making time in your busy schedule to grant an audience to me and my friends. I am glad to be in your country and doubly glad to meet you not only as a President of this great nation but also as a clergyman who still preaches in his hometown church."

The President again smiled shaking the hands of the prominent clergymen who accompanied the American evangelist.

"Evangelist Danny Craven you have chosen well using your life to serve your Creator. Exactly what message have you brought us?

"May we pray?

The earnest evangelist asked. A request which the President readily agreed to. When the prayer was over, in a booming voice Danny Craven announced.

"I have come to bring the hearts of the children to their fathers according to Malachi 2:6. To make men study war no more. To let your people know while politics can divide humankind, Jesus Christ our Saviour and Master can unite. Onesimus, a runaway slave was told by Paul to return to his master. His master was told by Paul in a letter to receive Onesimus not as a slave but as a brother, as a co- laborer in the Lord. I have come President Robert, to tell proclaim to your nation the message of God's love and the atoning sacrifice of Christ."

The President listened in rap attention as Evangelist Danny Craven espoused the teachings of the good book with infectious enthusiasm. Miles Spider was a natural born actor endowed with a tempestuous charm which endeared him to all people irrespective of their skin color. He spoke from the script at his hotel supplied by the agency's psychologists which he rehearsed for so long while his exterior brimmed with enthusiasm, his inner hood squirmed at what he was saying because he did not believe a word of it. "To whom little is given, little is expected," the President mused.

"Sometimes though for some of us to whom much is given we wonder whether much is not a curse rather than a blessing. I do not understand how boys I have singled out for their brilliance; provided scholarships for them to study both at home and abroad suddenly turned against me and my government, stirring the people. I know Evangelist Craven there are problems, historical problems between the children of the settlers and the children of the tribal people. But past inequalities cannot be reversed within a year. I cannot understand how people nurtured to correct these inequalities against stiff opposition from the old guard could exploit these very inequalities against their benefactor to gain political power."

"That is why my message of healing and reconciliation is so important for your nation."

The President nodded his head in agreement

Miles Spider wished he had never met this man. This man who was treating him with so much respect and being so candid to him, yet it was the downfall of this very man he had come to seek. Evangelist Danny Craven presented the President with a large gold leaf bible laden with microphones. "Call on me anytime especially before you leave."

The President then offered a short word of prayer before personally escorting the American to the elevator, an honor bestowed on very few visitors. A sleek limousine drove the American back to his hotel.

In the evening, Danny Craven had to deliver his first major outdoor sermon near the Springs Airfield on the Tubman Boulevard. Zero hours was just few hours away during which time his contacts already poised to act would move against the Executive Mansion around midnight to capture the President. President Roberts would live the rest of his life in exile. At least this gave the tough agent a little comfort. This man had to leave the Presidency because he was getting too friendly with the nations of the eastern bloc. The arms and ammunitions were already in the hands of the saboteurs. Key commanders have been separated into those to be bribed, those to be drugged and those to be eliminated as a last resort.

It was a balmy night in the capital, a day blessed with a kind of unusually calm,, fair weather; it was one of those days which the sun did not shine with her blistering intensity nor did the rain with her penetrating wetness come down. The weather could be described as pleasantly cool but the heavy relative humidity made it a fair day with a kind of vague efflorescence moodiness attached. This pattern of fair gray weather extended into a breezeless evening. By night cars still clogged the highways leaving the city center for the suburbs. The idle chatter of birds has been absent throughout the day. The President alone in his office agonized over the fate of the boys in prison if the judges came out with a guilty verdict.

Danny Craven was also deep in meditation in his hotel room memorizing his script for the crusade sermon.

President Robert was kneeling to pray when a weary Director Noring without appointment burst into his office. The President kept him at arm length still deep in meditation. Director Noring stood impatiently, but protocol demanded that he waited. The drone of the air condition made him uncomfortable. The President communed with his God for the next ten minutes oblivious to the presence of his police chief. Satisfied with his meditation he rose slowly to his feet.

"What is it this time?"

He asked in annoyance.

"Mr. President I have come to warn you never to meet with Danny Craven. He must be deported as an undesirable alien."

"You better be careful about what you say about the Lord's servant otherwise you may face the wrath of the Almighty."

"Mr. President we have photos. In fact there is a witness to prove that the so called evangelist have been contacting elements of the army for a coup. Cousin Robert that man is pure trouble."

The President peered over the pictures examining them for a while.

He hesitated before speaking. When he spoke, he chose his words carefully.

'Let the man carry out his evangelistic activities tonight. Tomorrow morning come with your witness and evidence. Watch his movements after the crusade. I am too stressed today to look into such matter. Contact the Justice and Defense Ministers to be here with you tomorrow morning. Leave me in peace right now."

"President Robert ah...

"I say leave Noring now before I lose my appetite."

"Okay sir"

Director Noring boarded the elevator with a sinking sensation in his stomach; he had failed to warn the President sufficiently about Danny Craven's nefarious activities. His evidence the Director knew were circumstantial, but his bones told him there was something more sinister about the evangelist with the beaming smile than meet the eyes.

Miles Spider listened with keen interest to the conversation between the Police Chief and the President. It was imperative action be taken sooner rather than later. The evangelist counter checked his plans to make sure everything was in order. Meanwhile, thousands of Liberians young and old, thin and fat, whole and crippled, sighted and sightless journeyed to the eastern suburbs to hear the good news of the message of God in a scary, uncertain time to be delivered by Evangelist Craven whose hope filled voice had saturated the nation's airwaves in recent days. The Platform for the occasion in the open air was constructed of planks. White clothes printed with bold letter filled with salvation messages encircled the platform filled teeming with singers, pastors, instruments and PA Systems. Huge speakers placed in strategy corners ensured that even those outside the perimeters of the crusade venue heard the message. Many people came with deformed children hoping for divine intervention. Bold printing on clothes throughout the crusade venue announce: "Jesus Can Set You Free!

Singing and dancing by an enthusiast crowd reverberated everywhere

Many hoped for a miracle and divine intervention. Banners announced "There is hope in Christ. The sheer enthusiasm of the crowd filled the atmosphere with an air of expectation. Local pastors introduced the evangelist with lavish praise at the end of an hour of intoxicating praise and worship. A sea of humanity of curly hair, thick lips, and gallant features became silent when the evangelist drew to the microphone. At that moment the chain smoking white saboteur, political missionary, and cold warrior dedicated to nibbling communism and socialism in the bud metamorphosized into a passionate advocate of Christianity. His voice echoed loud and clear interrupted by frequent cheers from an enthusiastic audience. Cripples were throwing their clutches away because of miraculous healing. Thousands came forward to receive Christ while many others came forward to renew their commitment to God. Trained counselors rushed to talk to them about their salvation. At that moment, a buzz sounded in the microphone hidden in Miles Spider ears. The dogs of war were moving on the President. He heaved. How he wanted to take a stiff drink: but how could he now?

CHAPTER 9

Liberia awoke to unprecedented, startling and revolutionary news shaking the very foundation upon which the nation state rested. The news swept the foundation of the old order, lock, stock and barrel. It was a joyous, spontaneous, tumultuous and extremely traumatic at the same time. It brought the unknown, the weak and hitherto powerless into the very den of power. Bringing the erstwhile rich and powerful into sudden subjugation, ridicule, and powerlessness never before seen in the land. This startling change made especially poignant by its dramatic manifestation and brute force. Listeners to early morning shows on the airways were surprised, stunned and stupefied by the announcement on the radio. Strange and dreamlike it seemed as if occurring in some distant land. The labored, unrefined, heavily accented voice with a strange twang, unrehearsed and unsophisticated belonging to one unpracticed in the diction of broadcasting echoed in the ears of listeners. But the voice carried a certain tone of ruthlessness and frenzied command bordering on morbid hysteria.

"The government of William Roberts has been overthrown due to nepotism, rampant corruption, favoritism, and economic mismanagement. Fellow citizens the People Salvation Council is in full control. All former government officials especially cabinet ministers, Legislators, and heads of security agencies are to report themselves to the nearest police station or the nearest military barracks effective immediately without the slightest delay. Any government official failing to adhere to this announcement will be dealt with most severely along with those harboring them. All political parties with particular emphasis on the National Whigs Party is banned with immediate effect. The Salvation Council is in control effective immediately. All governmental functions are now in the hands of the Salvation Council. The members of the Salvation Council are Master Sergeant Maxwell Forkpa, Chairman and Head of State, Sergeant Harrison Varney, Vice Chairman, Staff Sergeant Samuel Dahn, Commanding General of the Armed Forces of Liberia."

The unrefined voice continued to rattle the names of members of the new government. People held their breath. For those privileged to watch the announcement on television, the footage was even more dramatic. It showed the image of a man barely literate following the text of his speech laboriously with his fingers so as not to miss a line. Behind him stood his fellow young soldiers in uniforms holding M-16 Rifles with grenades hanging on their uniforms. Even as their action was surprising and unprecedented, it carried a tinge of mysterious profoundness of purpose. None of the low ranking soldiers claiming to have overthrown more that 125 years of National Whigs Party rule had ever come to national attention. The nations held her breath, somersaulted and exploded into rapturous joy. The recorded message was played again and again on state radio leaving no trace of doubt in the mind of even the most die-hard skeptic. The old order has been unceremoniously swept under the carpet by the terrible momentum of a people longing for change. Unsure of how the change would come, the country has been overwhelmed by the startling swiftness of the change coming from the most unexpected quarter. Unable to contain her joy crowds thronged to the streets yelling, dancing, screaming, ululation, jubilating and singing. Unlike the angry stampeding crowds of April 14 almost a year before; this crowd was crazy from hysteria borne out of sheer joy, spontaneous and explosive. A man dancing in the streets around Rally Time Market dropped and died. Died from too much happiness because his weak heart could not contain the flow of adrenalin was the autopsy report of his death. As the hours, dragged on more people thronged the streets waving hastily constructed placards of woods scrawled with chalks splashed on them. The slumbering nation has risen to a bright and beautiful day. An upbeat mood of optimism captured the imagination of the youthful population. Young soldiers in American made military jeeps sped through the streets amidst cheers from the crowds anxious to behold the face of her heroes. It was an exciting, interesting and glorious time to be young, to parade the streets condemning the old order. Even the voices of radio announcers announcing the momentous events carried the news with unbridled enthusiasm.

CHAPTER 10

Adonis Vonleh, Prof. Martins, Emory Lomax along with their other comrades had resigned themselves to their fate. However, they knew because of people power execution would not come to then, but a long spell in jail remained a very likely possibility. The tight clusters of men in prison sense something terribly amiss. Very unusual gunfire echoed in the distance breaking the eerie silence of midnight going towards dawn. Burst of automatic gunfire was followed by explosions. For once jailers and the jailed became united in their fear of the unknown terror being unleashed. The gunfire sounded very close. Just as abruptly as the gunfire started it ended in a similar manner. It became silent and the shrill cries of amphibians filled the air from surrounding mangrove swamps outside . Guards and inmates of the Post Stockade experienced one of man's basis emotions: fear.

Then it happened as if by magic as heavily armed soldiers burst into the prison compound

"Where are the prisoners? Open the door or we will

burst your heads open! The invading soldiers shouted at the wardens who cowered before the combat troops.

Adonis did not know what to make of the situation. There were sounds of approaching footsteps and hurried movement of keys in doors. Then, armed men burst into their cells.

"All of you hurry up!

A hesitating Prof. Martins was yanked to his feet.

"Who are you?"

He demanded.

"Never mind, just get into a single file all of you."

Like prisoners being led to a slaughter house the prisoners followed the soldiers. From their actions the prisoners could not deduce whether they had come on a rescue mission or whether they were government agents sent to secretly execute them before the court issued a formal death sentence. Rifles were pointed at them from all directions, harsh and menacing leaving no chance for conversation among the confused frightened men.

The blinding street lights outside exposed both the soldiers and their prisoners. A speeding jeep approached them from the direction of the Mansion and drew to an abrupt stop with tires screeching on the pavement. Soldiers having blood shot eyes leapt out.

"Get in!

For Adonis this was the time to take a stand.

"Tell us where we are going first."

"I say get in! a tall skinny officer roared.

"No, we are not going anywhere. If you want to kill us, shot us here. You are not going to shoot us like some dogs in some corners and throw our bodies into some gutter or better still into the sea.

"My God get in."

Adonis and his comrades stood their ground.

"We are not murderers but coup makers. Get in please. The leader says we will get kill if anything happens to you guys. Please get in quick."

Everybody waited for Adonis's reaction.

"Let us get in the car since these soldiers will not allow us to go back to prison nor can we remain in the open like this exposing ourselves to snipers"

The humming engine sprang to life speeding through the deserted streets.

In the cold chill of an April night each man kept his own counsel unsure of what fate awaited them. Driven at high speed to the seat of the Presidency where chaos reigned supreme with men running around shouting, trigger happy soldiers occasionally sending volleys of shots into the sky in an endless cacophony of confusion and happiness. It seemed all perplexing to the prisoners.

Adonis now knew for certain in this chaos a truly momentous event was taking place before their very eyes.

None of the men brought has seen so many soldiers assembled in one place like this before. Some of the soldiers already drunk were singing praises to their leaders. Jostled into the limelight Adonis and his comrades had not yet comprehended the monstrous complexities of the simplistic events unfolding before them. What tremendous relief it though to know it was not cold execution that awaited them. Soldiers were throwing biscuits, beer, and soft drinks to the emaciated prisoners. Adonis did not like the scene at the Mansion yard. He wondered aloud why they were brought there in the first place?

CHAPTER 11

Master Sergeant Maxwell Forkpa appeared to be living in a dream world too good to be true. His highest goal in life was to become a commissioned officer and if possible to obtain the rank of a Captain, that was all he longed for. His parents had accepted their poverty state. He Maxwell wanted to rise beyond where fate placed him in life hoping to better his lot in a modest way. By the time Maxwell completed middle school in his earlier years, lack of money forced the bright strapping lad to drop out of school to do petty trading. He wanted to attend the prestigious BWI Vocational school hoping to raise the money through trading on a small amount given him by his mother selling charcoal in Soniwein Market. His dreams came true. The lad gained admission into the school only to be back on the streets of Monrovia a year later selling cigarettes to survive because his mother had taken ill.

His educational ambition cut short by an evil monster that had pursued him all his life "no money Syndrome," desperate to survive and pay his mother's medical bills, the young man in his early twenties sought the army, but again gaining admission into this dump site was difficult. The young man spent a year in the house of General Prince Marwieh as his porter, houseboy, and butler before the General enlisted him.

Maxwell did not disappoint his benefactor for he quickly proved to be a dedicated soldier, yet a burning rage inside him did not endear him to his commanders. He raged at inequalities in the army where only the sons of Generals and Colonels got all the promotions while the children of sergeants remained corporals suitable only for sentry guard posts. This baggage of rage at society contributed to a vague sense of insecurity for he always felt like an outsider knowing his best was not good enough because he came from a no name background. His first child he had by a girl selling charcoal near his mother in the same market. Being father made him to ponder his future even more. If he wanted a good life he must conform to the norm, swallow his pride to become the ideal soldier. He vowed never to poke his nose at the sons of the elite who made up the top brass of the army so he worked hard. He soon teamed up with a group of boys of similar backgrounds namely: poor urban reared boys of tribal stock who sought solace in the army. These boys worked hard and bided their time hoping for the day of a truly professional army based on merit.

It astounded Maxwell on a sunny Tuesday morning during one of the Armed Forces Day Parade at the BTC when he was introduced to a queasy voice American by one of the Military Attaché of a friendly government.

They talked about many things during the cool of the day then he excused himself.

Few weeks again at a local club the American by chance came upon him. The American slow and sure tickled his imagination by waking up long suppressed dreams. This time he invited best friend Samuel Dahn. The American shared their desire for a truly professional army but refused to discuss any politics because in his words "Politics was a dirty game played by cunning politicians."

Intrigued by his sincerity and rambunctious charm, the young men hanged on to every word of the American. Little by little the American over bottles of beer in a dingy drinking spot convinced the soldier boys that the power to change the destiny of their country lay in their hands. But the young men laughed at his naivety.

"Since 1847 things have been like this and will always remained like this" Maxwell remarked laughing as he choked on a large morsel of fly infested roasted meat. Unknown to the young soldiers the chap who met Maxwell on AFL Day on February 11 was another person different from the one talking to them now. Miles Spider's voice was electronically process to sound like Mike Coker. A little hair dye and a few inches imbedded in the soles of the agent's shoes had made away with the difference between the two. Miles had come to take off where Mike left.

His job was to put finishing touches to their plans for the action. Again the antis have been raised. The serving American Ambassador Desmond Diaz in an illicit love liaison with a Liberian girl died from poisoning.

Ambassador Diaz's relationship with the increasingly non aligned was not so cordial. Were Liberian security officers somehow involved in the death of the US Ambassador? The death of an American Ambassador was not a small things. It was time to act, to unleash the dogs of war on the President.

In the dead of night while the nation's attention riveted on the crusade ground the American from information gleaned from his brief visit knew the exact location of the President. He was even listening to the heartbeat of the President.

Anxious the President usually slept in his hometown about 45 minutes from the capital. An inside informant working with the agency sent a coded signal. The president would sleep in his official residence that night. It was imperative to act.

Of the two leaders of the group of 17 enlisted men, Samuel Dahn was the warrior leading the troops. These group of men hailing from the east was armed to the teeth with assault rifles and grenades stormed an almost defenseless Mansion. They did not face much difficulty in penetrating the lax security of the Mansion. What the coupmakers did not count on was the presence of two Guinean bodyguards and two American trained security officers in the building that night. The men in the dead of night gravitated to the bedroom of the president thanks to the beacon implanted in the walking stick he was so fond of. A short fierce exchange of gunfight erupted. Thanks to the laser guns with silencers supplied by Miles Spider, defenders were killed.

Bursting in the room of the sleeping President; fearful and barbarous the soldiers argued over what to do. In the confusion that followed Samuel Dahn shot the President at close range in the head. Even as the President laid in a pool of blood in his own bed the heated argument continued among the soldiers.

Who was going to make the historic broadcast and announce himself President?

Maxwell Forkpa, Harrison Varney, and Samuel Dahn, the three most senior ranked members of the coup making team all coveted the position of Commanding General of the Army. The three men craved the soldier's post ;all loathed the political role of the President. The position of the President was a dead end since the purpose of the coup was to return the country to civilian rule as soon as the country became stable after the coup.

Maxwell like his friends wanted to continue to serve in the army when the country returned to constitutional rule.

"Samuel Dahn you are the one that killed the President and led us here, so I nominate you to become the head of State, President whatever you call it. You will be the best person for the job since this is a temporal role."

All of the guys nodded in agreement.

"I am mightily pleased that all of you including my friend Maxwell here want me to assume the role of the President. But aren't we missing something here?

Among us here the most senior ranked officer is Master Sergeant Maxwell Forkpa. I am a Staff Sergeant how can I become the head when there is a more senior officer?

"It doesn't matter who becomes the President since decisions will be taken collectively. The presidency is just a figure head." Maxwell retorted.

"Exactly, that why you our chief must become our head. You will guide us. And man Maxwell you are a much better speaker and reader than I am. I can't even read that speech prepared by that creepy looking white man."

Samuel was insistent while Maxwell was adamant.

"Guys time is running out, we cannot stay here arguing. Remember we need to go to the radio and TV stations to announce the coup."

At last his friends speaking with one voice prevailed on Maxwell.

"You are the most senior ranking officer of Master Sergeant - you have to be the President."

Maxwell was forced to accept the poisoned chalice of the Presidency.

"We need to put on trial all of the corrupt leaders of this country and execute them if guilty of crimes against the Liberian people."

"You could not have said it better. Isn't that what we all say?

Yea! Yea! Yea!

The new leaders filled with killer lust swift as an eagle sprinted in fast jeeps during the wee hours of the morning in the still sleepy city to broadcasting house.

Maxwell's slow uncertain fingers helped him to read the text of his historic broadcast. Oh how he felt so acutely aware of his lack of refinement for the highest office in the land! Even as he made the historic announcement his heart longed for the life of the barrack where he belonged instead of the suffocating, demanding, and absolute frivolity of the highest political office.

How he shifted in the executive chair of the Presidency. The soft velvety chair was too soft for his comfort. For a man used to the hard benches of the barrack, this seat was just too soft. Maxwell hated the endless meetings, his only comfort were his friends who like him hated a lot of things they were now doing. As the looting and confusion in the immediate aftermath of the coup died down Maxwell smiled. This meant soon he was going to vacate the damnable executive seat.

CHAPTER 12

Director Noring an early riser showered and made coffee. As was his habit, he flipped the large radio perched on a small glass table as a pleasant background noise not bothering to listen much.

He took his time to put on his clothes which oozed confidence; well pressed and starched.

Government officials must report themselves immediately!

Monica woke with a start shivering "Noring I had this terrible dream…..Ah" she recoiled.

"Men burst into your cousin's room at the Mansion and killed him in his own bed. Oh my God, what is happening? Where are you going?

Noring bent over and held his wife very close.

"I think dear you had a nightmare, calm down I'd get you some painkillers to help you relax. Nothing of that sort has happened before in this country and nothing of that sort will happen not under my watch." Director Noring managed to calm his almost hysterical wife stroking her head gently. He tried to call the Defense

Minister and there was nothing but silence. Another call to the Justice Minister and again silence. Director Noring then sensed something wrong and he fought to control his mounting panic.

It did not take long for the sound of a crowd rushing to their residence permeated the solitude of their room. A mob of excited people encircling their property.

The sounds of the mob were frightening like bloodhounds zoning for the kill. Husband and wife stood in their dream house they labored many years to build.

"Follow me I know his room!

Noring heard a very familiar voice.

Four soldiers burst into their room invading their privacy in an obscene manner.

Director Noring was in total shock. Standing before him was his houseboy of 10 years whom he gave his last name to -Sam Noring! Gone were the submissive girth he carried around until last night.

"Move off, you are under arrest!

Sam holding a rifle screamed.

Noring remained unruffled in dignified silence stagnant in his position. He was a man used to issuing orders to lower ranking officers and not the other way round. Sam angered by Director Noring's insolence struck him down with his rifle butt. Even then looters were now busy in their house. Sam Noring pointed his rifle.

"One move and I shoot you like a dog."

The Director's wife burst into tears and then fainted. A powerless Director Noring was led out of his own house a gun to his head into a commandeered vehicle. Forced into a waiting commandeered van captives and captors had barely cleared the imposing villa; when more looters pounced on the house with renew fury ransacking and looting on a systematic scale.

Though this military change has come as a surprise to many, the majority of the people had the élan to be brazen about it rejoicing in the streets. Any symbol of authority became fair game. Masonic lodges dotting the city and long symbol of power and political exclusivity came tumbling down.

However, it was the soldiers kept in the background for so long buoyed in their new power and prestige that were having a field day. Experiencing for the first time that a piece of wood and steel they call gun had the power to subjugate their civilian masters whom they had served faithfully, the soldiers became intoxicated.

Suppressed for so long the majority of Liberians of tribal stock had no second thoughts of mercy about the once powerful Americo- Liberians they once served. Scorn, irreverence, and downright contempt was what they received. All over the city government officials were being rounded up and hurled to prison by vigilantes styled group and soldiers. Army boys patrolling in commandeered cars cruised the streets at high speed picking up former officials and evicting them from their properties. Citizens were constantly bombarded by terse decrees issued from the enigmatic Salvation Council and her intriguing leaders through radio and television.

Excitement continued on the street. Rumor mill had it that Hon. James Jones Reeves; the avuncular Speaker of the

House of Representative had a pregnant dummy of a human being in his closet to enhance his political power. Skulls were being dragged out of the homes of former prominent government officials. These grotesque discoveries were given wide prominence in state controlled print and electronic media. There were suggestions that the former President even wanted to sell Liberia to a foreign buyer. Mysteriously, the new leaders had nothing to say about the fate of the former President. Director Paul Noring, his white Police Uniform shirt stained with blood was dumped onto an open football field in the barracks. With him was the incredibly handsome but aging House Speaker Hon. James Jones Reeves.

More government official found guilty of treason in a one day trial were being brought and dumped on the field. The acerbic Finance Minister, a brother of the late President scowled in a jeep along with the ministers of Labor, Foreign Affairs. Inspector Noring was handcuffed behind his back. Even in his captive and condemned state the former Minister of Finance echoed defiance. His words always caustic and strident lashed out. "Your own na finish."

A soldier mocked.

"I do not blame anybody but big brother Robbie. He should have killed all of the country as—s in jail long before Noko in uniforms thought on taking guns to kill him. I told Robbie not to buy guns for you good for nothing soldiers only fit to work as foremen on farms and to scrub toilets. I just do not understand what Robbie saw in those country bastards now who caused the coup sending them abroad on government scholarships."

An enraged soldier slapped the man being escorted to the execution ground.

"Oh my God how dare this animal strike me with his hands resembling those of a Monkey!

Frank sneered mustering all the contempt his voice could utter.

"You look like an animal on heat!"

The enraged soldier slapped him again for the second time this time drawing blood from the defenseless man. The former Finance Minister looked right into his eyes and spat there. "You are no better than a dog. I smell you even as you sit beside me!

Frank screamed. The incensed soldier wanted to strike for the third time, but another soldier stayed his hand.

"Stop beating the prisoner."

"Don,t you hear…

"Shut your mouth"

Director Noring vowed watching the scene to get even. One day his son Stephen presently at an American naval academy will get even with his torturers on his behalf. For days they have been kept in detention closed to the outside world not knowing the reason for their detention except for the fact they were prominent officials in the disposed regime. One early morning rounded up with impressive alacrity they were dragged before a court. Even before then, the versatile rumor mill had convicted them pleased that the hated symbols of oppressive authority would be executed for their crimes against the Liberian people.

A large groups of onlookers gathered at the golden sand beach behind the BTC barrack to watch in anticipation of a brutal spectacle. Like spectators in ancient Rome gathered to watch Gladiators in anticipation. Most rumors proved to be unfounded, but this one turned out to be otherwise. The blindfolded men mocked and abused were being escorted by soldiers. A soldier escorting one of the prisoners screamed in agony shouting one of the prisoners kicked him on his private parts with a back kick. The Finance Minister recognizable to the crowd by his slight stoop licked his lips in satisfaction. Director Noring prayed silently for a last minute reprieve still believing in a miracle. As the soldiers tied the irascible Finance Minister to the light poles he still cursed them calling them bastards, monkeys, rogues and using many other lewd invectives. Lined up neatly with their backs on the poles facing their executioners the condemned men waited. In a civilized world this could not happen. The condemned men could not see their executioners thanks to the blindfolds covering their eyes. Counting the soldiers cocked their rifles. Frank Roberts continued cursing the soldiers.

Fire! Came the dreaded command. Micro seconds later, the prisoners numbering thirteen in all slumped against the light poles. Small trickles of blood oozed from where the bullets penetrated snatching dear life away from them. In a bizarre scenario as the men collapse the spectators rejoiced. The collapse of the men meant the killings has been done. There would be no more state sanctioned killings.

The cool breeze blowing from the Atlantic Ocean bestowed a false sense of calm after a vile act has been committed. The bodies were then collected and taken to an unknown destination. The sins of the past has been avenged and expunged . A new society of egalitarianism would be built. But the bodies being collected would come back to haunt the nation.

With the most powerful men for they were all men sent to the great beyond the new junta felt secured from her enemies. But was it safe from itself?

Maxwell Forkpa on the surface appeared to a be an unassuming young man. His beliefs about things were never dogmatic. First and foremost he was a pragmatist and a man endowed with a sharp mind and the ability to learn and adapt quickly. He valued loyalty as long as that loyalty was pledged to him as an individual. Plucked from obscurity into the seat of power he somehow felt inadequate for the position thrust upon him. He rather envied his friend Samuel Dahn serving as Commanding General. Would this sense of insecurity come back to haunt him throughout his presidency? Samuel Dahn his unofficial number two was a quiet reserved man. He had an aversion to being in the limelight. His view of life was stoic. However, his aversion to publicity hid his vanity of imagining himself to be the protector of Liberian democracy. He was prepared to use violence to achieve that goal. His fierce determination and charisma inured him to the nuances of many things.

Harrison Payne like his two friends was at the peak of his physical strength in his late twenties. He too has grown up in poverty in the slums of Monrovia. His parents migrants to the city from the country like so many people found the dream did not match the reality. Harrison was the most leftwing member of the junta. He was stern and some may say dogmatic in his views. He was a man of fiery temper, a swift tongue and acerbic character. He believed that the purpose of the coup was to return the country to civilian rule after ridding the country of raffish politicians of the old order. He was determined that he and his fellow coup-makers did not remain in power too long. Thomas Payne also did not want to see anyone including Maxwell Forkpa though the nominal head to boss over him.

Alexander Kulah just happened to be lucky to be part of the council. He always wanted only to be on the winning side.

Outside the junta's office a group of supporters gathered again to present their statement of loyalty and support. The scenario seemed to come from a script. Groups of young people led by older people in vibrant mood waving placards always coming to the Mansion to praise the young President had become order of the day. The arrival of this group was expected. The President delayed in his office bidding time to meet them. He quickly learnt that being a big man meant people had to wait for the big man almost all the time. He smiled when he at last descended the stairs to meet the group assembled in front of the balcony. The group became ecstatic seeing the young President accompanied by bodyguards come towards them in crisp new uniforms.

"Native woman born Soya! Native woman born Soya!

The crowd chanted. Then it was time for the speech making. Speaker after speaker eulogized the new government using big words the President did not understand the meanings, yet he smiled listening in rap attention. The mid morning sun seemed to smile down on the crowd. Maxwell was a quick learner and charmer. Within days he learned to address crowd speaking fast to avoid hearing his own words which he knew did not sound refined. Would this insecurity about his background served a fly in an ointment during his Presidency?

"In the cause of the people!

The struggle continues! The crowd roared back.

"Well the time for flowery speeches are over; it is now time for action. We will guarantee peace and security for your children to go to school, for you to feed your children, go to the market. It is time for prosperity in the land! The head of state screamed . The crowd adoring her new leader broke into thunderous applause. Gone were the leaders of yesterday wearing suits hidden from the people they governed by their limousines and rigid formality.

Shortly after the outdoor rally, a distinguished looking man in his early 60s endowed with low cropped hair sprinkled with a fine maze of black hair interspersed with approached the President. A pair of large horn-rimmed glasses was perched on his high aristocratic nose. The man attempted to kneel down as he presented a prepared statement wrapped with gold ribbons. The President smiled receiving the bulky document from his guest. No two men could be so unlike physically. But Ebenezer Kum in the chance meeting could cast a long shadow on the intricate workings of the country.

President Forkpa invited the leaders of the delegation to meet him in his office. The new President did not like uppity politicians with toothy smiles. Ebie Kum knowing this from a source did not wear his favorite western suit. For this occasion his choice of clothes was an embroidered batik shirt. To add authority to his posture he wore a Fez cap with a golden tassel. He also carried a cane not really to help him in walking but to aid in his posture of being an elderly statesman.

The President in this casual meeting wore a stiff upper lip to hide his impatience making him look older than his 28 years.

"Well is great for our sons, brave and strong to hear the cries of the masses and act upon those cries to bring redemption to our people."

Maxwell gave the speaker a savage look which Ebie did not appear to notice continuing his speech in an unhurried manner. It would be rude to interrupt him.

"The position of President does not come just to anyone overnight. Some labor hard for it without success. Remember Thomas Faulkner? Liberia's perennial Presidential candidate in the earlier part of this century. Four times he vied for the Presidency without success.

He did not once get to the seat he craved for.

Your Excellency President Maxwell Forkpa God has sent you uncompromisingly swift into the position of Head of State. The future destiny of this nation lies in your hands. You may not realize it being young as you are how many people craved and envy you for the position God has thrust into your hands. Even some of your very friends like how Judas betrayed Jesus may even secretly envy you."

"Hold it right there! We of the Salvation Council are united; there is no division among us. I am strongly committed to handling over power to good civilians not crooks like you pretending to be in favor of the masses."

Ebie Kum flashed a brilliant disarming smile.

"Exactly handling over power to crooks like us who call ourselves politicians so soon can be a dangerous thing. Our society has to be rid of all raffish elements. A new future of peace and prosperity lies in store for the future of this land with you as the head. I sincerely believed you are the one God has chosen to usher us into this glorious era."

Blood rushed to Maxwell's face. Ebie Kum's enchanting words had a point.

"I am pleased my President to place my humble services at your disposal. The other men in the meeting did not say a word perhaps they had been handpicked by Ebie Kum.

President Maxwell Forkpa knew a crafty politician when he saw one. He decided to test the man's ability.

"Name me any position you want for your taking; a managing director of one of the public corporations, or the Minister of Internal Affairs will do for a man of your caliber," the President suggested in a wry voice. Who could resist the lure of a lucrative job?"

Ebie Kum displayed his disarming smile again

"Of course I am flattered by your generous offer Mr. President, a good one from a fine thinking young man. We politicians have messed up this country. It is an awesome task that has been placed on you young liberators to clean the mess we've made. But I will always be willing to give one or two pieces of advice I know with intelligent head like yours you will need very little tutelage in the craft of statesmanship. But I will be pleased to share part of your enlightened company instead of further helping to mess up this country by being a minister or a managing director".

The President thanked his guests smiling. " Mr. President can I say something to you in private?

"Sure."

The President signaled for aides and bodyguards milling around to leave the room. This act was most unusual for him especially someone he did not know so well. But this was his Mansion. Alone with the intriguing Ebenezer Kum, the man got down on his knees.

"Mr. President I have a very special message from God to you. Have you thought what will happen to you if you leave this seat? Which civilian government will feel secure with you being a general in their army knowing you have a track record of staging a coup? God has put you into this chair and only he alone can remove you. All your fellow junta members although they did not know it then wish to be in this seat. Guide this seat with your life for us the country people."

This man's words stirred deep feelings in him just like the American did when he and his friends were being goaded to stage a coup.. However, there was an important scheduled meeting with the American Ambassador, who previously hinted increased military and economic aid for

America's dependable ally' Ebenezer Kum's words had a profound effect on the President.

Maxwell flashed a toothpaste smile. Opening a bottle of wine he offered an enigmatic smile. "It is the Ambassador who requested this meeting. All we have to do is listen to what he has to say"".

"But?

"But what?

Outside the window the President spied the long dark Chevrolet van of the powerful Ambassador. Officials from the Ministry of State for Presidential Affairs rushed down to welcome the VIP guest, a middle age Caucasian man. Cheers, anthems, red carpets and pleasantries awaited the distinguished Ambassador William Lacey. He was escorted upstairs by no other than the President himself where the wives of members of the ruling junta were being entertained. Music and food circulated and there was so much infectious dancing that the reserved ambassador joined in the dance missing the dance steps which sent the assembled guests into rounds of hilarious laughter. Journalists' cameras flashed anxious to capture the excellent photo opportunity.

The music and dancing continued. The powerful men adjoined to the conference room away from the prying eyes and ears of the press.

"My government including the President Reagan is strongly supportive of your government Mr. President. All available support, economic and military will be given to your administration. We have a substantial assistance program for your country. Our experts will work along with your experts to work out the details of how and whatever budgetary support your government needs to the tune of ninety to hundred million dollars per annum."

The good news was always a delight to the hearer.

The ambassador then launched into a historical analysis of Liberian American relations.

"You see mutual understanding is crucial. Communism is a threat to the free way of life; it undermines the basic nature of human beings because it tries to take away from the individual and the family what rightfully belongs to them for a Godless ideology. To fight this battle against the evil empire of communism led by the Soviet Union, our Omega navigation Satellite station, the VOA transmitter sight and the Firestone Plantation are important assets in this battle ."

The young Head of State nodded vigorously yet his eyes stared into blank space. Ambassador Lacey rattled on with increased fervor. "The Russian and Chinese are ready to use devilish means to achieve world communistic domination. We in the free world, Liberia and America have nothing to lose in this struggle but our free democratic way of life. Col. Mengistu Haile Miriam, Eduardos Dos Santos, Samora Machel are their pawn in this game in Africa. Right next door Guineas Sekou Toure is a Marxist".

The ambassador paused laughing. "Sekou Toure though is not much of a communist; his chief concerns are staying in power and suppressing internal dissent rather than exporting socialism. The United States and Liberia have a mutual role in the foreign policy objectives of both our nations. The containment of Libya's maverick Col. Muammar Kadafi is important to America. This mercurial anti -western Arab extremist wants to gain a foot hole in Liberia. We would be deeply appreciative if your government distances itself from him. It will be difficult for us to procure further support for your government if you proceed with your pending visit to the Colonel's fiefdom. You know how difficult our Congress can be. Now the process of speeding up all the support to your government will be expedited if you do not go to Libya."

"Mr. Ambassador Liberia is sovereign country; therefore, we visit whom we want."

Ambassador Lacey remembered the young head of State dossier. "Of course we understand and applaud your independent stance. However, as friends we only meant well." Amb. Lacey smiled.

President Maxwell Forkpa became relaxed.

"No problem sir, I will consult with my cabinet concerning your request. I only want to extend the hand of African solidarity to Kadafi since he was the first Head of State to recognize our government. We need more M-16s Rifles, tanks… weaponry to protect us. As you can see, our barracks are in a awful shape. Ambassador, soldiers are human beings. Their lives must be improved especially their housing, pay equipments and general living conditions of service."

Amb. Lacey speaking through his nose took a sip of water to clear his throat. The exchange of views lasted for two hours.

The Americans kept their word. It was an enthused President Forkpa who visited the BTC Barrack to inspect a consignment of arms and ammunition from the US Military attaché assigned to the capital.

For every regime the most pressing initial concern was security. For these military men the best form of security was the abundance of military hardware. Molded and trained together in the same uniform and subject to the same stern discipline; these factors made soldiers develop a sense of solidarity seldom seen or attempted among civilians.

The young members of the junta had experienced the horrors of deprivations of the army firsthand. Hence, they were dedicated to improving the lots of their comrades in arms since they planned to return to that life anyway.

The President smiled feeling the smooth steel of the rifle in his hand. He strolled to his friend Samuel Dahn. All of the original men of the junta were present talking, laughing, and joking.

"Good Maxie, with these weapons we will soon be in to make the country safe so we can let the civilians do their job while we soldiers remain in our barracks," Samuel remarked smiling while examining a gun magazine

Maxwell did not smile back.

"It is true what you say, I am glad."

There was no conviction in Maxwell's voice .

"Samuel I just wondered whether you have taken the government house assigned to you in Sinkor? The barrack is too filthy for a man of your status. Why do you choose to stay such a filthy place?

"Maxwell it is true that the houses here are far beneath my position but you know I hate big show. All of us are soldiers and we must not care too much for the soft comforts of life."

"Yeah but the Bible itself says you must not muzzle the ox that pulls the plough. If our coup have failed we could all have been dead by now. Any privilege we have is justified."

"I am afraid Max that the more we enjoy the seat of power with all her trappings the more difficult it would be to leave power."

"Can we talk about that another time?

Right now we have to think where to store these new weapons."

"Max have you forgotten? We need to test them first."

"Look at me Sam. Test the weapons and meet with me soon for us to decide where to deploy them. For the time being let the weapons after you test them be stored at the national armory on Lynch Street. I am sorry to leave you guys so soon. I have some traditional chiefs waiting to meet me now ."

Maxie I am glad you are Head of State instead of me because these endless meetings would killed me."

"Me too boy but somebody has to wash the dirty laundry."

Samuel tapped his friend on the shoulders. Harrison Varney was coming over when the President got into his Mercedes and drove away.

CHAPTER 13

All of the men who staged the coup were cooped together in a secret meeting at the BTC Barrack inside one of those run of the mill shacks away from the Mansion and bodyguards. These hard driven rulers seemed to be the same comrades they were before the coup just few months back always finding time to be together. In their friendship rank did not matter when they met over cheap bottles of gin, they were just friends nobody higher or lower than the other. Their arguments were loud vulgar affairs more a test of rhetorical skills than logic. In times past, sometimes they met to play cards and exchange gossips about their bosses and women.

Having taken over the realms of power, the five core friends kept this tradition often laughing at those who did not previously count them as human beings now falling over backwards anxious to please them.

Sometimes they met in each other homes, public entertainment centers, and the like.

But now with more responsibilities, the friends were gradually drifting apart unknown to any of them. Only official functions were now bringing them together, but these changes were so subtle that even they did not notice them.

Early in their comradeship meeting it did not take long for simmering tension among ambitious young men now edged by equally ambitious courtiers to surface. Dave Paye, Alexander Kulah, Samuel Dahn and Harrison Varney wanted personal and junta relationships to continue as it was during pre junta days. Before the nation Maxwell Forkpa was the nominal head. Among themselves they were equal. Decisions must still remain a collective responsibility; a simple majority must carry the day.

Maxwell Forkpa on the other hand felt as President, Chief Executive his word should carry more weight and authority. His decisions were wise which he expected his friends to endorse without much discussion. In return their material comfort would be well catered for. The rumblings of discontent sounded in this casual meeting. Harrison Varney, the nominal number two and Maxwell were always clashing even before their successful coup; the passage of time did not ease the rivalry between them. Knowing his friend aversion to the issue of handing power over to civilians in recent discussions,this was the topic Harrison launched into it right away. Samuel Dahn changed the topic "The first time I slept in my official bed I did not sleep at all. The woman beside me smelt so soft and nice I was afraid to touch her." Me too I wonder where all those women were when we mere soldiers? Power attracts everyone like flies brother." The President smiled and took a sip of the strong homebrew liquor that attracted them those days because of the cheap price. They chatted and laughed and tension evaporated from the room but Harrison was not to be put off easily.

"Guys when are we going to hand over power to the civilians seeing things are getting back to normal? We have been in charge for a year now."

"Guys must we always discuss this issue of handling over power to civilians every time we meet when there are more important issues to talk on? We need to clean the rampant corruption from the Robert's years first before anything."

Harrison's lanky features showed disapproval.

"How long do you think it will take to clean this mess so we can return to the barracks Maxwell? For us to return this country to democracy?"

"Since when Harrison you started thinking so much about democracy?"

"Please this must not be a slinging march between you Harrison and Maxwell. I think we all can decide on this issue."

Samuel Dahn interjected snapping his fingers to make his point.

"I think this country is small. We must stay in power for 18 months of which 12 months are already gone. We have to start preparations for elections soon. Let's not forget, power is sweet. The other day one of the most beautiful girls in Monrovia came to my office asking me to take her for lunch." His colleagues broke into laughter licking their lips. "I am saying this to say," he continued when the laughter died down.

"To say the longer, we stay in power, the more difficult it would be to leave." Harrison suggested. Alexander nodded.

Maxwell Forkpa irascible temper took over.

"Now listen guys, is this a conspiracy I am facing here? Each time we meet Harrison must bring this topic about handling over power to civilians. I have no desire to cling onto power. I could hand over power right now, but we need to put into place certain structures before that can be done. We staged this coup to better the lives of our people which Harrison Varney is not in the least concerned about."

"Don't tell me that! Harrison shouted in anger.

"Was it you alone who risked your life on that fateful day? You know it was Samuel Dahn and myself who did the actual killing of the President. If I was not interested in the people's welfare why did I risk my life? Is it because you want to cling onto power you, you accuse me of not having the interest of the Liberian people at heart?"

"Harrison let me tell you, you must have some respect for me as the President. You just don't talk to me like that."

Harrison smiled. In a mocking tone of politeness he asked" Thank you your Excellency.

Mr. President when are we going to hand over power to the civilians since you have become our head to lord it over us?

"Yes I am lording it over you and so what?

Even in the army I was Master Sergeant while you were Staff Sergeant. You cannot force your views on me."

"Let us stop this argument guys and put this matter to a vote."

Samuel Dahn suggested trying to soothe tempers. "You sit there Samuel hearing Harrison Insulting me and all you have to say is let us put this to a vote?

"This thing about handling over power to civilians can be discussed later. If any change in government occurs Maxie will become Chief of Staff" Harrison replied laughing. The discussions switched to other topics. Gradually the tension subsided as the junta pillars joked like before. But the dispute between Harrison and Maxwell was far from resolved. Both sides believed in their own self-righteous indignation.

Harrison Varney wanted a conclusive decision on the matter of handling over power since he suspected Maxwell wanted to cling to power.

President Forkpa considered Harrison's behavior as a personal affront to his authority which must not go unpunished. The other three junta members did not want to take sides openly. All of them wanted power to be handed to civilians, but for it to be done in a cordial manner so they waited for another time since both parties were on edge.

"Guys we need to go somewhere to cool our thirst ."

"Yeah I think that will be a good idea. Maxwell and Harrison can shake hands"

"Go ahead guys" Samuel suggested. Both men appraised each other hesitating. It was Maxwell who extended his hand which Harrison took.

"We need to start setting up an election commission

soon and decide how to make this country normal again. Sometimes Harrison can be rude. But what he said struck a chord with me. Power I hear corrupts. We have to be careful before we get use to the trappings of power."

Samuel Dahn's comments seemed to support Harrison but if it irritated Maxwell he did not show it. Ebenezer Kum words came to his mind.

"Your friends are jealous of you, guard the presidency with your life."

Was Samuel Dahn the brain behind Harrison Payne's rant?

The five junta pillars shook hands and drifted to a local restaurant for a meal of goat soup and Rice. Maxwell sat down beside Samuel while the other three guys reclined on another table. Dave said an insulting word to Maxwell's mother. Maxwell replied in a similar vein, both of them were not serious. Alcohol and food lightened the atmosphere. Life was uncomplicated like before.

Even as they talked and joked plans were being formed in Maxwell's mind. From his BWI days he remembered an efficient soldier who served under him doing a short term training course. Maxwell dug deep into his memory. He took giant bites from a large morsel of meat on his plate.

Moses…..Moses……Moses Gabby was his name. He needed to increase his power base by surrounding himself with new men totally loyal to him. All of these men were potential rivals including Samuel Dahn. Samuel was a big fish. He will try go after Harrison first.

All of the gin consumed at the bar did not affect his thinking. Later that night in the company of his bodyguards the President let slip the names of certain soldiers he wanted to meet.

In the confines of his bedroom -four low ranking to middle ranking officers with no direct knowledge of the coup were with the President. These four were brilliant, ruthless and ambitious. Ambition was a dutiful servant but a terrible master. Even in the secrecy of his bedroom, they conversed in low tones. All four sat on the floor.

Pervasive quiet descended on the President and his men.

"Yes I think I have the answer!

The President announced with enthusiasm.

"Gabby you get me a good for nothing soldier whom you trust. Stashed up a considerate amount of arms and ammunition at a designated place."

He cleared his throat and continued in a determined voice. "Print some literature with Arabic writings on green and white paper. Include quotations from the Libyan Leader famous green book."

"I do not know of any green book by Kadafi."

Maxwell became incensed. "You stupid fool, you do not know much about the Libyans eh? The President asked in a high pitched voice striking out with his fist which landed on Moses Gabby's mouth.

Micro seconds later Gabby struck back. Instead of being offended the President laughed. Both men felt their jaws.

"On your feet Gabby."

Gabby rose up promptly.

"Keep an eye on the Libyan embassy 24 hours around the clock. I do not know Kadafi's motive. Good I have a solution. The Israelis our new friends just offered to upgrade our military surveillance equipment. We need to monitor that embassy. Doing that keeps the Americans happy. One day I will have to close that den of subversion. Take a photo of every Liberian who enters that embassy."

"I will send my secretary along with perfect copies of the leader's green book." Ebie Kum the overnight confidante of the President offered.

"Good! Gabby let this good for nothing soldier fire on my motorcade in broad daylight.

Make sure he is later arrested. We can nicely put Harrison Payne jail charging them with treason.

"President Forkpa this is incredulous. In fact downright dangerous" Ebie opined.

"Will it be necessary to take such a risk?

"I mean what if a stray bullet hits you?

Maxwell offered an enigmatic smile.

"Ebie you have forgotten the new jeep the Israelis gave me is bullet proof with hidden gun posts? If my attacker goes berserk, he will be mowed down with machine gun fire. Another unit from his rear will shoot him to rag. I am sure Gabby can arrange that. However, make sure no trigger happy Noko is among the rear gang. We need the attacker to be alive to implicate those we want. The rear guard is only to fire when it becomes absolutely necessary."

"Sir this plan is fraught with danger."

"Ebie you are a chicken?

Ebie Kum was a civilian at heart, a smooth operator who abhorred violence.

"You will sit with me in my convoy during the attack. 3 days from now I am going to dedicate a new lighting system for aircrafts at the Robertsfield. The attack will occur during my return to Monrovia after the dedication along the Robertsfield ELWA Highway."

Soon the meeting was over. Moses Gabby headed straight to the BTC Barrack to confer with trusted soldiers. Moses Gabby though not one of the original coup plotters had come to the President's attention because he had developed a reputation for quiet ruthless efficiency. He abhorred flamboyancy or publicity so typical of dashing operatives. Moses spent the next two days combing the barrack for the perfect soldier whom he found at last in the chocolate colored younger brother of the Logistic Commander Fred Knot. Physically strong, but gullible Daniel only joined the army because his older brother Fred was tired of supporting him and forced him to enlist just so he could draw a salary of his own. Apart from basic training at Schiefillin Daniel did not advance further, neither did he have the desire to do so. The younger Knot turned down every opportunity for career advancement thrown his way by his elder brother including one to train at the famous West Point.

All the dashing young fellow cared for was liquor, women, and a good life of partying. Of course, he was a consummate liar whose easy charms endeared him to many in spite of his decadent ways. Gabby's only doubt that he was the perfect soldier for the operation centered on whether the young man would stick to the rule and implicate only those they wanted him to? Or could he let his vivid imagination run wild when he faced the press?

His reservations aside, time was running out. He wanted a soldier who could take risks for easy money and not a career soldier.

The younger Knot agreed to the plan without hesitation since the amount promised was quite substantial. Half of the money was placed in a bank account opened in his name but which he could not touch until after the operation.

By nightfall,, a substantial arsenal under cover of darkness was being transferred. The managing director of the LEC was informed to switched the lights off in the designated location at a particular time the arms and ammunition was being transported. from the national armory on Lynn Street to a seaside apartment an odd assortment of arms including M-16s, rocket launchers, 30 and 50 caliber machine guns were transferred. Moses Gabby coached the younger Knot recruited unknown to his brother to repeat the names of his sponsors. His vivid imagination which the intelligence chief feared so far made things easier. He recited the names, date and venues of their meetings in a flawless manner. The individuals, dates and times were different but the methodology was the same.

$1000 lay scattered on the floor. A plain unmarked jeep with tinted glass window departed BTC to reconnoiter the site for the ambush. The vehicle to and fro along the highway selecting for a site for the ambush for almost an hour. A deep curve between Schiefillin Barracks and ELWA Station was chosen as a sight for the ambush. By nightfall machine guns were placed under the low bushes in the grassy field some distance from the road.

The driver of the last vehicle in the presidential convoy was told to get out of his vehicle when he heard the first gunshot sprayed in the air to allow the renegade soldier to spray the vehicle with bullets. "Everything in place."

Gabby called the President to inform him.

"Make sure the President's vehicle is some distance away before you shoot into the air."

Gabby warned the young Knot for the fifth time.

By Early morning Fred's eyes were cleared for once of its bloodshot alcohol infested look. Excitement and anticipation of his loot after the completion of the operation filled the thoughts of Fred. Bacardi Disco in Hotel Africa, the neon lights, the loud music, the girls were all good things he looked forward to. Even now the crisp feel of dollars in his pocket touching the skin of his thigh made him become all the more excited.

The operation arranged was going on according to plan. Crouched behind a low bush concealed behind his machine gun the 'assassin' palms felt wet.

Fred waited and waited becoming tired of the waiting game. The thought of abandoning the entire operation since his attempt at concealment made him feel cramp in his legs crossed his mind several times.

Then it happened. President Maxwell Forkpa speeding convoy dazzled under the clear midday sun carrying journalists, ministers, protocol officers and the usual large entourage of hanger- on appeared in his binoculars on their way to the airport. Unknown to Fred some distance away Gabby and a small team of soldiers had him in their binoculars. The Robertsfield highway gleaned under the mirage of the sunlight. The pale blue Atlantic unaware of the machinations of men along the highway frolicked rolling just as it has for ages.

A loud applause greeted the President when he turned the switch lighting the entire runway at the country's only international airport. Speeches, champagne, cultural dancers, and fanfare characterized the occasion.

By midday the fleet of vehicles which passed Fred earlier headed in opposite direction speeding to the capital. Ebie Kum smiled icily throughout the entire proceedings his mind fearful and pre- occupied. The sage whom they consulted earlier words were comforting but deliberately vague.

The President confident and relaxed ordered his officials to go ahead. Minutes later his convoy zoomed out of the airport terminal accompanied by three vehicles. President Forkpa made sure his gun ports were well stocked with ammunitions.

The sun beat mercilessly on Fred along the highway made him realize this operation was not just easy as he imagined. Fred Knot was becoming impatient. He watched the vehicles cruising along the highway hoping that the next one would be his target. As more vehicles passed him the newest one bearing no resemblance to the car he wished for his heart sank. As the time passed by impatience turned to disappointment. Fred wanted to rise from his crouched position which made his legs become cramped.

He toyed with the idea of just walking away from it all. But oh the lure of the money, and furthermore, his fear of Gabby's wrath kept him down. Anticipation at the next vehicle being the Presidential convoy and disappointment at it not being it made Fred tired and thirsty. He finally made up his mind to leave in the next 15 minutes if he did not see his target. Anger and frustration made him to rise from his position, but he soon fell back to the ground.

At last a small speck appeared in the horizon growing bigger by the second. The flagged motorcade appeared in his binocular.

Motivated by the urge to do the job quickly in order to take the money in his room and the balance $5000 in the bank Fred opened suppressive fire on the lead vehicle in the convoy. Presidential bodyguards rushed to their gun ports but the President ordered them not to shoot as bullets bounced off their car. The two cars immediately behind the President's car sailed through the rain of bullets. however, the third lost control. The vehicle swerved scalding of the tarmac unto the low bush beside the road. The driver bloodied figure jumped out of the moving vehicle straight unto where Fred was lying. That was the last thing he did. His body fell down in a hail of bullets jerking spasmodically. As the man died feeling euphoric Fred peppered his abandoned vehicle with bullets. The pressure of his fingers on the trigger stopped only when the gun belt in his machine gun became empty.

"Don't move!

A hoarse voice rang out in the calm after the storm of the short explosive reign of violence just experienced under the midday sun. Fred found the muzzle of guns pointed at him; he stared almost dazed at what he was seeing.

"Lift up your hands slowly, do not attempt to rise, otherwise; I will be forced to blow your head off."

"Is this some joke?

A rifle shot close to his ears reminded him it was no joke. Gabby, who had been lurking in the background, dawdled to the scene. Fred felt tremendous relief.

"Alright leave him boy."

Gabby managed to say through clenched teeth grateful for his black skin which hid the furious expression in his heart. It appeared Fred Knot wanted to kill the President since he was not supposed to fire directly on the President's car. The mountain of empty shells lying at his feet pointed to a more sinister motive.

Different thoughts flashed through Gabby's mind. Shoot Fred on sight to make way for one of his men to testify? But his men were soldiers and could mess up important details.

"Sir I could not wait to fire at the convoy. Where is my money?"

"Do not worry. You will be paid in town; we have to leave here quickly."

"But Sir?

"Keep your mouth shut! A soldier is to obey without question."

Gabby snapped at a questioning sergeant. Cameras flashed taking several close up shots of the bullet ridden jeep mangled along the road. Gabby knew the presence of several soldiers in battle gear beside a highway could raise suspicion along this well traveled highway.

Soon a disarmed Fred was led to a vehicle and driven at high speed to the barrack.

State radio was already broadcasting news on the latest coup announcement to a shocked nation.

A flabbergasted Harrison Varney at home upon hearing the announcement of his coup asked his wife. "What nonsense is this? Let me hurry and go to the Mansion to meet that scary bitch. Why would I want to stage a coup? Harrison hurried to the bathroom to shave and ended up cutting himself with the blade. Hurrying to his room he put on a new pair of uniforms. Minutes later he was prepared to meet the President having put on his clothes.

"It must be some mistake, an expensive joke" he kept muttering to himself. His wife's pleas and tears got on his nerves. "Guys c'mon we have to hurry to the Mansion."

He screamed at his bodyguards.

The loud tone of his voice was to assure himself that he was still in control of his bodyguards numbering six who were all within the vicinity of his bungalow .This stunning villa he seized from one of the executed ministers.

"Maybe I need to call S.D. and Paye to find out what this is all about." Harrison Varney, Vice Chairman of the Salvation Council looked around before attempting to board his car. Across the road coming from the opposite direction to which he was headed, a large convoy of soldiers drove towards him. Col. Harrison Varney whipped out an automatic pistol, his bodyguards followed suit cocking their rifles. Soldiers were jumping from the moving vehicle and taking positions around his yard. His children cried and screamed. Lt. Moses Gabby entered the yard on foot accompanied by twenty-five soldiers. Like a conquering hero he marched to the verandah where the hitherto number two man of the Salvation Council stood looking down.

"General Varney consider yourself under arrest!

He shouted nudging the machine gun in his chest.

"Is this a joke?

The general asked looking down on the soldiers crawling through his yard.

"I order you Lt. Gabby to turn around and head back to the BTC. I am going to see Maxwell myself!

Lt. Gabby smiled sardonically.

"General Varney if you surrender peacefully there will be no bloodshed. Your wife and children along with other family members are in this house. If we start shooting some of my men will die but all of your children, your wife and everybody around you will die. If you care less for your own life think about these people who depend on you now being dead."

Harrison Varney lapsed deep in thought as both parties held their rifles pointed at each other.

"Okay I will come down peacefully to go with you, but there must be no shooting in the yard, none of my children or any person in this yard must be roughed up in any way."

"Yes sir!

Gabby saluted. The General along with his bodyguards majestically walked down the stairs to the concrete floor. Once in power the junta members promoted themselves to the rank of generals. On the ground General Harrison and his men were promptly disarmed amidst shrieks and wailing in the compound. The General was not roughed up in any way; in fact he was allowed to sit in the front seat of the lead vehicle sandwiched between Gabby and the driver. His bodyguards were not so lucky. They were seen no more in this life. The few soldiers who stay behind after Harrison and his arresting officer exited the scene set to work dumping Russian and American Weapons around the yard. The weapons were mixed with seditious literature. Instead of being driven to the Mansion as requested, the captive General was driven straight to a threadbare prison where he was shoved into the filth of a bug, infected solitary cell and locked up.

"Some unpatriotic citizens motivated by satanic greed lay an ambush for the President's motorcade. Thankfully the President escaped unharmed, unfortunately Capt. David Sumo, a loyal and trusted motorcade driver was killed in the exchange of fire between the President's bodyguards and the diabolical attackers. One of the attackers Lt. Fred Knot was captured and is assisting government securities in apprehending the rest of his evil gang." the terse statement on state radio concluded.

Police, soldiers, journalists, ambassadors, people of every standing were rushed to the scene of the ambush by the government to gape horrified at the battered vehicle and the bullet ridden body of Capt. David Sumo. Abandoned machine guns some left in place by Gabby's crack rear guard troops laid scattered. Cameras flashed, mouth whispered into ears, fingers dug into sides. Tears accompanied the body of the slain motorcade driver to Monrovia. Majority of the people seeing the images on their TVs believed the authenticity now of the attack. The bullet ridden body and the mangled car were evidences of a real attack. The fearsome testimony of press agents in the Presidential convoy narrating their narrow brush with death left no doubt in the minds of most people. The stakes were indeed high. Fred Knot for his part was being kept high on booze.

A stunned country was sent into shock by an announcement by none other than the President himself that the Salvation Council number two Harrison Payne tried to stage a coup. People just asked in bewilderment why? Why? The aborted coup did not make sense. The swiftness of the countermeasure to neutralize the coup won applause though. The announcement stunned and surprised other members of the Salvation Council

———•◆•———

Inside the fortress of the corridor of power President Maxwell Forkpa was explaining Harrison Payne's treachery to an equally shock Salvation Council members. Within the twinkling of an eye power have been wrecked from Harrison Payne's bosom just how it came to him a few months ago. Government information machinery went into full motion to vilify Harrison Payne.

Baffled citizens seeing each other would shake their heads in amazement.

At 7 O'clock pm a curfew was slammed on the confused city.

Few regretted the curtailment of their desire to roam the city when such an attempt has been made on the life on the President. beer parlor operators mourned the loss of business cursing the soul of Harrison. Wives delighted at the opportunity for their husbands to stay at home for once at night. Pastors declared a day of national fasting.

Late into the night, Gabby and the President were locked in a closed door discussion planning and circumventing plans. The night dragged slowly in the capital. All over the country shock gave way to anger.

The next morning as it had become almost customary by people anxious to identify with the President and benefit from his generosity; crowds were assembling on the grounds of the Mansion to express their support.

The captured suspect was driven to the conference room of the Mansion for the major Press Conference to be held by the President, something which he very rarely did.

The entire country stood at a standstill glued to their radio and TVs. In homes when children cough they were being shouted at to keep quiet.

Foreign journalists filled the front pew in the section reserved for the press inside the conference room of the Mansion. Journalists milled around chatting gaily when the Light skinned press secretary to the President called their attention welcoming them. Minutes drag into hours and impatience nagged the atmosphere especially among the foreign journalists. Finally after what seemed like eternity the young President appeared at the podium magnificent in a western suit appeared his face somber, collected and serious looking every bit the leader he was.

A short press statement was read by the President. His Press Secretary announced the question and answer period which the assembled journalists was anxiously waiting for urging them to restrict their questions to the issue at hand and restricting further each journalist to two questions. "Please be recognized by the President before you ask your question and please state your name and the media house you represent before asking your question." The Press Secretary took his seat

"This is Nyenati Daniels of the Daily Observer Newspaper.

Do you think Mr. Harrison Payne alone is responsible for this dastardly act and do you think the suspect arrested acted alone or in collaboration with others?

"Well it is too soon to start blaming people. We are taking our time to investigate. Preliminary investigations revealed a well coordinated plot by socialist elements backed by a an Arab government. We have a suspects including the mastermind in custody who will give us information" the President replied.

"At what time was the attack launched and how did you survive?"

"Well the attack was launched around midday as me and my entourage made our way back to Monrovia from Robertsfield by men using 50 Caliber heavy machine guns, thirty caliber, grenades, Ak 47s you name them."

Allison Blay of ELBC News. How many persons were involved in the attack?"

"Our preliminary estimate suggests around 10 attackers. As for how I escape, I am a trained military man. My bodyguards and I fired back at the attackers. Superb driving by my chauffeur helped to save the day."

"Mr. President are the Chief of Defense Intelligence and the Defense Minister going to be fired? How come they did not detect the attack?

"We all knew evil persons were planning an attack but we did not know the exact place or time they wanted to strike, furthermore; we did not want to spread panic among our peaceful citizens. We want to remain approachable by my people, so we did not see the need to enforce heavy security around ourselves. I can assure you our investigations will not leave any stone unturned. There will be no sacred cows" the youthful President laughed. Soon the assembled guest joined in."

"John Kiazulu of ELWA Radio. What are the security measures being put in place to avert such an incident as this one from repeating itself?

"There are certain measures being put in place. Our surveillance equipment are being upgraded. Very soon the first batch of troops for anti terrorist training will be leaving for Israel. Measures are being put in place to safeguard our revolution which cannot be revealed to the public. There is not 100% effective measure against evil people. All of us security lies both in God's hands and in ourselves. But I can assure you we will deal ruthlessly with people who want to derail our freedom march. It is the welfare of the people we seek, the evils of the defunct government we removed was what made us to be willing to sacrifice life itself for the betterment of our people. We are against the syndrome of the elite against the people; the exclusion of tribal Liberians is done away with. We intend to restore this country to democratic civilian rule. We are committed to this vision."

A hush fell over the crowd. That was the first time the President had publicly mentioned those words.

There was a slight commotion behind the podium from which the President spoke. Gabby appeared to be conferring with the President. Security men with eyes inscrutable behind dark sunglasses and their jackets bulging with pistols positioned themselves better. The head of state nodded his head vigorously. Vehicles on the ground moved around in all directions. Security men and VIPs hurried about to the consternation of assembled guests. The President vacated the podium hurriedly. Adonis stepped forward and grabbed the microphone to calm the situation. Minutes later a sleepy eye soldier suited in an immaculate camouflage stood near the podium where the President was.

"Distinguished guests we have a guest for you."

A man with a face akin to a movie star emerged from behind the President. His handsome face, chiseled nose, cropped moustache, fine pair of dark brown eyes, a black upper lip and red lower lips and chocolate skin made the ladies in the audience to swoon in admiration. When he opened his mouth to speak his teeth milky white gleaned under the fluorescent beam.

"Now ladies and gentlemen we told you earlier we have one of the attackers captured, here is he to prove to you doubters."

The females and some men hushed in sympathetic tone for the suspect to one another. His body did not show any visible sigh of torture.

"There are skeptics who are willing to believe in anything as long as it is not from the government."

"My name is James Knot of A Company 1st Infantry Battalion. Two weeks ago I was contacted by Harrison Payne to do a serious job for he and his friends. I arrived in Harrison Payne the Vice President's home around 7pm on the Old Road. I thought I had gone to a social meeting. At Harrison Payne house, these were the –people I met in a meeting. The group invited me to share the soft drinks they had with them.

Maxwell whispered something into Gabby's ears.

More vehicles were seen departing the Mansion grounds.

"Harrison Payne put his arms around me saying he and his friends wanted me to do a piece of for them which they were willing to pay me handsomely for if I was brave and could keep my mouth shut. I replied I could be brave and do as they say as long as what they wanted me to do was not illegal. Drinks were brought. Under the influence of alcohol I agreed to their offer of $20.000 to overthrow the government. Each of the men I was to contact to help me in the operation would take $10.000 as their pay. Weapons, money and everything was ours as long as we agreed to do their job. I do not know how these people got their weapons. Two nights later on June 5th 9 pm at a greenhouse in Soul Clinic we were supplied in the dead of night with the weapons we needed from a dark blue Discovery jeep including rocket launchers. Half of my share of the money is paid in a bank account at Merchant Bank. I knew of the President's schedule so I and my boys set up this ambush near the Robertsfield Highway. I and my men opened heavy fire on the President's car with…. The suspect rattled the names of several weapons."

James Knot's voice sounded calm, calculated, and assertive speaking as if he was stating the gospel truth from his torrid throat. The calm assurance of his voice, the dead seriousness of his demeanor, and the sincerity of his tone were his perfect witness of truth. His voice did not tremble. His remarkable memory recalled dates, venues, and specific times even though the attacker's hands remained handcuffed in front of him.

Fred Knot had not finished his testimony when what could only be described as pandemonium of activities broke out. Journalists were anxious to ply the captured assassin with a thousand and one questions. Before they could do so the Defense Minister grabbed the microphone and announced in a firm voice. "All those named as conspirators and coup makers must immediately report themselves to the nearest military barrack or Police station. Wherever you are consider yourselves under arrest. There must not be any attempt, I repeat attempt by any of you to resist arrest or to flee from the forces of justice. Fellow citizens you are asked to report on the whereabouts of any enemy of the state. Any person or persons caught harboring or assisting a fugitive shall face the heavy hands of the law. Our borders, airports and seaports meanwhile shall remain sealed. However, peaceful citizens are free to carry on with their daily activities as government does everything in her power to safeguard the state and protect all lives and properties. The accused shall be granted a free and fair trial."

There was another round of discussion on the platform as senior government officials conferred among themselves. To everyone's surprise, the hustle suspect was thrust again in front of the microphone to respond to reporters' questions.

Again the captures suspect displayed remarkable savvy. His response to reporter's questions was terse, clipped and straight forward.

"Sir James Dahn of the Footsprint Newspaper. My question is not to the allege assassin, but is request to you Mr. President. Can Sergeant Knot take us to the house where he received the allege weapons."

The President did not like the word allege being used by the reporter. He winked at the Information Minister, who took the cue. Next year this Journalist would pay through his nose to get his accreditation as a journalist from the ministry.

The President conferred with his security men. He smiled when he spoke.

"Yes you will be taken to the house.

CHAPTER 14

Inside a small, airtight cell whose walls were decorated by spider web Harrison could not believe his eyes. The tiny window in the room was so high towards the ceiling. The poor ventilation did not allow much air or sunlight in rendering his cell a place of semi darkness under the brightest of sunlight. Iron bars, cruel and unyielding barred entrance to the room from both the door and window. Like a caged animal Harrison bowed his here and looked intently at the door leading to freedom as if his intense desire to be out of the suffocating environment could transform into reality. His pride was battered; but he remained confident the truth would come out and set him free he still had some powerful friends. In his minds plan were being formulated by him to punish Moses Gabby for humiliating him in front of his family. Those plotting his downfall would grate their teeth in shame when the truth rise to vindicate him. Still deep in thought he did not hear his name being called until a soldier entered the prison and tapped him on his shoulders. With all the promptness of military command he was taken to courtroom at a secret location.

Harrison Payne envisioned a better world beyond his cell and rejoiced for the small victory. How he longed for his children. Inside the cramped makeshift courtroom under a dim light he could make out the faces of the seven men whom he presumed were the jurors. Tribunal Chairman Amos Gbalaze large angular face dominated the court. His eyes which Harrison wished to make contact with were hidden behind a pair of dark sunglasses.

The 'judge' wasted no time in delving into the case.

"Will the Prosecution please state the charges against the two co-defendants?"

The high pitched voice of Capt. Thomas Paine echoed loud through the courtroom. "The prosecution representing the state of Liberia will establish that principal defendant General Harrison Payne, former Vice Chairman of the Salvation Council along with his co—accused James Knot connived and plotted with his bodyguards and certain foreign powers with the avowed aim of violently overthrowing and assassinating the Chairman of the Salvation Council Hon. Maxwell Forkpa. He along with his co- accused is also charged with illegal possession of arms beyond their assigned arms and producing seditious literature. Government stands ready to prove her charges.

The defendants were asked to enter a plea. "Not guilty, not guilty they replied. Harrison never felt so alone in life. Looking around the courtroom there was no family, no friend, no well wishers, nor independent observers or journalists. His co- accused, was a handsome mulatto guy he never met before. For a man being accused of the grave crime of plotting a coup, he seemed remarkably relaxed. The prosecution team briefcases were bulging with papers. Where was his defense team?

"The charges against me are all pack of lies" he screamed. This aspect of his plea sent the courtroom members into hilarious laughter. The Tribunal Judge, Col. Gbalaze and the principal defendant took military training together. Harrison was then his commander, now their positions have changed. His life lay in his onetime subordinate officer's hands. Proceedings rumbled on for another hour after which the case was adjoined. Harrison expected to be handcuffed; instead he was surrounded by half a dozen heavily armed men who bundled him into a jeep and drove him away.

Rough hands threw the former number two into prison like a common criminal.

In Monrovia and across the entire length of the country citizens shocked by the betrayal of the high ideas of the coup by one of her own brought disbelief and anger to the people. Thousands demonstrated especially in Monrovia some coming from the counties.

Inside the diplomatic fortress of Mamba Point in his well furnished office suite enhanced with rich embroidered rug and a huge American Eagle seal; the ambassador of the most powerful country to rule the world rested his long thin arms on the leather, velvet cushioned chair. His eyes were focused on the TV screen before him. Unfolding before him was the scene of the attack on President Forkpa's convoy picked up by the Omega Station. A solitary figure crouched in a low bush behind a machine gun belt. What piqued the ambassador's interest was the presence of crack soldiers looking like Presidential guards in a larger group some distance behind the solitary figure. He forwarded the video to the scene of the untrained solitary soldier firing volleys of shots at the convoy. Yet not one shoot was being fired by the larger body of troops behind him. Why were they not shooting? The camera zoomed further to reveal the shady figure of Moses Gabby the new Defense Minister and the attacker exchanging what looked like friendly greetings. It seemed the attacker and the President's man knew each other. They walked together to a parked jeep. Though he could not hear the dialogue between the two, their exchange appeared to be cordial. Amb. Lacey's training and many years as a diplomat in the political minefield of Africa brought a startling reality to his mind. The Political Counselor at the US Embassy Adolphus James sauntered into the office of his boss wearing an oversized cowboy heart. The bright yellow T-shirt he wore was tucked inside the Levi Jeans beneath held in place by a large leather belt conveying an almost boyish demeanor which infuriated his rather formal Yankee boss.

"I can tell you sir we have a guy who wants to be a politician for a long time. The soldier boy is beginning to love suits more than the starch of uniforms. Can we start looking for an alternative to him?

"The peace and stability of the country is still too fragile. I have to lean on President Forkpa not to execute any political prisoner."

"Brace yourself Ambassador Lacey." Adolphus quirked.

For the second consecutive day a now emaciated looking Harrison Payne along with his co -accused separated from him were taken to face the tribunal. Capt. Thomas Paine swaggered around ready to present his evidence. This time select journalists were allowed into the courtroom and given permission to take photos of the state exhibit. Rare Russian made rifles and ammunitions not normally used by the Liberian Army were displayed. Bombastic literature explaining the justification for removing Maxwell said to have been discovered at the home of the principal accused was shown around. Then it was time for one of the conspirators turned state witness to give evidence. Sergeant James Knot, the first state witness to take the stand was very detailed and exact naming dates, time and venues of their treacherous meetings outlining their plans to seize national radio and T.V.. Unknown to the principal defendant the testimony of the state witness was being broadcast live on state radio. People grouped in Taxis, buses, drinking places and schools discussed the trial's revelations in animated voices usually with no sympathy for the defendants.

"Can you produce a tape recording of our allege meetings or show direct evidence linking me to any meeting to overthrow this government?

"Yes apart from me there are witnesses to prove I was at your home and these witnesses were also part of the meetings".

"All of these weapons on display here can the state please tell me where were they found?

Harrison asked cross examining the first state witness himself since he had no defense attorney.

A voice came on state radio then announcing that because of technical problem the live broadcast of the trial could not continue. At this junction the press was asked to leave the courtroom.

"In your house and those of your co -conspirators!.

"Where are the pictures and why was I not taken to my house during the search for the weapons to be uncovered?

"Are you Harrison Payne trying to bring the capacity of our Police, military and intelligence officers into disrepute? I never thought I would live to see a coup plotter insulting Liberia's finest law enforcement agencies.'

'This is preposterous! Thundered Thomas Paine

"Any other question? Col. Gbalaze asked

"Your honor my first question has not been answered. I asked why I was not taken to the scene of the of the arms and ammunition cache purported to be kept by me for the purpose of overthrowing a government I sacrificed my life for."

"I have answered your question" James knot replied indignantly.

"The witness has answered your question General Varney" The tribunal chair responded.

"Please ask your question direct without making political statements next time." The judge warned.

It was the same thing over and over; questions being asked and the answers being evasive and the principal defendant being ridiculed with the acquiescence of the tribunal chairman. Frustrated Harrison stopped his cross examination of the state witness.

When it became time for the state Prosecution to cross examine the accused, it was a different scenario altogether.

"At what time did you have your first meeting to hatch the overthrow of the Salvation Council and to kill the Chairman?

"Which meeting? I have no idea of being part of any meeting apart from those held by the Salvation Council of which I am a part," there was a row of laughter.

"You know which meeting I am talking about. I am talking about clandestine meetings conveyed and spearheaded by you with the devilish aim of overthrowing the Salvation Council."

"I did not covertly or overtly take part in any subversive meeting for the purpose of a coup...."

"Defendant please restrict yourself to answering the prosecution's questions."

"How many rifles did you give....Thomas Paine rattled half a dozen names.

"I did not give weapons to anyone. All weapons I have are registered and assigned by the state. I do not have access to the national armory."

"Defendant answer the question" chairman Gbalaze ordered.

"How many rifles did you give out to your men?

"I gave weapons to no one."

"How much money did the Libyans gave you?"

"I did not receive any money from Libya or any other source for any purpose. I am satisfied with my pay from the Liberian government."

"I must warn you again Harrison Payne for the last time not to make political statements in this court room."

The Prosecution case rested on the aegis of presumed guilt. As the cross examination continued Harrison heart sank. Not once did his co -accuse take the witness stand during the entire trial.

"The tribunal announces the end of this trial. Tomorrow the court will meet here again to announce her verdict".

Captured attacker turned state witness Knot could not believe his ears. Of all places he hated jail especially this small untidy room with her low ceilings and dirty concrete floors he lay in. This had not been part of the bargain. He wanted to go to the beach with Korpo, a new chocolate colored girl he just met from Bong Mines of mixed German and Liberian parentage. He longed to take her to the Rivoli Cinema, to Holiday Inn pub for drinks and fine entertainment. Fred closed his eyes imagining he and Korpo strolling hand in hand on the sparkling, clean ELWA Beach with rollicking Atlantic waves splashing on their backs. As far as he knew he had fulfilled his side of the bargain, he had done a perfect job. What was he doing here? Since his childhood he hated confined spaces. Each hour brought him more discomfort. As the hours ticked by without Gabby's presence his discomfort gave way to guilt. If Gabby lied to him and confined him to this cage he had to find a way to free himself. The heat in the cubicle he lay in made his discomfort acute. Nightfall the cell's temperature dropped significantly. He missed Emily longing for her visit. But why has she not visited him?

Alone with his thoughts he listened to the conversation of two flippant soldiers conversing in low tones outside his prison's door. James slapped the mosquitoes taking liberties on his skin listening.

"You think James Knot and Harrison Payne really tried to kill the President?"

"Do no tell me you swallow that. The whole thing looks fishy to me."

James strained his ears to listen.

"Ba the way things are going I do not think James will come out alive…."

Fred strained his ears more, but he could not hear much as the soldiers drifted away.

Depressed, for the first time in his life he reflected on the deep meanings of life. It was there and then he decided to say the truth and repudiate his lies against Harrison Payne.

Late in the night the powers that be debated James Knot's fate. James fired directly on the President's car! Furthermore, he continued to shoot at the convoy long after he should have stopped. His display of trigger happy enthusiasm went far beyond acceptable limit. Letting him loose will release a dangerous sophisticated element into the army who now knew how to stage a coup. Something had to be done . The President and his advisors agreed. But exactly what has to be done? Was the question on the minds of these scheming men. Their plans worked simply too well. These men were head strong men utterly ruthless in maintaining their own. In the strange twist of human imagination and beliefs the dastardly violence they were quick to mete out to other human beings they felt could not come to them. Somehow they were above the fray even though they took elaborate precaution which somehow in their super magical beliefs could not come near them. And so the decision was reached after much deliberation on what to do to solve this little problem.

The verdict of the trial announced on radio brought relief to a worried population and extreme sorrow to a few. The young revolutionary government triumphed over the menace of coup plotting. Dark green vehicles plied the streets. Men with walkie-talkies and dark shades beefed up security at strategic locations throughout the city. Their presence re- assured rather than frighten the population.

Information Minister Adonis Vonleh stomach churned. Nausea welled in his throat. Every now and then he had to leave his seat to urinate in the bathroom. He and the Justice Minister clashed over the conduct of the trial. Of course, the trial has been held in camera. He as a civilian member of the junta had no direct part no access to it. But he was part of a system designed to convince the Liberian people on the authenticity of the coup and the impartiality of the tribunal set up to trial the defendants though he carried grave reservation on the matter. His uncomfortable feeling stemmed from announcing a verdict he had doubts about its veracity.

A cold gray morning greeted Harrison Payne. He was escorted like prized trophy to the courtroom for the announcement of the verdict for his trial. In spite of visible signs, Harrison still hoped for a miraculous reprieve. He could not believe his ears for he still had the naivety to believe his innocence would set him free. Maxwell Forkpa was his personal friend. They have eaten from the same bowl, gone to the same military training base and known each other for most of their lives. Maxwell Forkpa could not frame him to die. Tribunal Chairman Gbalaze bias against him was only for a moment perhaps based on some long-held grudge. Samuel Dahn was also still in authority, so was Dave Paye, Alex Kulah, all of them personal friends who would intercede on his behalf. Perhaps the reason none of them visited him in jail was due to the heated debates on his behalf.

"Will the defendant please rise."

The improvised courtroom became silent, so quiet that a pin dropped on the ground sounded like a tin can drop on the floor. The gentle breeze from the Atlantic filtered into the room.

"Defendants Harrison Payne and James Knot of the Armed Forces of Liberia are found guilty of the crime of high treason and hereby sentenced to death."

Harrison ears only caught the word guilty seeping into his consciousness. His legs began to wobble. Guards rushed to handcuff him. Men in dark glasses surrounded him on all sides.

Politics African style was a deadly game played without rules, conscience or qualms. The men guarding him had their fingers so perilously close to the triggers of their guns pointed at him it made him shudder. The pretense of civility vanished into thin air.

"Samuel some things simply just defy my imagination. I cannot believe after all we went through for Harrison

Payne to be the one plotting to kill me. I swear I could leave my wife with him and not have second thoughts. I could even leave my drink on the table with him and go in the toilet without thinking he could put something into it. Harrison of all persons? Maxwell beat his chest to show his surprise.

"Maxwell you and him were having lots of quarrel about this transfer to civilian rule lately and then he is accused of plotting a coup-"

"Samuel that you would even think that fills me with disgust. I swear on everything that I hold secret and sacred that Harrison.............did indeed want to kill me."

President Maxwell looked sincere and deep in General Dahn's eyes when he uttered these words.

"My friend I show you something. I have got my papers for admission to West Point. I am getting tired. Remember our conversation? But of us wanted only one position in this country and that's the position you currently hold while I am forced to endure the Presidency. You start as friends.....soon there is a quarrel and somebody has to die. I do not wish to see friends die. This power thing is consuming. Harrison such treason! You saw my bullet ridden car. It is only God Almighty who saved me. Samuel Dahn I need you my best friend for us to hold this country together now than at any time. Stand by me and we can get through this together. To show my sincerity, please help me to look around for a suitable person to head the commission to conduct elections. I will not participate as a candidate for office true to the intention of our coup."

Samuel Dahn has known Maxwell so long and he

knew his friend could not lie in such situations. Was it the trappings of power that he has begun to sub-consciously imbibed that made him believe Maxwell's words so easily?

It did not occur to Samuel Dahn and the other junta members that intrigues and maneuverings had entered the head of their comrade.

The beach that witnessed the execution of some of the nation's finest soon welcomed the bodies of Harrison Payne and James Knot executed by firing squad for attempting to overthrow the Salvation Council.

The bulk of the civilian collaborators accused of plotting the coup along with Harrison Payne remained in jail awaiting separate trial.

The friendship between Maxwell and Samuel became even closer after the execution of Harrison. The frequent visits, the hard drinking and late night talks resumed in earnest. Samuel Dahn continued to enjoy enormous popularity among the rank and file of the soldiers which some say eclipsed those of his friend the Commander in Chief, but the Commanding General remained unassuming and took the adulation on his sleeve. Maxwell the President was a natural born fast learner. He soon began to metamorphosized into a leader. Maxwell loved the attention and adulation of his people. He worked hard to improve his accent, his diction and his clothes. Ebie Kum again instrumental in the gatherings of the chiefs for the denunciation of the former number two managed to secure another meeting with the young head of state. Maxwell learned the rudiments of statecraft from him. Maxwell tried hard to interest his friend in these new exciting things.

Soon the young President dressed and spoke a little like a statesman. Samuel Dahn had no interest in all of these wanting to remain the simple faceless soldier he was. With each meeting between Ebie Kum and Maxwell the commander in chief, the President and his army commander began to see less and less of each other. The execution of Harrison Payne gave President Maxwell the opportunity to implement the next part of his plan to strengthen his hold on power.

God has chosen you and no one else to rule this country, the words again echoed in his ears.

CHAPTER 15

"General it is true, the radio just announced that you have been made Secretary General of the Salvation Council. You are to take your assignment immediately at the Mansion according to the announcement."

The easy charm on the general's handsome face disappeared. He stifled into an erect posture behind his desk. More and more soldiers poured into his office to offer their congratulations.

"Sit down soldier! Samuel ordered the latest well wisher. The General's tone puzzled Capt. Rodney Gweh who rushed to his boss's office to share in the celebration. He expected to be greeted by cheers not the stony face of the man behind a plywood vinyl desk.

"General what are we going to do now? Peyton asked exploiting his position as the General's favorite.

Samuel Dahn's suppressed anger exploded to the surface.

"Who does Maxwell thinks he is? If it wasn't for me, he would not be sitting in that f—k—g chair. That bastard thinks he can just wake up in the morning and do what he likes without consultation eh? An indignant General Dahn bellowed rising to his feet.

"As far as I am concern I am the Commanding General of the army. It t wasn't Maxwell who appointed me neither can he appoint me to any position without my approval. I and Harrison were the ones who entered the President bedroom while Maxwell waited downstairs saying he was there to kill escapees. I do not blame him because I made him President he can now use his power on me, but it will not be." S.D. thundered.

"Get me a jeep quick Peyton I must see that foolish man now!

The staff in adjoining buildings including the Chief and Director of staff heard the general's outburst. They too heard the announcement.

General Samuel Dahn too angry to say anything to stunned subordinates jumped unthinkingly into a small jeep driving to the Mansion at high speed. Those members of the government not part of the Salvation Council could neither understand Samuel Dahn's strong rejection of his promotion. In Samuel Dahn's eyes Maxwell Forkpa had no right to appoint him to any position without consultation and his agreement. Most annoying was the arbitrariness of removing him from a job he loved and cherished and giving him a bureaucratic job he detested.

This was the very reason the President had in mind for appointing him in the first place. By removing his friend from direct command of troops, the President was strengthening his own power base and checkmating a potential rival. He did not want Samuel to remain sleeping with soldiers at BTC so to create a bit of wedge he encouraged the general to move to Sinkor!

General Samuel Dahn ran through all the checkpoints erected along the route from BTC to the seat of the Presidency. Not one of the soldiers manning the checkpoints stopped or questioned him.

President Forkpa watched the snaking route from BTC to the Mansion in anticipation his move would infuriate Samuel Dahn. This was a high stake poker game. From the distance, President Forkpa glanced the small speeding jeep coming to the Mansion and recognized it instantly as belonging to his rival. In spite of himself, President Forkpa watched with a faint wicker of trepidation since he knew Samuel Dahn was capable of marching troops directly to confront his better trained but much smaller Presidential guard. In that case he was prepared to ask religious leader for their intervention. The President whispered to his chief bodyguard who nodded in response and hurried downstairs on an elevator.

The vehicle bearing the Ex Commanding General stopped at the main entrance to the parlors of the Mansion.

In the twinkling of an eye Maxwell accompanied by many bodyguards were heading downstairs running.

Alighting from the vehicle, General Dahn jumped to the ground and wasted no time heading for President Forkpa's office. Their rapid footsteps were blocked by soldiers who barred their path in the corridor of the third floor.

"Out of my way soldiers, I am on my way to meet Maxwell Forkpa!.

"Do you mean President Maxwell Forkpa?

The one who appeared to be leader of the men blocking the path of the general asked in a quiet voice.

"Yes whatever you call him, is he in?

"Yes Major General Dahn, the President is in."

The unperturbed soldier replied still blocking the general's path.

"Out of my way soldier!

"Hold it General Dahn. Five armed men cannot go with you to meet the President. You can go upstairs along with a single bodyguard. The President is waiting to receive you but not with all these men. After your meeting they can join you."

The general checked his side for his handset to call for more men from the BTC. There was no handset, in his hurry he had forgotten to bring one along. General Dahn wanted to do or say something awful to the soldiers blocking his path, but he managed to restrain himself biting his lower lip.

"Soldier you will regret this very much when I return.

Peyton you and the boys can wait for me. I will soon be back since these soldiers here seem to fear your presence so very much. I think this will please you Captain. I am going to meet the President alone." Peyton saluted. The leader of the men who blocked S.D's path saluted which the general ignored and this time he got into an elevator.

The President awaiting S.D. made several quick phone calls. President Forkpa returned to the Varendah fuming. His mounting anger held in check by an almost supreme will power.

Samuel Dahn filled with murderous rage shouted as soon as he saw Maxwell.

"How dare you?

Samuel asked closing the gap between them with quick strides. The two general faced each other, handsome and resplendent in their uniforms with pistols bulging on their hips the two men in their late twenties were almost of the same height. President Forkpa smiled broadly.

"Welcome General Samuel Dahn!

The President shouted opening his arms wide for an embrace. His false charm infuriated S.D. even more. "How dare you Maxwell relieving of my post without consulting me? You think you can run this government on your whim and caprices? I just came to let you know you can have both your Major Generalship and Secretary Generalship in your pockets. As far as I am concern, I remain the Commanding General of the Armed Forces of Liberia."

Samuel Dahn's actions were puerile; that of a man allowing anger to take the best of his reasoning ability. His former friend saw his exposed flank and took advantage of it.

"But Samuel be reasonable. I did you no wrong; I just increased your rank and gave you a promotion and now instead of thanking me you come storming into my office blasting words at me like I am some small boy staying with you?

I just told the staff to clean your office so we can be closer and work together in the same building. Maybe we can go there now together to inspect it. I made the guys do a thorough job cleaning that place and making it look the best because you deserve the best. Your office is a cool airy place you will love."

"Maxwell you must be out of your mind. You know I hate all of this publicity and political work. You know how I love to be just a soldier. We are supposed to be a ruling council where decisions are taken collectively and not a one man show. I do not owe my position to you."

Maxwell gave a quick wink.

"What do you mean Samuel coming to my office to insult me?"

"You deserve it, thank you indeed. You have me to thank for sitting here. Keep your office and adulations. Keep your promotions. I am going back to my troops, and never you try to play games with me. In front of the soldiers downstairs you are Mr. President. Let us keep it that way. Never cross me, and I promise to do my best never to cross you."

S.D. declared pointing his finger at the head of state.

"Wait a minute Samuel Dahn."

Gone was the affable smile on the President's face. Cress of frown covered the handsome face.

"You think you can come to the office of the President of the Republic of Liberia, and insult me in front of my staff and just walk away?

Realization hit Samuel like a ton of bricks. Incredulity at his own stupidity dawned on him. Quick as a flash his hand went to his gun. He intended to shoot Maxwell if even it meant seconds later his body was drilled with bullet holes. In that same flash Maxwell's hand went to his gun. Both guns cleared leather at the same time. A large object within the flicker of an eye crashed into Samuel's skull making him to lose balance. Strong hands whisked his hands behind his back. Maxwell stood his ground but beneath his expensive suits his legs trembled. Although sprawled on the floor; Samuel remained conscious. Elated by the presence of so many Presidential Guards rushing to the scene the President regained his confidence. Though he planned for something dramatic, the swiftness of what happened surprised him.

"Samuel Dahn you are a disgrace to the army. You are under arrest for treason."

"Oh yes Maxwell! Samuel shot back.

"You and I, who is a disgrace to the army? You are worst than a rat. I now know you kill Harrison under false pretence. You are not fit for the uniform you are wearing because you are shamelessly killing your friends. Those of you holding me right now beware because he will end up killing you one by one.

"Enough! Maxwell shouted. "Take this dog and put him under close confinement at the Post Stockade. That will teach him never to bite the hands that feed him."

Samuel Dahn's response was drowned out by the remarkable speed at which he was being dragged down the corridor.

Simultaneously at the two major barracks in the city, the Defense Minister along with the AFL top brass were arresting bodyguards, friends and relatives of Samuel Dahn. Some were receiving hastily typed letters of transfer to remote parts of the country even before they got to hear of the arrest of the popular general.

However, before the official media could report the arrest of the general, the ever efficient grapevine news service had spread it already. Soon civic and religious leaders were taking to the airwaves appealing for calm and reconciliation. President Maxwell Forkpa already gaining the upper hand in the struggle did not see the need to surrender his gains through negotiation which would still allow his rival to wield considerable influence. His advantage over his rival lay in his cunning while his rivals clung to the idea of collective leadership nurtured by their camaraderie. Each junta member looked out for his own. The president was using this individualistic nature, patronage and effective planning to outwit rivals and potential rivals. Anxious to be on the side of the man having the upper hand, the other members of the junta not affected by the latest action were prone to express outrage at what they considered the latest act of betrayal by a fallen colleague since the President was so good at demonizing his opponents. Samuel Dahn's dethronement from power came sooner and easier than expected from his nemesis. To the surprise of many 7 oclock news carried the news of the dismissal and arrest for treason of Samuel Dahn. The news bulletin also announced the promotion of Councilman Alexander Kulah to Major General and Secretary Generalship of the Salvation Council.

Anxious to forestall attempt by influential religious leaders for rapprochement the President of the Republic of Liberia his Excellency Maxwell Tarnue Forkpa departed Monrovia for a visit to Macias Nguema President of

Equatorial Guinea who staged a coup and executed his uncle to gain the leadership of his tiny island nation.

In Monrovia many could not believe their eyes seeing Samuel Dahn make his first court appearance for the charge of treason.

Loyalty can be fickle. Resilience can develop under the most trying circumstances. Alone in a cold cell ; his friends being purged and sent to prison far away from him- Samuel Dahn's self esteem hit rock bottom. He now knew what Harrison experienced before his death. Now he cursed his own duplicity in allowing the execution to go on.

CHAPTER 16

In a small zinc shack at Sonewein in a slum drained by a polluted creek, a small group of soldiers numbering about six were literally taking their lives in their hands huddled together in a clandestine meeting.

"Now there are about ten men guarding the prison at all times. In the early days, the guards were vigilant at all times."

The English being spoken by these men was so accented that it had to be transcribed for a non Liberian to understand.

"Now the soldiers spend most of their time playing cards."

A young Lieutenant with a wide gap in his upper frontal gum announced. He brought out a clean sheet from his pocket and drew lines.

"You, he said pointing to a Master Sergeant. "You will come from so, we will come from so."

He pointed to a line. "We need more ammo than we presently have. Can we contact Capt. Zoebadeh?

"The Captain is not in town known, gone to his village."

"Soldiers the fewer people know about this thing the better. We meet 12 O clock tonight at my place."

The soldiers exchanged handshakes. Each man walked casually out of the room as if coming from this den of opium smoking known as Ghetto. Filled with hope the men said goodbye.

Their plan faced a little snare. One of the conspirators chickened out of the plan at the last minute. However, not wanting to see his friends executed he kept quiet.

Midnight of that same day moving according to plan, a group of heavily armed soldiers quietly surrounded the notorious Post Stockade Prison. Despite this prison holding many prisoners awaiting death; there has been no previous attempt to storm the prison by anyone before. Using stun grenades and small arms the attackers took the defenders by surprise. The explosions and gunfire outside awoke Samuel Dahn from a tortured sleep. At first the general thought President Maxwell Forkpa had sent his men to execute him on the pretext he tried to break out of jail. The closer the shooting drew to his cell the more he realized it was perhaps a rescue attempt by soldiers still loyal to him. He lay flat on his stomach behind the entrance of the door of his cell jumping down from his previous position at the right corner of his cell. A bullet slammed into his vacated position. It was the rapid fire of an untrained soldier trying to kill him. There was silence followed by another burst of rifle fire followed by silence. He heard his name being called, but he remained silent. Then there was the sound of a man in agony and there were voices. Is the general inside?

"Yes"

"Are you sure?

Yes…..there was the sound of keys being inserted into a lock. The general recognized the voices.

General Dahn?

"Yes Capt. Gweh."

The two men embraced

Peyton standing behind Vonyigar another of the general bodyguards threw his commander a rifle.

"Yes you boys are good. I knew you would come. We have to get away from here fast before army reinforcements comes. I know the gunfire might alert soldiers."

Soon two of the other conspirators arrived. "Okay, men crouch low; we are heading to Mamba Point. For a man awaken from sleep his reflexes were good. He jumped over the body of one of the prison guards. S.D. and his men cleared a path for themselves with staccato burst of automatic rifle fire; there was no response from any defender. The wide steel door of the main entrance of the prison was flung open. However, from the direction of the Mansion along UN Drive there was the distinct sound of army jeeps rushing down towards them.

Hurry! Hurry! Hurry! Plans have changed, we are now heading for the national armory on Lynch Street S.D. commanded. Just outside the prison at the main gas station beside the Ford Motor Garage the escapees ran into a small team of government soldiers. Unable to make out each other in the semi darkness the two groups traded fire at close range. Firing as they ran the men escaped the ambush running through the back of the Public Works

Ministry yard into the other end of the LNRC building; they turned around heading north along the wall of the ministry from where they came. Tracer bullets being fired into the night skies brightening around them made the escapees to slow down. The soldiers guarding the armory ahead of them hearing the gun sound were now also shooting . Caught between the soldiers at the armory and those at the main gas station on the UN Drive near the Red Cross building, the escapees were in a mess. There was no way their small number could face these troops and any of them come out alive. Surrounded by drainage S.D. whispered to his men not to shoot. The men from the armory were heading in their direction while those from the GSA advanced towards them on foot. Squeezed between these two superior forces, the situation became desperate for the renegades. Facing certain death surrounded by drainage down into the filthy water filled with sewer they waded waist deep. The smelly group crawling through the drainage emerging on the lower slope of Sonewein behind the Rally Time Market and then ran upwards to Johnson Street, then unto Benson Street and to the Capital Bye Pass. It was at this time Samuel noticed the absence of Lt. Vonyigar.

"Where is Lt. Vonyigar each man asked his friend. There was a sound of an approaching vehicle. They fell to the ground spread eagle fashion with their weapons pointed forward along the wall of the BMC store primed to shoot. The men were shocked to see an unarmed man driving a car at that time of the morning. Shouting to block the path of the lone motorist the men rushed to the road. Peyton pointed his gun at the frightened motorist.

"Get out!

He ordered. The man was more than willing to comply. Stop that" S.D. order.

"Please sir would you allow us to use your car?

The general asked politely even though the tone of his voice suggested he was not prepared to accept no for an answer. The trembling motorist mumbled a yes.

"One day you and your family will be paid back for your services to this country." The man was scared to the bone. Peyton seated behind the steering revved the engine.

"I am afraid to be left here" the motorist managed to whisper. The men dragged him inside his own vehicle fast driving away. What was a lone driver doing driving past midnight in a city echoing with gunfire? This seems to be something one read in an adventure novel not something happening in real life.

Speeding down into the suburb of Gardnersville which offered an escape onto the interior the escapees drove at high speed. The American trained AFL was so amateurish in her approach to issues that there was no communication alerting all security posts in the country of the escape of the now fugitive general. Helped by the ineptness of the situation the men drove through Gardnersville passing right beside one of the strongest barracks in the nation, the 72nd Garrison without interference.

Now on relatively safe ground they dumped the car owner on the road with solemn apology and headed out of the capital. Now safe they could take stock of what happened during their escape.

Where is Vonyigar? The General asked for the second time.

General we may have lost him in the ambush at the junction." Peyton suggested.

"General what are we going to do now" Rodney inquired.

"Peyton there is a cut on your right arm, it is bleeding; I think you stopped a bullet." S.D. pointed ignoring Rodney's question.

"Nothing serious."

One of the guys replied wiping away blood from the affected arm.

"General we can overthrow Maxwell Forkpa tonight. Most of the soldiers at the 72nd Barracks in Paynesville love you, they could join us. We can rally them and then we can move on the radio station."

Captain Rodney Gweh emphasized with strong conviction.

Samuel Dahn had to do some quick thinking. All over the city bullets shattered the calm of the night skies.

"A man who fights and runs away lives to fight another day, we are not cowards but I am afraid for the lives of innocent soldiers who may have to die. Our number is too few. Overthrowing a military government is no bread and butter issue."

"You have done it before." Rodney persisted.

"Overthrowing a military government is not the same thing as overthrowing a weak, defenseless civilian government. By now the radio station is being heavily guarded. The Presidential Guards are already in action. Men…he paused for effect. We have to leave this city tonight."

"And go where?

"Those of you who want to go with me are welcome. I am going back home to Nimba."

There was complete silence among the men.

It was Peyton who broke the silence.

"General there is no future for us without you."

Tears welled in the General's eyes.

"Good I did not want for the blood of any of you to remain on my conscience. Such brave soldiers you are, risking your lives and those of your families for my sake. Soldiers you are true Patriots. One day we shall come back to Monrovia, the blood of heroes such as Lt. Vonyigar will not be spilled in vain. Now let us find transportation for our journey. We are running low on fuel."

CHAPTER 17

The word rage was not enough to describe the anger of the President on discovering the escape of his rival upon his return from Equatorial Guinea. Like a rabid dog, he snapped at everyone. In anger, he ordered the execution of the commander of the prison the general escaped from. The look on the faces of his aides as he issued the order puzzled him.

"Dogs what are you waiting for? Didn't I give you an order or could I reverse the order and have your bodies in the streets by noon instead?"

"Mr. President Major Toe died last night in a shootout with the fugitives."

"Did he die really?

Yes sir, there was a fierce exchange of fire between us and then. Four renegades were killed. We only lost two men."

The aides have seen an opening which they wanted to exploit to the fullest.

"Why was I not informed last night?

"We tried to call you last night but……..

"Shut up, go and confine yourself because it is only damn excuses you can give!

The President angered compounded by guilt. While his arch rival escaped; he whirled the night away in the bosom of one of his mistresses.

"All border points in the country must be sealed right now and any border crossing that dog passes through to leave this country; the commander on duty and all soldiers with him will be executed. Those are my orders!

Every soldier standing guard last night in Monrovia will be court martial!

The President kept shouting as he paced the floor of his office suit. Aides who could afford that luxury shied from his presence.

"You good for nothing Press Secretary you sit here and that dog Dahn name is on the lips of people. You are sacked! Clear your desk right now!

The poor man cowered before his boss hurrying and clearing his desk.

An extensive manhunt commenced for the fugitive general. Samuel Dahn has absconded to the safety of his own home county among kinsman who were willing to risk life and limbs to protect him. The corrupt border guards demanding and receiving bribes at the small forest clearing marking the border at the bank of the river allowed the group of Liberian traders to cross onto their shores for market day not recognizing the fugitive general.

CHAPTER 18

❖ ━━━ ❖ ━━━ ❖

Power zoomed into one's life as an unwelcome intruder for those who never dreamt of being entangled into its awesome grip: insidious and ruinous. Like wine few could resist her allures.

Maxwell Forkpa had had power thrust upon him and he was not willing to let it go . He possessed a determination to cling to what he had. Now the President sat as a pious worshipper at the Providence Baptist Church. In the game of politics appearances counted a lot. The transfer of the President's church membership from the obscured Baptist church he was baptized in the north to the prestigious church in the capital was both a religious and political act designed to gain some clout among the nation's influential but conservative clergy.

President Forkpa's relationship to God was neither intimate nor warm. God existed in his mind as a magnanimous all powerful yet interfering being that needed to be kept at a distance. His insincere soul wanted publicity because Maxwell the person wanted something more dramatic in terms of religion than the piety of organized Christianity. He preferred some connections to his ancestors; some form of fetishism as opposed to the regal formalism of Christianity. One could not place all of one's egg in one basket. A bit of traditional belief and Christianity mixed in an odious concoction appealed to the President. This was the reason he attended church today. He saw no contradiction if he visited a traditional shrine tomorrow.

The President however, did not have to wait that long to act on his practical beliefs.

That same evening the plain without bodyguards except two of his most trusted aides and another confidante huddled in an unmarked car. The hazy air of the evening air made the president incognito at the time most middle class people of the city were at home watching T.V. with their families. The President drove to the outer trading suburb of Dualla.

Driving down Johnson Street into the crowded Vai Town traffic down through the new bridge to the port. Traffic was light along the dual carriageway. The unmarked car kept along with the normal flow of traffic. At the famous Bong Mines Bridge, the President's blue Toyota Tercel veered left bouncing along the big gullies in the unpaved road. The vehicle proceeded at a snail pace through the maze of corrugated sheets buildings built without regards to convenience or beauty. All the urban dispossessed immigrants to the city dwelling in the overcrowded suburb wanted were a roof over their heads to shelter them from the elements and nothing else. Here lived the hustlers, the welders, the charcoal makers, drug dealers, the commercial sex workers, and the have-nots.

Old man Von Yakpah, an immigrant from the Forest Region of Guinea came here years ago, fleeing from the iron-fisted rule of Ahmed Sekou Toure with just the clothes on his back. Von did not find all he wished for, but he found enough to make him quite contented.

Today he wore his customary long white robe which made him look like an Islamic holy man. He sat crossed leg on his mat sewed together with Leopard pelt. Skins of cobras, Mambas, vipers and assorted snakes adored the wall leading to his cubicle; his consulting room. Cowrie shells lined a skull hanging in the middle of the room. Strange stones, dry Chameleon skeletons were positioned on four small stools in his consultation room. Jars lined with various powders and horns filled with black powders laid scattered all over the floor in controlled chaos. A huge white cow tail whose handle held cowries shells laid beside the fetish doctor on his right hand. All of these things had a role to play in his trade of being a fortune teller, a practitioner of magic, to this gentle family man of medium height.

Unlike many practitioners of their nefarious trade notorious for disclosing the names of their clients to boost their standing among peers and potential clients; Von was a discreet man of few words who kept his own counsel. Many of his clients; big and powerful people consulted him usually at night to avoid attention. Hypocrites these clients were, who cares as long as he got his money?

Von had the ability to detect his clients were even

before they arrive at his clinic. He braced himself to receive them and his palm usually became wet with anticipation. Even at night some of them wore dark goggles to hide their eyes. There were no chairs in his consultation room. It was important that any client who sought his services know he Von ran the show here irrespective of their status on the outside. Sitting on low mat facing him with expectation, their expectant faces made his clients look like children. The desire to know what will happen before it happens has been with mankind since time in memorial because human beings longed for the security of familiarity.

It was this desire for security which drove President Forkpa to this obscured corner of the city. Maxwell perched on a low stool in this dingy low ceiling room because for once Von chose to make an exception. Beside him on a mat, sat Ebie Kum also clad as the President in casual jeans. Maxwell focused his attention on the man in front of him chanting in a guttural voice. Von ignored the world around him chanting and throwing cowries shells into the air and letting them fall to the ground. He stared intensely like a person under a hypnotic spell at the cowrie shells on the ground as if fathoming some hidden messages from their positions on the ground. Their positions appeared random with each throw; some faced up while others faced the ground.

Von's facial expression vacillated from elation to sadness and elation and sadness fixed in a hypnotic trance. The President felt something cold touching his feet. He looked down to see a large hooded cobra nudged against his feet. Another serpent poised to strike with black and white markings beneath the hooded neck eyed him suspiciously darting her forked tongue. From the direction of the doorway still more snakes meandered their way into the room gliding smoothly on their thin long stomachs. The President's hands automatically went to his side to feel the gun which he knew were useless against so many slimy creatures. The serpents could inject their deadly toxins into his blood stream before his weapons could do much damage. Von smiled and waved his hand; in that second all of the snakes withdrew.

"I know want brings you here my son.......I hope I can be of service to you."

He grinned showing Kola nut stained teeth.

"Your demonstration here with those snakes were impressive, but I did not come for snake charm. I want you to fortify me and make me a man.' Von laughed.

"You are already more than a man, you are like a rock, and what can water do to rock? Before I do any work for you let me look again."

A tall strapping lad returned to the room almost as soon as the words escaped his father's lips with a candle. Maxwell watched the tiny pale blue flame flickering and Von seemed to communed with it.

Von then started to explain. "You want to remain President of Liberia. I see your opponents knocking and falling against you. The spirit inside you is very strong..... yes they are planning and plotting."

Many years in this business made Von to know clients who came to him were either bruised or they were unsure of something; he needed to boost their egos for his fees to be generous.

"I see people marching towards you."

He pronounced in heavily accented pidgin transcribed here. "I do not know whether they are in your favor or against you…. They are coming through one of the nations surrounding us…….

Suddenly Von stopped speaking and began rolling on the ground struggling to catch his breath. He mumbled some unintelligent words fuming at the mouth dripping with saliva. Maxwell gave Ebie Kum a savage look. Just as suddenly as he had fallen Von rushed back to his feet.

"Yes they are dying along the way … yet one of them is coming…he is still coming with his slanted eyes…Yes I see him clearly…..but his name keeps slipping……… from my mind…..

"It must be Samuel Dahn….The President suggested.

Von fumed continuing his halting speech oblivious to the President's suggestion.

"He comes from the northeast…..You can overcome him, but I need….

"Here take this money."

The President threw a wad of high denomination banknotes at Von.

He wanted to get out. Samuel Dahn was planning a comeback. He Maxwell would remain standing firm to meet him. The first time they (coup-makers) moved against a defenseless military regime. He Maxwell was different and Samuel would meet more than his march.

There were people destined to die and they would die

if necessary Maxwell fumed exiting Von's consultation room.

"Ebenezer this is a game of chess."

Back home an angry wife confronted him when he narrated what transpired in Von's place. The President's eyes were a little too bloodshot from being a bit too friendly with the bottle.

"I think it is about time you give the people ugly chair back to them."

"What did you say?

"You heard me right. Tarnue give the people back their Presidential chair."

Maxwell's temper rose to a feverish pitch. The muscle behind his neck bulged up.

"Someone wants to kill me and all you say woman is I must run away."

He lashed out at Nancy . Yet his wife did not cry out, instead she faced him defiant in her outlook. This woman schooled in the conservative school of subservience to her husband almost sheepishly followed him in most things. But Maxwell knew whenever she took a stand she was like a mule, in his blind fury he forgot this. He wanted her to cry out in pain but not this reaction.

"Yes he missed you today but God forbid what will happen the next time."

"And so you suggest?

Maxwell asked his eyes cold.

"Leave this place; go far away from this power thing."

"If someone wants to get you, you get them before he get you. Self-preservation is the first law of nature, woman."

"I do not want you to be where someone wants to get you."

This woman had a taste for the melodramatic. She knelt down to her feet holding fast to her husband's right knee. He tried to lift his feet to no avail.

"Don't you see what this job is doing to you? When was the last time you made love to me your wife? Your children do not know you anymore. When last did you have time to watch me cook while you play and laugh with your children? My children, our children? You are too busy doing good for other people chasing after useless girls...

"So this is it, your irrational jealousy disguised as concern for me."

Maxwell pushed aside yet she still clung to his knees. Tears broke on her fat face and her body heaved up and down. She began to wail. Maxwell did not love her intensely anymore, but he still cared for her and hated to see her so distraught.

"No Tarnue, it is not because of jealousy I say these things. It is because of what you are doing to yourself, to your family, to people who love you I am concern about. Ebie Kum, Adonis, Gabby all those men are only behind you for what they can get from you and nothing else. The late nights, the fiery temper, the blank pre-occupied stare, your children growing up without knowing you.

Now I have everything I dream about still I am not happy. If it comes to choosing between you and money, there is no choice. I will choose you. I want you back again."

Her voice dropped to a pleading whisper. There were few things moving or emotional disturbing to Maxwell than the pleading tearful eyes of this woman.

"Please husband of mine give the people chair.

Look at you and Samuel Dahn .You and him did everything in common but now oh my God….. I can't see his wife who was my best friend and say hello."

She burst into a new round of wailing.

"Honey I promised when we have this country working again for and behalf of the people, my job will be completed and I will gracefully step aside. I do not want to keep falling out with friends.

I have to plead with you to do me a favor right. Please do not ever call Samuel Dahn's name in my presence again ever!

I give this presidential chair over one day soon and we be together again like before."

"Do you really mean it for us to be together again?

She asked in an enthusiastic voice.

"Of course honey."

A broad smile spread across her face. Maxwell began to stroke her hair his hands rubbing down her body. She began to sing a cheesy traditional tune . She fell backwards on the king-size bed his demanding hands cupping her breasts.

The national mood was not in favor of any execution especially for the coup plotters still facing trial at the justice temple for their role in Harrison Payne coup and Samuel Dahn's escape. The mood in the country was somber and people went about their daily routine laughing less. Taxis lowered the volume of the music a bit as for in the changed political dispensation they awaited the verdict of another coup trial this time for the civilian collaborators of Harrison Payne.

The President aware of the mood in his country sent invitation to the heads of media organizations for a special news conference slated for 11 am in the parlors of the Mansion just a day before the announcement of the verdict of the coup trial. Somber music dominated the airwaves. President Forkpa remained alone meditating even when the time for the conference arrived. Worried aides baited their breath waiting wondering what the President was doing in his office when the nation was anxious to hear from him.

The President stepped forward to the microphone around 11:30 dressed in his now customary expensive designer's suit appearing collected. His somber, calm look and well groomed body made him resemble a film star. The country again held her breath for he alone could bring tears or joy. A poor boy from a village whom the nation did not know held the country under his feet.

The President began his discourse relax, not speaking hurriedly as he did previously "Sometimes people think the life of the President is an easy one. When this nation sleeps I am wide awake thinking about the good of this God blessed country. We all want to breathe free again away from coup plots, guns and soldiers.

But remember the soldiers are your brothers and sisters. They are part of the society which we cannot hide from. They are trained to safeguard our lives and properties. I must commend Capt. Peter Toe who gave his life in defense of his nation and President. Posthumously he is promoted to the rank of Lt. Colonel. His wife and children will continue to receive his salary and benefits. I will personally pay the school expenses of his children for this young man who made the supreme sacrifice of giving his life to protect and sustain our way of life.

There are others though who chose to tread the vile path of coup making, people who have no respect for the sanctity of life willing to go to any length to perpetuate their vain desire for power. They are not willing to wait for the time to restore democratic civilian rule. These diabolical people plotted and treacherously ambushed my car while returning from dedicating a development project.

Not long ago a military tribunal under the chairmanship of Gen. Amos Gbalaze found General Harrison Payne and other guilty of treason for which they paid the ultimate penalty. Sometime later Samuel Dahn and his co-conspirators were also found guilty of the charge of Treason and conspiracy to commit murder in absentia. General Dahn shall face the full weight of the law according to Uniform Code of Military Justice."

Many hearts in the audience almost stopped beating.

"In any civilized society we must also temper justice with mercy. Sergeant James Knot accused Prof. Martins, Antoinette Browne, Peter George, Taewah Dwalu of plotting against our government . While government has impressive evidence to continue with the treason trial, in the interest of peace and national reconciliation I now immediately by the power vested in me pardon and order release from further detention all persons within our borders accused of the heinous crime of treason!

The somber nation exploded into bombastic happiness. People abandon their homes and offices for the streets. The Liberian people were predictable in their response rejoice! The President's magnanimity was embraced by a grateful nation.

The released prisoners held shoulder high by family and friends were escorted to their homes accompanied by rhythmic dancing.

While the country rejoice the President placed a call to his trusted aide Moses Gabby

"I want you to recruit a special agent abroad to watch the activities of the fugitive former commanding general. This agent will watch who he gets into contact with. I know that one day we shall face an invasion from him. We have to prepare for that eventuality." These words would prove prophetic.

CHAPTER 19

The President had work to do which he wanted done fast. President Forkpa paused to receive a confidential call from the US Secretary of State. He dialed his Foreign Minister just a block away. "Doctor Emory come right over."

"I am just receiving the Zambian Ambassador, who is making a courtesy call on me. Please give me at least half an hour."

"It seemed you didn't hear me. I said I need you now. Zambia what and what I do not care just come right over….The President banged the phone down.

A flurried Minister passed an astonished Mr. Manawasara in the corridor heading to his office.

The Foreign Minister fought to control his temper. He hurried upstairs to meet his boss. If the President noticed the approach of his minister, he did not pay any attention. He remained motionless in a swivel chair, yet his penetrating gaze took in the entire scene. He seemed pre- occupied. Remaining immobile he acknowledged the greetings of the erudite professor with a slight murmur. Minister Emory perched down in the chair motioned to him by the President. The President did not mince his words. Getting used to the corridor of power President Forkpa looking magnificent in a western suit.

"What is our level of trade with the Israelis?"

The question startled the minister since this matter did not remotely featured in any discussion previously held with the President. What the Foreign Minister did not know the Israeli had requested full diplomatic recognition in exchange for security assistance.

"The Finance Minister is the best person to answer that question your Excellency the Minister thought, but he could not give such as answer to his boss.

"Well, we do just a little bit of trading with them but quite frankly not much."

Maxwell laughed. Not much eh? I think Israeli trade could be more important. After our discussion, you can show me Zambia on the map." - President Forkpa laughed.

"What do you think about Liberia re-establishing diplomatic relationship with Israel to boost our trade links."

"What? Mr. President the OAU unanimously agreed it after Israel went to war with a fellow African country Egypt in 1973 that all African countries sever diplomatic relationship with the Jewish state. You remembered the unprovoked Yom Kippur War in which Israel seized the Sinai Peninsula from Egypt? Since that time, however, all African countries have isolated Israel. We cannot unilaterally re-establish ties with Israel without the agreement of the OAU General Assembly."

The President stood up pacing the floor.

"It seemed to me Egypt is more an Arab than an African Country. Now if the OAU breaks off diplomatic ties with Israel in the name of shaky African solidarity with Egypt, Egypt goes behind the OAU and sign a peace accord with Israel at Camp David and re-establish ties with Israel without consulting the OAU General Assembly; what is there stopping us from doing the same?

I think we are wailing too much for a friend who lost a relative more than the friend himself. Instead of us stopping our friend from crying, we are the ones crying loudest while the friend who lost the relative is playing."

"True Mr. President but that position has to be argued at the OAU. Israel must also learn to treat the Palestinians better."

"You my dear friend is more learned and better able to deal with the hard questions of the Israeli Palestinian conflict. I am only talking about national interest."

"I am talking about principles- African solidarity. Furthermore, our volume of trade with Israel is so minute. I do not see the need for such haste in re-establishing ties."

"I am talking about Israeli arms, products and experts to boost our failing Agriculture programs. We need Israeli intelligence on Libya terroristic activities. If we take the line you are taking won't it will be better you are working in Addis Ababa instead of here."

"Mr. President an agreement is an agreement. For many years Liberia stood as an inspiration, a beacon of hope for colonized Africans destroying a myth that the black man was incapable of governing himself. It is important we continue to play that role. While I do agree with the points you are bringing I only say let us argue our case in Addis Ababa. Please Mr. President let us not act alone."

President Maxwell Forkpa sauntered to his seat. With careless ease he lighted a cigar. His press and executive Secretaries sensed the calm before the storm.

"Is that your last word on the matter Prof. Emory? The President's rich baritone carried a belle charm almost.

"I hope you understand. I will start liaison work in Addis immediately."

"Addis Ababa, Addis Ababa is that all you know. Go back to the university Professor. I want your letter of resignation first thing tomorrow morning on my desk if you do not want to bear the shame of hearing you are dismissed."

Maxwell laughed loud. His laughter sounded coarse and vulgar much to the embarrassment of his aides. Something of a man past always followed him like his shadow; some kind of unpleasant relic. Of course Maxwell had traveled a long way from the village and urban slums. Finer clothes, finer food, finer women, better speech, everything was available to him, yet he still laughed a bit too loud for a civilized surrounding. An astonished minister too stunned to speak made a hasty exit. He dared not argue with the President. A cardinal rule those close to the President never crossed. Had he known the President so well he would have cajoled him and agreed with him if he did not bulged. The Foreign Minister's foreign accent and education represented everything the President was not. Something which created resentment. An angry president wanted nothing but disgrace for him.

By evening hours the President called his new slumbering press secretary to prepare an announcement for the dismissal of Foreign Minister Prof. Emory.

The US Ambassador headed to a meeting with the Liberian President in a sour mood. His cooked burnt his beloved baked chicken this morning. It did not please him to again meet the young President with maverick ways. America needed the support of this staunch ally in their fight against the global menace of communism. His political machinations did not however, appear to bring the orderly transition and stable governance Washington wanted. The envoy had a hunch Washington was raising a Tiger as a pet. While their mutually beneficial relation continued because Washington gave him what he needed, if his desires clashed with the wishes of Washington he could be difficult to tame.

The envoy's dark Chevrolet meandered its way through the potholed streets of Monrovia.

President Maxwell Forkpa stood on the balcony of the presidential palace waiting to welcome his distinguished guest. He smiled and offered a handshake to the great man when he finally arrived.

"Welcome Ambassador Lacey we are very appreciative of your kind support during our period of national crisis."

"Mr. President we are very sorry for the unfortunate attempt on your life. The American government and people are happy that the wicked attempt did not succeed. We must also commend you for your bold decision to expel the Libyans from your country."

"Mr. Ambassador you have no idea how much trouble those Arab radicals have given us."

The President smiled broadly exercising the fabled charm of his dashing personality buoyed by his youthfulness. He showed the Ambassador around the Mansion with brilliant warm charm. Soon the photo opportunity was over; the Press was soon shooed away for the business for which he came for . If the Ambassador just wanted for his pictures to be taken he could do so abundantly in his seaside diplomatic enclave.

"Mr. Ambassador the attempt on my life by Harrison Payne and the revolt by our ex army commander I think should let you know with a sense of urgency our need to receive the surveillance equipment we asked for."

The ambassador smiled because he knew better.

"Mr. President he announced in his delightful southern drawl. Do not pull that crap on me. We know everything that happened. We have satellites that can photograph a needle from space with remarkable accuracy. Moses Gabby Defense Minister set this assassination thing up. As for Samuel Dahn's coup we know better. It was no coup. A small group of soldiers stormed and surprised your men guarding the prison. The general escaped from the country with a small group of soldiers to the Ivory Coast."

The warm smile on the President's face disappeared. Underneath his arms a thin layer of sweat poured onto his shirt. The toothy envoy smiled.

"Do not worry it is none of our business. We-my government is grateful to you for the release of the arrested detainees. What we appreciate though is a commitment from you no military man who had been part of the

THE FADING FLOWER

Salvation Council will run in any election organize by the Salvation Council."

"If I do that won't that be letting the cat out of the bag ?".

"It is crucial Mr. President we receive that commitment from you that no military men will take part in an election."

President Maxwell Forkpa's demeanor changed and he became very serious.

"Yes sir there will be no military man standing as a candidate in an election organized by the Salvation Council."

"Good Mr. President. I did not want to let the cat out of the bag. The US will accept 100 more soldiers for advance military training at Fort Bragg in North Carolina to improve your security in view of the unfortunate attempt on your life."

The Ambassador smiled.

This piece of information so delighted that President he hugged the Ambassador. The President was a man who always thought on things before their time. If he wanted to run in future he was already thinking of how to circumvent his promise to the US envoy.

From that day onwards President Forkpa made away with his now usual dark sunglasses. He abandoned his military uniforms completely. He also reduced the number of visible security personnel accompanying him to state functions.

Words such as effective immediately, in the cause of the people- the struggle continues, anybody violating this decree will meet the full force of the law quietly disappeared from his vocabulary.

Words like" Nation building, our common heritage, and constitutional order,

Democracy, civilian rule escaped his lips more often. The hurried speech to disguise his bad accent disappeared. To further boost his image the President embarked on extensive trips abroad. Offers of technical and financial support followed the President wherever he went to visit. He was the rooster in the country. All his junta rivals were either dead or forced into the ignominy of exile or were subservient.

Most Liberians were proud of their affable handsome young President. When he came back home acrobatic cultural dancers and citizens lined the route to welcome him back. He now often visited the countryside. The man exuberating charm excited his people and everywhere he went people waited in the sun for hours to welcome him and get a glimpse of the young President. Wherever he visited there was something good for the people he visited. Traditional chiefs in colorful robes received handsome bonuses. Crucially when the President was petitioned by territories seeking county status, he agreed to the request by ambitious local politicians to create more counties. More counties meant more Senators in the next election, Circuit Judges, Superintendents and their staffs, and simply more jobs which the President approved of. Cultural dancers received donations. New school buildings were dedicated. Some good works came out of every visit to benefit whenever the President visited a locality.

The young President was the unquestioned Captain of the ship of national affairs.

It puzzled some observers that for a military man desirous of handling over power back to civilians the President was adopting such populist agenda. His eloquent Information Minister, Adonis Vonleh assured the doubters that the President was sincere in his desire to restore what the minister called" Genuine Democracy." When the loquacious editor of the Daily Observer broke the news of the purchase of a Presidential jet at tax payer's expense he was condemned by almost every sector of society for being unpatriotic. An editorial on ELBC described the journalist as an unrepentant extreme left winger. The New Liberian Newspaper decried what it described as the editor's intemperate seditious outburst.

Press release after press release by people desirous of government jobs condemned the editor. It seemed surprising that in a nation of such high illiteracy rate where no newspaper circulation reached 5000, a little story like that could receive such vitriolic condemnation when the majority of the people had not even read the story. The President did not need to comment on the publication. He did not need to. One thing he and his advisers did not read too well was the determination of Liberians for a faster return to civil rule instead his snail pace structured returned to constitutional rule.

CHAPTER 20

The clamor grew louder and louder in the nation as military rule dragged into four years. Monrovia City Hall, a modest two storied building situated at the gateway to the eastern suburb was filled to overflowing with people who wanted a return to constitutional rule. The young and ambitious, the old and tenacious, the curious and the idle jammed the main reception area of the edifice resting their backs in the marooned reclining seats. Still others stood in the passageway in the corridors to listen. The released former Foreign Minister. Prof. Martins having completed the work of drafting a new constitution returned to his previous role of being an opposition leader. The Prof. Stood on the platform his hand raised in the style of "In the cause of the people" salute. The Political Officer at the US Embassy, and the controversial Lawyer James Chelly sat on the stage nodding their heads. The sounds of bells greeted the unfolding of a huge cloth banner. Outside the hall a discreet military presence prevailed keeping out of sight away from the main road. However, as the meeting gained momentum more and more military men took up positions along the St. Patrick High School Campus and just opposite the hall in the yard of the Libyan built Pan African Plaza. .

"We have come today to foster democracy. The baby of democracy has to be nurtured and fed. We the Liberian people demand an impartial free electoral commission. A transparent electoral process, early registration of political parties, along with a firm declaration from President Maxwell Forkpa of his intentions is crucial if our elections are to be credible. One cannot be a referee and a player in a match at the same time. If President Forkpa wanted to run in this election he must resign the same way he urged his colleagues."

The Prof. Martins spoke with the clarity of a focused vision, his emotion surging . Hundreds of his supporters urged him on with their support. Cameras flashed, tape recorders zapped. The Prof. spoke on without fear or favor. The crowd roared back with approval. Unknown to the people inside the hall, more and more vehicles filled with security men were surrounding the building. Even later when news of the growing security presence reached Prof. Martins, he remained unperturbed continuing his speech his voice rising. Using mobile radios the security agents were busy sealing off escape routes from the hall. The faint hearted onlookers on the periphery of the crowd began to quietly melt away.

"And so civil society demands nothing but a level playing field….the Prof. concluded his speech which was a paragon of brilliant oratory. His electrifying words spurred the crowd into chanting political slogans. The security agents outside waited impatient for the conclusion of the Prof's speech for they had their orders to obey. These security men stood by as the US Political Officer drove away in her diplomatic jeep. Prof. Martins stood in the corridor of the building leading to the main entrance waving to his party militants who cheered him on. Hedged in by party militants suspicious of the growing security presence he was escorted to a Renault Laguna.

He urged his driver towards the direction of Sinkor. A stocky man in the crowd signaled to a nearby Rodeo jeep whose driver switched his ignition on. As soon as the Laguna carrying Prof. Martins drove past, the Rodeo Jeep waited for another two cars before setting out in pursuit moving slowly with the traffic. There was a slow build up of traffic ahead with a break dancing Policeman trying hard to direct impatient motorists.

A uniformed officer flagged the Professor's car down. A Land Cruiser which was driving ahead of the Laguna also slowed down, the Rodeo SUV from behind closed in too leaving the Laguna between the two jeeps. Plainclothes security agents surrounded the Professor's vehicle.

"What is this?

An exasperated Professor Martins asked opening the door of his car.

"Sir, consider yourself under arrest."

A well built security agent wearing a sport trench coat announced. His large pot belly protruded from beneath a tight T-shirt. His face appeared to suit his frame and his dark kinky hair was combed backwards.

"On what charge? And where is the arrest warrant?

I cannot leave this vehicle unless you produce a valid warrant."

"I am Capt. Fred Kollie of the CID Division of the LNP. Please I have a lot of respect for you sir. I do not want the boys to get rough with you because I have an order to obey, a job to protect."

"Orders from whom?

"That I am not at liberty to say.

Would you please come down sir."

"This Professor is not going anywhere ruffians" an agitated young man riding with the Prof. shouted.

"Take it easy, just marked the car registration plate down."

Bulging biceps surrounding the vehicle pulled doors opened.

The Prof. alighted from the vehicle surrounded by men as if he was some prized trophy won by a team.

"I like to speak to my driver privately."

"You are welcome sir."

"Alert the US Ambassador of my arrest, phone the offices of all the newspapers and radio stations you know in this country describing the circumstances of my arrest."

The Prof. whispered quickly.

"Hurry up sir, I have my orders to obey."

Capt. Kollie urged. Seconds later, the Prof. showing no trace of fear surrendered himself to the arresting officers. An overzealous security agent slammed a cuff on the Professor's wrist. He slapped the Prof.

An enraged commander Kollie lanky and very dark ordered his arrest on the spot. "How dare you slap the

Prof. Take away his radio and slam the handcuffs he put on the Professor on him!

"And what is this?

His subordinate a sordid creature with a slit for a mouth asked baring his yellow teeth. His face pot marked by holes, scars no doubt of a Smallpox infection in his early years screamed in anger.

"We are told to come and arrest this thing, not to treat him like some VIP I will tell the boss when we get back!

The aggressive agent cursed when the handcuffs were placed on his hands.

"Kollie you do not know what you are playing with?

I will show you that I am the President's brother.

The engines of both Rodeo and Land Cruiser zoomed to life.

"Are you going to leave me here? The handcuffed officer asked.

"That is exactly what we are going to do." Kollie replied.

The men were respectful but thorough. Before the Professor could board their vehicle an agent frisked him. In seconds strong hands frisked his body for possible weapon.

"Suspect under custody, mission complete." Kollie announced on his radio.

———

The helicopter carrying President Maxwell Forkpa landed on the grassy rural airstrip of Voinjama. The noise of the rotor blades drowned out the noise of the energetic dancers that now sang and danced with more gusto upon seeing the Presidential party. Pride swelled in the hearts of the large number of people who thronged to the airport to welcome their President. The people had a reason to be proud. They were the first county in the nation to produce an indigenous President; Maxwell was not just a President for the nation, he was also their son. Long forbidden doors in the high echelons of the security sector had flung wide open to the people of Voinjama District upon the ascendancy of their son to the Presidency. Many heads of parastatals came from their district and county. Much money flowed into the district, thanks to the efforts of their son. The President disembarked from his aircraft amidst huge a huge roar of approval sweeping through the crowd clapping their hands. Many in the crowd have been waiting for more than five hours in the hot sun to see Tarnue. School children resplendent in their uniforms stood at attention. Many of them now were named Maxwell, Tarnue, or Forkpa. A young girl whose face radiated the vibrancy of holy innocence presented a brocade of flowers to the head of state who scooped down not only to take the proffered flowers but to also scoop the little girl into his arms. The little girl smiled and broke into a cry to the amusement of everyone present. Bosomy women danced sending a specter of dust into the skies. The arrival of the President energized their performance. Security men were having a hard time trying to prevent the crowd from mopping the President. Traditional rulers clothed in the finest traditional robes vied with each other to be the first to shake the hand of their famous son.

Their wives also clothed in the best African wax print money could buy and the best of the rare hand woven textile for which the county was famous for gazed with unabashed admiration for their son and husband dancing and singing the praises of the President. The county civil administrators dressed in western suits sweated in the midday sun . Like school children they lined up to greet the President beaming in his presence.

A boisterous toothy elder poured libation calling on their ancestors to protect the President. The Lormas were decent strongly conservative people endowed with a rich culture, and proud history spanning many years. They were justly proud to display their tradition. The President beamed with happiness every bit a homecoming prince. He savored every moment basking in the praises of young students singing special songs composed for the occasion. He outpaced his bodyguards moving into the crowd shaking hands and tossing money. Everyone wanted to touch him. He responded enthusiastically to the overt display of love by his brothers and sisters. His security men were beside themselves with worry. The President waded into the crowd oblivious to their concern.

A word here, a touch there, a joke here, and a word of praise there delighted the people. President Forkpa shook so many hands his palm became sticky wet. A jubilant crowd trudged behind the presidential motorcade through the streets, people lining the route sang and danced. He waved acknowledging their cheers.

Voinjama weather beaten streets high in the mountains of northwest exuded confidence. The administrative headquarters of the largest of the leeward counties throbbed with the festivities of a welcoming celebration for her favorite son. In the dusty hilly streets of this rural city, the President became once again an ornery Lorma boy contented to dwell among the Palm Trees and savannah vegetation of the north country.

President Maxwell enjoyed the pomp and pageantry of his welcoming knowing it was genuine adulation. The following day the ornery Lorma boy became even more ornery accompanied by elders who took him to the bush country north of Voinjama.

All of those present sat crossed legged in a semicircle under a Palm Tree in the Savannah. These wizened old men who were the high priests of the tribe relished the prospect of their finest son coming to drink from the calabash of wisdom. The famous traditional garment whose art of weaving had disappeared in most other counties in the nation adorned their bodies. Many held long thin silver swords, their bodies were decorated with cowries' shells. Many held Cow tails a symbol of their authorities: adding solemnity to their gathering under the open blue skies.

President Forkpa wore a short blue white raffia short . Tarnue sat cross legged in the semicircle on one side facing the elders on a Leopard skin mat. An old man poured water on his head from an earthen jar. Without warning a young man struck a savage blow to his neck. Maxwell stared in horror. His horror turned to unbelief when the cutlass used by the young man to strike him did not leave a single mark.

"Now you have power; if any man has not eaten salt that will be the only time anything they plan against you will work."

A toothless old man grinned.

"Our ancestor have a saying that it is a cat which has patience and a strong back catches a rat. A man cannot leave the road his ancestors made for him and try to make his own. We tread the path our forefathers made. We do not light fire in our houses and then close the door.

Tarnue you are our fire we bring to our houses. Elders is this not so?

The speaker asked in a voice which sounded so strong for his frail body.

"It is so!

The elders replied in loud guttural voices. The atmosphere around them echoed. Their united voices made the meaning of what was being said to sink deeper into the mind of the President.

"A man cannot have water in his house and use his spittle to wash his hands. Neither do you leave old fire burning to start a new one.

In our tradition when a neighbor's fire is burning and you need to start a fire of your own you do not begin to and start another fire. You simply go and get live embers to light your own fire.

You have become President Tarnue and must remain one!

"Is it not so elders?

It is so! It is so! It is so!

The elders replied their voices strong and united.

"Forget about handling power to anybody! Power is yours! Our sons and daughters are yours!

Maxwell's head swirled in a circle. The charismatic old man leading the chant words had a mesmerizing effect on the President. He started feeling drowsy and had a feeling he was being transported out of this world into another world.

CHAPTER 21

Refreshed by the visit to his ancestral homeland the President's return to the city coincided with the completion of the work of the constitution drafter and so he addressed the nation.

When the President rose to speak at the Conference Center, the audience became very silent. The entire nation stood still and listened.

The now suave, debonair, charming President spoke in a dignified manner.

"Two years ago when we announced our decision to return this country to civilian rule doubters and skeptics mocked our sincerity. Now with this document the Liberian people can now see tangible proof that our commitment to democracy is unflinching.

It my hope that the Liberian people will accept this draft constitution in a referendum on May 15 so as not to delay our forward march to democracy. Though I have not yet read the contents of this document I have every confidence in the men and women who prepared this document. We ask our detractors to return home and contribute their quotas to the nation building effort.

I now declared a general amnesty to all exiled opponents of our government. People who have committed treason against this nation are now pardoned….. Thunderous applause greeted this part of the President's address.

Maxwell smiled acknowledging the applause. He waited for the noise to die down before resuming.

I assure the Liberian people with God above our rights to prove nothing will derail our forward march to democracy. As soon as you my fellow citizens accept this document the date for general and Presidential elections will be announced.

Another thunderous applause greeted the President.

"May God bless the works of our hands and save the state!

The Police Band sprang to life with a rendition of the National Anthem.

Crowds hearing the words of the President lined the streets to cheer the President. All through the journey back to the capital from the Unity Conference the President made unscheduled stops to donate money and interact with his people.

At the Freeport, the President stopped his motorcade, walked into the crowd and donated a hundred dollars to an old lady who grimaced, smiled and thanked the President in an emotional voice crying. She had never dreamed of being face to face with a President before let alone receiving a donation in person from him. Will he run for the highest office in the land? Won't he run? The crucial question remained unanswered.

Ebenezer Kum rubbed his hand through his gray hair touching the dove collar of his Maoist styled suit. The task before them was not as easy as it seemed.

"We have to choose someone who is not remotely related to any of us, but, unfortunately, the space at the top in Liberian society is minuscule. We need someone who is neither an admirer nor overt supporter of the Salvation Council."

Maxwell lighted his cigar. The indecision of his civilian collaborators were baffling at times. He had asked them who he could appoint as chairman of the newly constituted election commission; instead of giving her names here they were analyzing and wasting his time without coming up with possible names. He just sat motionless as his advisors engaged in a wrangle.

"Barnabas Rudolph Trimes the long time former Foreign Minister is one of the best candidates for the job. He has experience and rarely for a top Liberian official; he is not corrupt."

"And you think his long public association with the powers that be in Liberia has made him a suitable candidate to conduct our elections? You want the Liberian people to say the Congo people coming back to rule the country?

"Now you have said what is wrong with the name I suggest, who do you think is best suitable to meet your stringent criteria?

The note of sarcasm in the new Foreign Minister's voice was biting.

"Yarkpawolo Howard remembered him? One of

Liberia's foremost academics, he presently teaches African History at Howard University in Washington D.C.

The guy has no known ties to any political party in Liberia."

The President laughed. "Even though I am a Tarnue I do not want a Yarkpawolo to head our election now maybe the next election because that name itself is a mouthful and he is not international known this is my first time hearing his name." Professor Yarkpawolo is the son of Ebenezer's auntie she had by a Kpelle man.

When Ebenezer Kum spoke at last after a long period of silence, he did so carefully to conceal his excitement.

"I know a man who once headed the Liberian delegation to Geneva. A very reliable and quiet man. These qualities proved valuable in his important but often overlooked Geneva posted. The late President Tubman wanted more UN Agencies to come and work in Liberia, so he posted a Mr. Everette Gray a distinguished product of the University of Liberia and Oxford Universities. However, I very much doubt if Mr. Gray will be willing to accept such a high profile job meaning if of course you could appoint him."

"You yourself stated the fact there is doubt in your mind Everette could accept such a job"

"It would be good in these days of women empowerment to have a woman as a commissioner."

The Foreign Minister countered.

"And who could that be?

President Forkpa asked in a low voice…. I am not too sure, but I think Eugenia Weade Thompson, a product of our own law, and former ambassador to Swaziland and Germany is one of the best candidates for the job".

"It will interest you to know Weade is now the head of UNDP for Africa.

The argument swam back and forth between the two men. The President was bemused. He liked the idea of his men fighting to gain his attention. His mind was already made up but he enjoyed the verbal jabs being exchanged though.

"The venerable ambassador is a man with a mind and will of his own. Convincing him to accept such high profile job when he looked forward to a peaceful retirement would not be an easy task. One thing is certain though. The old man cannot refuse a summon from the head of state."

"I think your suggestion deserves some thoughts." The President finally declared his mind was already toying with the idea of arranging a casual meeting with the elderly statesman. However, he discarded the thought. The Ambassador must know any request made to him has state authority which he could not refuse if he wanted to spend a quiet retirement he surmised.

Rising from his desk he made a signal to Ebenezer to know what interested the Old man as a hobby.

Music was at the top of his priorities Manny whispered. He had become a collector of Liberian Folk music over the years. The late Morley Dorley, Fatu Gayflor and Zaye Tetee are some of his favorite singers. By afternoon hours, a sizable collection of Liberian folk music wrapped up in fine gift papers were already packed in a corner waiting to be delivered To Everette Gray upon his visit to the seat of the imperial Presidency. These were some of the attractions of the power which made it extremely difficult for someone who had tasted her trappings especially in Africa to let go because as soon as one said the word for something it was done.

The President had many different appointments but he told his Administrative Secretary that the meeting with the Ambassador took priority.

In this time the president busied himself with the mechanism of an election, Samuel Dahn his principal remained an enigma to him. Other exiled politicians cast doubt and cynicism on the process on the country's much listened news program -BBC Focus on Africa Samuel Dahn remained extremely quiet. Not a word from him. No visit to neighboring countries. Nothing all of his known friends and associate still living in the country phones were tap but the surveillance produce nothing concrete. State intelligence found him in Maryland. In the last two months he relocated to Brooklyn Park. But he was not active in the large expatriate Liberian community. Has the president overestimated his relevance?

The guy still commanded the loyalty of many soldiers: why did he not command his loyal troops when he was freed from prison but instead fled from the capital? The president has kept a wary eye on the Ivory Coast. The assassinated President and his murdered son links to the eastern neighbor were strong. The son was married to Le Vieux Cote D'Ivoire President foster daughter, yet the fugitive general made no effort at least according to his intelligence sources to contact them. The Ivory Coast was not part of the non aggression pact he signed with Guinea and Sierra Leone. Something just did not seem right. The prolonged silence of Samuel Dahn worried, pleased and puzzled the President.

President Forkpa was busy giving himself an air of respectability. He wanted to appear to be listening to the demands of the Americans for a return to civilian while entrenching himself in power to worry too much. From afar he continued to watch his foe but so far nothing.

Samuel Dahn waited and bided his time and waited. While others debated and argued in the quietude of his home in Minnesota; there were some things that were crystal clear to him. He reclined in the garage of his modest rented flat watching the empty bottles of his favorite drink; Guinness piling up. It was hard for the alcohol to seep down into his troubled brain. His wife was scrubbing other people floor and toilets to support his kids on her work as a cleaner to keep the family up! He a general could not become a cleaner. He held a part time job working as a security guard at a mint company. A job he hated. Such work was more than beneath his person. His loss of status ebbed at his mind. Every day Maxwell Forkpa served as president of Liberia ate into his consciousness. He lived and dreamed about removing his foe from power.

Why has Maxwell bested him so far? He asked himself. The move from the barracks to Sinkor, the changing of his position in the Salvation Council, his imprisonment. Why did he and his men not try to stage a coup when he was released from prison and he has chosen instead to flee into exile while Maxwell Forkpa continued as Mr. President?

Maxwell had the backing of the Americans and a large powerful army. What did he have? Ha ha ha he laughed to himself like a demented person.

Maxwell was going to run as civilian in the election that was to be held in Liberia. Maxwell was going to win the election by a huge majority. The choice of the electorate was irrelevant, his one- time friend would never leave the Presidency alive. Everything going on was just a shenanigan. If the fact of the game unfolded as he envisioned it, than the chips of his secret plan would fall into place. The closeness of people who were friends rubbed salt into their bitterness when they became enemies.

Samuel was no fool. He knew all friends and associates of his were under surveillance by Liberian security operatives. He too still had his sources. Fred Knot, the chief of logistics of the Liberian army was one of his most effective mole in the government. Powerful friends of the men they executed were among his backers. The enemy of my enemy is my friend. But he had an ace up his sleeves. Miles Spider was one of the most powerful men in the agency. Miles proffered Samuel Dahn a phone that could not be tapped.

"Don't ever call me, I'd call you when we are ready."

The American warned him emphatically.

Samuel knew if what he thought came to pass he would get that call from Miles Spider.

He could never return to Liberia as long as Maxwell Forkpa was in power. His life was not safe.

"My life for his life" with that solemn pledge to himself he gulped down his 5th bottle of Guinness. He would wait with his dogs of war. The faithful men who fled with him to exile waited expectantly for his call. But the long wait made him tired. It was time to do something!

———————

"Sorry Mr. Ambassador you cannot go on your flight to Abidjan. The President send for you effective immediately."

A young man said tapping him on the shoulders.

"What the hell is this?'

An angry Ambassador Gray shouted letting out a stream of expletives.

"Sir please do not cause a spectacle. I have my orders. Please come with me quietly. You can come with me now. I am sure if your trip is so urgent after your meeting, the president can lend you his private jet. This way sir we already have a jeep waiting to convey you."

Ambassador Gray exploded on his feet upon seeing the rapacious young man called President Forkpa..

"Young man even President Tubman in all the absolute power did not resort to such practice as literally kidnapping an official, one of her own. I will not be coerced to accept your offer!

Raw anger flashed through the President.

"You Everette Gray have the audacity to call me a young man in anger and shout at me? Have you forgotten that I am President of the Republic of Liberia?

Do you think you are better than the thirteen men who were tied to the light poles and shot those days?

My government spared you and re -appointed you as Ambassador and now because I asked you to do a piece of job which you will benefit handsomely from, you try to run away and after being caught you have the audacity to insult me? Mr. Gray you test my patience too far. You may leave and go where you were going but you shall feel the fire I can warm myself with. I am sure you want to spend your retirement peacefully and not to just disappear. You understand? I need your name and status to make our elections, my election respectable. Plan the game well and you will be richly rewarded. I need nobody but you and this time I want you consent now!

The President turned and headed abruptly upstairs. The Ambassador's mouth was opened, suddenly he felt fear. He wanted to drink and urinate at the same time. That very hour Everette Gray accepted to serve as election commission head.

The days following the inauguration of the Special Elections Commission headed by Ambassador Everette Gray coincided with a new recruitment drive by the army targeting young men in the villages of Lofa. Young men and to a lesser extend young women tired with their parents sedentary, agrarian lifestyles ekking a living from poor heavily leached tropical Lithosols drifted southwards into the open bosom of the army. A paid lifestyle where the government supplied the recruits with the recruit's needs just for holding an M-16 or LAR Rifle looked more exciting than the joys of low skilled subsistent farming.

These recruits swelled the ranks of the army because the President felt he could depend more on the loyalty of his kinsmen from Lofa in times of crisis. The strategic noose of the military around the capital tightened. Schiefillin, 72nd, BTC, Bomi Hills barracks made the President breathe a bit better at night.

Again to the absolute delight of the President his army now possessed long range artillery and armor. Thanks to the good will of Dictator Nicolai Ceausescu of Romania. The army a long neglected institution but one of the few national institutions that was an amalgamation of tribes changed from a national body into a private domain. The new army wedged into an elite executive guard could be relied on to crush internal dissent in a much more vigorous manner. The new ethnic recruits were better armed that the rank of file of the army which was poorly armed and to some extend ostracized from the Presidency. To strengthen his hold on power, the President embarked upon another round of tour West Africa meeting with Togolese strong man President Gnassingbe Eyadema, and Nigeria's military strongman Ibrahim Babangida with whom he soon developed an excellent personal relationship.

CHAPTER 22

In the charming far away Ghanaian capital, just about the same time the President and his top civilian collaborators were meeting, a group of men was celebrating a birthday party. The Ghanaian security forces have been keeping surveillance on this group for quite some time now. Their actions it appeared did not endanger the national security of the leftwing revolutionary regime of Flt. Lt. Jerry John Rawlings.

Hotel Shangrila, their base offered quality food and discreetness away from the congested city center. The proximity of the hotel to the Kotoka International Airport offered an added advantage. The men assembled here wanted to avoid the exposure to a more diverse audience from the corridors of the classier hotels such as Golden Tulip, Labadi Beach, or the Novotel located right in the heart of the city. The fugitives meeting drowned down bottles of beer talking in low excited voices. Those who knew them better knew: the men were putting on a charade. Peyton Sey's brother had been executed for being an alleged coup plotters in one of many coups. Rodney

Gweh, a former intelligence officer declared a wanted man by the Salvation Council, and the now heavily bearded Samuel Dahn, former Commanding General of the AFL came to Ghana to explore" investment opportunities."

"Man we can launch a lightning assault on that traitor and remove him from power by force. Maxwell Forkpa is a very unpopular man."

Peyton Seh emphasized.

"We could consider the Ivory Coast as a point of entry. I had had discussions with some exiled Liberians in that country including the former Ambassador who has connections to the top of the Ivorian Government. Remember President Robert" son, Adolphus James was married to the foster daughter of President Houphouet. When the boy was captured in the French Embassy, despite personal appeals from the Ivorian President we still went ahead and executed him. Ever since that time Maxwell's relationship with the Ivorian President has been shaky."

The men residing in the Shangrilla were all hot-headed men whose raison d'etre was revenge. Former colleagues of the President tossed from their positions of authority and forced to become fugitives in impoverished neighboring countries, these men lived literally on their hatred of the Liberian President. None of them wanted to leave Liberia in the first place yet circumstances forced them into the ignominy of exile. If now their bodies were free, their souls were imprisoned by a sense of worthlessness as long as their former friend now arch enemy Maxwell Forkpa remained in power.

"We can consider recruitment. I have contacted some known and not so known opponents of the regime. Some of them are what you may call scumbags. Who cares as long as they give us money to do what we want to do. The enemy of my enemy is my friend."

The friends burst out laughing.

A shapely waitress approached their table in the corner bringing roasted yam and grilled meat soaked in Tomato sauce.

Samuel Dahn purposely raised his voice.

"I think the tourism potential here is great, we can think about investing in some travel and tours company."

The waitress with the delightful Ghanaian accent removed some drinks from her tray setting it on the table of the Liberian gentlemen.

"Akosua that is nice of you."

"Always a pleasure Mr.….."

"Mr. Harrison Dennis." S.D. completed for her smiling. He passed a tip to the waitress who lifted her face showing even white teeth. The ambitious driven men plucked knives into their food. Akosua still lingered. S.D. smiled.

"That is okay for now if you can please excuse us."

S.D. requested tapping her lightly on the shoulders.

"You really know how to serve. I will forget my wife's delightful serving touch if I remain here for long."

"Oh Mr. Dennis you know that is not true."

Akos replied giggling no doubt pleased by the compliment . S.D. waited impatient for her to leave.

"Now guys there is nobody who wants to see the back

of Maxwell more than me. I promoted him and then he turned around and stabbed me in the back. We will only decide to release the dogs of war if he decides to run in the election to be held."

"S.D. what are you saying? The sooner we move the better since you are still the most popular man in the army. Most of the men in high positions are still loyal to you. Let us proceed now without waiting for any plebiscite."

Peyton suggested banging the table.

Little did these firebrand exiled opponents of Maxwell know that positions of authority were like a lizard; when it lost its tail another one quickly grows in its place. No doubt Samuel was more popular than Maxwell, but time waits for no man. Maxwell Forkpa was making changes in the army to entrench himself.

"Peyton you have to go to the town of Danane to collect intelligence on government troops strength. From now Rodney you will be stationed in Abidjan though you have to eventually go back with me to the states to test the waters as it were. I know Maxwell's men are trailing me. You will have to learn to raise funds without my personal presence all the time. You know Oxford Roberts?

The two men shook their heads.

"He is the son of the former executed Finance Minister. Oxford abiding desire is to remove the man who killed his father from power. Since you were not part of the Salvation Council, his fat pockets will be an added plus if you can get him on board. We have to lay the ground work well. No hurry, no publicity what so ever, you understand? Go and listen and then I will direct the next steps. We need additional men to train."

———⋆———

Akosua re-appeared on the scene with ice cubes to cool their drinks accompanied by two other Ghanaian beauties who bowed curtsying before the men.

Back in the Monrovia at a dedication President resigned officially from the army at a colorful ceremony. The next morning, The Daily Observer Newspaper hit the streets of the capital with a blazing editorial "No old wine in a new bottle." The newspaper sold like hot cakes in the streets. A ghost article by Prof. Martins warned of the danger of military rule under the guise of civilian rule. By midday, all copies of the papers were sold out.

The editorial angered the powers that be and they planned their revenge.

At night four hooded figures climbed the steep slopes of Crown Hill from the densely populated slum of Slipway. The heavy object they carried was tightly sealed to prevent the contents from disturbing the neighborhood. The men with the nefarious intent waited for the dead of night to carry out their plan. During this time ;the good people of the land snored in their beds while those prone to questionable activities like these nocturnal birds went about their business. They climbed the steep slope on Crown Hill leading to the offices of the offending newspaper struggling with their buckets. The bold letterings on the front door of the offices of the

Observer finally appeared. The two men who were the leaders urged their companions to set their loads down. They scouted the main Broad Street road which appeared to be deserted. The men then branched left approaching the office of the newspaper. One of them picked up stone and threw it at the bright florescent tube burning outside the entrance of the front door shattering glass. A security guard inside the low fence building came out to investigate. The men were waiting. A powerful blow to the security guard head sent him sprawling into darkness on the ground. Using a combination of sulfuric acids, wrench, saw and screw drivers the gang broke into the inner offices of the Observer. The Mafioso type leader of the gang whispered the command to his companions who soon set to work. They tied their noses with heavy pieces of cloths and began to plaster desks, chairs, floors and walls of the building with their foul smelling cargo of human excrement in a thorough manner.

They did not tamper with anything in the offices. They just did their jobs and before the morning hours they were back at base soundly sleeping like babies. All of them rich by $200 while their leaders pocketed $500 each.

The foul scent of their handiwork polluted the neighborhood. Flies sent invitations to their relatives and friends for the feast before them. By morning hours when the good people of the cities woke up to commence their daily chores; the flies were having a jolly good time much to the extreme annoyance of journalists, photographers, cleaners, secretaries, along with other support staff who congregated in the Observer offices that morning.

The news of the "attack" filtered through the grapevine throughout the city. The attention loving Information Minister in a hastily arranged press briefing fumed his disgust out…"I cannot understand the reason for such cowardly diabolical attack on the premises of the Daily Observer. It is a heinous act which this government condemns in the strongest possible terms."

After the strongly worded statements were read journalists were ready with questions for the Minister.

"Sir don't you see a connection between the stinging editorials of the newspaper and this attack coming so soon afterward ?

"None what so ever, this government is one committed to uphold law and order. If we have a problem with the Observer, we will take the newspaper to court instead of resorting to such a barbaric act."

"Don't you think that some rogue elements in the security forces might have committed this act?

"There are no rogue elements in our security forces. We have a security force comprised of dedicated professional committed to upholding the highest possible standards in law and order. The Attorney General will make sure everything is done to catch and punish the perpetrators of this ugly act."

President Maxwell Forkpa listened with satisfaction to the spirited defense of his government by the minister. He turned to Ebie Kum sitting beside him on the sofa sipping a bottle of soda.

"What do you think?

"Fine performance by the chap, but his praise of that

garbage pushing newspaper sounded a bit too sincere for my liking."

The two men looked at each other and broke into hilarious laughter.

"I think by now they are holding their filthy noses, good for them to clean up some of the dirt they pour on other people."

"Gabby really knows how to operate."

The two men burst into another round of laughter.

The President looked at his watch.

"I will soon be meeting the Israeli Ambassador. I think our national team the Lone Star needs some attention.

True to his word, the new package of sports promotion for the country's senior national team coincided with a dramatic announcement by the President.

"I shall be standing as a civilian in the upcoming elections!

Ebie Kum mobilized people from every part of the country in return for cash and jobs to petition the President to run before the dramatic announcement.

The motion set in place by this dramatic announcement culminated with the holding of the People Democratic Party holding her party caucus to select their candidates in the historic but isolated city of Robertsport in Grand Cape Mount County.

CHAPTER 23

Election fever swept across the country. The genie of political activity bottled inside the cloak of military dictatorship released now wanted to explode. Thousands of people thronged the main street of Kakata, the capital of one of the newly created counties called Margibi. Many carried placards, wore bandanas and banners with portraits of President Maxwell Forkpa smiling broadly. President Forkpa's handsome image adorned hundreds of T-shirts and cheap paper caps. The atmosphere in the city center was festive, more a mood of celebration rather than a campaign rally. Loudspeakers mounted on cars and placed at strategic corners provided audio to those attending the rally and neighborhoods beyond stretching as far as the Bong Mines highway. Local county administration officials clad in their finest vied with each other to show their loyalty to the powers that be. Superintendent Dennis Palmer wearing an expensive hand woven gown led the array of local government officials. Big men from the People Democratic Party of Liberia which included the party chairman Ebenezer

Kum and Publicity Secretary Adonis Vonleh were very much in attendance also. Both men were clothed in sparkling white robes. All cabinet ministers of note wore the civilized mandatory three piece business suit of the Liberian elite greeting each other with a flurry of laughter. The main streets of the city were decorated with ribbons of the national colors of red, white, and blue. Balloons stretching from the ewes of Lebanese stores lined both sides of the main street. Every building around the venue of the rally was draped in national colors. Dancers masked and unmasked dancers entertained the crowd with their enthralling acrobatic displays. A large contingent of market women wearing lappas specially made for the occasion drummed and danced on the road added color to the occasion. The ubiquitous sounding journalists from state controlled media carried proceedings live; the fine line between journalism and public relations blurred into a thin gray one.

Political campaigns in the country have never been run on policies and platforms. Enthusiasm of supporters, pomp, color, pageantry and the generosity of the candidates in dishing out money and favor were more important than the message. This campaign was very much well attended and no different. Government officials along with most self respecting business houses have given their workers the day off. Local authorities made sure all of their workers were present at the rally. Promotions and longevity on the job required being present at the right place at the right time.

Ebenezer Kum's voice addressing the rally has lost

none of its booming vitality so reminiscent of his younger days. His voice boomed to address the party faithful gathered to listen.

"Ladies and gentlemen what is the matter with the PDP?

All right! All right!

The crowd roared back in unison. Spontaneous singing and dancing broke out in a spectacular manner among the youthful supporters of the President. Young girls below the wooden purpose built stage exercised the movement of their hips and buttocks gyrating as if they were moving their arms.

A short burst of applause greeted the impromptu welcome performance by the young girls. The colorful program continued with growing exuberance. The president rose from his seat to acknowledge the applause raising his hand in victory like salute. He waved a white handkerchief in the air which drove his supporters into a frenzy. All of the dignitaries on the stage stood up beside President Forkpa hugging and kissing his cheeks. The young President possessed a certain enigmatic charisma which elucidated deep respect and loyalty among those closest to him. Beside the President on the stage also was his wife with whom he rarely appeared in public, but the deeply religious Liberian populace liked to see a man and his wife together for respectability. Confusing though was the presence of the chairman of the election commissioner on the stage along with the President.

"Politics is not a game for the faint hearted; it is game for men with trousers not for boys who run like chickens.

Some of these politicians who want to be President of this country just ask them where their wives and children are?

The President's question was interrupted by derisive laughter.

"People think the Presidency is for someone who gets on a jet plane and come back home to occupy it for some time and then go back to America. They want to bring their Lawyer crookedness to fool to us. They are not only satisfied with filling our children's head with mischief; they want to bring their mischief upon us. But we will not allow them to do so, as long as the army is behind us to guarantee peace and security this election will not end in confusion.

This election will result in placing me, a young handsome President, who can play Football as President of the 2nd Republic. I can assure you I will make the national team-The red, white and blue colors boys qualify for the next African Cups of Nations. Some of those ugly people clamoring to be President like the poor school teacher who is broke as a church house rat wearing white man's clothes will never sit in that Mansion.

We will continue to build more schools, clinics, markets. You will eat well. In fact right now I donate 500 bags of Rice to all those attending this rally! Thunderous applause greeted this pronouncement. The crowd broke into wild dancing.

"This is our nation, the people and the Salvation Council government are the same. We are proud to identify with the dignified people of Margibi. There is a significant development package for Margibi after the election.

I am making a personal cash donation of $100.000 towards this development fund."

Another round of thunderous applause greeted this statement, though the volume of this applause did not match the previous one announcing the donation of rice.

Singing and dancing spontaneous again broke out in the streets.

Hours later, while partisans, supporters and hanger ons of the PDP celebrated in the streets, the President's convoy buoyed by the impressive show of his supporters headed back down south to Monrovia which lay 45 minutes drive away.

Curious villagers and settlement dwellers lined the route cheering and waving to the Presidential motorcade as it passed by their hamlets.

Ebenezer Kum was flushed with the joy of satisfaction at the success of the campaign rally. As it is customary with people, he called to share his sentiment with his friend.

"Yes this is Ebie Kum; He responded to the questioning voice on the other side of the telephone.

"How are you doing? "Just fine, but I know you didn't call me to find out how I am doing since we were together just some few minutes ago."

"Yes but I didn't have the chance to tell you-

"Tell me what?

Ebenezer laughed.

"Do not sound so alarm, apart from being the chairman of the election commission you are also a personal friend of mine. I just have this small request to make to you."

The line became silent, very silent until one could you hear the breathing on the other side.

"Just make sure you delay all those other parties clamoring for registration especially Prof. Martins party and those of other politicians whom you know could prove a formidable challenge to the president until the last minute. Come up with some bureaucratic bottlenecks you can think of to give my party the advantage."

"My friend you take your liberties on the phone too far. I do not trust telephones for such conversations. Just the other day you were within Robertsports when I was asked to register the other three parties."

"Everette relax, the opposition does not have the means to tap our phones. Any call I make cannot be traced or listened to by the telecom boys. I take it then that you are amenable to my suggestion?

There is a logging company which I want you to be chairman of the board for. I also intend to make you board chair for the National Port Authority through a proxy whose name you shall suggest, I mean if my idea is okay."

"Ebenezer Kum thank you. You know as chairman of the Special elections commission I must not say or do anything to impugn my sparkling clean integrity."

'Fine with me my friend.' Ebie Kum replied.

"I trust you to keep your word. By the way, how is your old lady doing? I heard you are too busy organizing elections and chasing young skirts to pay much attention to her anymore."

"Ebie Kum, you rogue must leave my private life out

of this. I only ask you to clean the log out of your own eyes so you can see better to clean the speck in mine."

That night armed men surrounded the chairman's house in Johnsonville patrolling close to make their presence felt. These contradictory messages to the chairman were designed to wear him down.

CHAPTER 24

——◆◆◆——

Adonis Vonleh lay in bed too tired to move or say a word to his wife. Today has been a very good day for him. The crusader had learnt his lesson slowly but well. Government was a perpetual institution while the individuals who occupied her high offices were temporal. There is a common saying in the land that where you tied a Goat it must eat. As a government official, he would not remain one forever hence he must profit from his association so that the virus of poverty could never affect him again. The latest consignment of goods imported by Shresst Brothers, the largest building construction materials importing business in the country has been granted duty free privilege and the far lesser duty paid to his bank account instead of the government. He lay in bed thinking. His eyelids gradually shut and he drifted into the unknown.

He was back at his alma mater, the University of Liberia among a large crowd of demonstrating students wearing red bandanas on their heads. The chanting students raised their clenched fists into the air singing their political defiance of the military. The students voices were raised to the heavens united and strong. Passing motorists honked their horns in solidarity.

Adonis Vonleh! Adonis! Adonis Vonleh! The students cried out shouting his name calling for transparency in government. Incredibly, instead of surging to the front to lead the young, idealistic students, Adonis found himself running away. The voices of the students rang louder and louder in his ears the more he tried to run. Darkness descended and enveloped the main campus of the university; even in darkness the students waved huge cloth banners into the air. Adonis ran and ran growing tired. His legs wanted to crash beneath him. All he wanted to do was to get away from the mob of protesting students; the urgency of their cries spurred his speed. Tired he spied a grey colored jeep on the opposite side of the road in front of the ministry of Foreign Affairs building. The engine of the car was still running so he lengthened his strides to reach the vehicle which offered him the chance of getting away from the students. To his amazement, a group of students from apparently nowhere wedged themselves between him and the car he was running to blocking his view. Another group of rampaging students closed in on him from behind. The student mob brandishing clubs advanced towards him. A burly fellow armed with a big stick at the head of the mob rushed towards Adonis. He step on something tripped and fell. Losing his chance of escape, the protesting students caught up with him encircling him while he laid prostrate. The burly student who fell down first regained his balance and raised his club to strike Adonis. On the ground, helpless surrounded by a hostile crowd Adonis braced himself for the blow; he did not plead for mercy. Just at that moment Elizabeth Iris Reeves appeared dropped from the sky by parachute looking petite, serene, and beautiful. She grabbed Adonis hand firmly in hers. She of a much smaller build raised the fallen Adonis to his feet. She shouted at the students in her strong high pitched voice to make way. Her voice carried weight with the students who parted to allow the couple to walk through. Adonis did not know or care for their destination as long as Elizabeth petite and forceful was leading him.

Through the student mob they walked down to a narrow street leaving behind the urban noise which grew faint. Now alone to Adonis's horror Liz began to cry. Her blood curdling screams wrenched his heart. She kept at it without stopping to explain the reason for her tears. The more Adonis tried to calm her down the more she cried.

Just then the jeep he first saw when the students were chasing him appeared and Liz left him.

Adonis woke up with a cold start sweat pouring down his shirt shaking like a leaf. Tears set in his eyes. Why has the heroine of the revolution come to him now?

CHAPTER 25

While President Maxwell campaigned, cajoled and courted the people to vote for him his most important constituency remained the army. He merely changed his starched uniforms for expensive suits. At heart he remained a military men. If the election did not give him the legitimacy he wanted the army would. It was a beaming President standing at the James Spriggs Airfield located right in the heart of Sinkor. The airstrip was sealed to private individuals. A green American built Cessna transport planes rolled on the tarmac of the runway.

Up the control tower, President Maxwell Forkpa clad in an olive green uniform with a colt .45 Pistol on his side had his eyes glued to the binocular in his hands. He watched his troops land. The first batch of soldiers from the craft was leaping out of the plane before the aircraft could taxi to a stop. These Liberian soldiers returning from advanced military training looked like black American servicemen in their crisp new camouflage. Their short butt M-16s and grenade launchers made them distinct from the typical African Buffalo soldier who held

Russian or east European Kalashnikov rifles. Beside the President stood his former chief of Military Intelligence now Defense Minister clad in uniforms like his boss. The Chief of Staff his three stars emblazoned on his arms with golden thread was a stereotypical defense chief. On top of the green pair of trousers, he wore a crisp white uniform shirt. His clean shaven face and gold horn rimmed glasses made him look every bit the civilian General he was. This role he relished. He loved receiving foreign dignitaries, reviewing troops and rhapsodizing about the strategies of great commanders in the past; Genghis Khan, Hannibal, Scipio, Douglass Macarthur. From somewhere in the low bush surrounding the perimeter fence of the airstrip, a shot rang out. The crack troops responded with swift maneuvers hitting the ground, somersaulting and forming a circle. Their backs turned to each other rifles at the ready soldiers advanced to the direction of the shot in a rapid manner. A low flying aircraft approached. In seconds the door under the belly of the aircraft opened and troops leapt out of the craft in parachutes. The American and Israeli Ambassadors and attaches exchanged glances. President Forkpa was beside himself with joy. He was preparing for the future, for the unknown. Samuel Dahn dare not think of mounting an invasion or coup against such crack soldiers.

"I will never be caught unaware like that stupid President Robert."

"What did you say?

"Your organization is perfect." Maxwell replied smiling.

"Mr. Ambassador, you see the best way to keep an army from rebelling it to keep them happy."

"Of course."

The tall Texan affirmed.

"But what role will the new troops play?

"They will serve on the Executive Mansion Guard Battalion and with the Ist Infantry Battalion."

The President added. Moses Gabby gave his boss a savage look.

"Amb. Larcy you have not responded to our repeated requests for long range artilleries or perhaps a helicopter gunship" Gabby asked.

The clean shaven diplomat with thinning silver hair combed back to conceal the baldness in the middle smiled.

"America is committed to meeting the defense needs of this country. We are testing new artillery with 95% accuracy. Allow us to finish our testing because this country could well be one of the beneficiaries of this new weapon."

The Ambassador lied for this was part of his job as a man of virtue sent abroad to lie for his government. He was just stalling for time. The gallant men of the AFL 60% of whom belonged to the President's tribe lined up in orderly fashion on the tarmac. From the control tower, the VIPs descended down the stairs to inspect the proud troops standing on the tarmac. Satisfied with the caliber of his new troops; President Forkpa departed the scene in a Cruiser Jeep accompanied by the top brass of his military along with his cousin.

He drove straight to the BTC Barrack staying until nightfall.

Inside the apartments of one of the non-commissioned soldiers where one could not expect him President Forkpa was huddled with his top brass. He made all those in the meeting to remove their caps.

The President opened a small briefcase producing a small leather Bible before the men seated in a semi circle. Among the group President Forkpa alone wore a cap in the meeting with the five silver stars of his rank - Commander in Chief of the army emblazoned on. He called out the names of the men facing him one by one.

"All of you believe in God?

This question puzzled his Lieutenants.

"I believe in God."

The Defense Minister replied. His response irritated Maxwell. Among all those present why did he have to reply?

But the President kept his irritation to himself. His gaze felt on his Chief of Staff.

"And you sir?

"Yes, yes, I believe in the Almighty God who controls our destiny."

"I did not ask you to sermonize.'

"Do you believe in God?

Dunbar armpits became damp.

"Yessir." He stammered.

The meeting hall became eerily silent.

"Place your hands on this book." Dunbar's stomach tightened into a knot.

"I promise…. Repeat after me….

"I promise to be faithful.….

Death and disaster await me if I betray my leader.......

The President veered towards his cousin and without warning kicked the chair beneath him. Daniel flopped backwards using the back of his palm on the wall to steady himself.

"You want to resign?

President Forkpa asked his gaze resting on Daniel.

"Of course not sir……'.

Maxwell was not finished yet. He struck Daniel with a powerful blow in the chest. Daniel flopped backwards hitting the wall. Anger flashed through his eyes. By reflex, his palm tightened into a fist. Maxwell smiled and stood over him. Daniel remained rooted to the spot.

"How many trucks and Mowaks (APCs) have we got now?

He turned to the dark muscular chap- Fred Knot the chief of logistics. Of course, the President knew him because his brother James was killed for plotting against him with Harrison Payne.

"Sir I have to check with…..

Shut up man. You must be able to tell me how many artillery pieces, how many trucks we have off head. Copy head is better than copy book."

The President circled around approaching the Defense Minister from his back.

"I am beginning to feel the Americans will not give us anything to run after our enemies. They only give us weapons we need to stay in the hole to fight. Can you help us get multiple rocket launchers?

Moses Gabby wanted to rattle the names of several possible suppliers. However, he checked himself…

"Sir I need to source around."

"And where do you have to do the sourcing."

"I think our friend Col. Mengistu could direct us where to look."

This answer pleased the President.

He returned to his chair all eyes following him.

"And men listen very well. An old man sent his son to go bring him a piece of dry stick. When the boy returned with the stick, the old man asked his son to break the stick. The strapping lad easily did. He asked the boy to put the two broken pieces together and break them. The boy broke the two pieces with some difficulties. The old man then told his son to put the four pieces together to break it. This time the boy could not break the bundle of sticks. This is how it is with us. If we allow greed and petty jealousies to divide us, we will fall prey to cunning politicians. The military needs someone who knows and appreciates the level of sacrifice we have made and continue to make on behalf of this country to protect her interest. Good salaries, uniforms, boots, and equipment are yours as long as I remain in the Presidency. I expect you soldiers, my soldiers to remain behind me 100%. Let me tell your something."

The President lowered his voice.

"The most important thing in this country is not who the people vote for on election day but who has the loyalty of the army.

Chief of Staff if you want to continue wearing those

sparkling white starched uniforms basking in the glory of parades while wining and dining, keep the army together.

Chief of Military Intelligence if someone farts in the army I expect you to smell the fart scent and let me know. That high nose girl of yours you know is only with you because of the things you can give her. Stop it today… The President snapped his fingers… And she is gone.

And you Gabby with your short structure and nose which look like baboon, you think people will look at you twice without you being Defense Minister? No way, boy forget it.

"And what about me lording it over you?

I am nobody from nowhere.

My parents are nobody, nothing, neither were my grandparents who migrated from Sierra Leone. I only became a soldier because there was nothing else to do.

Do any of you have a problem with my being in civilian clothes?

Maxwell waited for an answer. The place was quiet as a cemetery.

"No sir"

They responded in unison like school children.

The tension in the room evaporated.

'How then can we strengthen the military and our grip on power?

"Mr. President you put it right, more artillery pieces, armor coupled with surveillance equipment will do the trick instead of those inaccurate mortals the American gave us."

Maxwell smiled. His face radiated serenity. The man

had the uncanny changing power of a Chameleon. Just a moment ago fierce fire almost leapt from his eyes ready to devour anything that came before him. Now he became meek as a Lamb.

"And you…

"Sir I am thinking about us holding war games in the jungles of Nimba."

"And why Nimba?

Cold rage welled in the President's eyes.

"If there are battles to fight some will have to be fought there. The terrain there makes perfect ambush country. Our troops need that exposure."

"It is not who controls an isolated bush post but who controls this city. Monrovia is Liberia. He who controls Monrovia most especially Capitol Hill controls Liberia. True you will get your maneuver but not in that accursed county of Samuel Dahn. It will be staged right at Schiefillin". The two approaches of Maxwell and his Cousin were right. Perhaps it would have been good for the men of the AFL to concentrate on both bush and urban fighting, but now these planners did not have the benefit of hindsight.

Each of the men in the meeting spoke only when they are spoken to. The President had learnt from Ebie Kum that a leader must be strong, resolute, spiced with a touch of unpredictability if he wanted to last. Their meetings were not always like this. Now what the President wanted from his men was an oath of allegiance.

"When bush shake I want to know. When rain cloud gathers I want to know before the rain falls. There are lots of Liberian dissidents who I am sure are plotting our downfall. The Israelis promised to supply us with Uzi sub machines gun pistols for VIP protection. These, as you know, are guns portable enough to be concealed under clothes and yet deadly as an assault weapon."

"Sir our troop strength of 6500 men and women is not large enough. Look at a small country like Togo with troop strength of 12,000. When Hannibal attempted an invasion of the mighty Roman Empire, he crossed into Italy with over 70,000 troops. When General Douglass MacArthur and his nemesis Gen. Yamashita….."

The President again smiled raising his hand.

"I We will think about that. But we do not want to return to the days soldiers served as houseboys or head men on private farms. I want you all to know that all of the good things of life will go from all of you if I vacate from this chair. By the way, I hope all of you have began to build your own houses. Next week all of you will receive your brand new Discovery SUVs. A smile resembling those featured on toothpaste commercials spread across the faces of those present. They all attempted to rise to embrace the leader. He stilled them with the movement of his hands. The President exited the room returning shortly with a thick dark brew. A pungent smelling liquid in a white mug he proffered to the Defense Minister. "Drink it. What we say here let it remain right here."

Moses Gabby stared at the liquid wondering what the content of the liquid was because the odor nauseated him. He did not want to drink it. One look at his boss's face made him swallow a big gulp down. The liquid did not have a taste. Round and round the liquid went to all with each taking a mouthful. The President himself was the last to take a sip emptying the cup.

CHAPTER 26

The intelligence unit at the US Embassy complex was also busy monitoring. It was very unusual for the Head of State to be meeting with his lieutenants at such an hour in an unmarked building inside the barrack. Something must be going. From the files in his computer the officer with a fondness for bright colored clothes randomly clicked on files relating to the Salvation Council. He stared at the photo of Maxwell Forkpa and then he reverted his gaze to Samuel Dahn. The both of them looked energetic. He enlarged the two pictures before fusing the two. Maxwell Forkpa eyes looked bold forward-looking. Samuel Dahn's eyes instead of being forward looking appeared to recede inward giving him an introspective perhaps ideological outlook, but his rival's eyes were pragmatic with a tinge of cunningness attached.

Lt. Col. Dempster Brown sat staring into the bluish computer screen licking his lips. Then the revelation hit him with startling reality. Behind the veils of politics far away the eyes of the people a fierce battle loomed on the horizon. The attaché began to type his impression onto the screen. The ambassador has to be informed he muttered. Dempster clicked a key on his computer. Printed copies of his thoughts dropped from the laser printer in his cubicle to his desk. Col. Dempster read through his own words before setting the sheet ablaze and then deleting the files from his computer. From now on he had to watch the Liberian military very closely.

He ran to meet his boss the ambassador.

The Ambassador and his military attaché just tolerated each other. Col. Brown could not stand the Ambassador formal adroit ways, while the Ambassador loathed his young aide's brash, casual ways and informal dress code. The two men avoided meeting each other unless very necessary. The Liberian Military now possessed long ranged artillery from the eastern bloc. His earlier suspicions were justified. What troubled him was the fact the Liberian Government could obtain weapons from the eastern bloc which Washington was not willing to supply. The naïve young President was increasingly showing streaks of stubbornness which meant he wanted to cling onto power indefinitely with or without an election. The young attaché rubbed his blonde hair alarmed by the President's dangerous liaison with the eastern bloc.

"Mr. Ambassador we have got a problem. Maxwell Forkpa is going to rig the forth coming election. He is strengthening the capabilities of his army. He will win the election by hook or crook and then violence will again flow on the streets. Samuel Dahn will return with force."

The university of Liberia situated so close to the seat of power has always been a hotbed of political activity in the country. Situated on Capitol Hill it was just a stone throw from the Capitol Building which housed the legislature. The Temple of Justice which housed the Supreme Court was also just down the road, so was the Mansion the office and residence of the President. The Speaker of the House could stand near the fence and shout for his darling daughter to come to his office for lunch from across the road on the university campus. Events here were quick on gain national and international attention. Students wanting to gain national recognition, opposition politicians longing for change mixing together brought chaos to the campus. Professor Martins one of the stalwarts of the revolution spurned from political power used his lectures as a stage to advocate for a return to constitutional order. His actions soon attracted the attention of state security who promptly hurled him to jail. The third time in 3 years. Now students converged on the campus to demand the release of their teacher.

We want Martins! We want democracy!
Down with Maxwell Forkpa!
Down with Maxwell Forkpa!
A free and fair election is a must!
Education is a right and not a privilege!

Bright and patriotic, these students were easy prey for political manipulation. Professors were locked from their offices. A kind of carnival atmosphere prevailed on campus in spite of the underlying theme of political protest. The small security presence on the campus had long disappeared. Correspondents smuggled on campus hurried to cover the protest. The majority of the press though remained outside the campus interviewing anxious students from alongside the university fence, their microphones thrust over the low fence of the campus. The state media broadcast appeals from the authorities for parents to advise their children to forget about politics, disburse and go home. These simplistic messages were based on the assumption university students were children who listened to the dictates of their parents without a will or mind of their own. Contrary to this assumption, the students wanted their demands to be met.

We want Martins!
Give us Liberty or death!
Election today is a must!

In time, more people joined the growing agitation. Cold water and sandwich sellers made brisk business. Some students would come in the morning sing a few protest songs, go home and return in the evening for another round of protest.

At the Executive Mansion, President Maxwell Forkpa stood on the corridor of the Sixth Floor seeing before him what appeared to be a mob of drunken people. Anger burned in his bosom. He felt betrayed by the protesting students. Hasn't he increased the university budget 40%? More than 10% of those crazy mobs were people on his personal scholarships. What do they want from me now?

What do they want me to do? The President asked in an exasperated tone knocking his chest.

"To release political prisoners and set an election date."

Ebie Kum replied in a matter of fact tone.

"And are you suggesting I comply?

The President's voice was very calm, but the expression in his eyes was deadly.

"Of course not. Those bunch of kids over there are only looking for excuses to stop attending lectures. We could close down the university indefinitely."

"But how do we get the students to vacate the campus?

Their demonstration is illegal, a threat to the stability of this country. Their parents are not warning them strongly enough to let them know they are playing a game which is more than they think. If we allow a group of ruffians to hold this country to a ransom, if we allow their defiance to go on unabated next the workers, secondary students, everybody will go on the rampage."

The agitated President paced up and down the upper floor of his office.

"But Sir."

"Sir what?

President Forkpa asked. He turned abruptly to go back to his office with Ebie Kum close at his heels.

The President picked up the telephone to call. Ebenezer Kum knew what was going to come next.

"Mr. President pleased put the telephone down. I will speak to Minister Adonis Vonleh, he and I will talk to the students to end their protest peacefully."

President Forkpa hand remained on the telephone. A battle raged in his mind whether to obey his instinct emotion or to listen to the voice of his adviser. The President finally placed the receiver down and looked at his trusted adviser. He sensed the old man's mind was made up.

"Show people leniency and they think you are weak. I will teach them. I will teach them." President Forkpa continued to repeat banging on his elegant office table. His mood though was far from elegant. The anger burning in him was intense. "What more do they want me to do?

He kept asking. The infuriating part of the situation was here the students' chant was faintly audible invading his private lair.

Ebie Kum his trusted advisor loved being at the top by any means. He swayed with the wind like a normal tree branching flowing, following the direction of the wind. He always hanged his clothes where the sun was shining for it to dry properly. Power lay at the top bestowing upon her servants the best of material comfort. Like a chameleon Ebie Kum changed and adapted to his surroundings. Always affable, congenial, and loyal to those at the top. One of the cardinal principles he learned in his early years was never to disagree with the powers that be. If he wanted to express a view contrary to the powers that be he made sure it was sugar coated, laced with flattery and being ready to withdraw any offensive comment at the least sign of displeasure. Now faced with the prospect of young students being brutalized and possibly killed; the wizard decided for once to behave in an altruistic way and not out of avarice. He called another man determined to give respite to his soul.

The young man wanted to convey "I am one of you in the struggle" attitude. The two men put on jeans taking their lives into the own hands literally by walking unarmed and uninvited to the den of protesting students without bodyguards. They looked at each other as they boarded the jeep carrying them to the university. The chauffeur drove in a leisurely manner. Each of the men sat alone lost in their own thoughts. The voices of protesting students on the second day of their protests reminded them their task ahead was not going to be easy. The jeep conveying them now slowed down to an almost crawling pace veering left to the parking lot of the Capitol Building. Ebenezer Kum and Adonis Vonleh crossed the street heading to their Alma Mata.

Most people in this city were unemployed or underemployed sometimes with a grown man or woman selling few packs of razor blades just to make ends meet for the day. A small crowd of onlookers stood on the sidewalks. Fingers dug into sides, mouth whispered into ears. Taxi drivers and private motorists slowed down to watch the two government officials cross the street. Excitement bubbled in the ranks of militant students. The small team of security men observing the campus from the outside watched with keen interest the approach of Ebie and Adonis.

An officer toting a rifle approached the two dignitaries. His small face was inscrutable behind the dark sunglasses he wore.

"Sirs what are you doing here?

Her voice sounded respectful but firm.

"To talk to the students inside."

Already students were cramming the perimeter walls to see those coming to see them increasing the tempo of their chant.

"Sirs it could be dangerous. I have to keep my men outside to keep them from being lynched. There is no guarantee you will not be harmed without an escort. I have to send some men inside to escort you people inside or you could become hostages...

"Not necessary, young lady we will be perfectly safe. We want to talk to those young people inside to make them understand that their demands will be met though, not in the way they want."

"But sirs I cannot allow you to go inside. If anything happens to you, my head will roll. I have a husband and four kids to take care of. No, I will not allow you."

The hair on Ebenezer's head stood up in anger, but it was Adonis who spoke.

"We have the permission of the President to go to the campus. Now you will excuse us before your husband and children go hungry while you languish in prison."

Adonis pushed the smaller of the two gates leading to the main entrance. With a single step the two men were inside away from the outside sidewalk onto the concrete footpath leading to the law faculty. This single step was a momentous decision; government, law and order were behind them now. From all sides students pressed ganged them shouting hostile slogans. Ebie and Adonis felt no fear only an exhilarating strange feeling of doing the right thing. The Arthur Grimes School of Law was to their right, a little ahead to the left stood the multi storied girls dormitory. Nestled in a sea of green grass were the two famous campus palaver huts. Behind these huts were the large Teachers Hall and those of numerous campus based students groups including ULSU. The two men marched fearlessly to the smaller of the two huts. Two young men,one charcoal black with a thin frame and nervous brown eyes,the other short with light brown skin and a clean shaven hair, handsome nose and a protruding chin entered the hut upon seeing them accompanied by two bosomy ladies clad in tight fitting jeans trousers, A hush fell on the crowd.

Adonis recognized the two young men. Fred Tulay, a senior Political Science student, and Daniel Bayongar, a Chemistry major but political firebrand. Leaders of the two campus based political parties banished their internecine political infighting to unite in this protest.

"Adonis Vonleh and Ebenezer Kum what brings you here?"

Daniel asked casually as if he was with them that morning.

"To bring peace between you and the government."

"Have your soldier boy President sent you to sweet talk us into ending our protest?"

"We have not come to sweet talk you or anybody. We know you want political prisoners to be released and a date set for election. A few years ago I was right here doing the same thing you guys are doing. I will never remain a part of a government which keeps people in jail…"

Political prisoners will be released and election date announced but not immediately. It will make the President look weak," Ebie Kum interjected.

"So you want us to save your boss's face?"

"We want to prevent destruction and violence. We want you to continue your studies in peace."

"Does Maxwell Forkpa know you are here and did he send you?

"He is aware we are here but he did not send us. We are here on our own volition."

"And what is there to prevent us from taking the both of you hostage and keeping you in protective custody until our Professor is released…..

"Nothing. We came to you taking our lives into our own hands because we believe decent human beings can settle their differences through dialogue and negotiation. I have fought for justice and human rights in this nation. We brought down the corrupt Roberts regime. We broke down the walls separating the children of the rich and the poor so people like you and myself can have access to both education and the resources of this country. It was for this reason Elizabeth Reeves, a good girl from a privileged background suffered dying in the streets of Monrovia when she could have been at Harvard."

"And you think you are honoring her memory by working in a military regime that denies the most basic freedom such as the right to free speech and free assembly through the infamous decree 88A?

One of the student leaders sneered.

"We can assure you within 24 hours your Prof. will

be released and we will give 6 new buses to transport students to the Fendell Campus. Improvements for the library along with the lab…

The otherwise silent student body listening attentively to the exchange between the leaders and the government emissaries began murmuring and howling insults.

"When will the things you promised be done?

A strong voice student shouted, his voice echoing above the colleagues.

"As soon as possible."

"As soon as possible."

Another student leader mimicked and the crowd broke into rapturous laughter. Adonis and Ebie had to raise the tempo of their voices to be heard above the cacophony of voices. Student Fred Tulay stilled the unruly crowd with his booming voice which contrasted with his thin physical frame.

"These men……

He said pointing to the two high ranking government officials sent by the soldier boy President should we arrest and keep them here?

Arrest them!

Arrest them!

Voices echoed in unison.

"No comrades. They have come to us in peace and so they must go back in peace." Tulay shouted.

"They are liars!

All liars! They belong to hell and there we must send them!

There was movement in the crowd surrounding the dignitaries.

All of the neat lawns and flowers beautifying the campus crumpled under restless feet. Surrounded by restless and unpredictable students without armed protection Ebie Kum and Adonis were in mortal danger. The sea of eyes surrounding then began to press closer. In an ominous sign some students holding rocks and sticks were poised to pounce on the government emissaries. Boom! A rotten egg exploded in Adonis face.

The stench enveloped him. In the same instant a piece of rock grazed Ebie's head drawing a trickle of blood.

Daniel Bayongar witnessed the action, anger raw and defiant echoed in his voice. Adonis and Ebie were speechless. The atmosphere was perched on the precipice of violence abou to explode.

"These men have come to us in peace and peace they must leave. We will not end our protest. What we want is the immediate and unconditional release of our professor and all other political prisoners languishing in jail. These men he said pointing to Adonis and Ebenezer came to us in peace and in peace they must go. Any hooligan that wants to get to them will have to pass through me. Those rats that sent these two missiles must run to the hole they came from because they are not part of us. Make way for these two.!

"Yes sir! A thickset fellow bulging with biceps started to shove students aside. The crowd pushed aside left and right opening a small corridor for the now advancing men.

"Our demands are not for the eventual release. We want a full and unconditional release but you may go."

The two men looked at each other and started to leave

the same way they came back. At the entrance of the front gate a crowd of joy emanated from the crowd of worried security agents. Just before the sidewalk at the entrance a missile of dirty orange peeling landed between the two dignitaries . They were quickly hurled to safety.

But what could they tell their boss? That their mission failed and they have come close to being lynched? Squads of security agents swept them into waiting vans. The news of the humiliation of his aides by the protestors had already reached the President. The burning anger in him reached fever pitch. He had only reluctantly agreed to the mediation effort of his advisors with misgivings. Now his misgivings were confirmed. Using a binocular from the corridor of the sixth floor the President could not believe his eyes. A small casket emblazoned with his portrait being held aloof by the protestors in a mock burial for him while he still lived. The President took quick strides to his office.

"Whose speaking? The voice on the line asked.

"This is a direct order; clear the campus of the university of all demonstrators immediately!

I want the place quiet as a grave yard! You are authorized to use whatever force necessary to make the place quiet or your butt will be hanging to dry.

Move or be removed!

President Maxwell Forkpa screamed into the microphone.

The President returned to the balcony of the sixth floor eyeing the protesting radicals edged on by socialist and opposition elements below. The ignoble chant of their burial eulogy drifted to the skies. President Forkpa sipped an orange juice watching the crowd below dancing. Within minutes of the Presidential order the BTC became a beehive of activities. Soldiers equipped in battle gear mobilized for the important task before them. There were no rubber bullets or truncheon or even stun grenades for crowd control. The only non- lethal crowd control weapon was the rattan cane which some soldiers put into their cartridge belts on the spur of the moment. US supplied army jeeps packed with excited crack troops prepared for battle at the frontline of the university. The Defense Minister himself wearing battle gear sat in the front of those jeeps taking the straight route from the BTC down UN Drive branching left in front of the Labor Ministry climbing up to Capitol Hill and branching right passed the police headquarters up to the main gate. Another team of soldiers drove straight up Capitol Hill from the direction of Buzzi Quarters passed the Mansion yard and branched left at the Unknown Soldier monument. Here the soldiers disembarked from their vehicles crouching low, they positioned themselves along the low perimeter steel fence of the main campus. Another batch of troops coming from the direction of the Bye Pass picked positions along the sports pitch their rifles pointed and ready. Faint hearted perhaps wise students noticing the discreet movement of soldiers exited the scene quietly while the vast majority of their comrades united in their protest sang and danced unaware of the hostile encircling pincer movements around them. The group of troops heading from the police headquarters section of the hill was commanded by the Defense Minister himself. Another large jeep filled with soldiers came to an abrupt stop right in front of the main entrance of the school. Soldiers were leaping from the vehicle even before they stopped. It then dawned on the students they were in danger. Holding a loud speaker the Minister Gabby ordered the students to disperse. Seconds later, soldiers of the Armed Forces of Liberia opened fire on the students with automatic rifles running towards the unarmed students. Some fell down covered in blood while others fled for dear life. Pandemonium broke out. Protesting students ran helter skelter to protect dear life. The students were caught unaware; none of them expected in the least they would face armed soldiers firing live bullets as a crowd control mechanism. The worst they expected were teargas throwing police officers. But they did not anticipate the firm resolve of the military strongman, nor the eagerness of his men to execute his order.

Among the soldiers shooting at the students was a young, brave and sadistic James Tiatune who was experiencing a significant amount of pleasure shooting at the disappearing students running. He pursued his fleeing foes relentlessly. The soldier ran with no sense of direction, his feet propelled him forward onto a winding path which led him to what he did not know was the girls dormitory for he had never been on the campus before.

A pretty lady clad in tight jeans looking like a vanishing shadow floated across his vision. Soon he became the predatory hunter and she became his prey. One of his friends followed closely at his heels. Corporal

Tiatune stopped shooting; he did not want to shoot the pretty thing fleeing before him. At the basement of the dormitory's entrance he caught up with her. He viciously kicked her legs trapping her. He forced her to the ground. In the apartments above the shriek and cries of university girls mostly young women from bourgeois backgrounds screamed in pain. Tiatune sprayed bullets upstairs in a wanton manner. The Corporal turned his attention to the shadow laying before him. Though weak, she faced her attacker. Her eyes pleaded in a "please don't manner."

Tiatune looked away and kicked her again in a savage manner and she became still. The Corporal loosened his zip to satisfy his bestial, bacchanalian desires for at this time his behavior was worse than an animal. Elsewhere on the campus students were being shot, beaten, and raped. The citadel of learning cried under the yoke of violence being unleashed. College Freshman Gonlafale jumped down to the outcrop of rocks on the Jallah Town side of the campus to escape the soldiers no doubt falling down to serious injuries. His friend Dave behind him was not so lucky, his flight in mid air was cut short by a bullet to the heart. He fell bloody and wet to the ground near the fence he was attempting to jump over his eyes still pointing outside to the freedom just beyond. The university campus has turned into a war zone and torture chambers of unequal opposing forces. Within two hours the mission was complete. Complete calm returned to the main campus. The air smelled of cordite and used gunpowder. Here and there a pool of blood marked the grass or concrete pavement. Gone were the defiant protestors.

An embarrassed Defense Minister Moses Gabby called President Maxwell Forkpa to say the mission was a resounding success.

The calm of the campus was broken now and then by the heavy sound of boots thudding on grass. Bodies lay here and there in isolated groves and dormitory halls.

By nightfall the same mysterious guys from Slipway responsible for painting the Daily Observer offices with feces descended on the campus of the University of Liberia carting away dead bodies wrapped in plastic sheetings to prevent the blood from seeping into the vehicles transporting them. For the men involved in this clandestine operation, all of the bodies were the same lifeless corpse that needed to be disposed of in a hurry. Jeeps with tinted glasses filed with dead bodies hurried out of the campus with their macabre cargo. A severed hand from one of the bodies fell to the ground on the country's premier boulevard unknown to the transporters. Pedestrians and motorists heading for school and jobs the next morning watched agape in horror at the spectacle on the intersection of 9th Street. The bodies of the students were dumped into shallow graves in the swamp behind Matadi Estate. There were no bodies for family and friends of the deceased to mourn over and bury. Their pain and uncertainty stretched into eternity.

Government spokesperson's blithe denials and the request by the government for people to come out with bodies to prove that indeed deaths occurred and the offer to treat anybody wounded free of charge did little to ease the acute pain. That year 1984 is still mourned in Liberia today.

There was an outcry from the international community,

vociferous protest from civil society groups. The government promised an enquiry and soon people went about their normal business except for people who lost children, love ones and friends who are still suffering pain.

———•◆•———

The US Ambassador could not contain his disgust as he reviewed images, macabre relics of the brutal actions of blood thirsty soldiers. Yet in the twilight struggle of the cold war with cold warrior Ronald Reagan in the White house Washington was not yet ready to pull the plug on the maverick in the Executive Mansion. Washington suspended military aid and demanded the unconditional the release of all political prisoners and a firm date set for a return to civilian rule.

President Maxwell Forkpa's anger was appeased . He was in another of his numerous secret meetings with his security chiefs including his amiable but ruthless Director of Military Intelligence. At the end of the closed door meeting the President departed for an OAU Summit in Harare. In Harare, Zimbabwe the young Head of State made friends easily having lost his habitual shyness fostered by sense of inferiority among the rich and famous. Ebenezer Kum ensured his friend wore a magnificent coat in the finest tradition of Western Business suits.

President Maxwell Forkpa listened patiently to his colleagues addressing the famous African talk show. It pleased the President to be among the cream de la crème of the African continent.

CHAPTER 27

The Libyan Desert stretched as far as the eyes could see; sand dunes dotted the bleak, thirsty landscape. Even for sun bred Africans, the day time heat suffocated the lungs inflaming one's senses. Brown army tents enclosed in barb wires were the only available accommodation in the camp housing the motley trainees including Palestinian guerrillas and African Freedom Fighters ranging from anti- Mobutu Fighters to ANC Onkomto Wie Sizwe Fighters congregated together in a marriage of convenience. Each man and each group in their own way was an advocate of violence to achieve political means sponsored by Libyan oil money. The makeshift base was situated a little distance away from the huge Libyan airbase in the south eastern corner of the vast desert. Everything at the base was designed to blend with the desert to fool American spy planes. Libya did not yet have the sophistication of the North Koreans to build entire complexes underground away from the prying cameras of high attitude U2 Aircrafts. Tough looking Ukrainian, Syrians, and Russians instructors toting Ak-47s ruled their pupils with an iron fist in this school. This school did not teach her students to build; instead it taught them to destroy teaching the best means of killing another human being. The isolation of the base was so complete nobody could think of anything besides the skills for which they had come in this hot sand making the nostrils to burn. No women no booze, nothing just assortment of weapons, and weapons. Oh the intensity of the training, the sadistic no nonsense east European instructors training them like machines. The only pleasures allowed the trainees were video clips of American troops in Vietnam and the failed Bay of Pigs Invasion. To complete their isolation, the trainees were not given access to telephones. Many of the Liberian recruits such as Rodney Gweh were men whose desire for revenge kept them alive. To him the Maxwell Forkpa regime was evil, the devil incarnate personified. He could not stand for any argument or fine logic. All he cared for was his only pet brother Gongbaye has been killed in one of the many attempted coups on the President. Gongbaye pure and boyish with his perpetual cheerful smile gunned down by the devil and his fiendish demons. The heat in this desert was not anything bad for him as long as it gave him a chance to give the regime of his arch enemy a dose of their own medicine.

Their Commander Samuel Dahn now possessing a bushy beard was being driven by his alter ego from the relative peace of life in the Midwestern state of Minnesota in America to this intense heat. The pain in his heart was becoming an obsessive pre- occupation for him. How could he ever sleep in peace as long as Maxwell Forkpa remained in power? How could the years of his absence from Liberia now 2 years be restored? His presence uplifted the morale of his men immensely.

Few days later away from the base Samuel traded his favored military suits for civilian clothes. He looked quite attractive in his long lace gown, the flowing Agbada robe so typical of wealthy Nigerians. A stranger seeing him might have thought him Nigerian. He wore a dark spectacle to cover his slightly slanted eyes while toying with the dish of spiced Spaghetti mixed with grilled meat. He took a sip of the Lemonade drink on the table. Now and then Samuel Dahn looked at his watch. His contact was already 15 minutes late, something which was very unusual of the European. Maybe the infamous London Traffic had him stuck up somewhere. The time dragged on to 20 and 30 minutes. It was time to try initiating another contact. The disappointed Liberian fugitive rose to go his meal barely eaten. It was then he recognized his friend's Slavic features. His high cheek bones and almost ornamental features stood out. The Yugoslav carried his usual black briefcase in his right hand. His beautiful expensive tailored suit marked him out as an important business executive. Viktor's black hair was shampooed and combed in a telltale sign of underworld dandyism. The arms dealer smiled making his way to Samuel's table with a flurry of apology in excellent though accented English. Samuel forced a smile.

Viktor Stanislav waited deliberately somewhere outside the restaurant having arrived a long time ago; he killed the time in an antique shop across the road. Viktor wanted the African buyer to wait for him and anticipate his arrival thus making the buyer to feel the seller was in no hurry to sell. Impression was everything. Of course he was anxious to sell. How could he maintain the charmed, luxurious life he lived without those third world liberation movements?

Viktor cared nothing for ideologies, he cared for the good life of expensive threads on his body, first class travels to some of the most exotic spots in the world carousing with some of the most sensual women money could buy. Driving the latest SUVs, sleeping comfortable hotel suits, and meals at exclusive restaurants in all the fabulous cities of the world was what he lived for. Viktor offered his hand for the customary handshake and a big smile. Africans were an emotional bunch who still considered a warm handshake from a white man an honor in the world.

"Sorry for keeping you waiting; I am terribly sorry, this London traffic can be a nightmare. Anyway I should have anticipated this and left my hotel a little earlier. I hope there is no hard feelings sir?

"No Victor I was becoming a bit impatient but better late than never."

Samuel smiled.

If Viktor had seen his prospective buyer leaving their rendezvous he would have 'accidentally' bumped into him in the streets.

Outside the restaurant two of the arms dealer thickset accomplices waited for any sign of trouble though they have seen no sign of any since the African entered the restaurant. Viktor made his order. He brought his briefcase laying it on the table raising his voice a little higher.

"This world is a big place, also exciting to discover my friend. Some of the most spectacular scenes of natural beauty this world has to offer are in Africa, but you Africans have to let the rest of the world know what you have got to offer. When you attract visitors to come and see your natural beauty they must have accommodation. It reminds me of a trip I took to Livingstone years back, after seeing the great cascading beauty of the Zambezi we had to sleep on foam mattresses put on a dirt floor a far cry from the air conditioned rooms and flush toilets now available to tourists. My company has the money to build hotels for the time your warm,dry continent will be flooded by tourists from colder parts of the world tired of the bleached for tourist only natural attraction available in so many traditional tourist spots in the world."

From all indication, the two well dressed men conversing were businessmen contemplating a partnership of mutual benefits.

Pleasantries now done away with Viktor now brought his real brochures interspersed with those of fabulous hotels. The brochures included everything a guerrilla army needed: RPG 7 Rocket Launchers, machine guns, various assault rifles, Uzi automatic pistols 9mm Lugers, Beretta pistols ideal for urban street fighting, mortals, flame throwers, Sentex explosives, landmines even surface to air missile. Also included in the menu of There were also Swiss army knives famed worldwide for their durability, bullet proof vests, and high frequency VHS radios and army boots.

"All of these weapons I can supply you at any moment once you have the cash or diamonds, precious stones eh.?

In our business we are small but effective. Even if you want attack helicopters and soldiers of fortune to pilot them I can supply you at the right price of course."

Samuel Dahn smiled, the brochure suited his purpose well.

"We do not want to be bugged down by heavy equipments, what we need is an equipped highly mobile force depending on stealth, precision and surprise to achieve our aim."

"Take the Uzis and Berettas, they are good for urban fighting. Though I do not pride myself on knowing what use my clients have for the good gifts I give them. But I can sometimes give friendly advice. You are not planning a bush war, hence the need for these lethal urban weapons".

"Your choice is not bad, but I do not need the toys useful for assassinations or gang warfare. Perhaps Ak-47s, RPGs, five multi rocket launchers that can be fired using the foot instead of shoulder fire tubes. I do need lots of grenades, lethal and stun, I will also appreciate several of these hand held general purpose machine guns along with sufficient ammo. A few of these bullet proof vests will come in handy."

"Yeah your cause it right, you will succeed but how much are you offering my friend."

It was now time for the shadowy business man and his buyer to start the ancient art of bargaining over the time, price and delivery of the weapons.

Before I give you any of my weapons you have to give me half of the money. When I receive information from my bank account that you have made the deposit the weapons will be delivered. We can form a good partnership.

I can supply you with good slightly used weapons necessary to a bush campaign. If you make the initial payment for the used weapons I can supply you all of the ammunition that you need free of charge. I can even give you half of the weapons you need free, when your campaign is going well you can pay me back in Diamonds."

Your generosity surprises me. You see we the people of Eastern Europe have suffered a lot of oppression from both the west and Russia. I am prepared to help Africans throw away their yoke of oppression be it from western imperialist or from despotic rulers."

Viktor paused and fixed the Liberian general with a cold piercing stare famous to gangsters all over the world. He hoped his feigned message of political solidarity would do the trick, a long rebel war guaranteed a long term arms market. While Africans butchered each other he would be smiling all the way to the bank.

"When do you make the first payment?

"Wednesday."

"And if I pay you and I do not receive my shipment?

"Our goals are the same; I have weapons I do not have use for, and you have money you do not have other uses for. In our business we learn to trust, if I cheat or disappoint you who will be my next client?

"If you f-- k with me I will kill you and if I f-- k you I am sure have means of getting even."

Viktor smiled through clenched teeth. The two men

shook hands. Viktor exited the restaurant while Samuel remained to finish his sauced Rice Dinner.

Across the street in a small room adjacent to one of the British Capital's many pubs, two thirtyish men clad in jeans and T-shirts armed with portable communication gadgets were listening to a recording of the conversation between the fugitive general and the notorious arms dealer. Viktor was on the MI 5 watch list. But the arms dealer without peer had been careful never to violate any British law. He merely used London as a point of contact because of the city large expatriate community of Africans from the commonwealth. Insurgency groups and coups were much more frequent in former British colonies as compared to former French colonies. The paternalistic relationship between France and her former colonies guaranteed a much more interventionist foreign policy which in term guaranteed more stability in these countries compared to their British peers. Viktor made his living selling arms mostly small arms to insurgency groups as diverse as the Nicaraguan Contras anti -communist fighters to the Communist New People's Army in the Philippines, UNITA rebels in Angola, Tamil Tigers Separatist in Sri Lanka Viktor supplied them all.

The British did not have any particular interest in Liberia they were merely doing this to curry favor with their American Allies knowing full well America's interest in the nation.

Samuel Dahn having met with the arms dealer and given him his special list did not have much to do in London. He booked the next available BA Flight to the

JFK. Now he stood in a slow moving cue impatient to get out of the enclosure to brief his powerful backers, men and women implacably opposed to Maxwell Forkpa's Presidency but not willing to tie their name to the ignominy of coup making.

The queue edged forward slowly bristling with immigrants and visitors to the land of opportunity who like him were anxious to be out there with friends and relatives. A large uniform black man took Samuel's passport examining it for a rather long time. He lifted his eyes from the passport to look at Samuel Dahn's face. Samuel stood perplexed. He had never violated any American law as far as he knew. Furthermore, he was a frequent traveler to this country with all his papers intact.

"What is the problem sir?

"Nothing, I just wanted to make sure you are the rightful owner of this passport; never mind, we have to be alert these days."

He smiled.

"Here we go "he sounded cheerful as he stamped the general's passport. Something just did not seem right.

Samuel reached out to retrieve his passport. Two officers appeared on either side of him.

"Samuel Dahn sir?

The man asked flashing a security batch.

"Yes, but have I committed any crime? I have the right to my lawyer"

"Nobody said anything about arrest or crime sir. And let me tell you the United States and her laws are outside there after that door"

One of the two men replied testily.

"Here is not America, outside is America, please come with us we do not want to create a scene. The custom director wants to ask you some few questions that's all."

Samuel followed the two men down into a tube like glass corridor leading into a cubicle. The cubicle looked cozy enough with large drape curtains, soft carpets and two computer monitors. A small circular table with a miniature American flag stood in the middle of the room. A clean shaven man with blond hair combed backwards and tied into a pony tail sat wearing a business suit. Samuel knew him well. He motioned to a vacant chair facing his table. Samuel accepted the offer his heart still pounding in his chest.

"Would you like some coffee general."

"No sir, I am anxious to know why I am being pulled here."

"Gentlemen would you leave us?

The man commanded. In split seconds the two giants sauntered out of the room.

"You have been doing quite a lot of traveling lately.

On January 30 you were in Accra at the Shangrila Hotel. You have made two trips to London, and one to Rome. For a man on the run you have been globetrotting a little too much. Who pays for your travels."

"Can't a man have some privacy in America.? I have a family to support and I am doing my best to support them."

"Good I know your wife and children are living in Minnesota, a girlfriend of yours whom you have a son by lives in Monrovia, Sinkor to be precise. No attempt have been made by you to contact them."

"And my I ask why all this following me around is about?

"Precisely, this is why I called you here. I am in charge of the Liberia desk. I know you have been planning a coup. To stage your coup you have been soliciting support from various exiled Liberians. But what concerns my government is the men you have in training camps in Libya. We do not want Liberia to fall into the Libyan sphere of influence. We will not allow that."

"And if even that possibility exist my government will take action to neutralize your men before they arrive in Liberia. I could also put you in jail on some trump up security charges."

"I am not a man easily intimidated. If you want us to discuss you tell me what you want from me, and I will tell you what I want from you".

Miles stood to his feet and walked to one of the two large flat screen monitors in the room and flipped it on. S.D's conversation with Viktor played in perfect audio quality followed by pictures of the two men.

"Now you have to put all preparations for your coup on ice and wait for the election. We know there is a good chance Maxwell Forkpa may not win. Since you primary aim is revenge and returning your country to civil rule your dream may come true without bloodshed.

"But?

"Hold it General Dahn we will not tolerate a socialist or communist regime in Liberia."

"Miles you wait a minute, if the electoral process turns out to be a farce, if Maxwell rig the election and succeed himself as President then I can carry out my plans? In this case I will need America's backing especially with logistics."

Miles laughed. "General America is a democracy, there are laws in this country with prevents US government assistance to people such as you whom we label terrorist. The best I can say to you is watch your steps more carefully because if the information I have falls into the wrong hands my government will be forced to extradite you to Liberia. By the way what drove you to Kadafi and what does he gets from helping you remove your enemy?

"Kadafi knows America will never sit back to allow Libya's hands all over Liberia. All the Colonel wants is revenge, pure simple revenge. Remove the frisky Maxwell from power, good for his ego."

"Do I have your word?"

"On what?

"On not taking any action now against the President of Liberia?

"You have my word"

"And you have mine too"

Samuel Dahn rose to.

"Remember this meeting between you and I never took place." Miles sounded so officious without making any reference to their previous communications or the satellite phone he gave him. The question on Samuel Dahn's mind was why now? It was a time of uncertainty in the country. People were both elated and felt suffocated at the same time. Politics became an almost taboo subject in social gathering until one fateful day.

———◆◆———

In dingy run down shack in Monrovia's toughest slum named West Point where the lower slope of Cape Mesurado and sandy beaches collided, men and women gathered to drink in informal bars. Along the narrow winding street passing the head office of the Liberia Electricity Corporation lined by market stalls, chemist shops and Fulah shops nestled among a dense cluster of simple corrugated zinc shacks; the inhabitants of this tough place eke their living from petty selling, fishing and hustling. Seedy characters earned their living from thievery and pimping; the director of the secret police NSA inconspicuous enjoyed bottles of cold beer with some friends -street urchins whom years ago he roamed the streets with. The powerful government functionary looked casual in jeans and ruffled T-shirt and old jacket on top. He was devoid of any vestige of power. The small Toyota Corolla he drove was parked a little distance away at the borough's Police station. However, beneath his jeans jacket he wore a gun belt along with a portable camera and mini recorder.

"I can't wait to see this government fall."

Inside the den of an almost exclusive male customers out to drown the drudgery of casual labor missed with some habitual loafers who craved the pleasure of loud conversation and a free drink.

"Man look at all the suffering in this country, people graduating from college. I na say high school oh but college no job."

"Native woman born soya for true," replied a young man of average height with dark brown eyes wiping the foam of beer from his mustache . His friend a thin, wiry crook laughed showing his rough weather beaten feature. A big scar featured prominently above his left eye from an injury which he received from a bungled robbery attempt in his teenage years. He learned his lessons well because after that he had never been unfortunate again to target the strong in robbery, but the weak.

The atmosphere in the bar was relaxed, but filled with loud, boisterous conversations. But what attracted the most attention were the two young men discussing a time bomb of politics in a public bar. Opening your mouth too wide everyone knew could land you in trouble yet the two dudes speaking looked like ordinary hustlers who should know better like the rest of their drinking pals.

"You talking about college graduates not finding jobs what da one get to do with me? Me I na go to school, but I get my woman and five children to feed. The soldier boy na spoil dis country, thank God election time coming."

The critical conversation flowed smoothly between the two men their tongues loosened by alcohol.

A bearded man in his twenties with a large round head who have been trying very hard to remain silent popped up.

"What kinda election you talking about? In our country one man da de President, da de candidate, da de chairman of the election commission."

Daniel Kollie hands went to his side as if scratching his buttocks, his tape recorder was on.

William Tamba was by nature a very cautious man especially when it came to discussing political matters with strangers. However; the effect of alcohol and his anger at his cross border goods being confiscated by Liberian custom at the Ivorian border in Loguatuo loosened his tongue.

"Let me tell you my friend Prof. Martins will win this election hands down, nothing Maxwell Forkpa, Ebenezer Kum or Adonis Vonleh can do will make the President win."

A friend of the man talking coughed loudly and asked his friend to join him outside. Some men when they start a conversation did not like being stopped so he ignored his friend.

Daniel Kollie yarned switching off his tape.

"We…. The tape was back on-- wasting our time with this election business, it is President Forkpa today, tomorrow. The only person who can free this country and make us happy is Samuel Dahn and his men."

William Tamba as soon as he uttered this last sentence knew he had gone too far and shut his mouth like a clam. His friend who advised him earlier mumbled an excuse he wanted to urinate slipping away. The noisy bar became instantly silent. The two men who initially started the anti- government conversation broke the ice lambasting Maxwell Forkpa for being a military dictator talking and laughing like before. This time nobody joined their conversation. William Tamba sensed it was time to go. He rose from his chair his head nearly touching the ceiling. He hit the main street of the slum. The director of NSA headed for the bathroom which was a small circular enclosure.. The strong scent emanating from the pool of stale urine brought a fresh feeling of nausea to his throat. He flipped on his VHS radio giving a brief description of William Tamba. William Tamba was literally running to the main bus terminal at the Waterside. In front of the main market opposite the housing bank unknown hemmed men him in and bundled him into an unmarked car driving to an unknown destination. Just next another event was unfolding that would have consequences for the security operatives driving this man.

A British Airways plane slowly taxied to a stop at the Lungi International Airport runway. Samuel Dahn for all intent and purpose resembled a businessman who wanted to invest in real estate. His briefcase contained British credit cards, company listings, call cards, checks, and brochures. His dark conservative suit and clean-shaven face added to his cover. He emerged from the clustered pressurized cabin of the aircraft into the warm African sunshine. An hour later he was in a ferry with fellow travelers mostly Sierra Leonean exiles returning home for holidays and British holiday makers determined to enjoy the country's sparkling beaches, fine cuisines and abundant hospitality.

A white woman tourist sitting beside him on the ferry to Freetown asked. "First time visitor?

Yes but I am almost Sierra Leonean." Samuel replied. I am from next door Liberia."

Soon a contact picked the Liberian taking him to a safe house on Kissi Bye Pass.

Night time in the Sierra Leonean town of Kenema resembled festival time. A medium size city built near rich alluvial deposit Kenema attracted people from all over West Africa drawn by the lure of instant riches. Many soon found out that dreams are not what they seemed to be. While some achieve riches along the banks of rivers in the diamond corridor, many others became casual laborers digging mother earth notoriously fastidious with her riches. Middlemen and town based Lebanese merchants became the princes of the Diamond trade growing rich. The diamond while notorious difficult to find by men using primitive mining methods when came out came in the right quantity to keep dreams alive and maintain a fast, fabled lifestyle.

General Samuel Dahn set aside his smart suit resorting to the casual wear of the miners yet having on the big rings and chains so typical of the flamboyant dealers who were such a prominent feature of the local landscape. His companion was named Momoh Sesay, a brown complexioned man with thick curly lips and thin nose. He wore a long tailored gown typical of Muslim trader. Night time in Kenema brought reprieve from the suffocating daytime heat. Local bars attracted miners out to have a good time to alleviate the drudgery. Beer and local brewed liquor mixed with toxic cigarette fumes permeated the bar. Samuel allowed his tough control to slip in the heady atmosphere of liquor and loud music. The girls milling about in the bar had too much of everything. Too much lipstick, too much cologne and too much bare flesh tempting lascivious miners with plenty of money to spend and little brains.

Many of the girls smoked with their clients amidst loud conversations, laughter, music and dancing. Samuel and his guide sat in a secluded corner in the dimly lit room. A bosomy lady alone and alluring sauntered through the small entrance into the bar her stately appearance attracting hungry eyes. Samuel looked up smiling in her direction.

"You like her chief?

"I have a very pretty Mande girl just waiting to make you happy if only you say so just to make you relax."

Samuel again laughed.

"Sesay I have never learnt to relax. There is this overpowering intensity in me. An urge, a strong inner purse in me driving me crazy. What is in me is the desire to get even. This desire has become an obsession for me robbing me of the joys and pleasures of life including the sensual pleasure of women."

"Look chief there she comes!

Sesay pointed to the stately dame coming through the cloistered chairs to their direction stopping just short of their table.

"May I have a light," she asked whisking a pack of Rothmans from her small lady bag.

"Please put the cigarette down and have a seat."

Samuel offered shoving the vacant seat to her. The lady inspected Samuel's face before accepting the seat.

"Help yourself to a beer."

Samuel signaled a waittress who was struggling to walk through the congested bar her very tight mini skirt clinging to her skin. He ordered more beer and biscuits.

The night queen took a big mouthful of beer.

"This beer is freezing; this is what I love about Trawally's place...easy and convenient service. You see in a way I like what Trawally is doing. This is the real Ecowas; bringing all works of life together to relax and enjoy... The popular Freetown Teete collection tune hit the dance floor like a bomb. The chatter in the bar declined. More couples sauntered to the dance floor.

"Want to dance...? the large room seemed divided into two, the waiting area comprised of white wooden chairs and tables alongside the parallel easy,, convenient dance floor blurring out an opaque light made the white cloth to look purple. The ambience was charged. Night revelers freely moved between the two non separated compartments.

"Want to dance?

The beauty queen beside Samuel requested for the second time.

"Mr......

"Morrison Samuel" corrected.

The night queen smiled showing pouted lips inviting him.

"I am too old to dance... she giggled loudly.

"My name is Doris get that notion of being old out of your mind. I have seen men of sixty five hit the dance floor with the gusto of a 25 years old."

"It is not my body which is old, it is my mind."

She threw her hands up in a mock sign of surrender. This could be a rich client who offered her too much beer without making an overt or even subtle sexual advance. If she played her cards right she was sure could come out richer.

"You look different in these parts, surely you have come to buy diamonds. You don't look like a field hand. Our diamonds are so pure they do not need much polishing." As she spoke she bend on the table exposing her breasts through the low cut bras she wore getting close as if to put the nipple into Samuel's mouth.

"I am not a diamond broker."

"Every rich man in these parts is a diamond broker or has some connections to it. There is good money in it."

S.D. laughed "It seemed you are determined to make a diamond broker out of me or a dealer neither of which I am. I have only come to collect a debt from a former friend." Samuel's again laughed in sardonically.

"It must be millions of Leones he or she might have stolen from you eh?

"No it is not money my friend stole from me. It is something beyond that. He stole my pride, my dignity and myself self worth from me."

"Please sir I like to have a smoke and find myself something to eat" her long fingers covered the fugitive general's palm.

Samuel took a brand new $100.00 from his pockets placing it in her hands. Her eyes glowed with happiness.

"I am ready now to go to your hotel now if you say

the word; you look so unhappy. I can make you happy . I do whatsoever you want; I know a lot of tricks to keep a man satisfied in bed."

"Please do not talk like that, let us just sit down and enjoy the atmosphere for a while."

"How do you expect to get back what your friend had stolen from you?"

She asked out of the blue after a rather lengthy period of silence.

"If it was a house, car, your money these things you could easily get them back. But dignity and self worth are different.

Look at me, I have sold these two things you talked about to earn a living. At least my life now is more exciting than the forced marriage my father arranged for me to an old man old enough to be my grandfather."

"You see friendship is an almost priceless commodity. I had a friend whom we once did everything together until he lied on my name, took away my job, disgraced me and finally put me into jail. In choosing the ignominy of running away I vowed to get even by doing the same thing to him."

Doris laughed gulping another mouthful of beer. Samuel watched furious waiting impatiently for her to calm down. A frown creased his brow.

"And what so funny about what I said?

Doris hand shot to her chest.

"Please do not be vexed. I laughed because you men always take minor things to heart. You always look back at an affront wanting to pay back in a test of wills. If men could tune down their ego the world would be a much nicer and kinder place to live. If your friend stole your dignity he has sold his by betraying a friend which makes him the biggest villain in the world. While he has to live with a guilty conscience you can hold your head high as an injured innocent man who innocence shall be proven with the passage of time."

"In other words?"

"Mr. Morrison I am saying forget about him and let's enjoy life. Now let get on the dance floor. This is place of enjoyment where people come to enjoy themselves not a place of mourning.

Come out," she urged literally dragging Samuel to the dance floor. He attempted to move his legs which seemed stiff. Doris dance around him touching and holding him, laughing, gyrating, swaying Doris's dance moves were incredibly infectious. Gradually the stiffness edged out of Samuel. He responded to the funky dance beat. Doris was all over him bogging and whacking flaunting her decadent lifestyle of pleasure and immorality. S.D. stomped his feet to the beat he found himself holding tight to Doris holding her by her weight. Samuel never felt happier in life. The night slowly drifted away.

On the second night of his stay in Kailahun District the general ventured out of his hotel room. Borders in Africa were jealously guarded in many areas by gun wielding thugs wearing uniforms. Whether in east, south or west the scenario was the same; a plethora of armed security agents extorting money from travelers. Never mind these borders themselves were artificial creation of colonial mentality which had no basis in fact. These lines of demarcations were in many instances arbitrarily drawn without regards to genealogy, social or linguistic factor never more so than the border between Liberia and Sierra Leone where in many places the border point was a palm tree or a termite hill without the presence of any visible line of separation, not even a stone.

Samuel Dahn set aside his businessman cover wearing a pair of dark Levi jeans armed with a powerful torch light. His game tonight was very dangerous to say the least..

Persuasion for the very reluctant Lalugbah to take Samuel across the Mano River came in the form of the comparatively large amount of 5000 Leones. Lalugbah for that was his name was thin man with a perpetual frown on his face earned his living by being friend, and transporter for the smugglers who operated on both sides of the border.

It was a lucrative beneficial to all those involved in it except for the coffers of the revenue authorities. Sesay wanted to come, but Samuel would have none of it. The sleek dug out vessel glided almost noiseless except for the occasion shuttle of the canoe in the river barely touching the river before it was again raised for the next stroke of the paddle. The Sierra Leonean shore faded and the Liberian shore drew closer in the pitch darkness. Samuel squatted behind the canoe captain watching in silence, but he could not make out any other movement. His nearness to the Liberian shore brought a mixture of joy and apprehension. He grabbed the torch lying in the bottom of the canoe to shine the beam on the approaching shore.

"Please put the light away."

Lalughah requested without turning around in the Creole dialect.

"Shine that beam and you make us sitting ducks for anybody who wants to aim.

The general mind drifted to his wife and children sadness enveloped him for a moment. Laulugbah knew his route well even in the darkness gliding his craft to a large tree. The long roots of the tree hanging over the river served as an anchor on a cliff.

"Master I don't understand whatting you want do in the forest at this time of de night. That some sacrifice you want make?

The captain asking speaking his best English.

"Shut your mouth Lalugbah; you are paid to do a job, do the job and keep quiet. I James Morrison move alone, you hear that?

"I hear sah, dis na de place dem Liberia soya dem in de small village not far from here. I wait for you one hour, if you na come back one hour past I will go back for Sa Leone."

Me I na go stay long. But make you wait. Every thirty minute past one hour I go give you 100 Leones."

"Thank you master but please hurry oh."

Samuel stood in the canoe near the shallow river banks and heaved his body upwards using one of the protruding roots as an anchor and stepping stone to the shore. His feet touched Liberian soil far away from the watchful eyes of the international community. If he was captured no doubt torture and death awaited him.

Samuel stood still to get his eyes adjusted to the thick foliage of riverside vegetation. Before him lay a small footpath. He listened for a while for sounds of footsteps or human voice straining his ears to hear above the singing of insects including the mournful tune of the Owl .The palpable darkness enveloping him broken by the tiny glow of fireflies whose tiny sparks did not aid his visibility. Satisfied he was alone Samuel put on his powerful torchlight. He kept it on for just a little while bathing the vegetation in light and then put it out and began to walk deeper into Liberian territory. A few steps forward he put on the beam, looked around for a while and then shut it off before advancing further on foot. Nocturnal insects provided company for the solitary night traveler. A cluster of huts appeared ahead of him. By instinct he edged closer to the huts whose surrounding was lighted by a bonfire. Two Liberian soldiers were warming themselves by the wood fire their guns hanging a little distance from them above their heads on a bamboo rod. The two soldiers were conversing in loud voices. Two other soldiers snored beside them sleeping. The light from their campfire illuminated their presence. Samuel remembering his training days crouched down to his knees crawling within 18 yards of the soldiers to hear their conversation.

"I hope to be back in Monrovia soon for a promotion.. Samuel's heart missed a beat..Get a promotion with such reckless behavior being displayed?

"This bush is too remote. Let me go peepee. To Samuel Dahn's dismay, the soldier headed to his direction. He lay rigidly not daring to breath. The distance separating the two men was less than four feet apart. Only a thin foliage of bush separated the two foes. The armed one glanced around; satisfied with his inspection he opened his fly shooting a strong stream of urine some landing on Samuel's feet spattering on his shoes. He finished zipped his fly and returned to his post. Samuel crawled in opposite direction until he emerged on the main highway leading to Monrovia known as the Babangida Highway. Dead silence reigned now on this border which in the daytime was an epitome of trading. General Dahn looked into Liberia by passing all of the checkpoints along the border to emerge on this road, a task he hoped to someday perform with perfect ease. While Samuel Dahn carried out reconnaissance along the border, a man whom he did even know of his existence was in deep trouble because of him.

Brash, relaxed and restless Monrovia whirled around in a contradictory circle in her continuous dance with destiny. A kind of crazy dance in which the hundreds of thousands living in the city performed the dance in their own peculiar way at their own pace. In this quiet night time when the good people of the city retired to get a good night sleep a man screamed in an underground basement. He was hanged downwards his two legs tied by strong ropes attached to a ceiling. Blood and fluid seeped down to his brain. He was surrounded by a small group of men talking and laughing. The man hanging upside down still had his mental faculties intact.

"You know you are going to remain hanging in there until you tell us everything. Blood

Has a way of seeping into the brain until it enlarges the brain and turns you crazy before you die. Hang in there boy for you will soon start seeing stars."

"But I have told you everything please free me for God sake."

The heavy thudding sound of cartridge belt slamming into flesh made a piercing scream permeate the otherwise terse polite exchange.

"You must not talk when the chief talk."

A harsh voice cut through the air.'

"Sarge take time, this man here is a nice man who will tell us what we want to know"

Red paint decorated the walls of the basement room. The room was almost threadbare apart from two large tables. A couple of iron manacles attached to the wall held the man.

"When will Samuel Dahn and his men attack?

"I don't know."

The savage blow of the cartridge belt hanged in mid air just about to descend.

"Take it easy Sarge!

"We have all been through this before just tell me the number of men who are coming to attack when and where then you can feel some fat cash in your pockets. The electric shocks, the beating, all this suffering will end. You can now work for us because we are stronger than them."

The chief intelligence officer dangled a bundle of American dollars in front of the prisoner.

"All of these are for you as soon as you tell what I want to know."

"I have told you, I do not know anything. I beg you I am sorry. I was just too drunk and said some stupid things," the man pleaded.

Simultaneously the belt descended pounding his flesh in merciless waves drawing out pieces of flesh and blood.

The Prisoner begged for the blows to stop but they continued pounding his flesh till he descended into darkness.

"Bring some icy cold water put it on it and loosen him from the ceiling. The prisoner's huge body crashed onto the floor.

"Pretty tough guy eventually though he will talk. Put more water on him. The icy cold water tore through the sore of the prisoner piercing through his darkness to restore him back to consciousness. Moses Gabby was now more than angry. He knew the bruised man before him was hiding an important secret from him, something which his life, the President and the entire nation depended on. No means of expropriating information was vile as long as it served its purpose and saved life.

He's back! The chief torturer announced in a triumphant voice.

"Put some Cane Juice on the wound, it burns like isopropyl alcohol. The liquor burned the man's wound now bereft of energy to scream he moaned in agony

"Now tell me where is the base and how many men are training there?

I do not know anything except for the fact Samuel Dahn is training people in Libya to come to overthrown this government.

Please let me go," the tortured man whispered.

"Who are the significant people supporting him."

"I do not understand. Look I am only a trader what loose talk I hear is the one I am telling you."

The prisoner replied in short tortured gasps.

The Defense chief laughed.

"You are no ordinary trader. You are part of that dog Samuel Dahn's team sent to spy on us. You can gain more by working for us instead of against us. We are stronger. Sergeant give him the money.

Where is the training camp you are from?

"True to God I am a trader, please help me."

The cartridge belt again landed drawing groans.

"Sarge give him the money, now he will work with us. When will Samuel come?

The sadistic Sergeant pressed the wad of notes into the brutalized man slipping in and out of consciousness hands. In spite of his pain the tortured man managed to laugh. His laughter was ugly to see because his face already reduced to pulp looked grotesque under his twisted laughter. Several of his teeth hang loosely from the sockets ready to fall at the slightest touch.

His speech were labored coming slowly in spasm from a fractured rib.

And what is so funny ? One of his torturers asked. The tortured man continued to laugh. Perhaps his laughter was due to delirium, but it was a pretty absurd time to laugh during interrogation by ruthless men driven by fear and insecurity.

"Bring the wires, we will teach him nobody just laugh at us. Electric cables were soon attached to the man's genitals and this time the scream came out.

Remove the wires!

More cold water was poured over the dying man who could barely open his eyes. In his subconscious mind by a supreme effort of the will the prisoner sensed the end was near for him. For a long time he tried to be the ideal prisoner telling his torturers all he knew . Now it dawned on his half functioning brain that he would not leave this room alive. Already his dead mother in tears was calling him to leave his battered, broken body behind; a prospect which he now relished. He made up his mind to die like a man. His interrogators were hard driven men motivated by fear to the depth of extreme barbarity.

"Take the money."

"Yes what am I going to do with your money when I am dead you chickens?

The Sarge raised his hand to strike, but his commander stopped him.

The injured man continued to speak.

"Samuel Dahn and his two thousand men gallant men are coming, they will come to free this country and roast you dogs alive, you and......The last words were cut short by a nasty blow to his head. Blood, flesh and brain scattered on the floor.

"Get a plastic and get this thing to highway and bury it."

"Better still sir we can just dump him into the Farmington River."

"No!

"Give this dog a decent burial. Bury him six feet under the ground. If I get to know you guys bury him in some shallow grave the rest of you will regret the days you were born."

The Chief of Military Intelligence exited the scene heading for a drinking spree even in the wee hours of the morning.

Samuel Dahn retreated consciously back to the Mano River. His visit revealed to him the AFL checkpoints along the river were loosely manned. Among the groups of soldiers, he encountered he did not see a single communication gear. Small forward based troops must have radios to relay information of suspicious or unusual movements to headquarters or send for reinforcement at short notice. All of the soldiers he saw were not sufficiently vigilant with some even committing the unpardonable sin of sleeping on their guard posts. Those isolated border posts could be by-passed without much difficulty.. What rocked his brain walking through the forest in the darkness was how to neutralize the President's elite Israeli trained Special Anti Terrorist Unit. These men were highly trained, motivated tribal nationalists. If these men backed by the larger less trained greater AFL combined forces to combat his men, they stood no chance. He had to meet his friend at the State Department for some guarantees from the Americans.

Samuel arrived at their rendezvous spot at the

riverbank to discover to his horror that Lalugbah was nowhere around. He searched up and down stream without success. A scream swelled in his throat but dared not out of fear of exposing himself. The frantic man traversed the shoreline for another hour searching for his passport to safety. A dejected Samuel Dahn returned to the base of the tree he previously used as anchor. He stared at the river below flowing peacefully without regard to his worries. The driven impetuous man was effectively a combatant stranded in enemy territory. His body was worth any price to his nemesis occupying the seat of power. Daylight would soon approach; he vowed that he would rather die than be captured alive to be humiliated again by his arch rival. The river below was the main obstacle to his safety on Sierra Leonean soil. Back in the days when he was a child he learnt to swim but he had never swum in years. Furthermore, the creeks he used to swim in where midgets compared to the giant of the river below. Rescue needed to come before daylight. Samuel Dahn then decided it was better he died fighting for his life swimming in the river than to be captured. Lost in thoughts and still roaming he encountered two intrepid fishermen smugglers who agreed to ferry him across in a small raft. Now safe on Sierra Leonean soil a great overwhelming sense of relief came over him now he was away from the claws of his enemy. Standing on an insignificant part of Sierra Leonean territory away from the eyes of the authorities but it was so refreshingly good. Samuel Dahn the soldier did not fear death rather he feared engaging in an unfair fight with the odds stacked against him. That was the reason why he ran way in the first place. Though he escaped from physical danger, that small accusatory voice kept accusing him of not being a man for running away. In Monrovia itself was the government imploding on itself?

CHAPTER 28

In the strange world of political intrigue, no one could believe the identity of the man squatting on the unsanitary floor littered with the entrails of the many reptiles. The long false beard, small skull cap along with the flowing gown he wore suited him perfectly in his disguise. The equally strange man before him chanted in a strange guttural language. He appeared to be communicating with some unseen being in a diabolical fashion. This was not the typical witch doctor so frequently depicted in Nigerian films. This man's shrine was his own room in an uppity Sinkor suburb. Flying bats circled the room. When he chose to address his client before him, he spoke in a surreal, a bizarre unearthly voice which seemed to come from the ground below.

"A man must cut his coat according to his measurement. What you ask me is a very very hard task."

The man who came for consultation felt his head rising. His body felt like an empty frame. He just could not feel himself in his own body. Yet the client was dogmatic, determined in his quest.

"What you ask is a difficult task."

"But can it be done?

He asked his senses alert, tremulous, anxious as if his whole life depends on the response to that question. The juju man with the slit for mouth ignored the question. Smoke billowed from an unseen hole in the ground. Then the man squatting could no longer see the medicine man sitting across from him. He felt pangs of fear. The image of the medicine man looked like a blur until he towered above his client almost touching the ceiling. His long shaggy beard heaved up and down when he opened his slit for mouth. His clothes which have not been washed for days emanated a foul odor. Many wealthy clients came to his door because he had a reputation for delivering on his words unlike hundred of his fellow practitioners who were nothing more than charlatans.

"What you ask can be done, but can you afford the price?

"I can give you all the money you want."

A thunderous laughter escaped the lips of the medicine man. The ground again appeared to rise before him.

"You think money can do everything?

Behind power, there is power which must be more powerful than power. I see Maxwell sitting on a throne surrounded by Lions, fierce, angry, ready to devour anybody who comes to his throne. Before you get near him the Lions have to be poisoned by meat.

Do you have meat? When the meat is poisoned Maxwell Forkpa will die and then you can announced yourself President".

The Defense Minister was no longer naïve. He knew the medicine man was not referring to meat sold in the market,but he bit his lower lips waiting.

"I can do anything."

Moses Gabby again emphasized. From beside him he picked a wood carving that resembled a human being.

"You need to make human sacrifice. A sacrifice of a young man with strong blood running in his veins. Many people will ask you for the blood of a virgin. but we need the blood of a young man with power coursing through his veins."

The Defense Minister felt chill going through his body. A voice told him to run out of the wretched place he squatted by this juju man dedicated to the basest vice of human nature.

He catered to people who were desperate enough to sell their own souls battering others for the achievements of their humanly goals.

"Find a young man take out his tongue and then drain fresh blood from his neck into a pure white bucket. Not one drop of the blood being drained must drop to the ground. Make sure while his blood is being drained he is not dead. Let his life drain slowly out of him with his blood. That is how power will be drained out of Maxwell Forkpa. Reveal my name to anyone and you are a dead man. You have a week. Can you do it?

For a brief moment uncertainty swelled in the Defense Minister's mind. The forces of good and evil were fighting for supremacy in his mind which left his body weak. This period lasted for only a flash. The Defense Minister has come too far to stop.

"Yes I can do it, I can do it" Gabby's voice like the medicine man seemed to come from the ground. The medicine man extended a black bowl to him filled with a putrid liquid.

"Put your hand in this and lick it."

Gabby hesitated.

"Lick" this time the voice sounded a little more demanding.

Moses Gabby placed his pointing finger in the bowl and·licked the liquid.

The liquid tasted bitter with an aftertaste of salty acidity. Gabby weak body felt strength return. His heart felt more resolute in what he wanted to do.

What drove one of Maxwell's Forkpa's closest friend, confidante, collaborator and one of the most powerful men in the country to such extreme was unfathomable. Did Maxwell Forkpa steal a woman he fancied? Did the President insult him in a cabinet meeting?

Or was the Defense Minister simply tired of playing second fiddle to a younger less educated, less cultured man? Did any of these things drive him to such desperate measures, one could not tell for sure.

Back at his palatial riverside home Gabby invited five of his closest bodyguards to his white spacious verandah overlooking the St. Paul River. His boys knew from long association that their boss caring though he was, he did not accrue himself too much familiarity with his subordinates. He always maintained a careful dignified aloofness from his men. A man of small structure, he managed to maintain deep fear mixed with awe among men much bigger physically than him.

"Come," a surprised Gongbay the most senior of Gabby's bodyguards hesitated. His chief invited in a jovial mood to his upper floor verandah reserved for dignitaries, army generals and the President himself.

"Guys sit down and let us drink."

"Chief.....

"Oh,sit down Patrick.

Emily bring me some chilly cold beer," he announced in a jolly fashion for that was his wife's name.

"My boys and I have something to celebrate."

"Sit down guys," the Defense Minister licked his lips before continuing.

"You see years ago I was a junior officer like you guys are, happy to be where I was. But one day I realized I deserved something better than standing outside another person's door catching cold so that person can sleep in the warm comfort of their home. As a soldier I felt it was my duty, but I also wanted for people to guard me just as you guys are doing now."

More chilly, cold beer, Jollof rice, seasoned grilled meat filled the stomachs. And still their boss ordered more. Gradually the hitherto tensed men relaxed.

Patrick, Gongbay would you like to guard me for the rest of your lives?

Just then Emily petty, beautiful with a reserved manner appeared, her dark curly silky hair flowing down to her shoulders. A retinue of servant girls also appeared close to her heels armed with trays filled with drinks of all kinds which they placed on a circular plastic table adding to the mountain of food already there.

"Thanks Emily, charming beautiful woman of my dreams."

She giggled pleased with the compliments.

"Sir you have been so kind to us especially to me. I consider it a privilege to serve as your bodyguard for the rest of my life."

His friends nodded vigorously in agreement.

The Defense Minister smiled.

"Drink boys!

He gulped down a large mouthful of beer slapped his stomach commenting on the coldness of the beer.

"loyalty, loyalty, loyalty to family, to friends, employers are all good qualities.

Drinks boys, Momoh, Saah, Gongbaye, Wureh, Saye!

"Ah sir!!! They responded in unison

"You guys with minds and brains could become generals, Chief of Staffs….. He left the rest of his words hanging.

"Not me sir I prefer serving as your bodyguard."

Moses Gabby rose from his chair as if stung by a bee.

"Now you guys can serve me in better ways in higher positions. A man must have ambition. Without ambition, a man is no better than animals. What makes us better than Chimps? It is not because we are more beautiful than those wretched creatures, it because man has ambition. If not we would still be sleeping in trees like Chimps since genetically, we are so similar to them. While the

Chimps were happy to remain frolicking in the forest we humans wanted a better to place to lay our heads so we build houses. Imagine what this country would be like if Maxwell and his friends did not kill President Roberts.

Patrick Momoh felt like urinating. His boss was talking strange. He wanted something stiff to clear his brain instead of the sour beer in his hand. He just kept quiet listening to his boss. Every time he wanted to speak his tongue became tied to the hoof of his mouth. His boss seemed to be eyeing him. He fidgeted under his gaze.

"what is the problem Patrick?

"No sir."

"Patrick I ask you what is the problem?

"Sir…

"Sir what?

Speak up these boys look up to you for leadership because you are the oldest, what is bothering you?

"Sir this beer is too sour, it makes me want to pee often I want something strong."

"Such as?

"Cane Juice of course Chief"

Moses Gabby laughed until his sides hurt. He put his hand in his right pocket bringing out a wad of notes.

"You should have told me that a long time ago Patrick. At one time I used to drink a lot of that accursed brew. Boys let us go out. I will show you I can still challenge you."

Moses Gabby rose from his chair throwing the wad of money in his hand to surprised bodyguards. The Defense Minister hurried indoor returning later with words of rebuke echoing outside from his wife's reprimand.

"You are going to disgrace yourself with your own bodyguards?"

The chief seemed not to mind. He called out to his boys hurrying downstairs. Again to the surprise of his men he slipped behind the wheel backing the jeep effortlessly out of the fenced compound towards the capital to a liquor joint he knew at the Freeport. A rough area overflowing with seedy hustlers who thronged the port in the day time retiring to this joint at night for liquor boasting.

The chief in plain clothes challenged his men to a wrestling match of drinking spree.

In the morning in spite of his binge drinking in the night, a calm collected Defense Minister sat behind his desk on Benson Street looking at his nation's strategic arms balance with its neighbors from a computer screen. From information gleaned and pieced together from a suspect it was about time the country prepared for external aggression.

President Maxwell Forkpa was a shrewd man. The best men, equipment, and salaries were reserved for his Presidential guards drawn mostly from his own ethnic group and fanatically loyal to him. The bulk of the army under the nominal command of the Defense Minister were less trained, less equipped, and less motivated. What he needed to do to take over the government was a quick assassination, a word of assurance to loyalist troops to bring the killers to justice when the President was dead for him to take over power. To compound his problems the President turned each of his confidantes into rivals each not hesitating to dump their closest colleagues for the purpose of advancing themselves into the government without the slightest qualm about their action.

Hence Moses Gabby had to rely on his bodyguards along with the supernatural powers of his juju man to seize state power.

The Minister worked at a feverish pace meeting the joint chiefs of staffs, the Ethiopian military attaché and then attending meeting with his boss. Six more days remained for him to secure his human victim for the sacrifice. Even as he plotted against his friend their personal relationship remained cordial.

In the evening Gongbay received a rare visit from his boss who did not sit down. He gave the young man some money, did not say anything and then left the modest dwelling of his bodyguard. The ambitious man drove back home counting the number of days on his fingers.

Again during the week Moses Gabby closeted himself with his five closest bodyguards in a gray official Mercedes heading to Robertsfield. This highway had excellent tarmac, there were no potholes here unlike most highways in the country allowing precious time for discussions.

Walls had ears so he could not discuss his subject matter in the security of his home. At least the nervous sleep starved Gabby was sure his car was bug free. In spite of his valiant effort a self control his hands trembled on the wheel of his luxury saloon car.

"Loyalty to your boss is an important commodity."

He mumbled his eyes fixed on the disappearing asphalt.

"Years ago as a little boy growing up in Grand Kru

on the Atlantic Coast I heard a strange sickness began to decimate the ranks of the inhabitants of my village according to legend.

Our ancestors needed the assistance of a wily old man to stop the plague. I like my village years ago is suffering from a strange disease which is eating me up. If I survive this disease, it will be well with all of us. If this disease kills me, all of you will come tumbling down like walls blasted with RPGs.

"Chief if there is anything I and my boys can do to help we are willing to do. We are willing to do anything."

The gloominess in the tone of the Defense Minister lifted a bit because of the statement of his chief bodyguard.

"Do you really mean it?

"Yes," Gongbay replied.

"Hmmmmm… I visited the doctor, he told me I am going to die. The only thing that can save my life is the blood of a young man."

Moses Gabby eased his foot on the accelerator stopping his speech in mid sentence waiting for a reaction. His men were silent, not a shred of emotion showed on their dark faces.

"Sir after a long silence one of them raised his voice.

"we want you to get well sir."

No one else spoke a word. The Defense Minister parked his car, urinated on the road and then turned his car around returning to the capital.

CHAPTER 29

———◆◆◆———

Darkness, black and mysterious possessed a certain mystical aura which endured despite the best efforts of mankind to wipe away her vile threatening tentacles, the mystique of blackness night time brought reigned supreme. Not even the most powerful beam could wipe away the evil foreboding which night time brought. In the struggle for power and prestige in this tiny West African nation nothing was depraved, no act too heinous in the pursuit of the intangible quantity called power. There was simply too much to gain. As Defense Minister Gabby possessed power yet intoxicating as a strong drink, the more power one possessed the more a person wanted and the deeper one was prepared to do or go to any length to maintain or increase that power. The seat of the Presidency beckoned with too many good things--------prestige, opulence, luxury, the hands of sensual beautiful women waiting like yam tendrils to be plucked at will by the one in power, national coffers laid to be plundered at will. Grandiose projects that beat one's imagination waiting to be transformed by the magic wand of power, first class hotel accommodations, private jets, designer clothes, bulging Swiss bank accounts, foreign real estate to be acquired in exotic locations and attention oh attention from everyone small and big, people with smiling faces and outstretched hands eager to do your biddings. Newspapers, radios, and TV cameras to watch you wash your face, there was simply too much at stake. At times on the lower level this quest for power degenerated into a childish contest of wills for those involved.

This night like all nights people visited, chatted and enjoyed themselves. Lovers strolled through wide boulevards and small street corners oblivious to the evil waiting to happen known only by a few men who succumbed to the machination of evil power hungry men.

Train tracks attracted people everywhere. Their neat straight lines offered the quickest routes between two points especially the towns and villages strewn along her path from the mining town of Bong Mines to the Freeport offering a pleasurable escape for people who wanted to breath fresh air.

The tracks also offered a place for a rite of passage to drunkards who needed space to exercise their ghost of intoxication on the cold rock strewn iron beams. Trains did not run on the narrow gauge tracks from Bong Mines to the port passing through sleepy Caldwell, a suburb of semi rural landscape comprising of scattered houses nestled among trees.

Stockton Creek separated the sparsely populated suburb Caldwell from the densely populated Logan Town. The swamp and river separating the two adjacent pieces of land could not have separated two communities so different. Caldwell Quiet, quintessential, Logan and Sayon Towns bursting, dynamic, vibrant and more depraved.

Five malicious men hid in a low bush above the Bong Mines Bridge spanning across the main Dualla Central Monrovia Highway along the industrial Free Zone still awaiting development. Vacant lots coupled and mounds of Iron pellets still awaiting shipment dwarfed the surrounding low bush. A young hustler who earned his living either performing casual labor or engaging in petty thievery and sometimes engaging in both activities to survive decided at the end of his day's work to stroll to his place of abode in Logan Town. Unknown to this hustler, his routine route has been observed and plans have been carefully hatch to arm bush him. He whistled walking with careless ease dreaming of curling on his foam mattress placed on the bare floor he shared with three other friends.

"There he comes" the leader of the gang whispered. Then it happened very swiftly without warning. A large object rammed into the whistling young man's neck sending a flash of blinding sensation through his body. He fell face down off the track into a ditch. His attackers were soon upon him. Gongbay put his knees into the hapless man's groin. Another man sat on his ankle holding him down to make sure he did not move his leg though for the moment the precaution was unnecessary because of the state of their victim. His eyes were closed.

"We cannot get what we want, he may even be dead. Williams you have killed him. Check his blood pressure."

The leader urged Patrick. Patrick initially felt the man's purse shaking his head in disappointment." Leave the man alone for breeze to revive him.

We have to hurry before someone sees us"

"Shut your mouth, the chief says the man must be alive and aware of what we are doing to him otherwise the medicine will not work."

"What kind of medicine requires human blood self?

"Shut your mouth before I am forced to shoot you chicken. Whatsoever we are doing here is a secret only known to ourselves. If you open your bloody mouth we will let the chief know. We will just kill you and throw you dirty body into a ditch!

The men waited impatient beside the body which seemed lifeless. Suddenly signs of life returned to him. He took in a deep breath.

"Good, he's not dead."

The leader of the gang remarked with relief unmistakable in his voice.

The unconscious man slowly came to. One thing that perplexed him was the heavy weight on top of him emptying his supply of oxygen and making breathing difficult.

"William come here and hold the man's head down and give me the knife."

The young man on the ground saw the vicious blade about to descend. He pushed with all the force in his body heaving the attacker kneeling in his groins into the air. His sudden action disoriented the fellow sitting on his ankle causing him to lose his balance. In seconds the injured victim sent a vicious kick into the private part of the man holding the knife causing him to yell in pain.

Keep him down press him!

More force descended on the hapless wounded man.

"Grab his mouth Patrick!

Gongbay tried to force his hand into the man's mouth to draw out his tongue while Momoh shoved his hand into the mouth of the captive. He grabbed the tongue, but the pain of teeth tearing into flesh caused him to yell in pain. In that instant the young man made a terrible mistake. He tried to cry for help. In this isolated place his cries rang, but no help came. The echoes of his own voice ricocheted against containers returning to mock him. His shouting exposed his tongue. Momoh's knife primed for the kill descended on target slicing off half of the tongue. The sadistic killers then placed the neck of the man on the train track; place a white bucket under him performing an act too vile to describe here.

"All of us must take time to cut" Gongbay ordered. Blood poured into the white bucket. The severed head of the victim was placed on the train track inside the two iron beam to make it appeared the man was run over by a moving train.

"Guys let us get out of here fast!

In a Sinkor suburb whose street shall be nameless because people are still too sensitive for such a heinous act to be associated with their street, a medicine man; a servant of the devil performed a bizarre ritual. In his hand was a wooden carving of a human figure which he dipped repeatedly into the bucket of blood offering incantations while the Defense Minister danced naked.

Lying beside his wife in another part of town Maxwell Forkpa was turning and twisting fighting in his sleep crying out loud. His frightened wife tried to wake him from sleep but to no avail.

Lions were approaching his throne, the President was calling out to his own Lions to come to his aid and there was a fierce battle being fought between the two prides of Lions. One of the enemy Lions struck him on the throne drawing blood from his leg. In the real world blood oozed onto his bed. The President was fighting for his life.

The medicine man was confused by the mixed signal he was receiving. Had he pushed his luck too far?

The new Director of Military Intelligence for some unknown reasons rushed from sleep to the home of his boss at such unholy hour. Earlier he had seen his boss Moses Gabby ride with his bodyguards on the Robertsfield Highway.

There were some men who had unlimited access to the head of state one of whom was Daniel Kollie so even at such hour he drove out of his house heading to the seat of the Presidency.

Monrovia awoke to the horrific news of a ritualistic murder because of a mechanical problem the train scheduled to take the iron pellets from Bong Mines that morning developed. Casual workers frequented the rail in their bid to sneak into the port avoiding the main gate to gain access to the pier. It was one of these itinerant hustlers who discover the macabre remains of the murdered man. Soon the news griped the entire city. Police men, curious onlookers, press people soon invaded the scene. The murdered man had strong blood in more ways than his killers imagined. The train from Bong Mines being delayed was unusual. ritualistic killing in this society where secret societies abounded thrived because of many factors. Inept policing, lack of investigative equipment, lack of trained legal prosecutors and the involvement of higher ups made many such murders go unsolved.

Patrick of one of Gabby's bodyguards was not a killer or warrior by nature. A shy gentle boy growing up he hated violence. The sight of blood nauseated him. Even as a child he was always the first to run to his mother at the slightest sign of danger. Years later as a teenager he avoided fights by being friendly with the school bullies. Anytime his friends in class wanted to perform some mischief on the teacher they waited when he was out because he would be among the first to advice against it. It was a trick fate paid on him for such a boy of gentle nature to fall into the lap of the army. Urban joblessness and ingrained fear of hard physical labor were the culprits that threw him into the bosom of the army which at the time was the haven for the have-nots in society. His meticulous ways and desire for the easier part of military life made him want to be bodyguards to the powerful. As a bodyguard, one earned extra pocket money from the generosity of the boss. The bodyguard also had access to free food and spend a lot of time riding some of the best cars in the country with the boss. In return for these things, he repaid with an unquestionable loyalty to his boss. Now seduced by this life and forced to commit murder in one of the most gruesome manners possible his mind had turned into a demon of torture for him. The blood and scream of the dying man was with him everywhere. Even in his sleep he could not find any respite from his torturers waking up with a start sweating and searching for his gun. Fed up with his erratic behavior and his failure to explain to his wife what was happening to him despite repeated attempts by her to find out his wife left their matrimonial home going to her mother's place with their three children.

Now Sergeant Patrick as he was commonly wanted to confide his pain to someone. But the threat of Gongbay hanged over his head. He loved his wife and children too much to want them kill just because he wanted to ease his own internal pains. If he confided to his wife women with their love of talk, she could confide to another person. Having seen the capabilities of his friends he knew the threats from them were no joke. The stress he was undergoing was making him go crazy. His head ached endlessly like someone was beating something inside. To ease his pain, he took to the bottle something which angered Gongbay. This morning Gongbay issued him the latest warning telling him not to open his mouth wide in any drunken blabber.

A troubled man is not difficult to spot provided an observer take just a little bit of more than passing interest in someone.

Daniel Kollie, a shrew observer watching things from afar put two and two together. The death on the Bong Mines Bridge, the frenetic pace of the Defense Minister, the drive along the Robertsfield Highway, the erratic behavior of Sergeant Patrick. Something must be going on wrong. But the man was always in the company of the other bodyguards of the Defense Minister who seemed to be shepherding him.

Not being on duty, anxious to drown his mental anguish in liquor Patrick hired a taxi from the Defense Ministry building to Dry Rice Market. There was a new drinking spot across the road from the market itself. The owners capitalized on the availability of empty shipping containers to put one huge one down covered it with Zinc and plastered the front placing chairs and table for boozers to recline. Two large speakers were placed on both sides. Even though, the Diamond Spot was located along the road it was in an isolated suburb far away from the eyes of the rich and powerful. Daniel Kollie watching Patrick hired another taxi informing the driver to tail Patrick's taxi at a slow discreet pace. Patrick disembarked from his vehicle taking a seat in a corner away from the center of the spot. Women were preparing fish to roast with plenty of pepper on open fire iron tripods known locally as coal pot. It was still early evening. The place was only half filled. An overdressed teenage girl and a fat patron occupied a table in the middle of the Diamond talking and giggling. A man with dark shades on even in the fading light of the night slowly sipped his beer.

Patrick requested a big bottle of Club Beer. Daniel Kollie ordered his taxi to head for Barnersville Estate upon arrival at the Diamond. If he got down from the vehicle right away Patrick could be suspicious. Their meeting must appear like a chance encounter so he drove to a low cost estate to drop by an old friend in area B.

Patrick wished for inner peace. He wished he could confide in somebody. He wished he was somewhere far away from his mind and troubles. But how can one run away from one's mind? The murdered man's severed head screamed at him for the umpteenth time. The loud music soothed him a little but what he wanted most was somebody to talk to. Could he just turn to one of the customers and say oh man I participated in the gruesome killing of another human being for ritualistic purpose?

His thoughts were intruded upon by the presence of Daniel Kollie. "Excuse me. The last person I expected to see here is you Patrick."

"Why isn't this a public entertainment center? Patrick asked surprise.

"Of course it is, but I mean this place is so quiet and away from such places like Musu's spot."

"I like the quietness, the ability to drink in peace without prostitutes propositioning you." Patrick was grateful for the company.

"I discovered this place a while ago and whenever I can make it I do come here to relax. But strange I haven't met you here before."

"Perhaps we just choose different days to come here for a couple of drinks. Myself I am not a heavy drinker because alcohol is quick to put a deep hole on one's pocket. But whenever I am stressed out or I am being troubled by something on my mind I always appreciate a couple of drinks to ease the tension."

"Me too Daniel sometimes the long irregular hours of work get me stress out."

Patrick called the waitress over. The shining wig covering her natural head was tied at the center of her head into a bum. She wore a revealing blouse over a large jeans skirt.

"Two more bottles of beer and you can keep the change."

Daniel ordered in a boisterous mood waving aside William's attempt to pay the waitress.

The two men sat in silence drinking. It was Daniel who broke the silence.

"I once had a girlfriend whom I once loved. She was my childhood girlfriend. In fact we were neighbors growing up together on Totota. Our parents were friends and we attended the same school. Even in those early days as children we kept our lunch to eat together. People thought the older we grew our childhood fantasy of being husband and wife would dissipate with the passage of time. Time however, made our relationship grow stronger together until we both moved to Monrovia. Like most young couples in love we were both penniless. She stayed with her aunt in Sinkor attending a commercial school while I lived across the bridge in Duala doing odd jobs to raise money for college. I was completely faithful to her and she to me or so I thought until I caught her with a rich married man right handed. I wanted to kill myself. Deep depression came over me. Life had no meaning for me. To compound my sorrow my dearly beloved accused me of being sneaking dog who got what was good for him. My life was meaningless to me. I only existed and was not living. It was only with compulsion that I performed the slightest necessities of life like eating or bathing. I was slowly wasting away until a chanced encountered with a friend lifted me out of my dungeon of despair. A friend in need is a friend indeed."

"That is so true."

Patrick affirmed.

His tongue was already loosened by alcohol but he could not trust the man sitting beside him.

"And who was that friend?

"The lady whom I intend to marry next week in gratitude to her for my life is that friend. And where is your wife?"

"This is not the sort of place you bring your wife."

There was a queer silence each man concentrated on his drink.

"Mine wife is the opposite of your girl whom you wish to marry. The slightest problem I face she has run away from me and go to her mother."

"What kind of woman is that my friend?

"She says I talk fearful things in my sleep."

Daniel laughed out loud. The atmosphere in the Diamond was becoming rowdier more people returning from the city crowded into the bar. No one paid any particular attention to a stranger under the music and noise.

"Was she afraid of your dreams?

"My brother strange things can happen in this world."

Daniel Kollie became all ears his voyeuristic instinct alert. He carried a portable mini tape recorder.

"You know I cannot sleep. I just have this recurring dream of this man screaming and pleading being butchered by a group of man along the Buchanan Train track. His blood being emptied into a bucket. My God this dream is terrible. This is the dream I keep seeing and it is because of this dream my wife has run away."

Daniel took a large gulp of drinks. Patrick took a giant gulp of this also at least glad he had narrated his dream to another human being.

"You mean your wife left you because of a mere dream? Daniel asked laughing.

"You can't be serious. A mere dream and somebody run away from their marital home? She must be nuts."

Patrick did not like his wife being branded that way so he wanted to defend her.

"No actually it was more than a dream. You see the chief have this incurable disease which he said can only be cured by human blood."

Daniel wanted to ask which chief? But he held his peace. "The only disease I know is incurable is HIV. In fact it is gotten from the blood."

"That was the thing that puzzled me. The Defense Minister is fit as a fiddle yet he claimed he is sick and he needs human blood to make him well. Imagine the scream of that young man."

"Which young man?"

"Surely the President would not have appointed you to your position if you were that naïve. Everybody in Liberia knows the story. Haven't you heard about the man killed on the Bong Mines Bridge?"

"I have heard of that of course, but it has no connection to you because you are a decent law abiding officer. In fact we tell other officers to follow your exemplary example."

"I am that way that is why I told Gongbay and the others to leave me out in the first place. But Moses Gabby could not let us rest."

Daniel Kollie coughed loudly and excused himself to go and urinate. Patrick was by now quite anxious to talk. The delay of his friend in returning to their table made a slight feeling of uneasiness penetrate his alcohol infested brain.

His anxiety was eased short while later when Daniel returned ordering more beer.

"Daniel I think I have had enough and I think I have to return to that damn house again with this ugly dream."

"But why? The night is just beginning. I do not have a car to take me home just like you."

"Never mind I' ll give you a lift in my car."

"No, at least the liquor you bought is enough for me."

Patrick tried to rise, but he wobbled to his feet. Daniel's eyes were clear. While Patrick consumed the alcohol, he was actually pouring most of his beneath the table in the dull hazy light of the club. He helped steered the drunken man to his car. Four Police vans with armed officers leaping out appeared on the scene.

The President himself still dazed and pained from the gaping wound inflicted in his thigh in his own bed sat at his desk at the mansion waiting for Patrick while soldiers and armored cars were already heading to Clay Ashland. Blood oozed from the President's nose intermittently.

Another batch of security agents in Police cars with siren blaring headed to the Sinkor Suburb. Two of the government's spin doctors were preparing for a shock announcement with patriotic songs rocking the airwaves. The now savvy populace people sensed something was amiss. By now the populace was developing a stoic attitude. But even in this atmosphere inane to crisis, the announcement on the radio made people shake their heads in utter amazement. People could not believe their ears hearing the announcement that the Defense Minister Moses Gabby was arrested for plotting a coup. The President and Moses Gabby were not only the closest of collaborators but also the best of friends.

Skeptic contended the government was at war with itself again. A government filled with paranoia eating itself up. Daniel Kollie, the new Defense Minister was expecting such a reaction. He wasted no time putting Patrick and the other self-confessed murderers along with

Sekou Yonneh's taped confession. The pidgin voice of the medicine man was unmistakable."De time Minista Moses Gabby asky me to makeir medicine for him. Me I de tell him Gabby you egg, Maxwell da rock, you fall on him you bustit, if him fall on you, you crack. De man jam me, him swear say I mon make medicine for him. So I ask him to bring white chicken.

"What kind of white chicken you ask for old man?

Da dey human being blood we can call white chicken. Ah na know de man who die for train track me ah only want de white chicken I na care where it come from," the medicine man replied.

All of those confessing on radio were persons very close to the Defense Minister. To have all these men who had stayed so long with the Defense Minister with so much guilt in their voice their story remarkably similar being told in such natural voices when they were no actors was a tall order. The most damaging evidence came from the sorcerer who admitted he asked for and received human sacrifice. Even in the midst of these truths the President still played his ace when Patrick accused General Samuel Dahn and Prof Martins of being one of their backers. This statement virtually destroyed the Professor's political ambition. In the new constitution approved in a referendum, anyone with a criminal record could not contest in any election. A young nephew of the Prof. upon hearing before hand of this ace hurried to the home of his uncle. The new Defense Minister was waiting for just this, it played well into his plans.

Within minutes Moses Gabby became a jailbird.

For Samuel Dahn watching from afar it confirmed his belief that only violent means could remove his archrival from the presidency. There was no coup attempt against the President. He was simply at his game again and only he could bring liberation to the Liberian people and redeem his own image.

CHAPTER 30

A woman of privilege endowed with incredible beauty Emily learnt from an early age the impact her beauty had on men. When she became older she learnt to exploit this beauty to her advantage. Few men could resist doing a favor for a pretty woman with smiles. Her husband locked behind bars she remembered on the few occasions she met the President the impact she had on him. For this reason she avoided social gatherings where he was present as much as possible. With her husband in prison she risked coming out of her social isolation from the President to come and meet him excitement The men outside waiting for could not be kept waiting longer. A mixture of trepidation and expectation filled Emily waiting to meet the President whom the life of her husband depended on.

"I have been waiting for you for a very long time. Don't you know it is an offence for a visitor to keep the President of Liberia waiting for so long? Talk about the privilege of being a woman. Here you have one."

President Forkpa rose from his chair sauntering across to the woman entering his cozy lair. A broad charming smile spread across his face enveloped his entire body. He extended his right hand. A visibly nervous woman extended her small hand to meet his wide palm. The President rubbed her fingers a little too long than necessary. He ushered her away from the larger office into his private semi-detached office equipped with heavily cushioned chairs, the latest stereo and video sets. A small well stocked refrigerator amply stocked with liquor, fruits, can food, juices stood ostensibly in corner on the right side of the door. A large cushion chair which could easily be transformed into a bed just by loosening some screws stood adjacent to the refrigerator. Flowers pleasant but not lavish dotted the four corners placed on golden stands. The two bodyguards guarding the entrance snapped to attention as the President and his visitor entered.

"Guys don't you have manners? This woman Mrs. Gabby has come to discuss her husband's welfare and you want to stay and listen?

"Mr. President I do not mind having them around."

Emily words came too late; the two aides were already out closing the thick wood paneled door behind them. Emily surveyed the room and felt ill at ease. "Please sit down."

The President motioned to an empty sofa. His guest obliged. She mopped her face with a white handkerchief.

"I thought you really wanted to see me."

President Forkpa asked sensing her discomfort. He opened the fridge and brought a chilled bottle of coke which Mrs. Gabby accepted with a dimple smile. Maxwell smiled back. He relished the role of playing charming host to beautiful women. The woman sitting before him belonged truly to such a category.. Her silky long hair captured his imagination. President Forkpa knew she had a careful plea of mercy for him so he decided to throw her off balance. Contented he sat beside her and poured himself full blooded wine on the opposite side of the sofa. "You are holding on quite well under the strain."

"It's been a hell of a time with a sentence of death hanging over my husband's head for a crime he did not commit. I swear.....

President Forkpa interrupted laughing low. Emily in surprised stopped to look at the President. In between bursts of laughter he spoke in a halting manner "Stop the charade....You and I know he was planning a coup.

"But Mr. President you and I know he was so loyal to you.. I mean huh."

The President threw her a fierce glance which silenced her.

"Mrs. Gabby did you come here to plead your husband's innocence or to plea for mercy? I could have thrown into jail for co- plotting with him. You cannot tell me you did not notice the strange morning hours and meetings? Of course you and him are very close. He might have told you some of his plans which included making you First Lady."

Maxwell paused and took a sip from his glass. Emily in her well tailored African Lappa suit took a sip too from her glass.

"Mr. President, please have mercy on my husband. I do not want him to die neither do I want to become a widow for my children to grow up without a father."

Tears streamed down her face. She attempted to knee. Sensing her intention the President stopped her.

"Please don't, please get up."

The President helped her back to the sofa.

"Mr. President, please have mercy on your friend especially for the sake of the children and me. We women want all of the good things in life. But you men do not realize that the things we desire most is the love of a good husband and a place for our children to grow in peace. How we women craved for tranquility and the gentler things of life, but you men always want to do something to prove to us that you are somebody. In so doing you mostly bring trouble and sadness to those of us who love you. I am prepared to do anything Mr. President anything to save the life of my husband."

Emily pleaded looking extremely vulnerable under the smooth glow of the light. Maxwell smiled and put on a soft R&B tone on the large stereo in the room.

"Sir I want you to please accept my pleas so I can leave before I take too much of your time."

Color drained from the President's face. When he spoke he did so in a dismissive tone.

"Okay I see you anytime my schedule permits. There lies the door. Emily I thought you were sincere about Gabby otherwise you would have waited for a response to your plead instead of hurrying me."

"Sorry Mr. President it is the music which is making me uncomfortable. It is just too seductive."

She remarked in a matter of fact tone.

"I am sorry."

Maxwell apologized switching the remote controlled tape. An eerie silenced prevailed for a minute before the President resumed the conversation.

"I like the part you said you are prepared to do anything."

"I am sorry sir ."

"Do not mind. I too am sorry for the music, for the seductive surrounding. People call me Mr. President, but at heart I am still a country boy. I do not know how to woo a woman or act sophisticated. In the country where I spent some time growing up when a man wants a woman he simply walks to her house and boldly declares his intention without rose, wine, music or gifts.

What you ask me is a difficult thing to do. If I spare your husband it will send a bad signal to other men serving under me. If I show one sign of weakness nobody in this country will be safe. The death penalty is used as a deterrent to would be coupmakers; however, for the sake of such a beautiful woman like you I can bend the rule a little. I find you an attractive woman; forget the prestige of my office. I can fall to my knees to ask for your love."

Emily sat dazed and stunned by Maxwell Forkpa's words. She appeared to be in a stupor. Maxwell edged closer to her on the sofa and put his arms around her. She did not resist, but Maxwell felt her body stiffen. He whispered soft nothings into her ears, his breath heavy with desire. His hands moved on her body to her breast, his demanding hand prodding. Emily continued starring at the floor for a long time.

"Get away from me Maxwell Forkpa! Maxwell Forkpa obliged without a word and stood on his feet.

"I thought you and Gabby were friends. I never knew you were an opportunistic pig trying to steal your friend's woman when he is in trouble. So this was what all this was meant to be eh?

A knock sounded on the door. The President screamed at the intruder to get away.

"I am never going to do such a thing while Gabby remains alive." Emily bellowed in righteous indignation. She pouted and rose to go. Throughout her outburst Maxwell remained calm. As she stood to go the President smiled before speaking.

"If your husband was truly my friend he never would have gone to a medicine man to have me kill. Look," he pointed to his neck. "This neck of mine was almost choked to death through your husband and his medicine man's handiwork. It will interest you to know that Yonneh is already dead. If it wasn't for you and you pretty neck your husband would have long gone that same road. The evidence against you and your husband is clear. And still you come to plead innocence and insult me in my office because I made a simple request to you which will benefit you and your family? In a couple of days the verdict against your husband will be announced. So sad you not have done all that is within your power to save him."

Indignant Emily strolled out of the office of the President. The President closed his inner office door unperturbed by Mrs. Gabby's outburst. President Forkpa glanced through the day's newspapers' headlines. Most of the newspaper headlines concerned this Minister and deputy at loggerheads and so on. But the headlines printed in bold letters on the front page of the Daily Observer piqued him. The banner headline announced "Emory Lomax becomes Vice Standard Bearer for PDP did not bother him. Instead it was the smaller print beneath the headlines which pricked him. Bribery and intimidation involved.

In the story there was the usual according to reliable sources- agreement sealed at a Cape mount Hotel.

"Morris get all of my security men, the Defense Minister, the Police Director, the SSS Director along with the Commanding General along with his deputy.

And you get the editor of the Daily Observer now! Go personally to his office and get him here now." The President snapped at his under work Press Secretary. The hitherto subdued office became filled in that instant with a flurry of activities. Judging by the tone of his voice the President wanted immediate action. Coupled with the disturbing story a source had earlier informed the President of plans to hold a major opposition rally in the city.

CHAPTER 31

In the morning, the dreaded news hit her with the force of a lightning bolt. Though she expected this; she somehow wished the someway somehow something occurred to change the verdict. Now her thin hope hanging on the thread of good fortune evaporated. The voice on the radio was unequivocally clear.

"Former Defense Minister Moses Gabby have been found guilty on the charge of treason and have been sentenced to death by firing squad."

The news reader moved on to another news clip as if her husband's life was another news item to be read and discarded. Emily hurried to the bathroom and took a quick bath. She breeze through to her room applying as little makeup as possible, painting her eyelashes. She sprayed sexy smelling cologne over her body. Very soon her house would be filled with family and friends coming to sympathize and express their condolences. The madam of the house issued terse instructions and got into her car. She refused the assistance of her chauffeur driving her silver BMW out of the fence onto the main road straight down to the Freeport, Johnson Street down to the Bye to the Mansion yard. At the Unknown Soldier monument, crack Israeli trained Presidential Guards flagged down her vehicle.

"Madam what is your name? a young soldier no doubt a recent recruit since he did not know the wife of the former Defense Minister asked.

"Chief you do not know the old Defense Minister's wife?"

"So where are you going? I hope you do have some grenades in your clothes?"

The young soldier asked laughing.

"No, please officer. I am a civilian I know nothing of guns and grenades."

Emily pleaded gripping the wheel of her car tighter in panic.

"Madam private cars are not allowed beyond this point."

"I am going to see the President."

"Do you have an appointment card?

"No, he said I can come anytime to see him."

"But madam you must have an appointment card or letter before we allow you to cross our checkpoint knowing your husband is a coup plotter."

"Please I must see President Forkpa urgently, I must."

There was a mixture of panic and determination in her voice. She grabbed the young soldier who appeared to be the commander's hand. He stood rooted torn between his desire to help a distraught woman and his dedication to duty.

"Please officer."

The soldier pulled out a gadget yellow and black hand held gadget from his belt charging all over her body with the device. Other soldiers joined in the search thoroughly examining the car. The officer moved away discussing on a radio. After a short while he returned.

"The President is busy in a meeting right now. Go come back later I will allow you in."

"Please allow me in I can wait for President Forkpa."

"Alright if you insist."

The Roadblock was lifted. Emily drove through zigzagging through other roadblocks on the main thoroughfare in front of the Presidential Palace. Her vehicle was again thoroughly searched at the main entrance before being allowed into the fence.

A subdued Emily walked onto the first floor alone unsure of herself.

President Maxwell Forkpa watched her unsure footsteps and laughed softly with the contentment of a victor's laugh; later he would dispatch an aide to fetch her.

Locked in an artificial meeting the President was actually watching an action movie joking with his aides.

President Forkpa was in a jovial mood, those around him sensed it. In the past before men occupied the high office of the Presidency, they were groomed by the system and robbed of their spontaneous vitality and mostly advanced in age. By then these previous Presidents were steeped in western traditions to the extent they were actually white men in black men skin. Maxwell Forkpa's ascendancy threw all this aside. He was the spoiler of system with a penchant for ruthlessness and unpredictability.

Emily fidgeted in her chair staring at her watch just as she has done for the past hour regretting her sudden decision to come to the Mansion. She toyed with the many gold rings lining her fingers asking God to help her. Her fabled physical beauty remained timeless.

"Is the President still in a meeting?"

She inquired for the tenth time.

"Can I get you a coke?

"No thanks Minister Morris," she smiled at the Assistant Minister for Public Affairs.

"But you need something maybe a grape juice?

The Minister persisted.

"I am fine."

In response to the questioning look on his face, she decided to accept a little of his hospitality though she was in no mood for such. The Minister was in a way expressing his sympathy for her pain though he dare not say so openly. The man had seen the hurried greetings and strides of previous friends feeling awkward, unsure of their reaction at her presence here knowing her husband was a condemned man. The fly that sticks on a body gets bury along with it according to an old Gio proverb. So people avoided her until the minister sensing her predicament brought her in his secretary's office.

"Please give me a glass of water."

"Water and biscuits?

"Just water"

A chilling glass of water in her hands the Minister

rushed to see the President whose attention was still glued to his TV.

"Let her keep waiting."

He replied to Minister Morris inquiry without lifting his head from the set.

Two hours later the President was ready to meet Emily. This time the setting of their meeting was formal. There were chairs and lights. No refrigerator, no soft music humming in the background. High sofas, austere ornamental chairs, leather desk greeted Emily as she was ushered into the President's presence. The President looked formal in his business suit his hair combed neatly not one out of place. Papers were sprawled across his desk which commanded the Lion share of his attention. He acknowledged Emily's presence with a slight nodding of the head still riveting his gaze on the papers before him giving the impression of a man who took his responsibilities serious. All of the aides in the room exited leaving them alone. Emily waited for the President to say something, instead silenced prevailed in the room. She temporarily lost her voice folding her hands in her lap losing the courage to speak.

"Sir I have come."

She began in small tentative voice expecting the President to interrupt her. The President remained focused on the papers lying on his desk.

"I have been wanting to see my husband for sometimes now, but the soldiers would not let me. I have come to see you. Thank you for allowing time in your busy schedule to see me at such short notice. Your men are very thorough but polite."

Emily rumbled on receiving only stiff silence from the President. She wished she could say more, short of words she finally blurted out.

"You are such a charming man. I have come bringing myself to you for your pleasure. Please release my husband. Save his life I beg you!

For the first time the President lifted his head up from his papers.

"Look at these papers."

He gestured to Emily, who rose from her chair receiving the white paper smeared with black ink from the President. Her eyes skimmed over the paper only two words stuck to her mind death and Gabby.

"That is your husband's death warrant. I am pondering over whether or not to sign it. Such a fine treacherous man was your husband."

Emily lost all sense of control. She burst into tears begging the President who sat mute watching her.

After a while he spoke.

"Please Emily this is my office. What will people say if they come and see a grown woman crying in my office? Please calm down."

"Please spare his life."

She countered.

The President smiled.

"Last time you were so rude. Your request cannot be discussed in this office. Go home, I will come to see you tonight at 8'oclock so we can discuss as responsible adults."

"You mean you will not sign the death warrant?

"Please Emily tonight we shall discuss. I am busy and God knows I have given you sufficient time to plead your case."

The President picked Emily's arm escorting her to the door.

In the afternoon hours the President went to see the mother of a shoe shine boy he encountered. It pleased President Maxwell Forkpa to assist one of the poor nameless ones in society. The smile on the face of the young mother upon receiving the considerable amount of $1000.00 was ample reward to the President. Gladdened by the deep gratitude expressed by the single young mother and the beaming children; the President himself personally escorted brother and sister to buy their books, shoes, uniforms, and shoes on Camp Johnson Road.

By evening hours flushed from the feel good effect of his benevolence, President Forkpa convened a meeting with Adonis Vonleh, Ebie, and Kum some of the upcoming party militants to discuss politics. Of course this meeting was secondary. The President relied heavily on his military colleagues and to a lesser extent on the elders of his native village outside Voinjama for advice. In this Presidential year the President worked at feverish pace filling his Swiss bank account to ensure none of his descendants would ever again endure the malaise of poverty, appointing his relatives to some of the best money generating autonomous agencies. Cabinet Ministers were more politically glaring so he did not want to appoint his family members to that level.

True to his campaign promise in Kakata the President

signed agreement for the pavement of road links in the capital Bushrod Island, Gardnersville, Congo Town etc. These new roads were to traverse the swamp separating Gardnersville from Congo Town and the Capital Bye Pass. He mandated the Finance and Public Works Ministries to tarmac the streets of his village, build his dream Presidential Palace with the utmost urgency. Clara Town, Slipway soon received tarmac roads in the Presidential bliss of development. The President was out in the field in Jeans and sneakers to ensure the work was done quickly. In this form he resembled any young man in the prime of his life full of vital energy.

However, the Daily Observer and her editor continued to throw poison darts at the efforts of the President to reform his image with one negative story after the other.

"I wish someone would solve the problem of that newspaper and her editor for me!

An exasperated President screamed in the hearing of his ruthless security operatives.

CHAPTER 32

The Editor of the Daily Observer, a fearless Journalist reputed to be a frequent thorn in the side of the Liberian Government was in a joyous mood but his joy was tinged by a bit mysterious apprehension this morning. He knew full well his story would provoke a reaction from the authorities, perhaps the customary summons from the Information Minister or from the President. Journalism as a profession was meant to comfort the afflicted and afflict the comfortable.

His latest story did not bother him unduly preparing as it was for what promised to be an eventful trip into the interior where he rarely ventured. Not out of disinterest he did not visit the countryside. In the country's over centralized administration concentrated in Monrovia, a legacy of the Tubman years all things news and politics occurred in Monrovia. Publishing a small newspaper with a small staff where he played a role in everything from reporting, to editing, typesetting, solicitation of adverts and proofreading did not give him, chance to leave the city and venture into the countryside often.

Today though the situation was so different, of all things his first cousin was getting married to the doyen of Liberian womanhood one of those fabulous Lofa women in the town of Zorzor, north of Gbarnga. Preparations have been going on for months for the wedding between the coastal boy and the interior woman. Marriage in those parts was not merely a union between a man and a woman. It was a union between two families, clans and communities.

Up north, the venue for the occasion was decorated with cut plantains tree, palm fronds and flowers. Live stocks for the occasion bleat behind the house in dusty Zorzor. Cousin Korlubah insisted that Kenneth attend the occasion at all cost making incessant calls over the erratic phone lines urging his favorite Cousin to attend.

Kenneth gave his word and he was determined to keep it. His wife Madea, her sister Lydia, his other cousin from the mother side Harris doubling as valet and bodyguard were all set for the trip. Laughter coupled with excitement bubbled in the household which did not have one in the recent past. Madea wanted for her and Kenneth to return to North Carolina until after the election. Trained as a Journalist to tell the story Kenneth was determined to tell the remarkable story of the country's transition from a military to democratic civilian rule. Madea worried about Kenneth's safety because of his uncompromising stand on journalistic principles of objectivity and truth when other Journalists were engaging in pocket book journalism ie singing the praises of the high and mighty ignoring the plight of the poor and oppressed while they enriched themselves.

For the first time to appease his wife's incessant plead Kenneth consented to look into his wife's request for him to take a brief vacation in the states. Leaving Liberia permanently for now was out of the question he told Madea. Madea was more than pleased with the response. It was her hope once she got her husband into America to get him to stay through peer pressure, plead, tears and blackmail whatever. All that was forgotten now in the throes of preparation for the trip into Zorzor. She joined them in the Nissan Patrol with the tainted glasses. Even for the brief trip Madea's clothes, gifts and cosmetics filled the heavy suitcase being placed at the back of the battered old Peugeot 504 to the brim by Harris.

When the car started Madea remembered she forgot something in the house. It took her another ten minutes to find what she forgot.

Finally Madea came giving a final warning to their houseboy not to venture out during their absence.

Kenneth sitting at the steering drove at a leisurely speed from Congo Town to Paynesville along the single lane highway moving along with the relatively light traffic. He played his car radio low to participate in the easy conversation flowing so rapidly. Petty sellers, hustlers, and hawkers taking over the sidewalks forced pedestrians to walk along the main road at various junctions from ELWA Junction through Duport Road and Police Academy junctions. Kenneth meandered his vehicle through the overcrowded Paynesville parking station on to the outskirts of the city along the road through Coca Cola Factory down to the urban sprawl dotted with makeshift gasoline stations springing all along the highway to serve the growing number of motorist plying one of the main highways into the interior.

Kenneth slowed down drawing to stop to fill his car tank. Cousin Zazzay advised him to do just that since gas was more expensive and not readily available in the interior.

The Rubber Plantations and smallholder Rubber Farms surrounding the capital hugged the very outskirts of the city. Soon they were driving through the thick sea of green trees that sprouted everywhere, but in this case they did not just sprout but were planted by the largest Plantation owner of the world. The road was good yet very circular and it called for careful driving. Kenneth drove at the moderate speed of between 60 to 75 km per hour chasing Kakata. He did not have problem with the numerous checkpoints dotted along the outskirts of every major town a legacy of the military rulers. However, the corrupt Police officers and the plethora of security personnel called joint security manning the checkpoints did not bother much with private cars which sometimes meant trouble. A security agent could inadvertently cause an offense to a senior government official whom may not have known. To avoid this mistake, private cars were usually left alone for the rewards of commercial vehicles from whom these security agents extorted small bribes from the drivers and occasionally from foreigners traveling on those vehicles.

Kenneth's departure unknown to him was being watched by a group of men led by Daniel Kollie. The security chief and his men in a jeep watched him take gas and head for the highway sure now he was leaving the capital away from the prying eyes of the world tailed his vehicle. None of the four or so men in the vehicle wore uniforms which could make them conspicuous instead they wore respectable civilian clothes. The driver did not bother to keep the vehicle he was tailing within sight. The security agents laughed and joke. From Wealla Plantation they increased their speed to catch up with Kenneth's vehicle. As they planned sure enough the team caught up with Kenneth at the Salala gate which was one of those special anti rebel gates built. They did not exchange pleasantries with the agents manning the checkpoints because they did not want too much familiarization or recognition. With emergency lights flashing they passed through the checkpoint without stopping. Sure enough Kenneth's vehicle was getting back on the main road.

Daniel and his men drove at high speed to Malaika, rested for some time and drove straight to Gbarnga to the main Police Station located just at the intersection of the Gbarnga Monrovia highway and the Lofa Road which was a dusty untarred one. Taking charge of the station Daniel called the commanderfor a quick brief.

The briefing did not end when Kenneth's vehicle edged into view. However, instead of turning left the vehicle drove straight into Gbarnga city center causing Daniel to almost panic.

"This is a special operation. You have to arrest this man."

He showed Kenneth's picture to the slim light skinned

middle aged man with a bushy moustache who was the Police commander. Varney was a career Police officer with more than 20 years of service to the government.

"Arrest him on what charge sir?"

"Are you asking me on what charge? I have not time for stupid questions. You are the Policeman. You are the one to arrest him and charge him."

"A h sir there is the small matter of a judge order. I need to see a judge a for an arrest warrant"

"Are you crazy?

An angry Danny asked.

"You do not understand eh? This is a special operation. You are to do what you are told without asking stupid questions if this bushy moustache of yours must remain in place without it being cleaned by a knife. Arrest the guy on a charge right now. I would not have asked you to get involve but for the fact the man is headed on the Nimba Highway and not to Lofa as thought. Your job is to arrest and leave the rest to us. You understand?

Varney nodded his head. He knew the Defense Minister was not someone to trifle with if you wanted to survive in Liberia. Soon he was barking orders to his officers.

Kenneth just could not understand his wife's insatiable desire for procrastination. Suddenly she remembered she need to buy some gifts for the bride in Gbarnga. Passing the post office the car turned right to Gbarnga Broad Street. Kenneth held his anger in check and chose to remain in the vehicle for his wife and her sister to do their last minute shopping. His presence in the vehicle was an impetus for Madea to hurry up and come for them to resume their journey surmising that if he went with her she could find means of prolonging the shopping. "Harris you go with them to help tote whatsoever they want to buy."

The Police van chasing them drove straight through the city mistakenly thinking the editor vehicle has taken the eastward route. Policemen at the VP Gate told them that a Peugeot 504 did not use that route. They turned back driving at high speed to the city center. Sure enough they spotted the vehicle they wanted parking near the Mosque. Madea was coming out of a store with assorted items in her hands. Harris walked ahead with a bundle on his head. Lydia was collecting their change from the sour face Lebanese trader behind the counter.

Madea threw her luggage into the trunk. Harris locked the trunk taking his seat at the back.

"Darling I hope I did not stay too long to make you angry. Why are you so anxious for this trip like you are the one being married? Do not tell me I have a new rival in my sister in law." She kissed Kenneth on the check and then hopped to her seat fastening the seat belt. In spite of his anger Kenneth smiled. Just then two brutish looking officers with big bodies and small heads appeared on both sides of the vehicle.

"Kenneth Laye you are under arrest," the older of the two who looked like a man in his thirties announced.

"On what charge? This must be some joke."

"Come with us right now to the Police Station then you will be informed."

The man said in very accented nasal English. Four more Police Officers appeared on the scene along with two other plainclothes agents. Before Kenneth knew it he and his wife were wedged between two officers who commandeered his car with one driving. The two plain clothes officers sat at the back hemming Harris in. Harris attempted resisting, but Kenneth knew it was some mistake.

"Keep it cool Harris, this must be some mistake everything will soon be cleared at the Police Station.

"Lydia coming out of the store could not believe her eyes seeing her brother in law and sister being driven by Police man in their own car.

There was shock as an initial reaction and some quick thinking. Her initial reaction was to go to the Police station. Then she decided against it. Wondering what to do she imagined seeing something like a piece of paper being thrown out of the car window by Kenneth. Seeing that same piece of paper on the ground she picked it up.

"Go quickly to Zorzor."

That was the simple terse message on the paper. There is a time to think and a time to act. Without wasting any time Lydia chartered a taxi for Zorzor paying the money cash down.

Instead of being taken to the Police station the car veered right to the Lofa Road. Daniel Kollie radio cracked alive. There was a hasty transfer of people from the Police vehicle to an unmarked jeep and a transfer of men. The uniformed officers disappeared. All of the men holding them their faces inscrutable behind dark sunglasses wore civilian clothes. Kenneth was protesting loudly, his wife was expressing outrage at such barbarity and Harris was kicking when the unmarked jeep zoomed at high speed sending a cloud of dusting behind. The men holding the Laye's hostage instead of continuing their journey along the main highway branched off to a small Rubber Farm road covered swallowed up almost by the vegetation growing on both sides.

Kenneth a thoughtful man heart missed a beat. His life was rewinding before him, his childhood, his life and his wife all in a trance. The men ordered them out of the vehicle at gunpoint. Madea's face was filled with terror. In a strange mood Kenneth grabbed his wife and kissed her long and deep.

"You have brought us to kill us right? He stated in a matter of fact tone.

"You write too darn much garbage on powerful people."

Kenneth's response was cut short by a single shot to the head. The two others died in rapid succession. The brutish men with big bodies and small heads cracked open their radio.

"Mission complete sir"

"Good men. Put them in the car and burn them. Hold on a minute.

"How many persons did you... ah....

"Three sir."

"How could you be so dumb? There were four persons in the car. Two men and two women. You let one escape? The world will know about our beautiful secret mission if the other girl escapes. This is meant to be a smooth operation that nobody should live to tell the story."

Instantly the search began. A vehicle was dispatched to Gbarnga city center in search of Lydia. Security corundum was being set up around the perimeters of the city to prevent a girl of Lydia's description from leaving the city. The car on its way for Lydia passed the vehicle she was riding in right at the intercession of Lofa Road. The driver happy to drop his passenger whom he overcharged to make more money for the day could not agree less with his passenger's urged to hurry. He simply tore his lithe Japanese vehicle through the dust chasing Zorzor.

———————◆◆———————

Daniel Kollie pleased that the loquacious could write no more garbage had an amount of trepidation over the escape of Lydia, which threw spinach in what otherwise was a picture perfect operation.

Radio messages from Zorzor alerted the capital and by extension the international world of the nation's most celebrated Journalist Kenneth Laye's abduction and disappearance.

The calls to the President started to come in thick and fast because the outside world knew of his extraordinary powers. And for once the President did not know what was going on. He did not give an explicit instruction to eliminate the Journalist.

Even before he could answer the phones Daniel Kollie entered his office his face flushed with excitement usually reserved for people who achieve great victories or success.

"Chief no more garbage being used to thrash you esteemed reputation. That scoundrel called Kenneth Laye can only write his thrash in the next world. He and his wife are gone from the surface of the earth forever."

"You mean you killed them?

"If that is how you want to put it yes."

Adonis Vonleh and Ebenezer Kum watched their chief keenly. When the telephones started ringing these two were called to prepare the government's response to the crises.

"Why did you kill them? Gabby. I gave no such orders. Look, see what you have done. The man had parents. He is an only child of aging parents his death could send them to the grave soon. My friend I am changing from being a military man to civilian and such killings makes things difficult for me" Why Daniel?

Anger flashed through Danny.

"Are you telling me Maxwell you love your enemies more than those who sacrifice everything to obey your every whim? Wasn't it you who said just the other day you wish somebody could rid you of that scoundrel? And when we risk our all to please instead of thanking us you whimper?

"I said get rid, did that mean kill him?

"And how do you get rid of? Now I know your orders should be taken lightly. You stand there and tell me Kenneth had aging parents. Tell me people who have we kill before that did not have parents? Is it because his parents are old that makes him unique? If his parents die now at least, they have enjoyed life. What about other parents dying early death because of the loss of their children. We make your throne safe and you give us not even a thank you and you try to lay a guilt trip on us?

"Sorry Daniel. Thank you. I will see you tomorrow, go and have some rest something will be provided for you and your boys tomorrow."

Behind Daniel, the President turned to his two civilian collaborators.

"The public is becoming more difficult to fool, what can we do?

President Forkpa put his hand on his head perplexed. There was complete silence for good five minutes.

Adonis picked his words careful.

"Mr. President the Justice Minister has to be changed. A new guy fresh and handsome from college has to be named as the new minister. Suspects will have to be arrested for trial. Of course, the suspects will have to be innocent. A trial will take place in Gbarnga, far away from the vocal Monrovia based civil society groups and the vociferous press who may not be able to station a correspondent in the city during a prolonged trial. The public would see you like doing something for a brutally murdered couple. The killings will be condemned in the strongest terms on state radio. You will visit the parents of the deceased to personally express your condolences. The children of the brilliant journalist will be your personal responsibility and soon the attention would turn to other things. But please Mr. President these killings must stop."

"Adonis could not have said it better."

Ebenezer Kum nodded his head in agreement.

"Daniel is becoming too powerful."

President Maxwell Forkpa muttered under his breath.

"Damn it, Kenneth was a dirt pusher but in a strange way I like the man and did not want him kill with his wife like that." President Forkpa slammed his fist onto the desk. With that, he became an all business President dictating to his press Secretary turned green from hearing about the death of a colleague.

Before the multitudes of condemnation could start pouring in, Zubawo Flemister a young up and coming Lawyer was named Justice Minister. His strong, youthful voice denouncing the killings and the arrest of four suspects including a woman for the murder of the charismatic journalist.

CHAPTER 33

October 15 Liberians queue in long orderly lines to cast their votes in Presidentially and legislative elections. President Forkpa and three other candidates vied for the highest office in the land. With most worthy opponents of the President prohibited from running or either in exile the overwhelming majority of the Liberian people united behind John Momoh the poor teacher from Bong County. In every nook and cranny of the country the cries of the Rooster the symbol of Momoh's party crowed. Staring defeat the President ordered Everette Gray to declare him President and winner of the election.

In desperation Everette informed the people through the media that because of malpractices by some members of the Special Elections Commission Secon, a 50 man committee has been chosen to count the votes. Liberians were patient to wait for the commission to do her job.

Zayzay knees ached from the arthritis in his joints. From the day, he was born to the time of his old age Zazay loved the streets. He was a man motivated by action and in politics he was a leftwinger by virtue of his downtrodden status in life. He believed the government must provide essential services free of charge to the people. Free water, free electricity, free medical and free education for the people. He lived his life long enough to know that the promises of politicians were sugar coated empty words yet he did not lose his interest in politics. Even as a pensioner he spent most of his time on the streets arguing his beliefs in politics and football with the same passion as the listless young men who idled their time on the streets of Jamaica Road criticizing and condemning anything and anyone that represent, authority and the establishment. His boyhood friend Tokpah with whom he had lived his entire life within ten miles radius of where he was born spent most of their time playing checkers and enjoying the many cheap drinks offered by many of those idling the time by. True to form the hot potato topic was the past election.

All their talk is just to fill their pockets."

"The person God wants to be President of Liberia that person will be president no matter what people do."

"Zayzay watch your mouth before you say I won you because you were talking." Tokpa took advantage of his friend's exposed flank to send his seed to king. The two pensioner's views summarized the attitude of most Liberians in regards to the two week waiting period. Whomsoever God had chosen to lead the country would still lead in spite of a two week wait. People here firmly believed in fate and destiny; a belief which made them unperturbed and easy going. But such a crucial part of national life placed in the hands of an intangible few could wreak havoc on a fertile land bristling with natural resources.

The Chairman of the Elections Commission true to his words announced the names of the counting committee members the following day just as he promised.

The Co chair was Daniel Forster, a respected retired barrister who unknown to a lot of people was cousin of Ebenezer Kum. His mother was Ebenezer's Aunt married to a Forster. The Vice Chair was Emmette Weeks, a former Foreign Minister who served as a behind the scene consultant for the government. Others were the President of the local chamber of Commerce David Luogon, a businessman with close ties to Daniel Kollie. Ruthie Soloteh, President of the Dualla Branch of the Marketing Association was also selected to serve on the committee along with Evangelical Bishops Basher Grimes and Imam Ishmael Ayouba.

All in all clergymen, marketers, jurists, retired judges, civil society representatives, and respected Senior citizens comprised the committee.

On the surface, these were individuals with impeccable credentials. However, this benighted committee concealed an ugly flaw. Most of them had business, political as well as family ties to the government. Ebie Kum, President Forkpa nd Everette Gray have been shrewd in their selection. None of the committee members possessed any covert ties to the government. Some individuals who were completely indifferent were added to spice the group knowing they could be easily manipulated even if they had no ties to the government. This was done to counter any criticism from the opposition.

The President hours after the formation of the committee issued a terse statement promising to deal with anybody who hindered the work of ballot counting.

Smelling rat under the closet John Momoh issued a statement challenging both the validity and neutrality of many of the counting committee members.

The committee, however remained undeterred by the criticisms. They began their work at the sprawling leafy Unity Conference Center built to host an OAU Summit.

Government controlled newspapers carried pictures of members of the special committee counting ballot papers the day the committee began work. Otherwise, the ballot counting was done quietly out of the glare of publicity.

Meanwhile, disturbing photos of burnt ballot papers from known opposition strongholds, and ballot stuffing surfaced in the press and electronic media but the government and the committee were determined to continued their work unhindered. These quite credible reports were simply overlooked. The Liberian populace as a whole gave the benefit of the doubt to the distinguished men and women counting their ballots.

At the conference center itself, the careful act to sway the election results were in full motion. Members of the fourth estate and civil society representatives were barred from proceedings at the center. The pictures of ballot counting committee members earnestly at work counting ballots were taken on the same day they commenced work. Soon after, they launched into detailed discussions about their benefits and remuneration in the neat air conditioned rooms. The mostly senior citizens spent their day reminiscing, eating, and drinking and having a jolly good time consuming the best of everything sometimes coming out in the afternoons to enjoy the gentle ocean breeze. Chilled drinks of all kinds were served along with freshly cooked seafood prepared with the finest ingredients served regularly to the committee members to prepare them adequately for their task. The President was determined to reward handsomely these distinguished personalities. Most of them were former classmates who relished the opportunity to be together again at government's expense.

There were boisterous discussions about their children and grandchildren in America studying at prestigious universities. Ruthie Saye and a few other 'neutral' committee members were told to bid their time and think about their pay package while fresh unaccounted ballot papers lay on the floor remaining sealed in their boxes.

About the same time at the Unity Conference Center Ebie Kum, Everette Gray and the rest of the committee members with the kind assistance of an Accountant were putting finishing torches on the' Elections result.'

"If we have to pave the way for Maxwell's Presidential victory, we have to be careful with the Legislative results."

Ebie nodded his grey head in agreement. Some of the committee members were snoring in their seats.

"Now let see, out of the 26 Senators at least 10 must come from the opposition."

"10 is a bit too much, I think 8 it will do or maybe 6."

"What we have here confirms the two Senatorial Seats from Bong County goes to the National Renewal Party of

Joseph Momoh. Edwin Blayee of the Reformation Party wins a seat each from Maryland and Sinoe Counties. All of the Presidential candidates must win the popular votes in their home county plus seats along with a sprinkling of Representatives slot.

"I understand Commissioner Gray, but where will we get the rest of the Senators from?

"Ebenezer you sometimes surprise me. Look what our Accountant has here. Are you forgetting Buchanan, Kakata, and of course Monrovia are three of our most populous cities. Here is what our boy did."

He shuffled the sheet towards Ebie. "Look, popular Engineer Mel Gramie wins one of the Senatorial seats from Margibi."

Ebie Kum studied the results for a while and pushed it to Bishop Grimes.

"What is the percentage of the President's victory? Manny questioned.

The Elections Commissioner laughed in a soft voice.

"Just enough to ensure that there is no runoff elections. The President will win in the first round. However; at least the strength of the opposition particularly in the capital will be acknowledged. The actual percentage I will reveal to no one, not even you Manny and Ebie Kum."

The chairman laughed his false teeth glowing under the bright light of the florescent tube

"Commissioner Gray, the President will love to know the margin of his victory before tomorrow." Ebie persisted.

Behind the scene a contest of will was taking place. President Maxwell Forkpa was preparing for any attempt

THE FADING FLOWER

by Samuel Dahn to come back and try to remove him by force from power. Samuel Dahn for his part was planning and scheming for the day he would come to remove President Maxwell Forkpa from power.

CHAPTER 34

Inside a desert training camp in Libya, the former Commanding General of the Armed Forces of Liberia Brigadier General Samuel Dahn huddled inside a giant green army tent with his men pouring over maps discussing strategies without fanfare or protocol, pomp or pageantry prepared to unleash their barbarity. The trainees were now fit for graduation getting ready for their mission to the homeland which many of them have not seen for close to three years now. This was a confident bunch expecting a hero's welcome when they marched triumphant into Monrovia to remove the tyrant Maxwell Forkpa from power. Equipment was being prepared, strategic points on maps were tarred with red paint. Comrades on the camps were being waved goodbye to. Commanders were telling them to remember what they were taught. The long wait was certainly going to be over soon.

These men have been welcomed by Libya's mercurial Kadafi. Blessed with abundant oil wealth, a sparse population, the popular Colonel has enough money to keep his people happy and still possessed more to sponsor

African revolutionaries fuelled by his anti Western Imperialist dreams.

The Colonel also harbored a personal grudge against Liberia's Maxwell Forkpa. Hasn't he Kadafi been the first to recognize Maxwell's government and being paid back by the non-commissioned officer canceling a visit to his country? Maxwell had even gone further insulting the Colonel at an OAU Summit in Zimbabwe. Now was payback time.

Samuel Dahn cared little for the deeper maneuvers involved in the decision by the Libyan leader to assist him; all he wanted was the opportunity to get back at his enemy. While the politicians in Monrovia argued, Samuel Dahn had no doubt in mind who the winner of the elections would be.

Freetown chosen as the forward base for the operation was being besieged by top backers of the coup anxious to receive the collaboration and good will of President Joseph Saidu Momoh to allow the men free passage. Elaborate luncheons were being made to celebrate the demise of a man who put so many of the nation's best and brightest on light poles and summarily executed them by the descendants of these people and a group of early supporters with whom the President felt out at the Bintumani Hotel even before the dogs of war were unleashed.

Rodney Gweh and Peyton Seh were now in Freetown putting finishing torches on an important part of their plans. These men surmised that they had a small well armed, highly trained and mobile force using stealth and surprise to remove the entrenched Maxwell Forkpa from power.

The men they were preparing to face were strong and equally determined, dedicated to remaining in power. A clash of will between two strong willed, ambitious and motivated men who made up the core of the executioners from the east loomed. The facade of democratic elections had seduced the Liberian People but the two men knew better. The world is such a frenetic place changing so fast that one had to struggle to catch their breath just to make sense of it all. The seconds changed to minutes, the minutes to hours, the hours into days and soon the days turn into weeks and months. Liberia stood at another threshold.

Just about the same time Samuel Dahn was studying his maps with his Lieutenants at a remote suburb which many Monrovians did not know, Maxwell Forkpa too was crowded with his men in a strategic planning section. The hard boiled Defense Minister had of late begun to rise in prominence, the SSS Chief restored to his position sat to the right of the President leaning on his arm.

"Sir while we concentrate on tomorrow my humble suggestion is we replace the commander of Schiefillin with Moses Tweh. Remember he is one of our best officers trained in Israel. In addition to his military brilliance he has aggression; we need an aggressive officer in charge of that brigade."

"Man we came here to discuss what to do if Everette Gray proclaims John Momoh as President against all odds, this is not time to discuss our strategic balance at a barrack," the Commanding General interjected.

President Maxwell Forkpa in full military regalia remained silent listening to the two men.

"Seemed to me Daniel is suggesting the right thing, Commanding General make sure effective immediately Moses Tweh is put in charge as commander of that first Infantry Brigade. The Americans do not just give US$ 14 million for lame duck commanders to sit on the pride of our infantry. Give the new commander another APC and let him check with me personally at my office tomorrow."

In view of the momentous occasion to take place the next day, President Forkpa's appointment seemed weird; it signified the intense ambition and contradictions of the man.

"Daniel I expect you to personally lead the men to guard the conference center.

Station APCs at all roads leading to Virginia. Arrest anybody you think suspicious within your security radius. If Monkey wants to be a man let fine shot bring him down. As of tomorrow the Mansion Grounds are off limit to civilians until I say otherwise. I just have this feeling that one day we may have a sneak attack from somewhere which I do not know. Do not take any chance with Everette, if he says the wrong thing; do not let him escape the Conference Center alive. It will be your life for his life, you understand?

"Yes Sir." the wiry military man replied.

"Mr. President I think it will be necessary to establish a security cordon around the radio and television stations."

"Yelp" the President already had that in mind. "In spite of all our precautions if something goes wrong:

accidentally explode a grenade inside the conference hall. Let none of the clamorers vying for my seat called opposition leaders escape alive in the ensuing melee. From the beachfront let some plains clothes security agents open fire on the building, sporadic but not sustain. The APC at the front will evacuate me and my VIPs which you know. Targeted shooting made to look uncontrolled is our strategy. Use only crack soldiers for this mission, apart from the opposition leaders a few innocent people along with one or two of the attackers must die in the attack. Order in the midst of pandemonium men is the plan."

"Sir in such a situation communication is critical; we do not have sufficient walkie talkies."

The President laughed.

"We received a little bit of such equipment overnight. Payne will make sure men you receive all you need just after this meeting ends. The crucial announcement to wait for is the name of the winner of the Presidency."

"Chief do not worry. Besides you nobody will sit in that Presidential chair."

"I swear on my society chief," the youthful Director of Military Intelligence affirmed in the most determined of tones.

"Chief the word has spread among us that the army will never accept anyone as President besides you, but sir I have the feeling that the deputy Commanding General along with the Logistics Commander may not be so loyal."

The Defense Minister adopted a conspiratorial low tone. In the intricacies of human relations suspicion coupled with envy played an important role. The President had a soft spot for his chief of Logistics ever since his brother who happened to be one of Harrison's bodyguards was executed. He would not take action against his favorite colonel until there was irrefutable evidence against the young man. The meeting of the elite cream of the crop Presidential Council ended just how it started .

True to his word President Maxwell was declared outright winner of the Presidential election with a 6 years mandate as a civilian President. To further sweeten his victory, his party the PDP won a majority of the legislative seats in both the upper and lower houses of the lawmaking body. The president and his supporters engaged in choreographed victory dance in front of foreign journalists expressing surprise at their win. In another part of the world as soon as Samuel Dahn heard the announcement of his archrival victory he rejoiced. It was time to act!

CHAPTER 35

The Final Assault

In the south central part of West Africa two small interlocked countries with similar climates, endowed with relatively long coastlines that were sloppily guarded were small in size. But the machinations of their politics far exceeded their size. The conflict that erupted in those countries would eventually rack West Africa in turmoil for nearly a decade.

Liberia and Sierra Leone's long unprotected coastline offered more than just a haven for rogue foreign trawlers. The unguarded coastlines made it possible for smugglers operating fast speed boats to do brisk business with little hindrance. The few lightly armed vessels of the Liberian coast guard stayed close Monrovia around the port and behind the Mansion; Sierra Leone's coastal defenses were no better.

It was somewhere in the no man sea between the two countries a dilapidated Ukrainian vessel anchored in the Atlantic away from the shores yet technically within the coastal water of Sierra Leone. Two boats were lowered its deck into the choppy water below. Cargo wrapped in wooden cardboard boxes were hastily transferred from the bigger vessel to the two small fast boats below. The thick darkness enveloping the ocean meant other vessels plying the sea lane could only see the cargo ship in the distance as partner vessel.

A huge black man was in charge of the operation. His men trained hands worked efficiently in the darkness in almost total silence. Straining their backs in an hour their deadly cargo was ready. Five men sat over the cargo; their speed boats then headed for shore to a preselected rendezvous point. The cold sea breeze chilled their bones, but the excitement in the determined night riders wiped every trace of fatigue. The two boats moved along side each other unto a track of beach now visible to their eyes.

Their boats drew to a stop near the shallow coastal water; their engines were switched off. In too much hurry the men on the boats did not bother to drop anchor. Quickly the heavy boxes from the boats were placed on the heads of men standing in the waist high water. This part of their mission did not have any of the enchantment of chivalry for these men who considered themselves patriotic freedom fighters. Wading through the sea with heavy boxes taxed the men patience beyond words. However, years of training under the scorching sun have turned these men into a disciplined cohesive unit full of steely determination.

The big black man directing the operation opened the zipper of his jacket exposing his rifle. He stopped what he was doing to inspect his weapon and cocked it before putting it on safe. He did not want to be caught unaware even though he knew the area was safe. An advanced team which included his boss was already on the land. The commander blew a special whistle which was their coded signal. There was no response.

The huge man became alert; his keen sense of danger sharpened by living dangerously on the edge sprang into motion. Their card boxes being placed on the sandy beaches were not safe in that position. He signaled to the ten men or so with him to cock their rifles and lie down even as they placed their boxes down. Their getaway boats were shoved back into the water soon disappearing fast into the open seas.

Once the men landed they were on their own taking their lives into their hands. The surrounding coastal bushes were silent. The man in charge of the operation blew the whistle for the second time receiving silence in response.

Disappointment showed on their faces. Again their commanded blew the coded signal for the third time.

Distinctly, their commander crouched behind a cardboard box on the beach heard the shrill but clear response. The men rose from their positions in jubilation. Their commander shouted obscenities at them ordering them to lie back angrily. There was a muffled sound and movements in the bushes, men toting Kalashnikovs emerged. Samuel Dahn ran to Rodney embracing him warmly.

"Praise God you made it, all sorts of things have been crossing my mind. I was beside myself with worry."

"Good comrades we are together now. Maxwell days are numbered. We will show his penis to the people. Chief do you have the canoes ready?"

"They have been here since 6 pm this evening."

On the isolated stretch of beach trained Liberian dissidents embraced with the warmth of meeting a long lost brother.

"Guys get going, we have to move the cakes quickly! Samuel Dahn shouted to his men.

The exiled former Commanding General wore a complete military outfit; his army face cap carried the one star emblem of his Brigadier Generalship big and bold. A pair of glasses hid the slant in his left eye. A pair of binocular dangled on his neck. Grenades were attached all over his body. Two to the pocket of his baggy camouflage trousers, two to his breast pocket, three strapped to his belt, a Kalashnikov with two magazines fastened together with tapes slung across his back. under his armpit he carried a .38 Pistol. He held a stun grenade in his right hand. Inside the pocket of his bullet proof vest he carried a taped recording of a special message.

In his pocket also was a detailed drawing of the Executive Mansion, .the parts of the building which President Forkpa frequented were highlighted in red, there were also pale yellow dots highlighting the main security checkpoints leading to and encircling the Mansion. Careful to conceal themselves, the dissidents calling themselves the Patriotic Brigade had initially disguised themselves to look like fishermen, now their true identity came out. The heavy boxes of ammunitions were being hauled across the beach to the lush coastal vegetation just along the coast. The boxes concealed by the vegetation and darkness were opened to reveal their impressive contents under the beam of a flashlight.

Each of the men was given their obligatory 150 rounds of ammunition before being given their specialist weapon. Viktor kept his side of the deal. Russian made RPG 7 tubes were handed out to the specialist along with three rockets each wrapped in green moisture resisting bags, others received machine guns.

Rodney Gweh expected to become the new commander of Schiefillin exchanged his civilian clothes for an army uniform and the ziz zag criss cross of a machine gun belt that encircled his body like a serpent about to strangulate its victim.

Peyton Seh carried tubes of RPGs on his back in addition to his rifle. His bulky large frame gave him an incredible physical strength showing him as a brave African fighter. Among the arsenal of the invaders were night flares, small surface to air missile mobile launchers that could be assembled and disassembled in minutes. Every dissident carried a small mobile VHS radio because communication was crucial for such a small group of men who dare to invade their country and engage their national army. For some, this was a foolhardy attempt, to those involve it was an incredible act of bravery. Now Samuel Dahn's men were ready for action buoyed by the assumption Maxwell Forkpa was so unpopular with the people and army that Samuel Dahn's name was the magical catalyst for men to desert the army and join his rebellion. Surrounded by his heavily armed soldiers all itching for battle in this Sierra Leonean bush country near the Liberian border, Samuel Dahn addressed his men in a voice seeping with emotional discharge held in check only by military discipline.

"Africa is a unique continent. Liberia our country is a blessed land endowed with countless riches by the Creator.

We risk our lives for the redemption of our people years ago to overthrow President Roberts, our aim was to remove a corrupt regime and replace it with constitutional rule to benefit our people-Now! The emotional restraint broke through------

Maxwell Forkpa has betrayed our revolution killing us...Alexander Kulah is dead, Harrison is dead.... Their blood cries for vengeance, for justice men. Count it all joy men that you have been chosen to rid our nation of that dog called Maxwell Forkpa. No retreat no surrender. Anybody who fails in this mission will die for his failure.

Now! Samuel drew a map from his pocket, spread it on the ground shining his torch on it.

His key commanders crouched beside him.

"We will storm broadcasting house. Never for one moment leave the place unguarded when we capture it. There are two armor cars parked at the entrance. Use a stun grenade and mount a direct frontal assault. Surprise the guards and disarm them, do not shoot unless fired upon. Assure the journalists when you enter their studio that they are safe and let them perform their duty. Do not allow anybody to leave the compound once you enter"

Samuel pointed to a speck on the piece of paper representing the facility.

"Jeremiah you will lie in ambush. Take as many rockets as possible to arm bush any re- enforcement that may come from Schiefillin.

Now you will take over the refinery to block any military vehicle from leaving Seventy Seconds Barracks to head for town on the Somalia Drive Route. James and I will lead the rest of the troops to attack BTC and the Mansion. Maxwell Forkpa will not escape. Peyton Seh guard this cassette with your life.

"Any question men?

No Question?"

Thank you"

He responded to his own question after a brief silence.

"As a last resort if we meet overpowering resistance you know where we shall assemble to decide next? A sardonic smile crossed Samuel Dahn's thick lips.

"We shall all fall back to the BTC. Got it?

"Yes sir!

"Now Fred Knot will have three large army jeeps waiting for us at this point" he indicated the spot on a dot on his map.

"The Commanding General along with the Chief of Staff will remain in their positions."

"No chief the best thing we can for them is no to shoot them, nothing more, nothing less." Peyton shot back in anger.

Samuel smiled back. "We will need them if we want the army to desert to our side en mass. Forget it man, a week later you will become the Chief of Staff. Cool your temper boy. Any questions?

"No sir!

"Now let's move!

The men broke out of camp in a long thin line their rifles pointed in opposite direction. The main barrier between the dissidents and their native land was the Mano River. The dissidents were mostly Liberians except their Ghanaian communication specialist and a couple of Sierra Leoneans. Under the cloak of darkness, the men glided their canoes paddling upstream to the sight Samuel reconnoitered months ago.

They disembarked at the arranged sight easily evading the officers at the first checkpoint inside Liberia.

On Liberian soil, the men offered a short prayer. Samuel Dahn radio soon cracked alive.

"Yes the vehicles were ready."

Fred Knot confirmed. "The trucks are fitted with M-16 Rifles. Hurrying to the designated point the driver of one of the government army truck stolen broke down crying upon seeing General Dahn.

Fred Knot embraced his soul brother; the man on whose behalf he has taken his life into his own hand. The months of worry about being caught for his treachery and being tortured to death have left their marks on his physical features, his uniform hanged a little too loosely on his frame.

The task before the dissidents was too grave for much conversation apart from operational planning. Later there would be wives to kiss, mothers to embrace, and sisters to see, comrades and brothers to embrace and friends to rejoice with when their mission succeeded.

The men climbed aboard the vehicles testing their communication sets. Instead of these men setting their base in some obscure corner fighting their way to power inch by inch, so confident of victory they were that they headed straight for the capital. They drove down to Monrovia through abandoned checkpoints, undermanned barriers and soldiers perhaps too drunk or too intimidated by the presence of the Logistics Commander of the army to say anything or examine the tarpaulin covered trucks. The road in this part of Liberia was good.

Soon in the distance Monrovia shining and beautiful appeared like a bride waiting to be ravaged, it beaconed to the dissidents with irresistible charms. Approaching the city from the northwest direction they drove down from Clay, Poe River, Iron Gate then unto the settlement of Brewerville down through to the densely populated trading suburb of Dwalla.

Soon the men were at the Freeport Junction. To the east of the Freeport Junction branching left laid the route to broadcasting house sight of the nation's sole T.V. station whose beamed images did not reach even half of the country. Her two radio outlets periodically covered the entire country.

This deserted junction was the first place the dissidents separated. Peyton and his team headed east in three stolen vehicles commandeered from a used car garage at the Freeport. He along with his small band of intrepid attackers drove east listening to ELBC their target playing soft, sentimental music. Samuel Dahn along and his conquering Lions drove straight through Vai Town going to the Mansion. For a group of armed men to invade the capital unchallenged, it seemed like a work of fiction written by an author with under worked imagination. Yet it was true, the nation up to this point has never experienced an invasion launched from a neighboring country. Checkpoints around the immediate perimeters of the city were nonexistent. The military government brought to power through a coup against a defenseless civilian government had always been aware of the possibility of internal coups and had therefore; taken the best of care to prevent this possibility. An elite troop of highly loyal tribalists, a policy of divide and rule, and the buying of patronage ensured longevity for the powers that be. Though intelligence on planned invasion by external aggression has filtered through security planners expected conventional attacks on military bases with the attackers using massive firepower not a sneak pre- dawn attack.

Fred Knot's treachery has remained uncovered because of the President's partiality to him because of his brother whom he executed. Having withstood the test of time; the president had relaxed his grip on power a little in regards to external aggression. Hasn't he signed a non aggression pact with his neighbors protecting his rear flanks?

The invaders drove unchallenged through the deserted streets into the city center. The few night security guards assigned at the LTC building on Broad Street watched the passing military vehicles without much cause for concern since they were accustomed to seeing military vehicles ply the city's streets at night. Furthermore, the markings on the trucks showed they belonged to the national army.

The tarpaulin covered vehicles drove through Crown Hill to the Bye Pass stopping at the intersection of Haile Salesie Avenue. The armed men on board jumped down out of their vehicles clutching their rifles. Each man checked his ammunition and radio before moving forward back to back heading to the seat of power. To fool government soldiers all of the men at the front of the advancing men held M-16 Rifles and wore AFL uniforms.

Fred Knot radioed ahead. One of his men at the Mansion infiltrated the SSS men manning the security cameras position within the central viewing point designed to pick up movements and alert the soldiers below. Advancing fast the dissidents divided themselves into groups of threes. One group approached the Mansion from the direction of the Temple of Justice, their aim to position themselves between the barrack and the Mansion while another group approached from the direction of the Capitol Building, still another group approached from the direction of the University Campus. Samuel Dahn led the larger group from Capitol Building. A small single lane highway separated the Mansion fence from those of the Capitol Building. Landscapers with eyes for horticulture planted shrub of trees which had now grown to a thick cluster Using the flowers and exotic trees as cover, the attackers slowly slithered between the flowers inching ever closer to the body of troops manning a barrier across the road. The spiked iron fence surrounding the Mansion was neither high nor did it possess barbed razor wires. Across the street activities in the Mansion yard was visible to the attackers. All seemed quiet; an eerie silence pervaded the atmosphere. Samuel Dahn shrouded by the under foliage stared at his enemies through binoculars. Overpowering this small group would not be much of a problem but if there were a larger body of troops which was certain, crossing the road to the Mansion fence could be dangerous under sustained fire. They did not want to alert the main body of troops in the fence. Fred Knot whispered into his radio. The trained saboteur electronic engineer inside working for the dissidents inside the Mansion unplugged a switch plunging the whole yard into darkness. Since there has never been a power shortage at the Mansion before, the soldiers on the ground did not have flashlights.

The attackers most of whom knew the Mansion intricately before fleeing into exile infiltrated the yard hastily since they were dressed and armed like those defending it. Anxious AFL commanders unnerved by the darkness tried to maintain contacts with their men in the darkness in the ensuing confusion. Within minutes many found themselves staring into the muzzles of strange guns. Using silencers the invaders cleared the main gate. The three prone attackers using stun grenades on the defenders soon took over the Mansion without a fight. Their accurate marksmanship and equipments have given them a crucial advantage aided by the element of surprise. While his men disarmed the defenders urging them not to die for another person, Samuel Dahn and a huge trusted man followed by two others were running upstairs: their target the President of Liberia!

President Maxwell Forkpa did not allow himself the luxury of deep sleep. No matter how deep asleep he was the moment he woke all trace of sleep disappeared from his eyes. The ring on his finger was burning him. The President knew something was wrong. What was it he did not know? By premonition he quickly donned his military uniform picking the phone for his special line to the SSS Director. The line was dead, he cursed under his breath pulling his silver pistol. He called out to his bodyguards. Commander Korlubah's mumbled response infuriated him. The President carefully opened the door leading to his bedroom to investigate in the semi darkness.

"Maxwell Jerome Forkpa if you move a muscle you are dead! Drop the gun!

The harsh steely voice sounded from behind him; before he could react he felt the cold muzzle of a gun on his head.

"Drop the gun Maxwell."

"Who are you and what do you want?"

The President asked his voice still commandingly steady. In view of the circumstances, he was in the tone of his voice was remarkable.

"I thought Maxwell you would recognize my voice. Two years is not such a long time."

"God breath !

Samuel Dahn how did you get here?

"Never mind how."

The President attempted to turn to face his attacker.

"Drop the gun before you force me to shoot."

The submachine pistol dropped from Maxwell's hands.

"Tiatune search him!

Expert hands frisked his body bringing out a silver pistol.

"Now take a step forward and turn around slowly" Maxwell Forkpa obliged.

Samuel Dahn laughed.

"Here I am Maxwell; you thought by framing me up you could have executed me as you did to others eh?

But God had other plans. Now it is payback time."

"Well, General Dahn you look so good. If you could beat my entire security network catching me in my own bedroom, it means you are still the best. You could come and work with me again. Right now I fire all those useless as… Who are with me. You could have any position you want in the Salvation Council."

"Give you enough time to plot another means of killing me?

"Chief what are you wasting your time for? Chief let us kill this dirty dog and get out of here quick! Fred Knot shouted.

"This dog framed my brother up and killed him."

"No, no, no, Fred it is not simple revenge we want. This man has to stand trial to account for all the people he killed, the money he stole, the election he rigged, and the subversion of our revolution. This thing goes beyond you and myself Col. Knot."

"Chief as soon as this man is dead our coup has succeeded, let us use the old try and tested way by killing Maxwell like we did to President Robert."

"I said no, he must stand trial!

Samuel's refusal was clear.

"You know there is no personal animosity between us, only Gabby tried to spoil between us. He is now in prison so we can rule this country together like before. You can be Defense Minister, Chief of Staff, even your old job of Commanding General is all yours."

"Maxwell Forkpa you think you can bribe everybody with your sweet words and forked tongue? The only thing preventing me from shooting you is to shame you before this nation for your uncircumcised twisted manhood to be seen by the entire nation. You will die in prison like the common criminal you are."

"Samuel Dahn we were once best friends as far as I am concerned we are still friends."

Unable to contain his anger any longer Fred gave Maxwell a vicious slap on the back of his neck which sent him sprawling forward falling on his hand. Too much of good times had made the President slacken a little bit his physical fitness.

"Take it easy Fred."

Tiatune and Zoebadeh tie this dog up quickly. I must rush to ELBC."

The words did not escape Samuel Dahn's lips when quick, strong hands and clothes from Maxwell's own body bind the former President. The former President's hands and feet were tightly bound to his body which made him look artificially erect. As the rope tore into his flesh Maxwell Forkpa cried out in pain pleading for mercy. The men tying him laughed. Just then the radio in Samuel's pocket cracked alive.

"Roger, radio station not taken….. heavy resistance….

Help on the way… Samuel put the radio back into his breast pocket.

"Tiatune, Zoebadeh keep this man bound. Never dare to loosen him up for a second, if he wants to urinate or shit let him do them on himself, I am coming back soon. In fact put a piece of cloth into his mouth before he utters any word to you guys in my absence. If you hear any unexpected action or noise shoot Maxwell first before you investigate. Your lives for his life.. if anything happens and he escapes I will castrate you alive. You understand?

"Yes sir! Zoebadeh and Tiatune saluted.

"Come! In the twinkling of an eye, Samuel Dahn whisked a bayonet from his side.

"Show me your thumb"

The dissident leader plunk the tip of the knife into Tiatune's exposed thumb drawing out blood.

"Your blood for his blood soldier"

Samuel wiped Tiatune's blood on Maxwell body lying on the floor.

"Fred come with me, I do not trust you to guard this prisoner before you kill him in your anger. You are going with me to the radio station."

The two men hurried downstairs out of the Mansion to the radio station.

Peyton Seh and his group of 15 men earlier approached the small broadcasting facility from the narrow Redlight end of the Paynesville-Monrovia highway. The invaders disembarked from their vehicles at the Joe Bar. Streetlights cast a faint shadow on them. Now instead of using the darkness to their advantage sneaking upon the small contingent of soldiers at the entrance of ELBC, Peyton's men hastily shot up flares illuminating the area. While the flares revealed the position of the defenders, the attackers lost the element of surprise. Wasting no time the cream of crop of the Liberian Army opened fire immediately on Peyton's men. The attackers were forced to drop to the ground crawling on their bellies across the road. The small arms fire from the facility was augmented by shells from the two APCs parked before the entrance. The shells were not well aimed as they flew harmlessly over the attackers wrecking havoc in the swamp across the market building opposite them. Peyton's men replied with automatic rifles, machine guns, and RPGs rounds. In more than half an hour of sustained fire, the attackers made no progress. The battle quickly reached a stalemate with the defenders of the station making no attempt to break out of their defensive position.

An AFL soldiers trying to call for reinforcement received a direct hit from a rocket tearing him into smithereens. Two of the attackers lay wounded groaning in pain, the attackers had met their match. Journalists inside the facility cowered on the floor in sheer terror.

The attackers at this crucial stage were reinforced by the additional men Samuel brought in from the Mansion including some AFL deserters. The pressure on the defenders increased significantly. Realizing their predicament, the defenders concentrated their firepower towards the main highway attempting to break out. Abandoning their APCs two defenders dropped to the ground after receiving direct hits; their volleys dropped two of their attackers dead.

The now larger group of attackers split themselves into three groups. Even though, the fence protecting the back of the facility was quite high another group of attackers by-passed the main entrance shooting from the back of the facility as a scare tactic to let the defenders know they were outnumbered and there was no hope in continual resistance.

Exhausted, running low on ammunition and disappointed by the lack of reinforcement the defenders fled.

Samuel Dahn met no resistance now as he entered through the Iron Gate. He ran to the studio guarded by six men to the white broadcasting facility not bothering to go the administration building ahead of him to his right. The Eucalyptus trees lining the road to the house swayed under the gentle ocean breeze oblivious to the violence exploding around it

"We are freedom fighters of the Patriotic Brigade. Nobody will be hurt, just stay cool and do your job."

The new President, Liberia's latest coup maker announced to shocked but relieved journalists inside the cozy studio.

Peyton produced the priceless transparent blue, black cassette tape. The frightened journalist on duty could not insert the seditious tape into a large tape deck in the small studio tape recorder. His hand trembled badly. The new President spoke softly calming him down and he managed to insert the tape.

The national Anthem played then the explosive announcement beamed.

The clear booming voice of Samuel Dahn bold and free no longer a fugitive but an advocate of political violence announced with all the exigency of a triumphant conquering hero. A hero delivering a message which brought joy to a still sleeping nation.

"Maxwell Forkpa is a man who has denied the Liberian People, robbed our nation of its values and significance… The tape launched into a long diatribe of the litany of abuses perpetuated by the ex-President.

"You shall have yourself worth and dignity restored. I Brigadier General Samuel Dahn, Commanding General of the Armed Forces of Liberia have seized power and have overthrown Maxwell Forkpa's despotic regime. I am now your President until free and fair elections which I will not be a candidate are held within a year. Maxwell Forkpa is in hiding. There is no escape for him… Then the names of key military commanders were announced in addition to the heads of security agencies.

"All soldiers are advised to remain in their barracks and take orders from their new commanders. All former government officials including the SSS Director, Police, NSA Directors, cabinet ministers, and heads of autonomous government agencies are to report themselves to the nearest Police station for their own safety. Maxwell Forkpa and his cohorts shall stand trial to account for all the things they have stolen from the country. Our revolution is not about revenge or bloodbath, we only aim to give you fellow citizens a government you can truly be proud of..'

Why President Samuel Dahn did not obtain a tape recording of Maxwell's voice asking his loyalists to surrender and why he said the former President is in hiding instead of has been captured remains a mystery.

By the time the momentous broadcast ended in the early hours of the morning few of the intended audience heard it. Samuel Dahn was enjoying his finest hours reaching the peak of Mount Everest viewing the world from its lofty heights while Liberia lay in his hands.

The recording announcing the coup was being repeatedly played on radio.

The new Head of State journeyed from the studio to inspect his men at the refinery.

There was no firing at the country's sole petroleum refinery; government troops simply joined the invading coup makers. By this time dawn began to break upon the land. Within a few hours, Samuel Dahn coup had succeeded beyond his dreams. The speed, the efficiency, the willingness of soldiers though expected still brought happiness to Samuel.

By 6 am Samuel entered the fortress, the nation's premier barrack, the seat of political power of the military called the Barclay training Center. But this barrack was not the strongest barrack.

Resplendent in his uniform, swift and authoritative in his movement, the charismatic new President entered the barrack in a small tactical jeep amidst cheers from troops. The barrack was a multi tribal institution of soldiers. Soldiers from the new President's tribe were ecstatic. Significantly, though, the new President's appeal when beyond ethnic affiliation cutting across ethnic divide. Soldiers who wanted to be soldiers and wanted the military out of politics rejoiced seeing the blazing commanding sight of Samuel Dahn floating to them like sweet heavenly dreams. All of the top echelons of the military were now at the General's mercy.

The imposing General........................ The Chief of Staff, the Defense Minister, Police Director.... The Foreign Minister and even the Vice President were now in handcuff dumped into the football field in the middle of the barrack sitting prostrate at the feet of the man they vilified for so long pleading for mercy. Within the few hours of the coup, all of them were now speaking from the other side of their mouths. Adonis Vonleh one of President Forkpa's best friend became one of the most enthusiastic supporters of the coup. Samuel Dahn had no time for them. The Vice President was made to make a statement which was recorded calling on all concerned to cooperate with the new government and accepting the legitimacy of the Patriotic Brigade government. These senior government officials' homes were never invaded nor were they arrested by the invader. The invaders were far too few to spread themselves that thin. In another bizarre twist of fortunes erstwhile loyal bodyguards in a repeat scenario of 1980 arrested, handcuffed, beat, and presented their bosses to the new authorities at the BTC. Strange emotions and power can be. Samuel Dahn was such a busy man he could not take personal charge of these shriveling men whose status evaporated into thin air. Issuing terse instructions the new President departed the barracks to secure the ELWA Radio Station. By now most of the inhabitants of the capital were aware of the coup but the vast majority of the people in the countryside remained ignorant.

Radio ELWA, their only outlet to the capital only played somber gospel music. Local and international news broadcast relayed usually broadcast on the station remained silent. The monotony of music devoid of an announcer's voice continued.

Some keen observers in the countryside sensed something unusual happening in the capital city because of this. The majority of the people though continued with their daily activities as usual in the morning. Marketers cleaned their tables to set up wares, school children in colorful uniform were on their way to school oblivious to the events in the capital.

In the interior with high illiteracy, people did not pay as keen attention to their radio as their urban counterparts.

On his way to the smaller ELWA facility, the new President of Liberia noticed crowds beginning to assemble on the streets in celebratory mood. Soon a copy of the momentous cassette became inserted into the tape deck at ELWA Studio. The message of the coup now beamed from Voinjama to Harper, from Yekepa to Buchanan. By mid morning; huge crowds of civilians and soldiers alike thronged the streets to celebrate. Almost every hamlet in the nation rejoiced. In Lofa, the news of the coup was received in silence for the most part. For a momentous and dangerous event as a coup, the guns were silent, the line of demarcation between civilians and soldiers, between invaders and AFL soldiers blurred, the tight discipline of the invaders flushed like a commode. Overwhelmed by their staggering success discipline built over the years soon faded. Wives of the invaders, relatives and friends besieged their love ones with kisses, tears, rejoicing, and showing rapturous joy even though many of these long lost love ones were still in the delicate act of consolidating their hold on power, or performing sentry duties. The crowds in the streets were just too large to control. Peyton Seh and his men began to flirt with the civilians especially the beautiful women who hero worshipped them. Samuel Dahn returning from ELWA hastened to return to the BTC, but the adoring crowd could not allow his jeep through Their infectious praises, their presence overwhelmed his vehicle such adulation was hard to ignore even though their action impeded his progress. He waved and smiled. Women took off their lappa clothes and placed them on the ground for him to walk on. The crack of communication radio could not be heard over the deafening voices of the celebrating, ululating, and dancing mob of people. Peyton Seh, Rodney Gweh. Fred Knot -key commanders threw caution to the wind drinking and dancing.

CHAPTER 36

At the Executive Mansion, the rope on him tore into Maxwell Forkpa's flesh. It seemed the circulation of blood to his body's extremities had stopped. For the twentieth time, he attempted to speak to his captors through the gag of cloth in his mouth. Wiamie and Zoebadeh laughed. Their captive shifted rolling on the floor hoping that his body movement could loosen the tightness of his cord. Forcing his breath through the gag,he laid face down rubbing the edge of the cloth on the floor. His mouth has become sore from rubbing it on the ground in an attempt to loosen the gag a little to allow him to speak without much success. Former President Forkpa was a determined man. There was nothing he dreaded than for Samuel Dahn to come and meet him tied. His salvation lay in his being able to communicate with the young impressionable men guarding him. Even though, it pained Maxwell continued to rub his mouth on the ground to the amusement of his captors who did nothing to restrain him. Gradually the cloth slipped a little from his mouth. Maxwell turned to stare at the muzzle of gun pointing at his nose.

"How much money are you being paid Tiatune?

"Dog this is not for money, you hear that?"

To emphasize his point Tiatune kicked Maxwell in the groin. The former President groaned in pain.

"Teach you to keep your mouth shut," he bellowed.

'If Samuel Dahn becomes President what will he do for you?

"I am a patriot Maxwell. The wishes of our people are paramount not our personal gains." Tiatune boasted.

"After this coup you don't have to risk your life again. Anything can happen. You two are poor. The day has come for you your family not to suffer again."

"How?

Tiatune asked in a gruff voice.

"I can give you and your friend 1 million dollars each, that will make your rich for life. Because after this coup Samuel Dahn will have you guys retire from the army. I know him better than you two."

"Shut your mouth !

Tiatune bellowed.

"Zoebaded put the gag back on before his forked tongue."

"Listen men, look at Daniel Kollie, he was not one of the coup plotters in 1980, because of his loyalty to me I made him Defense Minister and he is also rich. I can give you any rank in the army. Pretty soon this place will be crawling with my men. Samuel Dahn and his men are too few to confront my men. I can save you two and also make you rich. If you loosen my rope now I will give each of you $10.000 right now."

"You heard what our chief say. Our life for this man's life. I am too young to die. Tiatune let us put this man's gag back on."

"Okay put it back on."

The young soldier folded the gag to make it bigger to shove it into Maxwell's mouth.

"Hey at least let me show you where I put the money for you to take it before you tie my mouth again."

Zoebadeh hurried to put the gag back on looking up to Tiatune for approval.

"Let him show us the money first before you put the gag back on. Where is the money Maxwell?

"You stay here and guard me and let your friend go in my bed room cover. If he does not bring $10.000 in cash then everything I have told you is a lie."

The two young men conversed in low tunes some little distance away from their captive. Maxwell baited his breath and waited though the ropes in his skin burned like fire.

They came back.

"Okay we shall leave the gag out of place until we can get the money."

Maxwell heart leapt in happiness for the small victory. He directed Tiatune into his bedroom showing where the key of the cover with the cash in was.

Alone with Zoebaded the captive sought to maximize his attack.

"Zoebadeh you are too young to know all the ways of men. Samuel Dahn and me were the best of friends; the reason he and I fell apart is he wanted to make love to my woman. My woman did not agree to his love and told me about his attempt. I want to make you a General in the AFL."

Zoebadeh annoyed by the frequent chatter of the prisoner kicked him in the mouth drawing out a little blood from a bruise inflicted . Maxwell did not cry he pain. Instead he faced his captor.

Zoebadeh cracked his VHS radio alive to talk to his boss. He could not hear a thing something which made him to panic. Were he and the small band of men at the Mansion yard being abandoned?

He tried for the second time to hear the voice of his chief to dissuade the negative thoughts beginning to form in his mind.

Just then Tiatune arrived with bundles of money all over him. The two of them set to work fast stuffing the money all over their body clothes and even into their under pants.

"Now you see my words are true. Whether this coup fails succeed or fails now you have some money in your pockets. I have more money in my room I can give you if you could only loosen this rope a little".

His captors cringed at the suggestion.

"Now you can keep your guns pointed at my head, just release one of my hands for me to open my suitcase. It has a special code which can only detect my finger print for it to open. There is so much money in there for your taking. At least I want you guys to have it instead of Samuel Dahn. If even he kills me before my men get here I want you guys to have it instead of him laying his filthy hands on my money."

"But we have to untie you hands and feet before you can get to that room and we can't do that."

"No, no, no, you can even leave me tied and carry me into that room. The only thing is at least one of my hands should be untied for my fingers to open the special combination numbers."

"Your hand should be free for you to take your gun? Tiatune asked greed already insipid in his soul.

"Of course your guns will be on my head, with my body including one of my hands tied I stand little chance against trained marksmen such as you two."

Maxwell had uttered the truth. We keep your hands tied. We bring the suitcase to you. Your tied fingers can still punch the code. The former President was tote to his room two guns pointed at head. Maxwell knelt beside his bed praying that that special telephone line beside it was not cut, he fingered the bag he came for touching the real purpose of his visit to the room, a hidden line connecting him to his men at Schiefillin. He just could not feel the line and for the first time bile filled his mouth . He tried for the second time with one of the soldiers poking his shoes under his butt. Yes he felt the line, through a pre-arranged code he signaled to Moses that he was still alive in the Mansion.

"Hurry up ! Tiatune shouted. Maxwell then opened the suitcase filled to the brim with money. As the men stuffed the bundles of cash the former President for the first time since his capture clung to a faint glimmer of hope. Escorted back to the corridor Maxwell kept on talking to distract the men and establish rapport. Frustrated by his persistent chatter Tiatune shove the gag back into place. He tied the cords binding the former President back together but not as tight as before. Maxwell lay face down on the floor, the ring on his finger that warned him of danger burned now with less intensity.

At Schiefillin Barrack, the aggressive commander had sat mute since the announcement of the coup. He did not relish the thought of giving in to the coup makers without a fight. However, realizing the finality of the coup and his own hopelessness he waited for his replacement to arrive. Now with the confirmation his boss was alive in the Mansion, the news galvanized him into action.

Within minutes heavily armed troops were being mustered to storm Monrovia and confront the invaders. A convoy of troops riding a top armor personnel carriers headed to the city about 20 minutes drive away. In her path to Monrovia, just a few meters away from the road laid ELWA relaying dangerous messages about the coup.

In Monrovia proper; some observers noticed a dark green Chevrolet jeep filled with white men plied the streets on a continuous basis. Revelers waved the car by. A dangerous situation soon began to unravel. Something strange began to happen, and some electronic devise began jamming the simple VHS signal of the invaders.

The group of coupmakers at BTC could not hear from their comrades at the radio stations; neither could those at the Mansion hear the signal of those at the LPRC.

The lack of resistance had buoyed the confidence and wane the steadfastness and coordination of the invaders.

Samuel Dahn slammed the radio in his hand

hard managing to extricate himself from the adoring crowd. He could not issue a command or monitor the communication of his men. A s soon as he tried to pick up signal a loud crackling sound emitted from his radio and he could not hear a thing.

As the minutes tickled by the General knew something was seriously wrong. He dispatched Fred Knot to ELBC with a message warning the garrison at Schiefillin to surrender or be invaded.

Loyalty and allegiance were tricky companions, while Samuel Dahn was still without doubt the most popular man in uniform; Maxwell Forkpa had quietly built a powerful base among the new recruits drawn mostly from his tribe. It was these soldiers that were now putting their lives on the line on his behalf heading to Monrovia. Samuel Dahn stranded somewhere between Congo Town and the barrack was frantic; trying to maneuver his way through the throngs of civilians still hungering to see and touch him. At the Lutheran school in Sinkor his jeep came under a freak attack. This diversionary attack by renegade soldiers delayed some crucial time.

The main body of troops from Schiefillin atop armored cars coming to reverse the coup were approaching the outskirts of the capital.

Their hitherto unchallenged progress was ran into an ambush at the ELWA radio station market. Rodney Gweh ELWA shortwave broadcast was the only radio station that covered the entire country. And if it fell to enemy forces the unraveling of their coup would start. The AFL's

APCs were almost useless against the nimble Patriotic Brigade snipers picking up soldiers a top the convoy.

While the battle raged on the main highway; other crack troops of AFL rangers advanced on foot along the beach front. Another group of commandos using commandeered canoes landed at the unprotected sea coast rear of the Mansion.

These Israeli trained soldiers, some using spiked hooks attached to ropes began to scale the walls of the impressive building housing the Presidency. The small group of invaders at the Mansion who did not joined the partying in the streets having judged their coup a success numbers were outnumbered. Almost the entire Patriotic Brigade troops stationed at the front entrance of the Mansion. Their numbers thinned; demoralized by the lack of communication to their colleagues the invaders only realized the presence of the crack infantry troops almost too late. A short but fierce fire fight ensured .Small arms fire reverberated around the seat of the Presidency. From the sounds of the echoing gun fire below Maxwell Forkpa sensed his men have arrived on the scene as his avenging angels. He thanked his God, his medicine, his protection his just anything.

Buoyed by the sounds of M-16s clashing with Ak-47s he faced his captors.

"Tiatune release me now and I will spare your precious lives. You guys can go in peace finding your way out of here with the money I already gave you."

"We have to shoot you as our commander Samuel Dahn ordered."

"No come on guys don't do anything you will regret."

There was real panic in the former President's voice which he tried to suppress. Surprising that people who sent other people to death with callous ease always fear death.

Zoebaded released the safety catch on his gun off to shoot the former President.

"Drop you guns dogs!!

The voice of the intruder startled Tiatune and Zoebaded who found themselves looking into the muzzles of 10 M-16s with M203 grenade launchers.

"Put your guns down!

"Never!

Tiatune shouted.

"Any of you move a step and your boss is dead!

The soldiers laughed although none of them took a step forward.

"Guys your coup has failed."

"Liars!

Tiatune shouted.

"Sergeant Murphy put on the radio........This is Colonel Moses Korlubah of the 1st Infantry Battalion of Schiefillin. We have seized ELWA radio station and are calling on all citizens and loyal soldiers to join us combat Samuel Dahn along with his group....

The soldier put his small transistor radio off smiling.

"Soldiers your game is up. Downstairs is crawling with my men."

"Liars I can still hear the heavy exchange of fire downstairs, our men are also fighting."

Fighting where? Your communication is not going through. Your friends on the outside have all fled. Give your guns now."

"Soldiers take it easy with these guys, they are the ones who saved my life.

Treat them well and we will enlist them in our army."

A soldier sprang forward and attempted jerking their weapons.

"A step forward and I will shoot."

"Ok and then we will drill your body with holes. Call your commander now and see if he will answer."

All Tiatune and Zoebaded heard was loud crackles.

"Take their weapons but let them keep their money because they save my life-".

The untied President commanded.

No sooner have their rifles been taken when Zoebaded and Tarnue were bound hands and feet. Slaps and kicks rained on their bodies.

"Charge those bastards and take my money off them, the money belongs to you now."

"Guys take me to the radio station right now! I have to inform the Liberian People that the invaders and imposters and usurpers have been crushed!

The situation is still fluid chief. Let us get to your room; there is something far more important for you to do then going to the radio station

"Soldier take it easy you are talking to your commander."

"Yes sir! How Chief Maxwell Forkpa look?

"Alright! Alright! Alright!

The overjoyed men raised their rifles in the air in a salute. Maxwell stretched his fingers to restore the circulation in them. In a fit of anger he sent a vicious kick into Tiatune's groin. The tied coupmaker screamed in pain. The disputed President entered into his room and put on a new uniform. Handsome and commanding he looked as a re- incarnate Greek god flashing brass and weapons.

"Captain make sure no harm come to my wife and children."

The soldier saluted.

Guarded by his soldiers, the Commander in Chief of the Armed Forces of Liberia descended the stairs. The shooting outside has now become sporadic. Maxwell watched his men driving the invaders away inch by inch. Though he was courageous he was not a warrior by nature. He remained at a safe distant watching the battle protected by six men.

———————◆◆———————

On another side of the city convoy from Schiefillin has by now cleared the ambush along the highway on the main highway heading to ELWA Junction. Rodney Gweh wounded in the leg fled the scene with his few remaining men. From this junction ELBC was not more than 5 miles away. This body of troops from Schiefillin made rapid progress meeting almost no resistance. They bulldozed their way into the broadcasting facility. Just as the coup has taken place rapidly it began to unravel in a similar fashion.

Seeing strange grim faced soldiers appearing now on the streets civilians, began to see the writing on the wall.

Samuel Dahn tactical jeep speeding along the boulevard was also some writings on the wall. He turned to Fred Knot beside him. "Fred we have to kill Maxwell."

He finally admitted speeding towards the Mansion.

"We should have killed him this morning as I suggested."

"It is not too late since we have beaten back that diversionary attack. We shall have the pleasure of shooting him when we get back to the Mansion." The short lived former President remarked. The two men became silent .Their speeding jeep slowed down at the Unknown Soldier monument to make a left turn.

It was the wrong time to slow down, a fiery Bazooka round hit the jeep. Samuel Dahn jumped out in a flash along with Fred Knot and another soldier. Three other soldiers sitting in the back of the jeep did not have that luxury; they were blown into smithereens along with their vehicle. Samuel Dahn fell on the tarmac sustaining bruises; even in that instant his rifle was in his hand blazing. Samuel fought for his life shooting. The three soldiers with him pinned down by enemy fire continued to reply rolling on the road, shell landed all around them. Then Samuel in suicidal move ran forward on the road drawing enemy fire. He ziz zag crouching below the big bronze Unknown Soldier statute. Now he could see his attackers from the Mansion fence. A frown crossed his brow. It pleased Samuel that at least Maxwell Forkpa was dead. Taking advantage of his excellent marksmanship he thinned the ranks of his attackers fortunately giving the chance to his own companions to run for cover joining him as he covered them with suppressive fire. The world at the moment existed for only he and the attackers in the Mansion fence. Samuel emptied one magazine replacing it with a brand new one. When his third magazine was getting empty it dawned on him he was alone, both Fred Knox and the other soldier had disappeared.

Disgusted Samuel rose from his position and walked straight ahead not caring to dodge another bullet thus exposing himself to danger. The coup-maker did not mind or care. By then darkness began to descend on the city. The coupmaker whose coup was an overnight success few hours ago was now in effect a fugitive again.

He flagged down a private car whose owner was too frightened to refuse him. Inside the vehicle the coup maker ordered the driver to head for a Pharmacy on Broad Street.

True to his word he got off the vehicle strolling in the direction of the barracks alone.

At the BTC barrack inside a small room protected by fiercely loyal troops, Maxwell recorded his historic speech which he wrote himself on cassette. By 6 pm the two premier radio stations in the land were under the control of loyalist troops. These stations broadcast the speech which shook the nation's foundation and prepared the scene for a civil war. The fearless voice boomed. President

Maxwell Forkpa words at the end of a brilliant recital of the National Anthem was this. "When the cockroach dance there is no purpose or direction the President began. A sad event which rudely invaded our lives in the most diabolical, violent and satanic fashion this morning in the form of an invasion has been crushed. This morning as we are all aware a group of ruthless men with no sense of duty and loyalty to their own nation ganged up with foreign aggressors and illegally entered our nation with the sole aim of overthrowing our constitutional democratic government through brute force. Seeking to destroy our freedom and replaced it with a mindless military junta comprising of crooks and criminals led by the treacherous former Commanding General of our army Samuel Dahn.

I am pleased to announce to you fellow law abiding citizens that the plans of the invaders has failed. Their invasion and attempted coup has been completely crushed. I, your President Maxwell Forkpa is in complete control. We therefore, urge you fellow citizens not to welcome these dissidents on the run in your homes. Any citizen caught harboring; accompanying, aiding or abetting these dissidents in any way will be dealt with in the harshest possible way. A dust to dawn curfew has been imposed from 6 pm to 6 am. Curfew breakers will be shot on sight…..

A deep deafening silence, still, pale, and unnatural, like the enforced calm that follow immediately after a thunderous explosion descended on the city and across the Country. Gone were the revelers dancing in the streets. Gone too were the hooting motorists. Business and residential buildings closed. Now and then in the city, a military vehicle disturbed the enforced calm. The guns of the invaders became silent; the coupmakers threw away their weapons, and uniforms and melted into the population. Never in the history of this oldest African independent republic have the sound of music, conversation, traffic, children and street cooking so completely disappeared in this West African city famous for its vibrancy. Even babies were not allowed by their mothers to utter a word or emit a shrill cry from their tiny innocent mouths. A clueless nation had swallowed the bait and hook of Samuel's coup. So many shivered now in bed fearful of the repercussions of their reckless expression of euphoric joy. Under the peaceful tranquility of indoor darkness many rested safe for now. But what would tomorrow bring?

Maxwell Forkpa again alive in the Mansion contemplating in the quietude of the night felt raw consuming anger burning in his released soul. It was inevitable dawn would break for the sheep to be separated from the goats.

Alone and deserted Samuel Dahn sought refuge in an old zinc shack. The disappointment and anger in him was too consuming for his oppressed soul. His mind reviewed the entire events of the day. How could he face his wife and children?

His countrymen and women? his soldiers? His backers?

Now how many were going to die because of him for he was now powerless to stop that. How could he get out of his present claustrophobic environment?

He toyed with the idea of seeking refuge at the US Embassy and then tossed the idea aside. He could not face the many small, hardworking people abroad who scrubbed floors and cleaned toilets to finance his debacle. The horizon looked bleak. It even surprised him that the old lady owner of this shack allowed him into her home knowing it meant instant death for she and your family if he was discovered here. They only hauled him inside whispering to the fugitive general President Maxwell Forkpa was speaking on national radio.

Alone in the threadbare room given to him in the rat infested shack, Samuel searched for the faintest ray of hope and found none. His hand went to his breast pocket. Slowly he mumbled a short prayer. Maxwell Forkpa would never have the opportunity to humiliate him again. He put the vile content of the tiny bottle to his lips and drank copiously of its contents. His intestines were on fire, something exploded in his brain.

And then, the charismatic general and leader of men was no more. Dying a frustrated, sad, and disappointed man and alone.

Around the capital loyalist troops spent the night consolidating their positions. The coup success and failure had come about with little bloodshed. Many coupmakers and their supporters were in hiding contemplating their escape from the furnace of retribution.

Calm and silence began returning to the battered city which experienced her worst orgy of violence ever experienced in its long, turbulent history. The days following the immediate aftermath of this aborted coup far more vitriolic than the coup 5 years earlier. Loyalist government soldiers combed the streets settling old scores under the guise of rounding up invaders. Most Liberians believed the principal authors of the coup had fled the country. The whereabouts of their leader Samuel Dahn remained a mystery.

The President and his men happiness were tainted by their failure to capture the coup leader. His destination remained a mystery. If the fugitive general left the country, there was every possibility one day, he was going to return bigger and stronger. Therefore, an intense manhunt and a media barrage was launched asking people for information leading to the arrest of the general. Embassies were being watched intensely to prevent the general from seeking asylum in one.

Information was given to friendly intelligence service for information on Samuel Dahn. Every known accomplice, friend or anyone remotely connected to the general was under surveillance down to his home village. Even captured invaders did not have a clue to what happened to Samuel Dahn or his whereabouts. Nothing concrete about the general surfaced. The icing on the cake was spoiled. The initial high hope of capturing and killing General Samuel Dahn faded and the President was forced to content himself with the fact he remained secured for now in power.

Maxwell Forkpa sat alone in his over furnished executive office alone chain smoking or to put it accurately chain inhaling. He always love the aura and mystic of a good acrid cigar smoke. The big bone tobacco made feel like one of the urban elites whom he so detested and admired.

The whitish smoke curling upwards from between his fingers made him think better. Plucked from obscurity into the seat of power through brute force that same sudden brute force has come almost within inches of wrestling his cherished throne from him.

The humming sound in the background annoyed him. Moments from his younger years passed with cinematic clarity lasting only momentarily to vanish. He and Samuel Dahn playing Football together, dating two friends at one point including two sisters, eating GI boogie together. A fleeting sense of their companionship and camaraderie lost in the struggle of power appeared. A sense of nostalgia about the simple days back then swept across his mind. But those thoughts vanished into oblivion replaced by cold, callous hate.

"Samuel Dahn is my enemy," he whispered.

The die has been cast. Only the death of one or both of them could bring calm to their Country. Having been a survivor so long, the young President developed a sense of invincibility. That illusion was shattered by the entry of the roguish general into his fiefdom with such ease and he almost losing his life in the process like his predecessor.

The President banged hard on his sleek polished mahogany desk drawing blood. He licked the blood too absorbed in thoughts to feel pain.

If he Maxwell Forkpa was a fugitive, a hunted man being pursued by fanatical hunters during the most intense man-hunt in Liberian history what would he do to survive? To catch the prey, the hunter has to think like the prey. Would he go to one of those fabled western embassies located at Mamba Point?

Samuel would remember the son of the assassinated President-Adolphus Benson who sought refuge inside the French Embassy in Monrovia? What good did it do the young man when ignorant soldiers burst into the embassy seizing him in full violation of the embassy and the ambassador's diplomatic immunity?

Worse still they put him live on air after his capture soon before his mysterious death.

The last thing Samuel Dahn would want to do is to have that same fate befall him. If he fled to the most secured spot in Liberia : namely the US Embassy, the Americans would surely reject him. The only option open to him would be flee across the country's porous border as he did years back. Now the country's security forces while momentarily caught off guard were better prepared and beefed up in the aftermath of the coup. To escape, he needed accomplices which were extremely dangerous to do now. One by one the President formulated plans and discarded them. The hours flew by without him realizing it.

Then it hit him! The answer laid in their underprivileged upbringing in Monrovia!

A cornered being-man/woman or animal always returned to its roots, to familiar surroundings. Maxwell Forkpa smiled. He issued commands to his men on tender hooks worried about what their boss could do when he came out of his catatonic state sprang to action.

He picked the best of the best his own fanatical tribal nationalist who made the bulk of the elite presidential guards. Soon every notorious slum forming a ring around the BTC-Buzzi Quarter, Coconut Plantation venturing even further down to West Point were combed with house to house search. However, Samuel Dahn's whereabouts remained a mystery. The President's elation at hitting the jackpot of his idea of capturing and killing Samuel Dahn became like stale wine. To make matters worse how long could he remain in disguise blackening his already black face armed with assault rifle and grenades leaving his palace? Despondent and becoming a short fuse with taut nerves an unexpected break -through came in the form of a phone call. Sonewein just across the road from the BTC was the place to look. Marketers going to Rally Time market and the parallel open air market beside the road were surprised to see heavily armed soldiers wearing flak jackets speeding by.

A rusting zinc shack in the middle of the slum where raw sewer in open drains provided a backdrop was completely surrounded by heavily armed crack soldiers. The President did not want to take any chance. There was no order to surrender. A salvage barrage was opened up on the suspected zinc shack made of corrugated roofing zinc nailed to pieces of wood. President Maxwell Forkpa fired the first round of Bazooka followed by grenades and small arms fire. It was over in minutes. There was no return fire. Only the smoldering remains of a shack razed to the ground. President Forkpa hemmed on all sides by the best of his warriors entered the still burning wreckage. Remarkably, the body inside did not show any bullet mark. Preseident took one good look at the body and he did not need to ask any more questions for he knew who it was. He could recognize it even in the dark. The two of them shared the same bed during basic training. Seized by an unreasonable fear that the dead man could rise up from the dead, Maxwell Forkpa opened fire on the body. The dark almost congealed blood told them the victim has been dead for some time before their arrival. How the chief look? Alright! Alright!

The jubilant men cried out raising their M-16 rifles into the air. A man took his bayonet to cut the dead man's private part.

"No! No one should mutilate or touch the dead man in any way to dishonor the body. Call an ambulance to take the body."

His men used to mutilating the bodies of their enemies could not understand their boss's reaction. He issued strong commands and hurried out of the scene. Even when the bullet ridden body of General Samuel Dahn appeared on state TV news it was a very brief clip which did not even showed the general's face. Unknown to the public the directive has come from above. Maxwell Forkpa could afford to be magnanimous, his Presidency was now safe and secured.

———

To the majestic hills of the north country to be with his own people to celebrate his narrow escape from death went President Forkpa.

Back in his small ancestral village near Voinjama, the President put on raffia skirts. Cattle and other live stocks were killed by the hundreds and the entire town was enveloped in a pulsating mood of celebration.

President Forkpa himself joined in the dance himself taking off his shirt. He gyrated with full gusto to the pulsating and intoxicating drum beat. Females whose bodies were decorated with colorful chalks, beads, and shells beat their salsas, cymbals and tambourines; their thundering steps sent a crowd of dust behind them through the narrow streets of Voinjama. Cows, goats, sheep, chickens, fowls, and ducks were at the receiving end of the festivities with people feasting, singing and dancing. Their son and hero had survived a violence coup attempt. What more good news did they want in order to throng to the streets?

Emily Gabby a frequent companion of the President along with all the other attractive women from the city threw aside their western sophistication to share in the exuberant dance of their rural sisters. Nancy and her children were all dressed in colorful hand woven robes. In her hand, the First Lady carried a large cow tail whose ornamental handle was decorated with cowrie beads which represented the symbol of power and authority held aloof in her hands. She waved the symbol of authority to enthusiastic dancers who carried her shoulder high. Clean white rice, the symbol of riches thrown into the air by old ladies landed on the revelers. It was a spectacle, almost every human being present from far and wide jubilated, their thundering, ecstatic voices sealed together in unison ascended to the skies. Their sweat and voices mingled together in the mesmerizing spirit of oneness; even the feeble tapped their feet to the rhythm permeating every street corner.

Maxwell Forkpa was a man born under a lucky star, nothing his enemies could do had any effect on this magnanimous young man who in a short time swept and transformed the political landscape of his country and made the shoemaker son to dream of becoming President The highest office in Liberia was no longer a preserve of the rich and famous and their descendants.

Maxwell Forkpa still under 40 made this dream possible.

The mood back in the capital Monrovia was much more somber though than those in Voinjama. People wondered? Fate determines our destiny. Destiny determines our lives some say. But can fate as unpredictable as it can be entrusted with so crucial a part of our lives as destiny? If so, could we conclude that fate had it along for Samuel Dahn's life to end in the ignominy of suicide and for his body to be grotesquely disfigured by the holes of hundreds of bullets on the head, chest, stomach and the legs like a painting by an amateur graffiti artist? Fate has brought their lives together Samuel Dahn and Maxwell Forkpa; two brilliant young soldiers, their lives and careers intertwined together in a bizarre dance to death.

Samuel Dahn's body was dumped into an unmarked grave while Maxwell Forkpa continued to live a charmed life at the top only to dance to his death in turn too.

POSTSCRIPT

Maxwell Forkpa ruled his country for 10 more beautiful years after the abortive coup. Sadly, he too was captured and killed in the capital by rebels who were remnants of the Patriotic Brigade in a terrible rebellion which brought so much more violence and bloodshed. This rebellion using arms purchased from Viktor destabilized the entire West Africa sub- region.

President Forkpa's wife Nancy and their three children now live in London where his son Junior is a respectable Banker. He funds his father's PDP. Many people are urging him to run in the next election.

Ebenezer Kum is today Liberia's ambassador to Cameroon. The venerable old man also doubles up as an advisor to President Paul Biya. He is a man of enormous wealth and influence.

Defense Minister Daniel Kollie was killed in the rebellion that took his boss's life. Kollie died with his boss having remained fiercely loyal even to the end when friends and family deserted President Maxwell Forkpa in his last days when rebels besieged him in the Mansion.

The Chief of Defense Intelligence was last seen with Chadian rebels in the north of that country; others spoke of him being in eastern DR Congo. There is one thing which is certain about him; he is a feared and much sought after guerrilla leader and gun for hire.

Professor Martins teaches Political Science at Harvard in the states. He still plots his return to political dominance which he hoped will eventually lead to the Presidency. His children are grown now and call him occasionally but the Professor is an unpopular man now in Liberia.

Both Samuel Dahn and Adonis Vonlehs' sons are in the US army. They are brilliant, but angry young men who vows to one day avenge the death of their fathers.